Happy Utopia Day, Joe McCarthy

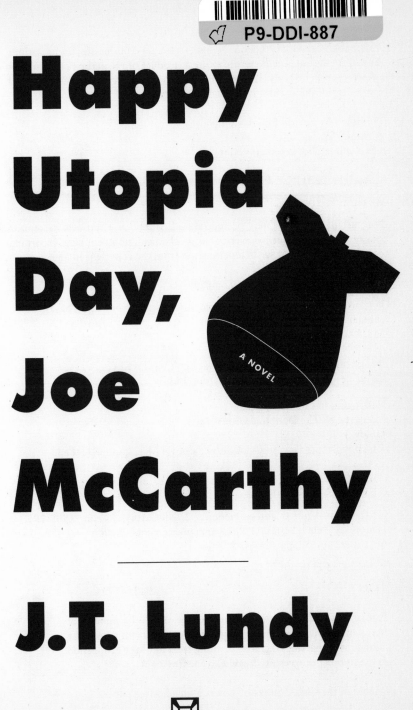

A NOVEL

J.T. Lundy

EMERALD
BOOK CO.

Published by Emerald Book Company
Austin, TX
www.emeraldbookcompany.com

Copyright ©2013 J.T. Lundy

Distributed by Emerald Book Company

For ordering information or special discounts for bulk purchases, please contact Emerald Book Company at PO Box 91869, Austin, TX 78709, 512.891.6100.

Design and composition by Greenleaf Book Group LLC
Cover design by Greenleaf Book Group LLC

Cataloging-in-Publication data
(Prepared by The Donohue Group, Inc.)
Lundy, J. T.
    Happy Utopia Day, Joe McCarthy : a novel / J.T. Lundy.—1st ed.
    p. ; cm.
    Issued also as an ebook.
    ISBN: 978-1-937110-53-6

    1. Spies—United States—Fiction. 2. McCarthy, Joseph, 1908-1957—Fiction. 3. United States—Politics and government—Fiction. 4. Political satire, American. 5. Spy stories. I. Title.

PS3612.U54 H36 2013

813/.6   2013941794

Part of the Tree Neutral® program, which offsets the number of trees consumed in the production and printing of this book by taking proactive steps, such as planting trees in direct proportion to the number of trees used: www.treeneutral.com

Printed in the United States of America on acid-free paper

TreeNeutral®

13 14 15 16 17 18   10 9 8 7 6 5 4 3 2 1

First Edition

For Renée, Calvin, Cooper, and Colin

I wonder how ridiculous we can get here.
—SENATOR JOSEPH McCARTHY

"MR. THOMPSON. It's the White House!"

I shoot up from my official United States Customs Office chair and look over my cubicle wall toward the administrative assistants, where Glenda has a phone to her ear and looks directly at me. Glenda and I are not on formal terms; normally, she calls me Chris. Her shout though, brings the occupants of the entire cubicle pond, and the cubicle sea beyond, to their feet. Heads bob out of the powerful window offices, and people on the move come to a stop.

My jaw drops. "The what?"

Glenda's mouth forms the words with exaggeration. "The. White. House—for real. Line two."

I look at the telephone and see line two blinking next to the stack of immigration files on my desk. The weighty stares of my nosy office mates press me slowly into my seat. I wet my lips and reach for the phone. "Chris Thompson."

A gravelly voice barks. "This is Vance Slater, President Wright's chief of staff."

"Hello, Mr. Slater. How can I help—"

"Are you the Chris Thompson who graduated Georgetown with a not-too-shabby 2.37?"

Why does the president's chief of staff know my GPA? "Yes, well, I had some trouble my freshman year," I say.

"No excuses," Slater bellows. "Hell, round it up to a 2.4. I would. Chris, President Wright wants to see you straight away."

I stand at attention. "I don't understand."

A recording beep sounds in the phone. "There's a car out front. Don't mess around. I'll see you in ten minutes."

I look around the office and feel like I'm balancing on a life raft. All is calm but for me. "I need to tell my boss."

"National emergency," Slater says. "I'll take care of your superiors. You've got two bosses now—the president and me. Now get in that car."

The phone goes dead.

I sit down and hide from my staring coworkers. I tap the desk. My knee bounces. Why would the president be interested in me? Could it have to do with the resume I sent to the CIA in college? Those spooks did give me a series of interviews, though none of them came to anything in the end. I didn't put my GPA on my resume. I didn't think the government had a minimum, which was fine, because without the grades or gumption for grad school, I'm lucky to call the United States Customs Service home.

I hear the rumble of a truck passing outside. Is there really a car waiting to take me to the White House? My throat is dry. My water bottle is empty. I pick up the phone to call my wife, Karen. No. I have to go right now.

The file shelf shakes. I look up and see my coworker Archie's long face hanging over the brown wall from the adjacent cubicle. "What was that all about?" His mustache twitches with curiosity.

"I don't know."

"Oh, stuff it. What the hell's going on?"

Archibald Lamb III is an East Coast blue-blood flunky sitting on the sidelines of the fast track like myself. He can be a real pain in the ass, but I count him as my only friend in the place. Vance Slater didn't say I couldn't tell anyone, but I feel reluctant to divulge the conversation, as if it's top secret or something.

"Nothing, Arch."

"You mean to tell me that Glenda yells out 'The White House, line two,' and you say it's nothing?"

I feel guilty. We're friends. I should trust Archie, and besides, we both have security clearance. "All right, if you must know, the president wants to see me."

Archie slaps the top of his bald head. "Holy shit. The president?"

I stand up and run my hands over my baggy khaki pants in a vain attempt to press them. I'm sporting a blue button-down shirt and scraped-up burgundy penny loafers. Technically I should be wearing a coat and tie, but I've been in violation for years.

"Think you're in trouble?"

"Why would you say that?" What if I am in trouble? I can't afford trouble. I have a wife and kid. I see Archie's blazer hanging on his wall. "I don't know, Arch. He did say that they were my bosses now."

"Who said?"

"Vance Slater."

"That was Vance Slater? Double damn."

Archie and I are about the same size give or take; five foot ten, medium build, a hundred and eighty pounds. "Hey, can I borrow your blazer?" I ask.

"No," Archie says. He strokes his mustache. "Maybe it's about those apple pies from Bangladesh. I bet that's it. They're going to give you a medal for good relations or something."

The apple pies. Last month the deputy ambassador from Bangladesh requested my assistance establishing approval for Grandma's American Pie Company to import apple pies. The good old boys running Grandma's American Pie wanted to outsource their labor, and the idea was that baker boats would sail from Bangladesh filled with Bangladeshi workers baking apple pies to be delivered fresh for distribution in New York. I felt bad about outsourcing apple pies, but all was in order, and I efficiently filed and approved the paperwork, for which I received a sincere letter from the ambassador commending me on a job "well done." I duly framed the letter and hung it in my cube between the photograph of my lovely wife and my wonderful son and my autographed mini-poster of Sean Connery, the ultimate James Bond.

"Seriously, let me borrow your navy blazer."

"No. That's my Brooks Brothers one."

If the White House wants to know about the apple pies, the meeting might not be as pleasant as Archie thinks. Either way, I need to look decent. I walk into Archie's cubicle. He stands up and positions himself between his jacket and me, folding his arms like a nightclub bouncer.

"Just let me try it on."

"No."

"Slater said there was a national emergency. This could be the biggest meeting of my life. I can't be demoted because I'm not in proper attire. Karen's hours have been cut in half as it is."

"A fine-looking woman like Karen never has trouble finding a job." Archie chuckles. "If she's looking for extra hours, I've got some things she could do."

Archie sometimes gets this hound dog look on his face that makes him appear stupider than he really is and you can't help feel sorry for him. That look added to a childlike smile lets him get away with offensive statements like this about people's wives. "I don't think you're her type," I say.

I step left to get closer to the jacket, but Archie blocks my way. I quickly step right, which he counters as well.

"That hot redhead sure thought I was her type last night," he says.

Archie and I had hit a bar after work yesterday, which we do once every month or so. I laugh. "She was hitting on me the whole time."

Archie raises an eyebrow in a victory arch. "But she went home with me." He smiles and twirls a finger. "Hook, line, and I sunk her."

"Good for you, Ahab."

I try for the jacket again. Archie and I shuffle left, right, left. His shoulder bumps into mine.

"I'm going to see the president, you oaf," I say. "I'll be representing the Customs Department. Have some pride. Give one up for the team."

Archie releases his grip. His face relaxes as he reconsiders. "Maybe you could put a good word in for me."

"You think the president is looking for an expert on pirated tennis shoes?"

"Who knows?" Archie says.

"Who knows?" I say.

"Who knows?" Archie says. He shrugs and steps aside.

I reach for the jacket and put it on. Perfect fit.

Archie brushes a piece of lint off the lapel. He pats my face with a good-luck slap. "They say Slater is one of those Big Mac guys."

Archie's always full of conspiracy theories. "I never heard that."

"Big Mac is more than just a movement. They've turned into a real political party with congressmen and everything."

"A couple representatives is all," I say. "Trust me. They'll disappear in an election or two." I straighten out the jacket. "How about your tie?"

Archie reluctantly unfastens the knot from his solid brown knit tie. He pulls it through his collar and hands it to me. "That's it."

I wrap the tie around my neck and twist it into a double Windsor. "What's this tie, like, from '82?"

Archie's mustache scrunches irritably into his nose as he talks. "You're looting me and have the nerve to complain about the quality of the merchandise?"

My phone rings and I backstroke around the worn fabric wall into my work area. Perhaps the White House is calling again—Vance Slater checking up, or even the president himself unable to wait for my sage advice. I always wanted to be a spy like James Bond, and even though the CIA was less than impressed by my resume, I'd still like to be a part of something exciting, something big. Maybe this White House meeting will be my chance. I clear my throat and answer the phone with patriotic zeal. "This is Chris Thompson."

"It's me," my wife says crisply, confident I will recognize her from the other *me*'s in the world.

I'm dying to tell her of my meeting with the president, but I play it cool. "What's up?"

"Just checking. You're still leaving early, right?"

"Three o'clock. I'll be there."

Archie's face plops over the wall like a lazy catfish. "Is that Karen?"

"Scotty was so cute this morning. He's excited for you to be at his concert," Karen says.

"Tell Karen I said hey," Archie says.

I wave at Archie to go away.

"He practiced his violin before school without being asked. I can tell he's nervous to be playing in front of all the kids at the assembly. He's never had a solo before. At breakfast he—"

"Tell Karen I said hey."

"Archie says hey."

"Hi, Archie. He's so sweet."

"No. He's not."

"Now you absolutely cannot be late."

I lean back in the chair importantly and put my feet on the twenty-gauge-steel-topped desk. "Listen to this, honey." I pause. "I will be there right *after* my meeting with the president of these fine United States." I put my feet down and lean forward, excited for her reaction.

"Okay, perfect. Oh. I have to go. See you at three."

Oh, well. Karen is on autopilot and all wrapped up with Scotty. We both are. He's our center, our creation, our connection to life beyond us. Still, I'm disappointed, but it's okay. I can tell her the details about the presidential meeting later.

I stand up and push Archie's face back over the wall. I grab my black plastic briefcase, textured to appear leatherlike, and traipse triumphantly past dumbfounded coworkers and salute the row of bosses who are menacingly mulling the improbability that I have indeed received a call from the White House.

I descend in the elevator, bewildered by the preceding events and irritated that Archie has cost me five minutes. Surely Slater had been flippant; it would take thirty minutes to fight through DC's traffic. I push open the entrance doors I like to imagine are bulletproof and emerge into a God-forgiving sunshine and mild spring day. A lanky chauffeur stands next to a black Cadillac limo, and a pair of motorcycle police escorts wait fore and aft.

"Mr. Thompson?" A clean-cut dark-suited man wearing the special Secret Service sunglasses that imply he packs multiple firearms has sidled up to me unnoticed as I stare at the limo.

Bond, James Bond, I think. I'm all about 007.

"Thompson, Chris Thompson," I say.

He puts his hand on my back and guides me toward the limo. He opens the rear door, and I scoot across the black leather seat. Sunglasses sits next to me, and we are off.

"Identification, please."

I produce a laser-engraved polycarbonate Virginia driver's license portraying me with an eight-year-old photograph of pre-gray-streaked short black hair parted to the side, baby-sleep-deprived-let-me-sleep-in-once-this-year eyes, and I-am-no-longer-the-important-man-in-the-house frowning lips. Not that I'm complaining. Scotty's our world. But if I hadn't almost flunked out my freshman year, I could have ended up a pay grade or two higher—like at the CIA or the State Department— and had the spare coin for a nanny when he was a baby. Karen and I could have gone on a date or two, or slept in more. As it was I had to scramble for nearly perfect grades my final years to end up with a C+ average. Damn Slater for busting my balls on my GPA. One year of partying still haunts me. I look out the window as we wail along through red lights while traffic guards, used to the drill, hold back less important citizens and wave us on our way.

Slater knows his business. In less than ten minutes we drive through the side White House gates and a car wash full of nuclear sensors, coming to a perfectly placed stop in the middle of more dark-suited sunglasses-wearing heat-packing clones. I step out and am immediately patted down and violated as never before with wands, brushes, swabs, needles, and a Geiger counter. On cue, the clones disperse, and another plastic-faced man steps forward. "Welcome to the White House, Mr. Thompson."

I reach out my hand. "Thank you, Mr.—"

Plastic Face shakes his head in disdain. "No need for shakes or names. Security, you understand."

I feel like a neophyte. "Of course."

"Follow me, sir. This is the West Wing." Plastic Face leads me down golden-rug-surfaced marble hallways, turning left, right, left, left, right, until finally he spins me around twice and pushes me through a door. "The Roosevelt Room," he says. "A shortcut." He leads me around a long conference table and past a row of flags. A painting of Native Americans riding horses bareback hangs on the wall.

We exit the Roosevelt Room out an opposite door to a marbled-floor reception area. I find myself standing in front of a meticulous-looking aide sitting at a desk. A presidential flag is posted left of the desk. The United States flag is posted to the right. Two wide dark-stained doors are behind the man. Above the doors it says "Oval Office" in some old Yankee-style letters.

"Have a seat, Mr. Thompson." Plastic Face steps back and stands against the wall. I sit down and watch the man at the desk work, too nervous to look anywhere else.

The man types on a computer and talks into a Bluetooth headset. He says the same things over and over in an abundance of ways. "No. He's not. President is out. Three thirty in the Rose Garden. Not in. Out. No. Three thirty. Rose Garden. This afternoon. Busy. Not available. No. Don't know when. Out."

The man looks like he could keep it up forever. The passing time only increases my nervousness. I twiddle my thumbs and continue to stare at the president's unflappable gatekeeper. It seems everyone wants access to the most powerful man of the most powerful country on earth. Why the hell am I here? Am I going down for selling America out to Bangladesh? Or maybe the Bangladeshi agreement is spreading goodwill and helping repair our relations with the Muslim world. My hopes rise for a second, but I know I'm being unrealistic.

An hour passes. I am in severe danger of missing Scotty's concert. Karen is going to kill me.

A buzz sounds from the man's desk. He picks up a phone. "Yes, sir." He sets the phone down and looks at me. "Any moment now."

I'm going to see the president. President Wright's public persona defines sophistication. He's polished, professional, and articulate. He presents critically acclaimed speeches, and when asked a question, he always has the appropriate response. I should be respectful, but confident: a take-charge guy. I can accomplish whatever he needs done. I need the president to see that I'm intelligent, too. I need the president to know that I'm his man. I take a deep breath.

The Oval Office door opens. Vance Slater fills my vision. I'm tense and alert. The old University of Michigan linebacker barrels toward me wearing a gray pinstriped suit, power red tie, and white Hermès pocket kerchief, all of it calculated to make someone like myself extra insecure. On television Slater is oily smooth, and in person it's doubly impressive, like a grease slide in an alley behind a Waffle House. There's a pin on his lapel: two blue letters, *BM*, superimposed over the American flag. He's never worn this pin before; surely the press would have covered it if he had. Archie was right. Slater is a part of the Big Mac Party.

"Thompson! What the hell took you so long?"

I try to explain that I'd been waiting. "Sorry, but—"

"Don't let it happen again."

"No, sir."

Vance Slater walks me into the Oval Office. It smells like fresh flowers. A blue oval carpet with a presidential crest covers most of the room. President Wright sits at his desk, hunched over a mini arcade game like a scientist examining a petri dish. He shouts at the game, "Bring it on, sucka!"

I look closely at the president. He looks strange playing a game and shouting. I look at his gallant photograph on the wall. He has an unmistakable bump at the bridge of his nose. I look to the man playing the game. Same bump. Same man as the photograph. This man is the president of the United States. Maybe he's sick.

I step with Slater onto the carpet and he guides me to the president. We stop five feet in front of his desk. "Let's hope this round is a good one," Slater whispers.

Out of the little game a throaty movie-tone voice roars, "Are you ready to play Bulls-Eye Ball?" At the same time energizing carnival music pulses.

The president has four marble-size steel balls in his left hand and one perched ready to go between his thumb and finger in his right. He stares intently at the round yellow rubber pad, placed before a skee-ball like concentric circle target. "Thirty seconds and . . . go!" says the voice. Quickly paced go-as-fast-as-you-can music plays, and the president begins bouncing the steel balls off the launch pad into the target.

I look at Slater. He stands calm, looking on as if all is normal.

The voice calls out the escalating score, and the balls return to a tray in front of the launch pad for the president to grab and shoot again. "Two, five, ten, thirteen, fifteen, twenty, twenty-two . . ." The president shoots a ball over the target. It rolls off the desk and onto the floor. Vance Slater picks it up, reaches over and places it into the president's left hand. The president transfers it to his right hand and shoots without looking up. The spectacle of him playing Bulls-Eye Ball is surreal. My eye twitches. I put my hands inside my pant pockets. I return them to my side. The president is under extreme pressure. Many powerful men have quirks. I take a silent deep breath.

Ding, ding, ding. "Time is up. You scored seventy-two points, a new record."

The president jumps up and raises his fists toward the ceiling in an Olympic victory salute. "Yeeow!" He double-punches the air, places his knuckles on the desk, and glares at the game mockingly. "Take that!"

Vance Slater clears his throat. "Mr. President, allow me to introduce Special Customs Service Agent Chris Thompson." The president looks at me for the first time. My heart thumps quickly against my chest. Slater continues, "Chris, the president of the United States, Oscar Wright."

The president straightens up to his full five-foot-four height, smiles to reveal the pearly whites that enhance his movie star good looks, and transforms into the respectable-looking man whom I recognize from multiple forms of media, though in person his short stature is much more apparent.

"Oh, yes. Special Agent Thompson. It is a pleasure." The president scoots around his desk nimbly and sticks out his hand. I try but fail to swallow in preparation for saying something intelligent at this momentous occasion. My limbs feel numb. President Wright has to reach for my hand. He shakes it and my arm waves like a Slinky. I attempt to say, "Pleasure is all mine, Mr. President," but I get stuck on the "Pl" part and, as my face turns red in a strenuous attempt to speak, I say something like "Plisss" before coughing.

"Water," the president calls unnecessarily, for a man places a bottle of Hawaiian volcanic-filtered water in my hand within seconds. Embarrassed, I take a drink and hand it back. The president slaps my back. "No worries, Thompson. This room humbles even the most important people. I could barely speak the first time I waltzed in here. Ha, and remember Schwarzenegger, Vance? Tough guy passed out cold from fear."

President Wright guides me to a couch and sits down next to me. Our knees touch. Vance Slater sits on the opposing couch. A cherry-finished coffee table separates us. George Washington in his general's uniform stands regally in a painting, sternly looking down, as if threatening us to do the honorable thing.

"I love that little skee ball game; calms the nerves, reminds me when I used to take my second set of kids, from my third wife, to Chuck E. Cheese's when I was a junior congressman. Those were the days . . . I love skee ball. The kids turned out for shit though, just like the first. Damn hooligans nearly cost me the election. Thank God for my last baby. She's a great kid— graduating Arizona State this year with straight As. I couldn't be more proud."

My mind is thinking so many things. I imagine telling friends about this White House visit and how they'll react. I'm not following everything the president is saying, something about his kids. I feel slightly more comfortable, though far from ease. I hadn't noticed before, but several men stand stationed around the room, silent and staring straight ahead, blending in with the wainscoted walls and gold-colored drapes. "The whole country is proud of your kids, Mr. President," I say.

"Yes . . . they're a great asset. And I understand you have a nice little family to be proud of, Chris."

"Karen is great, and Scotty will be turning ten—he can be a troublemaker at times, but he's—"

The president interrupts. "Chris, look. We could talk all day about kids, but we need to stay focused on what's important to the country. All kids turn out to be troublemakers sooner or later. Mark my word." The president looks up and points at Vance Slater.

Slater writes something in a notebook. "Marked."

I smile and feel out of place. I gather my courage and say, "I'm a little curious what this is all about."

The president looks at me matter-of-factly. I worry I've been too forward. "Chris, do you remember that CIA interview you had as a senior at Georgetown?"

I've always dreamed of working as a CIA foreign intelligence officer. I wanted to be an American-style 007, but they wouldn't give me a chance. "I had a series of interviews with the CIA," I say.

"Yes, I know. But the final one—do you remember that final day at headquarters in Langley?" The president looks at me expectantly.

"I remember they never offered me a job."

The president waves his hands in impatience. "Yes, yes, but do you remember that analyst exercise they gave you?"

Boy, do I ever. I'd had a half hour to respond and I've always regretted my answer. "I do. I was supposed to brainstorm a scenario not yet conceived that could be a threat to the United States."

"Exactly." The president snaps his fingers. "What was his analysis titled, Vance?"

Vance Slater brings out some sheets from a folder. "'The

Two-Phased Stealth Invasion Threat to the United States from Mexico and Canada.'"

My face feels warm as I confront this failure from my past. As best I can recall, my response had highlighted our preoccupation with Russia and the Middle East to the neglect of our friendly neighbors to the north and south. In the scenario I projected, Mexico and Canada used computers to "stealthily" steal control of our industrial infrastructure and military capabilities and divide up the land of the United States between them. So maybe it was my fault I'm not a spy. "I think my response ruined my chances for a job."

"It did," the president says. "But it's brilliant, and it's now officially classified as a top-secret security analysis paper."

They don't care about the apple pies. The president said *brilliant*. He looks at me with a smile of cheerful expectation. Slater stares like he's assessing me. "Are you sure?" I ask. "Classified? My paper? I don't see how my old analysis applies to anything."

President Wright looks at his chief of staff and nods. "Vance?"

Vance Slater nods back importantly and stands. A sly smirk escapes his stoic countenance, and I think he might laugh, but then he recovers. "Please stand, Mr. Thompson, and raise your right hand." I comply like an eager immigrant taking the citizenship oath. "Special Agent Chris Thompson, with your duties in the Customs Service you have already been granted top-secret clearance."

"Yes, sir. That's correct," I say.

"I am now about to grant you the highest-level security clearance possible: the Delta Delta Delta—or Tri-Delta clearance."

"I've never heard of that."

"I just created it." The president strokes his chin. "I named it in honor of my first wife. She was a Tri-Delt back at Indiana University. I have fond memories of that sorority house."

Slater continues, "Anyway, there are three people who have this security clearance: you, me, and the president. Tri-Delta documents are for our eyes only."

"Hoosier president?" shouts the president. He slaps his knee and laughs.

I'm not sure what is happening. I think they are trying to fluster me. "This is all very confusing."

"It will be clear in a minute," Slater says. "But first you have to take the Tri-Delta oath."

My right hand is still raised. The president places a musical triangle in my left. "Here, hold this. It's one of my relaxation devices, but it's appropriate, don't you think?"

Slater reads from three purple Post-it notes he has stacked on top of one another. "Do you, Special Agent Chris A. Thompson of the United States Customs Service, hereby agree to abide by the absolute Secret Code of the Tri-Delta security triangle, consisting of the White House chief of staff, Vance R. Slater; the president of the United States, Oscar I. Wright; and yourself?"

The president can barely contain himself. "And I'm in charge, right Vance?"

"Yes, Mr. President, you are in charge."

President Wright grabs my wrist. "We want you to be a part of our inner triangle, Chris."

Images of chartered jets and power dinners with world leaders flood my mind. "I do," I say with pride.

"Do you agree to maintain security and not communicate any confidential material, or anything you have ever heard, seen, learned, or imagined, whether secret or not, regarding anything to do with Tri-Delta security information, whether written, coded, taped, videoed, texted, emailed, hologrammed, or implied, to any other person living or dead, or partially dead but not really dead due to a near-death experience, no matter what law, judge, or means of coercion, or extreme torture, may fall upon you?"

"Um, what?"

"Just say 'I do,'" the president says. "We both did. Hooyah!"

I look at Slater. He looks like he might laugh again.

Okay. I've been ignoring it. The president is off his rocker. He's a total nut. I'm being set up. I'm the fall guy for the coming apple pie outsourcing scandal. I look nervously around the room and feel like the smallest guy in the jail yard. Slater regains his stern expression. The president smiles. "Ain't America great? Bet you thought it was going to be another ordinary day." The president says this with such good nature it's worrisome. They're still trying to shake me. This must be one of those high-stress interviews to see how I will react. I stay strong and vow not to let them faze me. Maybe this is a legitimate ticket out of my rubber-stamp job.

President Wright opens his hands in a welcoming gesture. "Well?"

I'm due for a lucky break. And it's not like this opportunity will ever come again. This is it. I've got to take the chance. "I do," I say softly.

"Hooyah!" the president says.

Slater hands me a glossy laminate identification card that displays three red triangles, my picture, and the words "Special Agent Chris Thompson, Tri-Delta Security Clearance." I've seen better fake IDs in college. I flip it over and see an embossed sketch of a large sorority-looking house. On the bottom in small red letters is a toll-free phone number and the name "Indiana University."

"What is all this?" I ask.

Vance sits down and motions for me to as well. "Your contact number."

The president slaps his hand on my knee. "What this all is . . . is that right now you're the only man in the government to have predicted what happened."

"What happened?"

"Your CIA security analysis paper. It's come true."

"My security analysis paper? You don't mean that Mexico and Canada have invaded us?"

"Phase I, exactly as you predicted, has happened," the president says with all seriousness.

"I'm sorry, I forget Phase I," I say.

"Mexico is invading us as we speak," Slater says.

I'm flabbergasted. "I haven't heard a thing."

"It's a stealth invasion. Simply genius how you foresaw it," the president says.

"A stealth invasion?"

"Your term, Chris, but yes, a stealth invasion," Slater says. "In the past three weeks, a hundred thousand Mexicans have stealthily invaded this country. We think millions more plan to enter soon."

"Millions?"

"Could be as high as ten million."

"Ten million? I can see a few dodging the border patrol, but ten million?"

"The border patrol lets them through," the president says.

Slater stands up and starts pacing. "Somehow the Mexicans hacked into our computers and obtained a shitload of tourist visas. It's all perfectly legal to the border patrol."

"They give 'em a handshake and tell 'em to take what they want," the president says.

"All very peaceful," Slater says.

"Just like when that Gandhi dude made 'em sit around all peaceful-like, and the British had to leave Mexico," the president says.

"That was India, Mr. President," Slater says.

The president's lips quiver. "I saw the movie, Vance. It was Mexico. And to think the British would get up and leave because a lot of people just sat around acting like hippies is plain absurd."

Vance Slater takes a deep breath and sighs. "Well anyhow,

this is what we believe." He closes his eyes for a moment as if in an attempt to add credibility to what he is about to say. "The Mexicans plan on implementing an electronically enhanced version of what the president likes to call the Gandhi scenario, until they get what they want."

I look back and forth between the president and Slater. They both appear sincere, seriously so. Could it be real? "What do they want?" I ask.

"They want to enter our country illegally without any hassles," Slater says.

"They want their land back," the president says.

I chuckle. "Like the Alamo?"

The president looks at me without a hint of sarcasm and says, "Yes, the Alamo! And everything else we snatched fair and square, out in the open, with guns and cannons and bayonets back in the Civil War."

"Mexican-American War," Slater says.

I can't help but laugh it seems so unlikely. "That's a lot of territory," I say.

The president does not think it so funny. He jumps up. "From El Paso to San Francisco, and everything with a Los, La, Las, El, or San in between." He slaps his forehead. "My God. They probably want Las Vegas." He looks petrified.

Slater tries to pacify him. "Mr. President. I don't think they—"

"Damn, we can't lose Vegas. That's as apple pie as we get. Thompson, you've got to stop this."

I put my hand to my chest. "Me?"

"Yes, you. Why the hell do you think you're here?"

I have no idea and that's the truth. "It all seems unreal."

"It is all unreal!" the president says.

"Perhaps we should break for lunch," Slater says.

"Taco Bell! Who's up for Taco Bell?" the president asks.

Vance Slater clears his throat. "I should remind you, Mr. President, that Taco Bell food is un-American."

The president holds up his index finger. "One last time." He shouts out to nobody in particular. "Two Nachos BellGrandes to start, Cheesy Bean and Rice Burrito for Vance, a Volcano Burrito for me, and how about you, Thompson?"

"No, thank you."

"And get Thompson the half-pound Nacho Crunch Burrito. He'll love it." The president, using the trademark ending he employs after all his campaign promises, points at me and winks. "I guarantee it."

I stand to join them and throw my arms in the air. "Mr. Slater, Mr. President. Mexico—Canada—invasion—Nachos BellGrandes—with all due respect, it's a bit much."

"All at once, a little overwhelming," Slater admits.

"Ass-toot of you not to forget the Canadians," the president says.

An efficient woman with black rectangular glasses enters the room. "Excuse me, Mr. Slater, the speaker of the house has arrived."

Slater looks uneasily back and forth between the president and me. "I'll take care of the speaker. Back in five."

Slater leaves the room. As soon as he's gone, the president rushes to his desk and sits down. "Come here, Thompson."

I pause.

The president calls me over. Suddenly he's looking at me with a seriousness he had yet to display. "Hurry. It's time for the truth."

He motions for me to take a seat. I sit down in one of the two wingback chairs in front of his desk. The president ruffles through some papers and looks around. His gaze stops at the painting of George Washington. He begins to say something, but a tornado-like roar from outside vibrates throughout the room. Out the side window, I see a presidential helicopter landing on the lawn. The president waits for the noise to die down. Then he looks me in the eye and speaks with gravity.

"Chris, do you remember Senator Joseph McCarthy?"

*It is like pulling teeth. I should not have to ask several
questions, in order to get to the truth.*
—SENATOR JOSEPH MCCARTHY

THE PRESIDENT TURNS on Bulls-Eye Ball. "So Slater doesn't
become suspicious."

I scoot back farther into the chair to be more comfortable.
"I studied about the McCarthy period in school."

"Good, good. I'm not an idiot, you know."

"No, sir."

"Cut the crap, Thompson. I've been yapping around here
like a mad cow in a funny farm, and we both know it."

He sure has, but I'm not going to say anything.

"I get confused sometimes," he says. "A lot more lately. I
might not be the smartest president, but I'm a damned good
speaker. Used to be a TV anchorman in Jackson."

"I recall that, sir."

"Said what they told me, and said it good, and played stupid all the way to the White House."

What is he trying to tell me? "Who are they?"

"Slater and the Big Mac Party. They're always watching every move, making all the decisions."

The Big Mac Party appeared in the 1980s, when Reagan called the Soviet Union the "evil empire." These old zealots, mostly men who had been supporters of Senator Joseph McCarthy's 1950s witch hunts, got all fired up on the anti-Communist bandwagon again. They spouted on about how McCarthy was right about all the Communists infiltrating America and about how we were doomed to collapse from within. In the late 1990s their ranks grew, and they formed the Big Mac Party and turned their un-American rhetoric to more contemporary issues. They have a few people in the House and Senate, but they've made little impact nationally—even with their greater electoral presence these days, the Big Mac Party is still on the fringe. It's incredible to learn that Slater's part of Big Mac.

"I thought you were a Democrat," I say to the president.

"I am. And I was a Republican my first two terms in Congress. Slater didn't care what we were—winning was the only thing that mattered. Don't look so shocked, Thompson. Everyone's a sellout sooner or later."

Regardless of the situation, I'm not going to argue with the president. "Why are you telling me this?"

"Emergence."

The word means nothing to me. "Is that like a support group or something?"

"No. It's a secret program." President Wright looks around the room. "So secret, even I don't know about it."

"But . . ." I stop myself from pointing out the inconsistency of his statement. An antique grandfather clock indicates five minutes to three. I need to get to Scotty's concert; presidential meeting or not, Karen will be pissed. "I have another appointment, sir."

The president raises his index finger. "A few minutes. I want to explain the invasion."

"What about the invasion?"

The president chuckles. "It's a complete farce."

"What do you mean a farce?"

"The invasion is not real," he says, as if it's no big deal. "It's a program inserted into border patrol surveillance computers that mimics illegal crossings. Some kid from Arizona State created it for me."

"A college kid created this emergency?"

"One of my daughter's friends I met out in Mesa during parents' weekend." The president gets a scared look on his face. "At least I hope he's just a friend. That kid's a real wacko. He's called Wizkid."

"Wizkid, huh?" That's it. I've had enough. I've obviously been called here because the president is completely out of his mind and he needs someone to entertain him. Who better to make a fool of than the man who outsourced apple pies? I want to go home. I need to talk to Karen. "Perhaps we could discuss these issues when they become more readily defined?" I say.

The president looks at the ceiling. "McCarthyism!" he shouts.

I can't help myself and laugh. "McCarthyism?"

"The issue has been defined." The president puts his hands in the air and flutters his fingers. "McCarthyism is alive and well within Big Mac. And they keep popping up everywhere."

"Is this a joke?"

"No. It might be unreal, but it's no joke."

"No offense, Mr. President, but I have to leave for my son's concert."

"Your son will understand."

"My wife won't."

The president strokes his chin. "Probably not." His face is calm. He touches my arm and looks at me with sincerity. "Your country needs you."

I reconsider. Despite the craziness, something in me trusts him. I decide to hear him out. "Why me?"

President Wright points his finger at me. "The Big Mac Party. They're more powerful than you think, Thompson. You'll find that out soon enough." He swivels his chair around and types on his computer. "Check this out."

I look over his shoulder to an email.

"This must have been sent to me by accident. The sender's address is blocked, but it has to be from someone who has my classified email."

Tim,

Emergence program is Big Mac's greatest asset, but also a huge potential liability. We should consider terminating if Big Mac Party becomes self-sufficient. Thoughts?

EAGLE.

"Do you know anything about the Emergence program?" I ask.

"It's on the books as a CIA intelligence-gathering center, but I can't figure out its true purpose. McCarthy started the program in 1951 and had it funded to last a hundred years. The program is self-sufficient and exists outside the known command structure."

The president confiding in me relaxes me somewhat. What he has been saying is mysterious, thrilling even. McCarthy's insidious influence and support were far and wide. Congressmen, senators, the army, even the president were afraid to take him on. And now the president is implying that a secret McCarthy program that's somehow tied up with the Big Mac Party is still influencing the government. It frightens me. I suddenly feel inclined to help.

"But what can I do?"

"You're my best shot."

"Best shot for what?"

"To find out what's going on at Emergence. I've heard Slater mention it on the phone before, but every time I try to find out what it is, I get blank stares. The bits I've picked up were from some old classified Truman files I was able to get access to."

I close my eyes for a second. "If you can't find out about Emergence, how am I supposed to find out about it?"

The president points at me. "I'll tell you. I just found out in one of these files that the president can send a liaison to Emergence, but only in times of a national emergency. I want you to be my liaison. I want you to find out what this program is all about and how it relates to the Big Mac Party. From what this email says, it could be a weak point for them. I've always wanted to obtain something I could hold over Slater."

"There's an actual national emergency?"

"The stealth invasion."

"You said it's a farce."

"Only you, me, and Wizkid know that."

"Not Slater?"

"He's actually concerned about the stealth invasion. Concerned enough to let me prepare to declare a national emergency. Having Canadians and Mexicans running over the border any time they want is the last thing Slater wants." The president smiles. "Smartest thing I've ever done."

"You're going to declare a national emergency over a farce?"

"Wizkid's virtual invasion is real enough for the government to prepare for a national emergency. And that's enough for me to send a liaison to Emergence. What do you say, Thompson? You'd be helping out the president of the United States. Let's see some American pride, my boy."

He's right. I've always wanted to help my country in an exciting position that mattered. I could be the president's spy in a secret world. James Bond images reel through my mind.

Thunderball! Dr. No! I'll never again get a chance like this. I clear my throat. "I feel honored to be chosen."

The president frowns discouragingly. "Let's face facts, Thompson. You're not exactly super-spy material. I requested a liaison, and Slater found you to appease me. He did a search through the government's ancient HR database and came across that bad analysis you wrote. He probably figures you're harmless. You're the best I'm going to get."

Ugh. I feel small. My shoulders sag. "You're the president. I wasn't good enough for the CIA."

The president punches me in the shoulder. "Cheer up, Thompson. I checked you out and looked beyond what Slater saw. Cub Scouts, Boy Scouts, computer club, all-conference high school football player, and straight As your last three years at Georgetown. Chris, you're the all-American, smart, athletic boy that I need."

"But I'm a lazy-ass man."

"A straight-up honest family man. And what a coincidence—you predicted a stealth invasion and I made one happen. We think alike, Thompson."

"Well, I . . ."

"Sylvia Fontaine! You passed the Sylvia Fontaine test." The president raises his voice when he says the name.

"Sylvia Fontaine?"

"The most beautiful operative in the world. And sex is her only weapon."

"I can only imagine."

"Oh, you did more than imagine. You met her."

I try to think. "I did?"

"Met her and rejected her."

"I did?"

"Remember last night when you and your friend Archibald went out for a couple of beers?"

"The redhead!"

"Sylvia Fontaine!"

"She's fantastic looking. And she did hit on me."

The president rubs his hands together greedily. "Sylvia Fontaine. And you snubbed her. Simply amazing."

"I'm a married man."

The president looks bewildered and shakes his head. "Pshaw! Didn't stop me."

"You and Sylvia?"

The president rubs his temples. "Another thing Slater has on me."

"Archie said he hooked up with her."

The president slaps the desk. "Ha! Archibald's a big fat liar. He took the female bouncer home."

I laugh. "So I finally passed the CIA test?"

"Absolutely. The right stuff is still inside you. Chris, I need someone who will make the right decision when it counts. Now, are you with me?"

The president sure knows what to say. I remain silent as I consider. *They keep popping up everywhere*, the president had said. I think of Hitler and Stalin. If the people aren't vigilant, a dictatorship could happen here in the United States. McCarthy nearly proved it.

"There are few pivotal moments in life. Step up or squirm back," he says.

The president is right. So what if this is all a little odd? It's time to stop being a mope and do something that matters for a change. *Tomorrow Never Dies! The World Is Not Enough!* Bring on the adventure. "I'm in."

The president smiles, and we shake hands just as Vance Slater walks into the room.

This is the most unheard of thing I have ever heard of.
— SENATOR JOSEPH McCARTHY

"DOUBLE OR NOTHING," the president says.

"Deal," I say.

The president winks at me and begins playing Bulls-Eye Ball. He fidgets back and forth to the music and bounces the steel balls toward the target. "You win," he says when the game ends.

The president rises. Vance Slater walks over and the three of us form a triangle, like we're at a cocktail party.

"I think Thompson has a grasp of the situation," the president says.

I have no experience with politics and even less with deception, but I have agreed to help the president, so I join in his charade. I think back and try to remember the main points of my CIA application. "The Canadians are the ones to really worry about."

"Exactly," the president says.

"Mexico wants their land back, but Canada wants it all."

"All the way down to New Orleans and their Cajun

brothers." The president rubs his eyes. He looks tired. "The Frenchies are still pissed off about the Louisiana Purchase and us swiping the Statue of Liberty. I'm not worried about the Canadians who think they're Americans—it's the ones who think they're French that scare me."

"They could be working together," I say.

"The American Canadians and the French Canadians?"

"No, Mexico and Canada, Mr. President."

"The bastards!"

Slater has been raising his finger wanting to talk. "Fellas. You're getting ahead of yourselves."

The president does not seem to hear him. He walks back and forth clenching his jaw. "Let's deal with Mexico first. I think we need Thompson on the front lines."

"Front lines?"

"You're the only one to have predicted and understand the whole situation. We need you as our liaison at our secret Emergence post at Area 51 right away."

"Tell me you're not going to bring aliens into this," I say.

"Area 22," Slater says.

"No aliens," the president says. "Like I told you. Emergence is a strategic intelligence operations center. Who knows what they do? Probably high-tech stuff that I don't understand. You ever Facebook or Twitter, Thompson?"

"My wife is on Facebook, and I signed up for Twitter only to follow Lance Armstrong."

"A true American hero, disgraced by drugs," Slater says.

"Could have been remembered as the greatest Tour de France rider ever," I say.

"Now he'll only be the first man on the moon," the president says. "Or did they strip him of that too?"

I pause to stop myself from correcting the president. "Area 51 is in the middle of nowhere. What's so strategic about its location?"

"Area 22," Slater says. "Not 51."

The president doesn't look pleased. "But it's right by Area 51, and Area 51 sounds much cooler."

"Yes. But it's at Area 22," Slater says.

The president rolls his eyes. "Okay, Area 22, exactly half as cool as Area 51." He gives me a nod. "It's strategic, Thompson, because of the invasion from Mexico. Emergence is right behind where we want to make our last stand."

"Last stand?"

"Vegas, baby!"

"Are we actually considering giving up all that territory?"

"Listen." President Wright grabs me by the lapels of Archie's blue blazer and puts his face in front of mine. "Bottom line—I don't want to give an inch, but if we have to give up all those Mexican-sounding places, then so be it. Hell, with California's debt, it'll be like cutting spoiled fruit off the great pineapple tree. The wife and I will sure miss staying at the Del in San Diego, though."

I find it difficult to tell whether the president believes what he is saying or not. A characteristic, I suppose, of a true actor. "I understand," I say.

The president lets go of the jacket and points at me. He has a foggy look in his eyes. "Understand this. Last stand is Vegas. The showgirls at the Flamingo and the buffet at the Bellagio are the only things that keep me going sometimes."

Vance Slater looks exasperated. He runs his hands down the side of his face. "Thompson, listen. The invasion is not about land. The real threat is about mass illegal aliens entering our country. They'll steal jobs, overwhelm our support system, change the language, and ruin our American way of life. That's the real emergency. We need to keep the un-Americans out."

The president takes a step back and looks at me strangely. "What's up with the clothes, Thompson?"

"Clothes, Mr. President?"

"And that tie? Are you a special agent or a PetSmart manager?"

"I, I . . ."

"Slater, call the magic-making people."

Slater grabs a phone, and within minutes two women and three men have surrounded me with tape measures, chalk, mumbles and orders, snips and pokes. When they are done I stand only in my boxers.

"Where's your gun?" President Wright asks.

I spread my hands out. "No gun."

"All special agents should have a gun. Vance, it's firearm time."

"Yes, sir." Slater loosens his tie, fishes his hand down the front of his shirt, and lands a key from a silver necklace. He walks to a mahogany cabinet on the far wall. Slater unlocks the massive doors and opens them to reveal guns galore.

"Hooyah!" crows the president.

There are M1s, M16s, M60s, Uzis, rifles, pistols, muskets, shotguns, and a few Daisies. The president pulls three long guns off the rack, places them in my arms, and grabs some more. He talks the whole while. "You need this to pierce armor, and this if you're pinned down, and this if you need to hunt for food, and, oh yeah, this has a laser-guided target finder. You could line up four of them squatters at a time."

"Mr. President, I can't possibly take all these guns."

Slater takes the guns from me and replaces them.

"Pistol is what you need," the president says.

I relent. "Okay, one pistol."

The president reaches into the cabinet and pulls out a silver beast of a pistol. "Smith & Wesson .44 Magnum—Dirty Harry special." He twirls the gun in the air and gazes at it with a gleam in his eye.

I point to a small black handgun that I instantly recognize. "How about that one?"

The president looks disappointed. "That little thing?"

"Walther PPK. James Bond, 007."

The president places the PPK in my hand. "I like how you think, Thompson."

The wardrobe team marches back in and attacks me in an haute couture bombardment. They are about to place a suit jacket on me when Slater says, "Wait." He drapes a leather-strapped shoulder holster over my neck, positions it against my left ribs for a right-handed quick draw, and slides the PPK inside. "Now you're ready."

I button the top of my jacket and walk over to a full-length mirror the magic makers have brought in. I reflect upon a perfectly tailored Armani suit, a white button-down Dior shirt, an Hermès tie, Versace socks, and Edward Green wingtips. I pack heat, and for the first time in my life, I feel like a special agent. The magic makers, the Secret Service guards, the president's personal pages, the White House chief of staff, and the president of the United States all stand back and admire me. I have arrived.

A suitcase and hanging bag are brought in. "Six more suits, shirts, and ties, with a couple extra belts and pairs of shoes," a magic man says.

Someone gruffly clears his throat. An ancient-looking man with wispy hair and a zombie-like face stands in a white lab coat. He holds a silver tray with plastic cups, a syringe, and a bottle of water.

"It's time for your medicine, Mr. President," Slater says.

"Excuse me for a moment." The president walks with the doctor and a plastic-faced man out of the room. I watch them go, frowning at the tray.

"You're ready," Slater says.

"For what?" I ask. "What's my cover?"

Slater reaches inside his jacket pocket. He hands me a piece of paper. "This should explain everything. You're an EPLO."

Emergency Preparedness Liaison Officer

```
Emergency Preparedness Liaison Officer or "EPLO"
is a generic term used to refer collectively to
Service and other DoD Agency personnel who coor-
dinate military assistance to other Federal Agen-
cies and State governments under an ALL HAZARDS
disaster or Federal emergency environment. The
EPLO refers to all DoD personnel serving with
the military and civilian headquarters having
primary planning, coordination, and execution
responsibilities under DoD Directive 3025.1(ref-
erence(c)). The CINC establishes EPLO authority
during Presidential National Emergency decla-
rations (or immediately prior to declaration).
EPLOs, at the discretion of the CINC, can inter-
face with the regional structure for planning and
coordination, and may be located at or operate
from FEMA National headquarters, FEMA Regional
headquarters, CINC, FORSCOM, CONUSA, STARC, or
DCE. These positions are established to: coordi-
nate the military response to ALL HAZARDS, coordi-
nate provision of resources as required, maintain
effective communication between the DoD compo-
nents, the Commander in Chief, the Department of
Defense and other Federal and/or State governmen-
tal agencies, and promote mutual understanding
among various organizations tasked with providing
and coordinating emergency support functions in
national or civil emergency situations.
```

I look at Slater, then to the paper, and then back to Slater. "What the heck? I, I, I'm . . ."

Slater slaps me on the back. "Nothing to it. Listen." He pauses and looks like he might tell me something important. "You might have noticed the president's not his usual self."

"Well, I . . ."

Slater puts his arm around me. "It's okay. The president's been having these, uh, moments. Which we of course want to keep absolutely private."

"I understand. You can trust me. I'm a member of Delta Delta Delta."

Slater gives a forced laugh. "Yes. And the CIA has many secret facilities. We don't know why the president's so focused on this Emergence one, but by law, he can now send a liaison out there."

"That's me."

"Yes, you. Look, I don't really know what this Emergence place is about either. We're going to send you out as clandestinely as possible, and whatever you find out there, I want to know before anyone else."

"Okay."

"I'm serious. Don't fuck this up. Straight out. Couple days and then back. I want to know everything you see. Then we'll report it all to the president together."

I look at Slater and think about what the president said about him. I try to figure out exactly what his angle is.

Slater still has his arm around me. He gives me a squeeze. "Don't worry. We won't keep anything from him, but you've seen the president's condition. We need to present information to him in a very specific way. Okay?"

This doesn't seem okay. "Okay," I say.

President Wright walks back into the room with a big smile on his face. "Fire up Marine One! No more lollygagging and wasting time, Thompson—we need you on the front lines now."

Vance Slater and the president usher me out into the hall. A page follows with my new wardrobe. Doors open to the South Lawn, and I can see the rotors of the presidential helicopter starting to turn and hear its engine beginning to whine.

The president looks at the helicopter with admiration. "Technically, it's only Marine One when I'm inside. But you can pretend if you want to."

"Where should I pretend Marine One is taking me?"

"That's the spirit!"

"Andrews Air Force Base, and then by jet to Emergence," Slater says.

I try to stop walking, but the old linebacker bulldogs me along.

"But—"

The president interrupts. "Don't worry, we're taking care of you. We've upped your pay to senator level, and we're throwing in a hazardous-duty bonus on top of that."

Wow. Senator level. I can't wait to tell Karen.

"From now on, you're deep undercover. You will cease all personal communications."

We walk out to the South Lawn, where Marine One perches in all its magnificence.

"Wait. I need to talk to my wife."

Vance Slater and President Wright look at each other. "Probably okay," Slater says.

"Go kiss the missus." The helicopter-induced wind blows the president's hair straight up. "Take the chopper to your house. No more than fifteen minutes though."

Slater shakes my hand. "Good luck." He begins to walk back toward the White House. Watching him go, the president shakes my hand and places a metal object in it.

"What's this?"

"It's a ring," he says quietly. "Put it on."

A Super-Bowl-size gold ring topped with an American-eagle-stamped shield rests in my palm. "You want me to wear it?"

The president looks to Vance Slater, who's still walking toward the White House. "Yeah, don't let Slater see."

Only my middle finger is large enough for the ring. I slide it on my left hand. "Why am I wearing this?"

"Ever hear of an LRAD—a long-range acoustic device?"

"Isn't that what cruise ships use to thwart pirates?"

"Exactly. This is a miniature one they made for my personal security. I call it a PRAD. *P* for puny. All I have to do is slap my hands together and point." He laughs. "And one hundred fifty decibels are directed in a beam of earsplitting noise."

The front side of the thick band is encased in a slightly protruding black mesh that looks like an electronic speaker.

"Does this really work?"

The president laughs. "Hell yeah. Knocked my kids flat." He gently pushes me toward the helicopter. "Now get out of here."

I start to walk.

"Wait." He grabs my arm and puts his lips next to my ear. He cups his hand over his mouth. "Don't forget this. Cannonball loves a roast beef sandwich with red peppers." He turns and walks back into the White House.

Confused and thrilled, I follow the page with my new bags toward the open door of Marine One.

4

I don't claim to be a master of words.
—SENATOR JOSEPH MᶜCARTHY

THE MARINES SHUT THE HELICOPTER DOOR and the president comes running out of the White House. He has a Taco Bell bag in one hand and is waving the other. The Marines open the door, stand at attention, and salute.

The president sticks his head through the helicopter door and hands me the bag. He shouts over the noise. "Your burrito. I put some nachos in too."

I look down at the bag, at a loss for words.

"You like margaritas?" the president asks.

The question takes me off guard, and I have to think. "Um, yes."

President Wright looks to the back of the helicopter, where a steward and more plastic-faced men sit. "Fire it up, boys." He looks at me. "I had a frozen margarita machine put in— you'll love it, Thompson." The president gives me a thumbs-up and backs away. The door shuts.

"Where do you live?" the captain asks.

I start to respond, but I am awestruck by her beauty. Her shoulder-length blonde hair cascades down from her helmet, and her skin glows with a gorgeous Miami Beach tan. I start to stumble over my words when the equally attractive brunette copilot gives me a notebook and pencil. "I'm Lieutenant Singer," she says.

"Special Agent Thompson," I say, wondering if the president personally selects the pilots.

She gestures to the captain. "Captain Pearson."

Captain Pearson gives me a salute. "Welcome aboard."

I write down my address and hand the notebook back to the lieutenant.

"Rock 'n' roll," Lieutenant Singer says. She reaches out her left fist to Captain Pearson, who reaches out her right. They touch knuckles and shout, "President's big green dream machine!"

The helicopter lifts into the air. I look out the window and watch the president become smaller and the whole White House come into view. The president waves excitedly. Plastic-faced men and women look on stoically from behind windows, the roof, and various spots on the lawn. I watch DC pan under me as we propel toward the Virginia suburbs.

I've been called out of my monotonous job on a secret mission for the president of the United States. I'm on Marine One. The government is about to declare a national emergency on the pretext that Canada and Mexico are secretly invading us, a ruse known only to President Wright, me, and somebody named Wizkid. Vance Slater is a part of the Big Mac Party, which has some sort of influence over the president. The president believes that the Big Mac Party is somehow involved with an old clandestine McCarthy program called Emergence, and I, while officially acting as a liaison to this program, am supposed to spy on it for him. There are a thousand guys in the government better qualified than me to be a presidential liaison, probably more, but I suppose that's why Vance Slater chose me. I'm wearing a secret-weapon ring, and I'm supposed to remember that Cannonball likes roast beef or something. And to think I've always laughed at conspiracy theorists. My head swirls with the rotors.

My neighborhood comes into view. We fly over the high school, the civic pool, the small downtown, and the park next to our subdivision. I find our house by counting three in from the park. The roof slants strangely from this angle, and the trees are indistinguishable, arranged similarly to those around the other houses. It all looks like a real-life version of an architect's 3-D model for a planned community. These buildings, places, and trees are home. They come at me all at once as we descend, and I take it in with a sense of pride and belonging.

The captain confidently drops the helicopter toward the middle of the street. The new subdivision trees below me bend like reeds in the downdraft. Newspapers and small debris twirl up into the air. The Campbells' side patio next to our house has a red canvas gazebo that I have never seen before. It shakes in the wind and then flies into the side of their house. The legs bend, and the gazebo rolls upward and lands atop their chimney. Paper napkins, plastic bowls, and plates scatter everywhere. Marine One touches down directly in front of our house. The Secret Service personnel pile out and station themselves around the green machine.

The captain flips some switches, and the engine turns off. "You have reached your destination."

The neighborhood's residents spill forth out of their houses. Stay-at-home moms and dads, men and women home from work early, children just returned from school, they all stand and gape. I see Karen standing behind Scotty on our front porch, her arms folded around his chest. These two are my family, my reason for being. Yet I have to leave them—for what? Duty? Adventure? Honor? Self-aggrandizement? Will any reason matter to Karen or Scotty?

Lieutenant Singer opens her door. "Need a stretch." She steps out, takes her helmet off, and shakes her head. The light breeze from the slowing rotor blades makes her hair float like a cover girl's.

I climb out of the helicopter and walk up the front sidewalk toward our three-bedroom seventy-eight-percent-mortgaged ranch-style-with-finished-basement home. Time slows down as the wind from the helicopter subsides, and I glide dreamlike toward my family. The steward walks behind me, two frozen margaritas in his hand. The neighbors look on astonished, their faces sagging with respect and jealousy. I used to dream about arriving like this at a high school reunion, but this would do.

I walk about five paces before they recognize me. Karen puts her hands to her face, and Scotty comes running toward me.

"Awesome, Dad!"

I reach out and give him a high five. "Hey, sport."

Karen walks toward us, her eyes scanning the neighbors and then Lieutenant Singer and me. "Honey. How? What?"

I put my index finger over my lips. "Let's go inside."

We walk through the living room back into the kitchen. I place the Taco Bell bag on our round glass table. The steward hands me the frozen margaritas in salt-rimmed glasses. I hand one to Karen. "Cheers."

I take a sip of the margarita and set the glass down. Karen quickly puts her glass down without trying it. She opens the curtains and looks out the window at the Campbells' house. "Phyllis is having book club in forty-five minutes. Her patio is ruined."

The steward starts to leave. "Can you clean up next door?" I ask.

"Of course, sir." He leaves and closes the door on the ridiculousness outside.

I breathe and sigh, relieved to be alone with Karen and Scotty. "There. No harm done."

Karen continues to look out the window. "Cleaning it up

won't do any good. She's been cooking and making things all day. There's potato salad and brownies plastered all over the side of their house."

"It's an accident. She'll get over it. Karen, I have bigger things to discuss."

"She went to buy wine. She'll be home any minute."

I put my arm around Karen and guide her back to the kitchen table. "Someone will take care of it."

"You're late."

"I'm sorry."

"Twenty minutes! That's all. You'd think you'd be able to find twenty minutes for your son."

Scotty pulls on her arm. "That's all right, Mom."

"Three concerts." Karen pushes three fingers in front of my face. "You've missed three concerts."

"I told you I had a meeting with the president."

"Phyllis is going to be hysterical. She only has book club once a year."

I spread my hands out to plead innocence. "I couldn't break away. President Wright kept talking."

Karen puts her hands on my suit. Her brown eyes take in my designer clothes. "Are you having an affair?" A clip holds back her silky black hair, and her ponytail shakes accusingly.

"An affair? I land on the street in the president's helicopter and that's the first thing you think?"

"Are you?"

"No!" I shake my head and roll my eyes. "Scotty, want some nachos?"

Scotty digs into the Taco Bell bag. "Is that really the president's helicopter?" He looks at me with heartwarming pride.

"Yes—one of them, anyway."

Karen's voice pleads. "Why did you have a meeting with the president? Why is that helicopter on our street?"

I wink at Scotty. "I'll tell you why." I snap my fingers and point at my chest with my thumbs. "I have been selected for a secret mission by the president of the United States."

"Yes!" Scotty says.

"No," Karen says. "There must be some mistake."

"It's true. There's a national emergency that requires my services."

"Turn on CNN, Scotty," Karen says.

"Of course we have to keep this quiet," I say. "If anyone asks about the helicopter, tell them I won Federal Employee of the Month."

Scotty lifts the remote from the gold-speckled Formica counter and turns on the TV that sits on a fiberboard shelf at the far end of the kitchen. He changes the channel to CNN and takes a large bite of nachos.

I cut the burrito in half and share it with Karen. Now that we're eating together and things seem slightly more normal, she relaxes, and even takes a sip of her margarita. "Not bad."

"Compliments of the president."

"Stop it, Chris."

"It's true. There's a frozen margarita machine in the back of Marine One."

"Oh, please."

CNN switches to the White House lawn as President Wright steps in front of the press corps.

"Turn it up, Scotty."

The president speaks. "Today the United States is eliminating federal contracts with corporations that disrespect our embargo policies, particularly those companies that continue to conduct business with Communist Latin American governments. In the spirit of the Monroe Doctrine, the United States is committed to subverting threats and guaranteeing freedom for all people throughout the Americas."

I watch him continue to speak, amazed that he's suddenly this eloquent. "It's hard to believe."

"What's not to believe? Those countries are a thorn in our side," Karen says. "Doesn't look like any national emergency though."

"The threat isn't public yet. But I meant the president. He seems so normal."

"What's that supposed to mean? President Wright is always the consummate statesman."

"President Wright might have some issues," I say.

Karen puts her hand on her slender waist and swings her elbow out like a school-bus stop sign to keep me in place. She rolls her eyes, extends her jaw, and sighs. Boy, does she look beautiful. "Just because you don't agree with the president's policies doesn't mean he's an idiot. That's at least one thing the whole country can agree on—our president is an extremely intelligent man."

I shake my head. "I was with him a half hour ago, and I know it's hard to fathom, but in person President Wright is completely unpredictable. He jumps around like a madman, but then wises up and claims it's all an act."

"What's wrong with you, Chris?"

"Listen, I'm telling you the president plays Bulls-Eye Ball and a musical triangle. He thinks Lance Armstrong landed on the moon."

"You expect me to believe this?"

I try to veer the conversation. "The president also promoted me to senator pay level."

That perks her up. "Really? That's over six figures."

"Really. See? This could be good."

"Maybe we could redo the kitchen?"

"Maybe," I say as noncommittally as possible.

She juts out her lower lip, exhales, and blows a loose strand of hair out of her eyes. "I want to believe you. I really do."

"I just landed out front in a presidential helicopter with margaritas and Taco Bell. What other proof do I need?"

"That's not proof. That's just craziness."

I pull out my new Tri-Delta identification card. "Look at this."

Karen takes the card. She flips it over a couple times to further examine it. "It looks like a doctored-up sorority ID to me. How'd you get this?"

"It's my new position. I have ultra top-level security clearance. Might be crazy, but I think the president made that card himself."

Karen closes her eyes and pinches the top part of her nose. "My God. You're carrying around a sorority ID. You must be having an affair."

"What?"

"And with a Tri-Delt, even. How ironic. You know they rejected me in college?"

"I thought you didn't want to be in their sorority."

"Of course I didn't want to be in their sorority if they didn't want me to be in their sorority," Karen sniffs.

On CNN, reporters raise their arms and clamor with more zeal than usual to ask the president questions. "*President Wright announces switch to the Big Mac Party*" scrolls across the screen.

"Wait," I say, and we both start watching more closely.

The TV returns to a close-up of the president. "As the newest member of the Big Mac Party, I will work to ensure that American core values are at the forefront of every government decision. America shall be first in our thoughts, our families, our work, and our world. Senator Joseph McCarthy, although some may have questioned his methods, had a spirit and message that we all, as true Americans, can believe in. The Big Mac Party discourages un-American activities. The Big Mac Party will make America number one again, now and forevermore."

The president refuses further questions and walks into the White House.

Karen looks rattled. "This is the strangest day."

"I got a Big Mac sticker," Scotty says. He proudly holds up his backpack. It has a round sticker with the words "Big Mac Attack! America #1" written in a circle around an American flag.

"Where'd you get this?"

"School. For eating an American lunch and not using any foreign words all day."

Someone knocks on the door, and a plastic-faced man sticks in his head. "The press is on their way, sir. We need to leave."

I look at Karen and Scotty. "I'm sorry I have to leave. I don't know how long I'll be gone, and I might not be able to communicate with you. I don't really understand all that is happening, but I'm pretty sure the president doesn't mean what he says about this Big Mac thing. And don't believe everything they tell you at school, Scotty. There are plenty of good foreign words you can use."

"Hasta la vista," Scotty says.

I point at him. "Exactly."

Karen is pacing. "Why would the president want a desk man from the Customs Service? Scotty. Quick. How many Chris Thompsons are there around here?"

Scotty runs to the computer in the family room. He moves the mouse and confidently clicks. "Five Chris Thompsons in Washington, DC, sixty Chris Thompsons in Virginia, and twenty-four in Maryland."

Karen points her finger at me with authority. "They've obviously made a big mistake. You're not the Chris Thompson they want." She whips her finger to Scotty. "There must be other Chris Thompsons in the federal government."

"At least sixteen," Scotty says. "Do you have to kill some people?"

"Won't be anything too dangerous, sport."

Karen's hands shake. "You have to tell them. It's a case of mistaken identity."

I grab her hands. "No. They've researched my past and are impressed with some of my talents. I can't explain it all now, but I'm confident they want me."

Karen pulls her hands out of mine. "Okay, assume they want you. You've seen all the spy movies. The random guy always gets killed. If there's another double-0 agent in any Bond movie, you can be sure he's the one going down."

"I'm sorry, Karen. I have to do this." I pat Scotty on the head. "You're the man of the house now. Be good for your mother."

Scotty salutes me. "Yes, sir."

I reach out to give him a hug.

Karen wipes her eyes. "What is she, like twenty-one?"

"Who?"

"Your sorority girlfriend."

"There's no sorority girlfriend," I explain again. "Trust me. I'm not having an affair. I'm on an assignment from the president and I love you."

She puts her hands on my chest and clutches my white dress shirt. "You're no James Bond," she says. "You think you are, but you're not."

I want to say she's wrong, but I can't.

Karen holds on to me tight. "I didn't marry a spy. I married an average Joe, and that's the way I like it."

"Well, maybe I don't," I say.

She taps my chest. "James Bond is fiction, and you're real. You're a knucklehead, but real. James Bond is invincible, and you're not." She shakes me. "Do you hear me, Chris?"

I reach out, fold her into my arms, and kiss her long on the lips.

The front door opens. "Sir, we have to go now."

I pull away from Karen and high-five Scotty. "I'll try to contact you guys somehow, but if not don't worry."

"Awesome, Dad," Scotty says.

I walk out the door and across our front lawn. I fight through the rotor-induced wind and step into the noisy helicopter.

I hear Karen yelling. She runs toward me with her finger pointing.

"Karen, please."

I start to climb out, but two Secret Service men each grab one of my arms and pull me into the helicopter.

"Don't you leave us," she shouts.

The mighty grips of the Secret Service men hold me in.

The pilots click knuckles. "President's big green dream machine!" We lift off the ground.

Today is my day. I've gotten my big chance. A chance to prove myself and to make a difference. But right now, leaving Karen and Scotty for who knows where, it feels wrong. Does President Wright have any idea what I risk losing?

The helicopter rises further into the sky. I see Karen fall to her knees. Scotty comes up and puts his arms around her. I wave feebly and force a smile. Scotty waves back, and they both disappear into a speck. I feel as small as they look.

5

*This must be a product of a great conspiracy, a conspiracy
on a scale so immense as to dwarf any previous such
venture in the history of man.*
—SENATOR JOSEPH McCARTHY

THE HELICOPTER LANDS next to a hangar at Andrews Air Force Base. Adjacent to the hangar is a sleek, black metallic Gulfstream 6, the world's premier private jet. The United States Air Force seal is on the fuselage, directly behind the cockpit window. The cabin door is open, and the steps are folded out.

The pilots kill the helicopter engine and take off their helmets. The Secret Service team exits, stretches their legs, and begins to chat. The sun beats down on the hot cement. We are at a remote section of the field; the quiet is disrupted every few moments by a distant plane engine's roar.

The great doors of the hangar part slightly, and a lone figure emerges and walks confidently toward us. He wears a green air force jumpsuit and looks thin and sinewy, like he can do a hundred pull-ups.

"The immortal Fixer," the captain says.

"The immortal asshole," the lieutenant says.

The captain shakes her head. "I told you not to go out with him."

Fixer walks up to the helicopter and stands next to the captain's open window. He has a strong jaw and short black hair that spikes up slightly in the center. The outside of the helicopter reflects off his Top Gun shades. "Hey there, Captain Pearson."

The captain looks at him with disdain. "Fixer."

Fixer cocks his head. "What do you say to me and you getting together for a few drinks at the officers' club Friday night?" He looks over to Lieutenant Singer. "Last couple of dates I had were duds."

Lieutenant Singer angrily flips him off.

"For the hundredth time, *no*, Fixer," the captain says.

"Only thirty-eight, if we're keeping track."

"Don't you give up?"

"Don't see why I should. Your rejections are much less spirited than when we first met. Someday Captain Pearson you'll say yes, and then we'll party like real pilots." He looks at Lieutenant Singer. "And not like amateurs."

"Go to hell, Fixer!" the lieutenant snaps, glaring. "I'll fly your ass out of the sky anytime."

Fixer lowers his sunglasses and winks at her. She clenches her fists.

"Don't you have something better to do?" the captain asks.

"Yeah," says Fixer. "You have a suit for me?"

She points her thumb back at me. "I have a suit, but he's for Captain Riley." She nods her head toward the Gulfstream. A tall male air force pilot climbs down the stairs.

"Riley, of course," Fixer says. "But I'm involved in it too."

"Aren't they lucky," Lieutenant Singer says.

"Damn right." Fixer steps over to the open door and sticks his hand in for a shake. "They call me the Fixer," he says to me.

"Some say 'the Faker,'" Lieutenant Singer says.

I shake his rough hand. "I'm—"

"Wait. No names," he says.

"Names are way too personal for Fixer," the lieutenant says. "He prefers to keep everything on a purely superficial level."

"Security for everyone," he says. "Are you ready?"

I hop out of the helicopter and grab my bags from the efficient steward. Fixer and I walk toward the Gulfstream.

I wave to the pilots, steward, and Secret Service team. "Thanks."

Fixer blows a kiss to the pilots. "Until next time, you superficial, super-luscious, super-licious ladies."

They ignore him, and the helicopter takes off.

"Hang on a second." Fixer walks over to the Gulfstream pilot. He shows him something on his smartphone and then nods to me. The pilot, whom they referred to as Captain Riley, brings out his cell phone and makes a call. Fixer points to the presidential helicopter flying away in the distance. He and Captain Riley slap hands and laugh. Captain Riley hangs up his phone. He shakes hands with Fixer and climbs back into the Gulfstream. The stairs go up and the engines start to whine.

Fixer walks back to me. "Change of plans."

"I'm supposed to be going to Emergence," I tell him.

Fixer starts walking toward the hangar. "You will. Mr. Slater thought it would be better for you to travel a little more inconspicuously."

I follow Fixer a step behind. The Gulfstream taxis away toward a distant runway. We reach the hangar, watching over our shoulders as the plane roars into the air. Fixer turns and leads me into the dark hangar. The silhouette of a large airplane looms in front of us.

"Stay here." Fixer walks along the hangar door into the dark. A light turns on inside an office.

"Don't move," Fixer yells.

I hear a clunk, a screech, and then a dull rolling rattle as the hangar doors separate. Daylight illuminates the inside. An old jumbo airliner with a faded United Airlines logo from years ago comes into focus.

Fixer appears next to me. "Ain't she a beaut?"

The cavernous hangar is silent. The monstrous plane looks content in her resting spot. "So peaceful," I say.

"DC-10. I'm told they're one of the sweetest planes to fly."

"Doesn't look like she's flown in a while."

Fixer claps his hands. "We're going to change that today."

He's joking. The silent hangar is devoid of any preflight activity. Yet Fixer takes my bags and walks toward the plane. "Stay here."

He climbs up a mobile aluminum stairway to the plane's open door. He turns and calls to me. "Hey, suit. Push the stairs away and close the hangar doors after I bring her out."

I stare at him.

He points. "There's a big switch in the office."

I continue to stare at him.

He shoos me with his hands. "Go!"

I turn mechanically and push the stairs out of the way.

A small hatch opens underneath the plane, directly below the cockpit. A leg protrudes and steps on one of the front landing wheels. Fixer bounces out and onto the ground. He walks to the back of the hangar and hops on an aircraft tug.

I step inside the office and wait.

Fixer drives the tug to the front of the plane and hooks it up. He slowly pulls the DC-10 out of the hangar. When it clears the doorway, he comes to a stop.

I look out into the distance across the airport's cement sea and search for mechanics, or a flight crew, or anything officially related to flying this airplane. Nothing. I flip a large red switch that says HANGAR DOOR to the "Close" position and walk out of the building as the doors rumble shut.

Fixer parks the tug next to the hangar and walks back to

the open hatch. He climbs up onto the landing wheels and motions for me to follow.

I hesitate. My mouth becomes dry. He really thinks he's going to fly this thing.

He motions me over. "Come on."

I look down the old plane's long fuselage. I imagine an engine falling off during turbulence.

"President's orders," he says.

The commander in chief. As a United States Customs Service agent, I long ago pledged an oath to defend the Constitution against all enemies, foreign and domestic, a promise I had assumed to be a mere formality. Fixer has called me out. With a sense of duty I walk over to him. "This is not exactly inconspicuous," I say.

Fixer chuckles. "After you."

He helps me stand on the wheel. I reach up and grab hold of a small metal ladder, place my foot on it, and climb up. Fixer follows, closing the hatch behind him. I emerge in the cockpit, just behind the pilot seats. I step out of the cockpit door to make room for Fixer, who climbs up, closes the hatch, and joins me just outside the cockpit.

The plane's cabin has been stripped. There are no chairs, overhead compartments, flight attendant workstations, or cabin separators. Only a metal floor and a ceiling of dangling wires and tubes remain.

"I don't think this thing is going anywhere anytime soon," I say and hope.

"Nonsense," Fixer says. "I tuned up the engines this morning. She's fueled up and ready to go."

How could only one man prepare this huge plane?

Fixer walks forward to the cockpit. "Let's fire her up."

I grab his shoulder and spin him around. "You can't be serious?"

"Of course I'm serious."

"But you're just going to fire the engines up, right? You're not thinking of flying this thing."

He walks away and enters the cockpit. I quickly follow. "Mr. Fixer? You're not thinking of flying this thing."

"How else are we going to transport you to Emergence?" He sits down in the captain's chair and opens a DC-10 flight manual.

"I don't know. Maybe a car, train, or an air force plane like that nice G6 you sent away. You know—something legit, with a real pilot."

He flips switches, and the cockpit comes to life. "Oh, that hurts. Look, I'm not too shy to admit that I'm the best pilot in the country, and probably in the entire world."

"But—but you previously stated that someone *told* you a DC-10 is sweet to fly. This implies that you have never flown one before."

"I checked it out last night with my laptop flight simulator." He flips a switch and there's a loud whirring noise. "There's nothing to it."

"What's that noise? You broke something."

He flips a few more switches. "Auxiliary power unit. Need air pressure to start the turbines." He pushes a throttle forward slightly and presses a button. "Firing up number one."

"I can't believe this is happening."

"Hey, you need a code name. Is that an Armani suit you're wearing?"

"So?"

"So I'm calling you Giorgio."

"I don't care what you call me as long as we don't take off. Don't we need help? Don't we need to tell somebody?"

"You want to be copilot, Giorgio?"

No, I want to be ground crew. "Do I have a choice?"

"Sure, as long as you're on the plane, you can do whatever the hell you want."

I sit in the copilot seat, and we buckle ourselves in. Fixer pushes on the throttles, and we begin to taxi.

"You sure we don't have to talk to someone? Shouldn't you be wearing headphones or something?"

"Nah, no need to talk to anyone. They always ruin the fun."

"We're just taking off?"

"Relax—we're clear for runway 24W, and once in the air we're a free bird straight west. Controllers have moved all other traffic out of the way for us. This baby is going to the airplane graveyard in Arizona, so this mission will serve two purposes." We turn onto a rubber-streaked runway, and Fixer jams the throttles forward. "It's her last flight—let's make it fun."

The plane rolls and picks up speed. Fixer has a huge grin on his face, one hand on the yoke, the other twirling in the air. "Yeeoww!"

We race down the runway. The tire streaks blur underneath us; I dig my fingers into my pants and find it difficult to breathe. Fixer puts both hands on the yoke and pulls back. We rocket into the air and are silent for a few minutes.

Fixer pushes the yoke forward and our ascent becomes gradual. "Nothing to it," he says.

I spin my new PRAD ring around my finger. It's okay. He seems in control.

Fixer banks the plane left, straightens her out, and begins checking dials and pushing buttons. He flips one last switch. "Good afternoon, Captain Casper." He climbs out of his seat and exits the cockpit.

What the hell? "Hey!"

"Don't worry, Casper's got her. Come on."

Alone in the cockpit, I'm afraid to touch anything. I carefully slink out of my seat and follow Fixer back to the cabin. He opens window shades. "Do the other side."

The cabin fills with warm light: tranquil, yet eerie in the empty space.

"I need to work out." Fixer stretches. "You want to work out?"

"No. Shouldn't we watch the plane?"

"Relax and have some fun." Fixer sprints to the end of the plane and stops to do push-ups. He sprints back and does sit-ups. He does this over and over.

I go to check the cockpit. Although the plane appears to be flying normally, the sight of it doing so without any pilot terrifies me. I run back to the cabin.

Fixer has his hands on his knees, gasping for breath. "Whew."

"How about resting in the cockpit?"

To my relief he agrees, and we return to our cockpit seats. Fixer jabbers on about nothing but happy things, while I remain silent. After a while he inquires, "Why so glum?"

"I miss my wife and kid."

A storm of confusion passes over his face. "It's only been an hour or two since you left them, hasn't it?"

"I know. It's just that she didn't want me to go. She didn't believe me. She didn't think any of this was real."

"It's not real," says Fixer.

Maybe not to him. "Don't you have any family?"

"Nope, no problems," he says with macho disgust.

"Parents or siblings?"

"Nope. I'm the last Fixer left—a requirement for the job. How about you?"

I picture Mom and Dad in their pajamas from Christmases years ago. "My parents have passed, and I have no siblings."

Fixer smiles. "You're almost like me."

I wonder.

Fixer punches me in the shoulder. "You need to drown your sorrows, Giorgio." He reaches behind his seat, opens up a compartment, and lifts out a blue Igloo cooler. He pulls two cans out and tosses one to me. "PBR, Pabst Blue Ribbon. As red, white, and blue as a beer can be."

"Is this legal?"

"We're way above the law."

"Nobody's above the law."

"I am. I assure you. And you're about to be too." He hands me a metal pen. "Let's shotgun 'em."

"You're not serious?"

"Live a little, Giorgio." He holds the PBR in his hand. "Ready, on the count of three."

He thinks I'm pathetic. I can do this. I sit in the copilot's seat of an empty DC-10 flying thirty thousand feet in the air and prepare to shotgun a beer for the first time since college.

"One, two, *three*."

We strike our pens into the bottom of the cans and lift them to our lips. I open the top tab. Beer rushes down my throat, and within seconds the can is empty.

"Whoo!" Fixer crunches his can and throws it behind him. "Again."

I hold up my hand. "Enough."

Fixer opens two more beers and hands me one. "You're right—we should enjoy this one."

I sip while Fixer chugs. He opens another. "Time for some fun." He pushes the throttles full forward and pulls the yoke back. We start a steep ascent. He starts punching keys into a small console.

"What are you doing?"

"Programming the autopilot." Fixer pulls back on the throttles and pushes the yoke forward. He presses one more button on the autopilot and climbs out of his seat.

"It feels like we're falling," I shout.

Fixer runs toward the cabin. "Exactly," he shouts. "Perfect parabolic flight. Get in here—we only have thirty seconds."

I'm slightly buzzed, and it makes an odd kind of sense. I bounce into the cabin like I'm walking on the moon. Fixer does somersaults in the air. "Weightlessness!"

I do a little jump and float, twisting my body like a spinning torpedo. The zero-gravity thrill, coupled with the abject fear of flying on a diving, pilotless plane, is a walk on the fine line of insanity. It feels addictive. Quickly my fear overcomes my amusement-park desires. "Fixer. The time!"

"Push me."

I push him, and he sails into the cockpit.

The plane pulls out of its dive, and I land on the floor with a thud. I feel nauseous and return to my cockpit seat.

Fixer puts another PBR to his lips.

"How can you drink after that?"

"Party never stops with Fixer."

"You have to land this plane. You can't be drunk."

Fixer laughs and reaches for another beer. "Who said anything about landing?"

He's trying to scare me. "I did. You've got to land this thing."

"I lied about the airplane graveyard. Instead, we're going to ram this plane into the side of a mountain."

If he's joking I fall for it. "No. That makes no sense. That's crazy."

"It's well thought out, I assure you."

I raise my voice. "I can think of no good reason to crash a perfectly flying plane, especially one with me on board, into a mountain."

"Here's some sense for you," he says. "For one, the government, for whatever reason, needs this plane to disappear." He pauses. "And two, you need to die."

Die? I grab the yoke in front of me and prepare to thwart any sudden flight maneuvers by Fixer. "I'll give you a hell of a fight. You may be stronger, but I've got more to live for."

He slaps his knee and laughs. "Man, you are domesticated."

I remember the PPK. Holding the yoke with my left hand, I draw the gun with my right and point it at Fixer. "Joke time is over."

Tell me what you want and I'll say it.
—SENATOR JOSEPH McCARTHY

FIXER STOPS LAUGHING. "Whoa, cowboy. Relax, relax, nobody is going to die."

"But you said I needed to die."

"Not literally. We jump out, the plane crashes, and on paper you're dead."

"We jump out?"

"In a parachute, Giorgio. Now put that gun away."

His face softens, and he appears truthful. I slowly put the PPK into its holster. "Why do I need to die?"

"Everyone dies."

I sigh. "Is this a game to you?"

"Yes." Fixer's eyes light up. "And the key is not to win or lose, but to stay in the game and keep having fun."

"I'm more concerned about the dying part. The president didn't say anything about dying."

Fixer leans forward and gazes out the window like he's looking for something on the ground. "Haven't you figured out that the president doesn't know anything about anything? That's why he's sending you to Emergence—so you can find out something about something."

I look at him, trying to figure out how much he might know. "Vance Slater's sending me, too."

"Slater's sending you to find out nothing about something," Fixer says.

"What's that supposed to mean? What do you know about Emergence?"

He pulls back slightly on the throttle. The engine whine lessens and the plane slows. "Forget about it. You'll find out soon enough. And don't worry about the dying part. Death is hope. Death is the good part of our job. Everyone at Emergence is dead."

"Bullshit." I point at him. "Talk straight for once."

Fixer holds up his palms. "Government dead, I mean. Emergence is so secret that it technically doesn't exist, and if you're going to visit there, you can't exist either."

I breathe in deep. "So, what you're saying is that the government fakes their deaths."

"Exactly. And trust me, a government death is the best kind."

"Well, sure. You're not really dead."

"But the beauty of it is you get to be reborn." Fixer gestures with his hands like an animated preacher. "Really reborn. Not just some hopeful Jesus-Bible-beating, Hare-Krishna-dancing, matzo-ball-eating, Muhammad-Ali-punching redemption. Real government forgiving rebirth."

"Like with a new name and everything?"

"Yes. They give you a new name, new clothes, a new place to live, and new friends. Think of it! No more debts, grudges, taxes, paternity suits, or psycho stalking women who don't understand what really being single is all about."

"Isn't being single a temporary state while you're in pursuit of a meaningful relationship?"

"You're hopeless, Giorgio. I should be calling you Ward."

"Whatever." I shake my head. "Look, I don't want to die, not even a blessed government death. What about my wife and kid? They can't think I'm dead. I'm not giving them up."

He looks perplexed. "You're serious, aren't you?"

"Of course I'm serious!"

Fixer raises his arm and looks at his titanium Kobold Polar Surveyor watch. "It's time." He runs into the cockpit, and the plane begins to descend.

"I don't want to die," I shout.

Fixer emerges with a tangled web of straps. He tosses me a helmet, and like an evil spider he entombs me in his harness.

I think of Karen and Scotty. I'm a fool. I wanted to be a spy. I wanted danger and excitement, and now I've got it. I've left my family in order to jump out of a crashing airplane with a half-cocked thrill seeker. "I'm not leaving my family."

"Deal with that later." Fixer runs to the rear emergency exit and opens it. My ears pop as the pressure changes. The wind howls. "You can die with me or die with the plane."

I'm frozen.

"Now!" he shouts.

The plane is going down. Fixer is crazy, yet oddly competent. I have no choice. My knees shake uncontrollably as I walk toward him. How does Bond remain so cool? "I've never jumped," I yell through the noisy wind.

Fixer lassoes me and then shackles me to him. He stands behind me and wraps his arms around me in an uncomfortable hug. "We go together."

"My bags."

"Government waste."

"What?"

"Government—" Fixer shoves me and we both tumble out. My stomach seizes and my breathing stops. I fall into blackness worse than any bad elevator dream. The freezing air buffets my face like an arctic storm as I fall in the bottomless night air.

"Whoo!" Fixer shouts.

I catch my breath, and then I scream.

The chute opens and jerks us like a jackknife. Our fall becomes a float.

"Shit," Fixer says.

I look up: A line restrains the chute, and a quarter of it remains collapsed. We spin in circles as if we're on a miniature flying chair ride at a carnival.

Fixer screams.

A terrific fireball erupts as the plane crashes into a distant mountain. The sounds of the explosion reach us a few seconds later.

The ground rapidly approaches. Fixer continues to scream. Fear so paralyzes me I cannot utter a sound. A forest of pine trees welcomes our landing.

Fixer takes the brunt of our crash into the top of a pine. The tree catches us, and we tumble down through its needle arms, free-falling the last twenty feet when the branches end.

Fixer hits the ground first with a thud. I land on top of him. I unlatch and roll over. Fixer looks delirious. His face is a bloody mess.

"Fixer."

His eyes laggardly roll as he tries to focus on me. He coughs and spits up blood. His face turns a white-streaked purple.

"Fixer!"

"Time to die," he whispers.

"You can make it," I say, not believing it he looks so awful.

"Top pocket." He clumsily rests his hand on his top-left flight suit pocket.

I open the pocket and pull out a small green Gideons New Testament. Post-it notes with sloppy handwriting protrude from the pages.

"My mother's. From the Motel 6 where I was conceived."

"And these are notes from her?"

"No. Lancaster signed off on this, so it should be official."

"Lancaster who? Official what?"

His eyes open and close. They can't seem to focus. "Lancaster said I could go with the chosen ones if I brought you. I could have lived forever."

I don't understand what he's talking about. He's delirious. I look and the top note says: "If you have found me dead or in a perilous situation where my death is likely, please be kind enough to read these last rites."

"I'm going for help."

"Read the rest," Fixer gurgles through blood. He looks at me, smiles, and gives me a thumbs-up. He whispers. "It should cover me." His eyes look up to the sky. "The stars." He stops blinking and his eyeballs freeze. I touch his forehead, face, and neck. I have no idea what to do. I put my head on his chest and listen. Nothing. Fixer is dead.

I've never seen anyone die and it's bewildering. "Fixer," I say, knowing he won't respond, but not believing it either. I feel obligated to read his last rites. I speak loudly and look to the sky:

"Dear God, have mercy on the soul of the human known as the Fixer, the best pilot in the world, undoubtedly the best pilot of all time. Fixer was an absolute expert at solving world problems. Every living being on earth is indebted to him. His uncanny good looks and amazing ability to survive the most harrowing situations known to man led to the belief by some of his immortality. Whoever is reading this may want to double-check if he is really dead, for it is most likely a famous Fixer prank."

I reach down and double-check Fixer's neck for a pulse. Nope, he's dead all right. I continue reading:

"Okay—so it's not a joke. Damn it! Okay. Fixer was a holy

warrior for the United States of America, a nation formed in God's image. And although he may have broken some rules, his heart always beat to the rhythm of the rockets' red glare. Please accept Fixer's soul into the hereafter, where he promises to continue his good deeds and get things done in the American way."

I've only known him for a few hours, but tears well up in my eyes. "You stupid son of a bitch. Thought you could play forever?" I gaze up through the cool crisp night air and to the stars he had looked upon. I imagine Fixer's soul racing to the heavens and hope someone up there will take him.

I put the last rites in my pocket. That's it. The plane is gone. Fixer is gone. I'm stuck alone in the middle of the forest. Mission over. President Wright can send another liaison to figure out what Emergence does. They might even think I've died, too. Could I wipe the slate clean, like Fixer said? The thought is tempting. I look to the sky for a few moments and grapple with the immensity of it all. I touch my chest as if to feel my heart; as if to check that I'm still me. I shake my head. I've got to get out of here. I need to go home.

A hard stick hits the back of my knees and knocks me off of my feet. A person in a black ninja suit, complete with head wrap, lands on my chest. The ninja grabs my hair with one hand and presses the blade of a knife to my neck with the other. "You move, you die," she says.

I am listening with one ear.
—SENATOR JOSEPH McCARTHY

"UNDERSTAND?" the ninja asks.

I don't understand at all. "I understand," I say.

She releases my hair and puts the knife away. She grabs her bo staff and steps over Fixer's body. "Your friend didn't make it," she says nonchalantly.

I stand up and rub my sore legs. "Who are you? And why did you attack me?"

She does a flying karate kick and lands in front of me. "I'm Ninjenna. Are you impressed?"

"I'm more sore than impressed."

"Shit. Look, I'm sorry about the knockdown. It's just that I wanted to impress you."

"You scared me, though. Who are you?"

"Ninjenna! You haven't heard of me?"

"No."

She whacks her bo staff against the ground. "Damn. I'm trying so hard to get a reputation. I'm sort of the protector around here."

"I'll remember you," I say, thinking out loud.

She perks up. "Really? Could you put a good word in? I so want to move up a level. Picking you up is the most exciting thing I've done since I arrived here two years ago. Is it true what they say?"

"I have no idea what you're talking about."

"Don't be coy. I've heard the stories."

"What stories?"

She points at me. "You know. The rumors are the government has figured out the secret to everlasting life. And that your level is in on it."

I roll my eyes and flick my hand in the air. "Look. I've had it with you nut-job spooks or whatever you are. How do I get out of here? I want to go home."

Ninjenna drops into a karate-ready pose. She looks at Fixer's body and then back at me. "Aren't you Fixer?"

I point to the body. "That's Fixer."

Her soft padded ninja shoes tip-tap over to Fixer. She kneels down and feels his neck. "He's dead." Her head slumps. "I can't believe it."

"I'm sorry. I only knew him a few hours. He seemed like a nice guy."

Ninjenna stands up and faces me. "This was my first chance to work with him." She paces. "I should have known. You were so easy to take down." She sits on the ground and crosses her legs in ninja fashion, resting her bo staff over her knees. "All hope is lost."

"How'd you get here?"

"Ten years of ninja training for naught."

"Do you have a car close by?"

"I renounced my religion. My parents won't even talk to me. All for some pipe dream."

I raise my voice. "Hey. Where the hell are we?"

She jumps up and checks me with her bo staff. "You don't understand."

"Ow!"

"Fixer is a legend. He supposedly had the secret." She checks me again.

"Hey." I back away and around Fixer. His body separates Ninjenna and me. "What secret?"

"I told you before. Everlasting life. Fixer couldn't die. He had everlasting life. I've worked ten years and gone through three levels to reach this point. I only had one more level to go. I wanted to live forever too!" She whips the bo staff over her head and twirls it in the air. "You *are* with the government, right?"

"Customs Service."

"Good enough. Somebody needs to pay." She lunges across Fixer's body and swings the bo staff at my head.

I duck and she misses. I turn and run into the woods, dodging pine trees for two hundred yards. I stop and hide behind a tree large enough to conceal me.

"You're playing my game now," she yells.

She's right. I think about using the PPK, but the dark precludes any accuracy, and it seems excessive. I call out, "Maybe those rumors had the secret wrong."

Silence.

"Fixer said something about being reborn," I yell.

"He did?" she asks, whispering in my ear.

I scream, jump, and spin around.

"What's this about being reborn?" Ninjenna continues, inches from me.

I try to calm down. At least I have her interest. "I don't know. I thought it was a load of crap, but Fixer said with a government death you get to be reborn."

"Really?"

She's buying it. I feel a little bad twisting the truth, but hell, I want to get out of here. "Yep. Fixer claimed he had been reborn several times."

She whacks the bo staff against the tree. "I knew it. Holy shit." She runs toward the landing spot. "Come on."

When I reach her she is digging through Fixer's pockets. She holds up a small black box with a blinking red light.

"His transponder." She flicks a switch on the transponder and four red lights, one on each side, blink rapidly.

"Our table is ready," I say.

She sets the transponder on Fixer's chest. "Let's go, smartass."

I follow her into the woods. "Are we doing anything about Fixer?"

"Not my department. I turned his transponder to emergency mode. They'll come for him fast as they can. Damn. I should have followed procedures and fired it up right away. They probably want to cryo-freeze him or something. Why didn't you tell me about him being reborn?"

"You were beating and stalking me. And I did tell you."

She ignores me. "Hope this doesn't hurt my chances for the next level. Think of it—being reborn. And we were a part of it."

I want to point out I had only witnessed a death, but think better of it.

We emerge from the forest next to a two-lane highway. A white 1978 Volkswagen Rabbit sits on the side of the road. Ninjenna unlocks the car and we climb in.

We ride in dark silence. "What exactly do you protect, Jenna?" I ask.

"Ninjenna!" She slugs me in the arm.

"Ah, sorry, Ninjenna."

She gestures with her index finger as she talks, pointing at unseen locations in the dark. "Mostly shipments from the airport to the Big Top and the Alien Center." She slams her fist on the steering wheel. "I can kick ass, you know. I tail along in case anything happens, but nothing ever does."

"Are the Big Top and the Alien Center government centers?"

Ninjenna looks at me and then at the road. She does it again. "If you don't know, how am I supposed to know?"

I try to sound legit. "I'm new to this section. Need-to-know basis, I suppose."

She seems satisfied. "I don't know what they really do, but officially the Alien Center is a bookstore and novelty shop for tourists and other nut jobs. And the Big Top—well, you'll find out about that soon enough."

"That's all you do? Escort deliveries?"

Her hands clench the wheel and she leans forward. "Sometimes I make them—special packages. I get to ride a sweet-ass ninja motorcycle then, back and forth between the Big Top and Alien Center."

I see a neon light far down the road. "Civilization," I say.

"Anything but," Ninjenna says.

We pull into a parking lot next to a dilapidated brown wood-sided building. A ten-foot neon sign rises from the roof. The sign blinks in red and blue: BIG TOP LOUNGE. Neon signs in the boarded-up windows flash GIRLS, GIRLS, GIRLS.

"It's a strip club!" I say.

Ninjenna pulls into the parking lot. "What a pervert."

"Pervert?"

She brings the car to a stop. "You're excited, just like all the delivery drivers are when they find out. Their five-minute breaks always seem to turn into hours."

"I just wasn't expecting a strip club, is all."

"Whatever. Here you go."

"Here I go? What am I supposed to do?"

Ninjenna ignores me and brings out an iPhone. She shows me a picture of a large man in Harley leather wearing a red bandanna. "My boyfriend." She points angrily at the Big Top Lounge. "I caught him leaving this flesh hole a month ago and had to beat the shit out of him."

"Oh."

"People call him Joemore. You see him in there, send word to Ninjenna."

"Joemore?"

"Yeah, Joemore's big. Joke is only thing his mother ever said to him was 'Joe, more?'"

"Is Joemore someone I should talk to? Is he like one of the inside guys?"

Ninjenna laughs. "Joemore don't know shit. He drives one of the delivery trucks. But he's interesting. Likes to get into trouble and raise hell—keeps me entertained, anyway, in this godforsaken place."

"Okay, but how would I send word to you if I see this Joemore? What am I supposed to do now? Is someone going to contact me? Should I go into the lounge?"

She punches me hard in the shoulder and then slaps me on the head. "You know that's exactly what you want to do. Now get out, pervert."

I open the door. Ninjenna kicks me in the ass, and I tumble to the pavement. She drives off in her Rabbit. I stand, brush the dirt from my suit, and walk toward the red door of the Big Top Lounge.

I reach for the worn door handle. It reverberates with Western music. I step inside a dark room lit up in front by a brass-poled stage containing two scantily clad cowgirls swinging and sashaying back and forth. When the song reaches the chorus they lock arms and high-kick together before turning around, bending over, and waving their butts at the dozen or so silent, miserable ranch-hand-looking dudes who are ogling them from their seats.

Not that I look any better. I walk forward with a bloody face, tattered suit coat, mud-stained trousers, and scraped-up wingtips. I expect a raised eyebrow or two, strip club or not, but all eyes remain glued to the stage.

"Drink, mister?" asks the bartender. He is a short rotund African-American dressed in a tuxedo. He has a neat and tidy appearance that looks out of place here.

I have no wallet, ID, money, or cell phone. "No thanks. Do you have a phone?"

He points his head as he dries a glass. "Back left corner."

I walk past the bar to the far wall. Colored lights spin and flash from the stage, lighting up a metal-beamed ceiling. Old-fashioned circular metallic lights reminiscent of a 1950s diner hang from the beams. Modern track lighting is attached to cables below the older, unused lamps. There is a short hallway with bathrooms. Across from the bathroom doors is a relic of a pay phone.

I walk over and lift the phone handle. I press zero, listen to my options, and press more numbers for even more confusing choices, rambling around in Ma Bell Hell until I finally reach a devil of an operator. "I'd like to make a collect call," I say.

"Say what?"

"A collect call."

"Hold on for my supervisor."

After a few clicks a raspy female voice comes on the line. "Hello, old-timer."

"I'd like to make a collect call."

"Let me guess. Never had a cell phone and you're flat broke."

"Can I make a collect call or not?"

"Sure, old-timer. Took us by surprise. Collect calls don't happen much anymore."

I give her the number, and my home phone rings; one, two, three times. Please don't go to voice mail. I'm alone and broke and I want out of this place. I need help. Four, five—

"Hello?" It's Scotty.

"I have a person-to-person collect call from Chris Thompson," says the operator. "Will you accept the charges?"

"It's Dad," I say.

"Will you accept the charges?"

"How much?" Scotty asks.

"Scotty, say yes."

"Yes."

"Thank you," the operator says.

"Hey, buddy," I begin.

"Hey, Dad. What's a Big Top?"

"What? Why do you ask that?"

"Caller ID says Big Top, Nevada."

"It's just a government building, bud. Go get Mom, will you?"

"Is it a secret building?"

"Yeah, it's like an undercover building. Now go get Mom."

"Mom!"

Karen comes on the line, her mood still sour. "Yes?"

"Hi, honey."

"Where are you?"

I look around and see men sitting at diner-like booths along the wall. Strippers dance on the tables between them. I choose my words carefully. "Um. I'm not sure. Some sort of restaurant."

"Are you in DC?"

"No. Somewhere out west. Look, I can't talk about it."

"I can't believe you just left us like that."

"I'm an agent for the government, Karen. I have to follow the president's orders. But in any case, I'm kind of in a bind here. Can you wire me some money?"

"What happened?"

"Long story, but I have no wallet or cell phone."

"Why? Why are you alone?"

"Guy who was escorting me didn't make it."

"What's that supposed to mean?"

"Nothing. Listen, can you call Western Union? They still wire money."

"Archie called today," she says.

"What does he want?"

"He wanted to make sure you brought his blue blazer back tomorrow. He's worried you're not going to return it."

"I'll have to buy him a new one. But forget him. Are you going to call Western Union?"

"Archie said his mother gave him that blue blazer."

"Karen, please."

"How am I supposed to wire you money if I don't know where you are?"

I hear Scotty's voice in the background. "I know where he is."

"Oh my God! Scotty, get away from that computer!"

"Mom!"

"Out! Out, out, out! Go to your room!"

"What's wrong?" I ask.

I can hear Karen crying. "I can't believe it."

"Is Scotty okay? Is everything all right?"

"Of all the nerve. Scotty googled that place you're calling from. It's a strip club in Nevada!"

Damn kid is smart.

"You bastard! You want me to wire you money in a strip club? Are you out of your mind?"

"Honey, no, listen."

"And you should see the pictures Scotty saw."

I feel something rubbing along my thigh. A blonde in a thong sways her rear end back and forth against me. "Private dance, fella?" she asks me, way too loud.

"No thank you," I whisper.

Karen screams, "I hope you die penniless in the Big Top Lounge!"

"I said no. Did you hear me? I said no."

"And I'm saying no too, Chris."

"Karen, please. Baby, honey, listen for just a minute." But it's too late; she's no longer there.

*I think they should get a man with a net and take
him to a good quiet place.*
—SENATOR JOSEPH McCARTHY

I WALK BACK TO THE BAR and hear a yell from the stage. "Yeow!"
Four girls surround a large man in leather. I recognize Joemore
from the picture on Ninjenna's phone. He has a huge grin on
his face. Strippers gyrate their hips against him and paw him
with their sparkling-nail-tipped fingers. Joemore raises his fist
into the air. "Cannonball, my man." He looks too happy to be
concerned about a beating from Ninjenna.

The bartender raises his fist into the air and salutes Joemore. It hits me. The bartender must be Cannonball, the one
President Wright referred to before I boarded Marine One.

I pull out a stool covered in red vinyl and sit at the far end
of the bar. Two men sit at the other end. They face the stage,
drinks in hand, their backs leaning against the bar.

"Are you ready for a drink?" Cannonball asks me.

"I'm a little short on cash. Could I have a water?"

"You're in the wrong place to be short on cash, mister."

"I'm not sure if this is the wrong place or the right place."
I look around and lower my voice. "I'm looking for some sort
of government program."

He sets a glass of water in front of me. "Program?"

"Fixer brought me. I'm sorry. He didn't make it. He died
on our landing."

Cannonball scrutinizes me. "If I did know anything about
a Fixer, I wasn't expecting him today."

I remember the change of plans at Andrews Air Force Base.
I try to think of that Gulfstream pilot's name. "Riley! Were you
expecting Captain Riley today?"

"Maybe I was, maybe I wasn't."

"The president sent me," I say in frustration. "I'm a liaison.
I'm supposed to visit Emergence."

"Shh." Cannonball looks around. He walks to the end of
the bar to fill a waitress's order. His dark brown skin is smooth
on top of his hairless head. The waitress laughs at something he
says, and a smile spreads across his amiable round face.

Cannonball returns. "There's nothing I can do for you. If
this Captain Riley of yours were here, then maybe things would
be different. But as you are alone, I'm afraid you'll just have to
be on your way."

Red candle lamps flicker from the tables that surround the
stage. Joemore dispenses dollar bills. He whoops and hollers.
An urge to flee grows inside me. What the hell am I doing here?
Joemore leaves the stage and a new dance routine starts.

Cannonball returns to washing glasses.

"They call you Cannonball?"

"What of it?"

I look him in the eye. "I was thinking about a sandwich."

He looks up. "What'd you have in mind?"

"Roast beef with red peppers."

Cannonball raises an eyebrow. "My favorite."

"I know."

"And how would you know?"

"Would you believe the commander in chief told me?"

He dries his hands with a towel and throws it down on the counter.

"Okay. Time to go." He walks around to the front of the bar, all business all of a sudden. "Ready?"

I stay put and look into my hands. I spin the PRAD around my finger. I'm confused and unsure of whether I even want to resume the mission.

"Yo, fella? You all right?"

I look weakly at Cannonball. "It's just that . . . I'm not so sure about this."

He walks over and stands next to me. "Not so sure about what?"

"This mission. I have no idea what I'm doing. I thought things would be more official."

Cannonball leans over and puts his face in front of mine. He looks appalled as he sizes me up. "I thought the president sent you? What kind of agent are you?"

I think of Bond and Fixer and feel embarrassed. A true spy doesn't need hand-holding.

"Pull it together, friend," Cannonball says.

I look at my fingers again.

He slaps me in the face.

I look up, scared. His eyes are alert and searching. "We're on the same side, right?"

I stand up angrily. "I'm no traitor."

Cannonball puts his hand on my shoulder. "All right, then."

I'm an agent for the United States of America, and I've been sent on a mission that might have something to do with the power of the presidency. Forces greater than me are at work, and what part I play I can only guess. But I will do my duty. I take a breath. "Sorry. I'm a little disheveled." I put my game face on. "Let's do this."

Cannonball stares at me, thoughtful. He smiles, rubs his thumb and finger on a diamond stud earring in his right lobe, snaps his fingers, and points at my chest. "Follow me." We walk through a door behind the bar to a kitchen. Two cooks busily work. They nod at Cannonball with respect. A waitress walks in silently, picks up an order, and leaves. It all seems very regimented, like the military.

We walk to the back of the kitchen, where there is a freezer locker. Cannonball punches in a code and opens the stainless steel locker door. It is a foot thick and looks more like the door to a bank vault. A frosty plume of steam flows out. I follow Cannonball through the steam cloud into a deep cold. He closes the door, and it makes a solid *ka-lunk*. The room is brightly lit, but I can't see any lights. A neon glow emanates mysteriously from behind stainless steel walls. Neatly stacked cardboard boxes full of frozen meats, vegetables, and a variety of prepared meals are in metallic bins. Computerized inventory displays on each bin indicate the quantity remaining. A hologram-like video floats in the air, showing the kitchen outside the freezer where the cooks work, unconcerned.

At the back wall Cannonball puts his hand into the air, palm up. A laser beam shoots down from the ceiling and rapidly scans his hand. A whir sounds, and the back wall slides up into the ceiling. There is another formidable stainless steel door. Adjacent to the door is an electronic pad with a telescopic eyepiece. Cannonball places his hand on the pad and looks with one eye into the eyepiece. "Fingerprint and retina scan," he says.

He opens the door to reveal a small futuristic-looking chamber with an elevator door. An identical scanning device is next to the elevator.

"Your turn," Cannonball says.

I place my hand on the cold glass pad and look into the eyepiece. My hand shakes in a very un-Bond-like way. Going through exotic security scans is exciting in the movies, but instead of anticipating the mystery on the other side, I now fear it. I worry how I'm going to get back out. I breathe deep, calm myself, and steady my hand. The government had my fingerprints and had given me eye tests, but I didn't remember having a retina scan. Would I remember that? The scanner beeps and clicks. The sound of an elevator moving vibrates through the room.

Cannonball pats me on the back. "It worked. You definitely must be the liaison."

The doors open. There's a black metallic cage-like collapsible door protecting a freight elevator. The walls are army green. The ivory-colored floor tiles are warped.

Cannonball slides open the squeaky door. He motions me inside. "Take the elevator down."

I step in. The elevator bounces slightly. A fan inside the ceiling light clicks. A moldy grime covers the intake vents. "Down? To what floor?"

"Just press the down arrow. Only one place to go."

"Aren't you coming?"

"I'm not allowed."

"You don't have clearance?"

"Nope. I only have the important job of sending the food down." Cannonball says this with disgust.

"Food's important."

"It's pure discrimination."

"It must be a coincidence."

"No, it's unwritten policy. Nonwhites are not allowed in the grave. There's one exception, as you'll see."

"The grave? Why would you want to go in the grave?"

"Secrets." Cannonball's eyes open wide. "They've got stuff figured out down there."

"What secrets?"

"Don't know. Only rumors. But it has to do with eternal life."

Hocus-pocus, just like with Fixer and Ninjenna. At least I would be going to the source of these rumors. Maybe they are doing longevity studies.

"When do I come back?" I ask.

Cannonball shrugs. He doesn't know. "Probably when the president orders you back."

"When will that be?"

"How am I supposed to know? He probably wants a liaison here until this national emergency is over." Cannonball shakes my hand. He smiles, touches his earring, snaps his fingers, and points at me. "Good luck. I envy you." He leaves the chamber, steps into the freezer, and closes the door.

"Hey, wait!" I shout from my cage with no effect. I want to ask him more questions. I'm in an old freight elevator within a small, futuristic, antiseptic chamber, and it's frightening. This is insane.

But there's only one way to go: to the grave. I press the down arrow and the elevator doors close.

I didn't think I could be touched very deeply.
—SENATOR JOSEPH MCCARTHY

THE CAB BEGINS A SLOW, RUMBLING DESCENT. Down and down. The air smells damp and earthy. My ears pop. The vent fan clicks above me. One minute passes, and then two, and still I move down. This death trap might go on forever. I look at the control panel: no stop button or up arrow. I'm never coming back. The cab rattles, and then stops with a thud. There's a clicking sound outside the door. I take a deep breath and compose myself. Courage. The doors open.

I step into a room dimly lit with yellowish light. The elevator doors close behind me, and I hear the cab automatically start the long ascent back. The clicking is louder. I feel like I'm in a hazy dream. I expected Emergence to be an electronic paradise with bright lights and clean walls like in a Silicon Valley research lab, but it looks like I'm in a decaying dormitory stuck in time. Cinder-block walls are painted a drab, sandy beige. I stand before a common room of sorts. A wide American flag covers a wall. Two men sit on a worn orange fabric sofa. One is reading a paper. The other leans over a coffee table and looks to be playing solitaire with real cards.

On a wall next to the men looms a stainless steel bank-like vault door. It is adorned with blinking Christmas lights, a locked present that looks impossible to open. Next to the vault door is a black-and-white photograph of Senator Joseph McCarthy, smug and confident. In front of McCarthy are two rows of gray metal desks with a black manual typewriter on each. Two desks are occupied by men. They rapidly tap and click away on the typewriters. A ding sounds, and then a ratchet as one of the men manually returns his carriage.

I watch the young men, each in his own world, silent, content, and unaware of me. I clear my throat. A man on the couch jumps up.

I give a short wave. "Hello."

"Liaison!" he shouts.

The other men stand up. They look at me like I am a strange being, like they haven't seen an unfamiliar human in their space in a long time.

A hallway extends in both directions with open doors to rooms that look like sleeping quarters. Three other men emerge from these rooms. They gravitate toward the others until they form one group. They all scoot toward me tentatively and then stop a few feet away. Seven twenty-something men stand before me in a line for inspection. Six are skinny, clean-cut Caucasians. Most have crew cuts, as if they're a 1950s glee choir. They are dressed in black pants with white long-sleeve button-down shirts. The last man is a Native American with black hair down to his waist. He wears blue jeans and a tie-dyed T-shirt.

I give them a friendly smile. "Hi, I'm—"

"Liaison," someone says. "Nicknames only, please."

"Oh, yes, silly of me. I guess you could call me Giorgio, or Ward, or—"

"Liaison."

"Or Liaison," I say.

They all nod their heads in agreement and say "Liaison" to one another to affirm it. They remain where they are and take turns introducing themselves.

"X-ray." X-ray's eyes are beady cobalt blue and look like a hunter's. We shake hands. His is cold and limp.

"Clutch." He looks stern, menacing almost. He shakes my hand and nearly crushes it. "Clutch," I say as he continues to clutch my hand.

A friendly blond-haired kid rescues me. "Flipper." He shakes my hand with a big smile and laughs like a dolphin. "Welcome to our world."

"Thanks."

"Noodles." Noodles is extra wiry. I think he could be called "Slinky" just as well.

"Beach." Beach has longer hair than the rest of the white men. His shaggy, sandy locks cover his ears. "Dude," he says.

The last white man moistens his lips. "They call me Juice." He shakes my hand and smiles. "I don't really drink juice, you know. What I really like—"

"Shut up, Juice," X-ray says.

Everyone is quiet. They stare at me, and though I sense a certain sense of wonder, mostly they appear hesitant, reluctant, unwilling to admit anything to an outsider.

The exception is the Native American man. He approaches me with confidence, shakes my hand hard, and looks deep into my eyes. "Land," he says. "Nickname and real name." He nods and steps back. I get the impression he's lonely.

"How far down are we?"

"One thousand feet," Noodles says.

"Enough to handle a nuclear blast," Clutch says.

Land covers his ears. "And not hear the screams."

"Are you a dead man?" X-ray asks.

This takes me aback, and then I understand. "I jumped out

of a plane that crashed into a mountain, if that's what you're getting at."

"Sounds like Fixer's work. Yeah, you're dead all right."

"But not really dead, just government dead," I say.

"You're catching on quick."

"I'm sorry to tell you that Fixer is really dead."

X-ray smiles and chuckles.

"What did he say?" Clutch asks.

X-ray laughs and points at me in a mocking way. "He says Fixer's dead."

I've had it with these government nuts and their everlasting life nonsense. "Why is that so funny? I'm telling you he really died."

They all smile dumbly at me.

I point to my eyes. "I'm not joking. I saw it with my own eyes." I angrily tap my open palm into my face. "The back of my helmet smashed his face in. There was blood everywhere, for God's sake. I saw the life drain out of him. I read him his last rites."

"It's possible," Flipper says.

"Who's in charge?" I look to Land. "Are you in charge?"

"It's a free-for-all down here," Land says. "But if anything, I'm the last man on the totem pole."

"Fixer wasn't a chosen one," Juice says. "You have to be a chosen one."

X-ray looks at Juice like he just revealed a secret. "Shut up, Juice. Fixer was promised. He was to go in with us."

"He had to make it here first," Flipper says. "If he didn't make it here, he might be out of luck."

They all look at one another, unsure.

"It's not our concern," X-ray says. "He was promised. That's all I know. We have to have faith." X-ray looks me up and down and seems to see for the first time my disheveled appearance. "No bags?"

"Government waste," I say.

X-ray looks at me hard. I don't think he likes jokes. "Settle him in, Land."

Land nods.

"Everyone else go back to what you were doing. Lights out in half an hour."

The white men disperse, leaving me alone with Land. "I thought this place would be more high-tech."

Land shrugs. He walks down the hall, leaving me where I am. After a dozen steps, he stops, turns around, and looks at me as if wondering why I haven't followed him.

I walk toward him. We are at the hallway's end. Open doors are on each side. He motions toward one door. "Library."

I stick my head inside. There are three long metal collapsible desks. Metal bookshelves line the room. There are books and old magazines. There is a 1951 set of *Encyclopedia Britannica*. I see a rack of *Life* magazines and *Reader's Digest*s. An old red Bell rotary phone sits on a desk.

"Does the phone work?"

"Emergency hotline only," Land says. "But they call us, mostly."

"Who calls you? Why do they call you?"

Land shrugs. He motions to an open doorway on the other side of the hallway. "Kitchen." He starts walking back down the hall toward the elevator. I follow. We pass the common room on the right. "Lounge," he says. After the common room there are individual sleeping quarters on the left. On the right is a doorway that opens into a room about the same size as the lounge. "Game room," Land says.

Inside the game room is a circular table. Board games are stacked on a shelf: Monopoly, Yahtzee, Scrabble. Old comic books are strewn around: Superman, Sky King, Captain America, Flash. In the corner I see an Erector Set and a Lionel train box.

We continue on. On the left there are still more dorm rooms. On the right is another open room. It's about half the size of the game room. Inside, gray mats cover the floor. Flipper has changed into a gray sweat suit. He holds an old tan leather medicine ball above his head and is doing knee bends. "Howdy," he says.

"Howdy," I say.

Flipper smiles broadly.

There's a vibrating belt machine in the corner. A punching bag hangs from the ceiling. A pommel horse stands behind Flipper.

Land continues on.

"Good night," Flipper says.

"Good night," I say.

I catch up to Land. A green metal door is on my right. "Bathroom and showers," he says.

And that's it. We have reached the hallway's other end. Covering the end wall are black-and-white photographs of large bombs. Paired with each bomb is a black-and-white photograph of a nuclear explosion. Underneath each mushroom cloud is a sign: "Buster Dog," "Buster Charlie," "Buster Easy," "Buster Baker."

I step around Land and look at the photographs. "Very welcoming," I say. I see one photograph of a round Fat Man type whale-like bomb resting on its side. The bomb is all gray and has four stubby fins. There is no corresponding mushroom cloud photograph next to it. Underneath the bomb it says "Buster Able."

"A fizzle," Land says.

"Excuse me?"

"Buster Able. It failed to explode. Nuke guys call that a fizzle."

"Are you guys nuke guys? Is that what you're doing down here, working on nuclear weapons?"

Land walks into the last open dorm room door, the one we've been standing outside of. I follow him into a sparse cell-like room. The walls are white painted concrete blocks. Land unfolds a metal bed that hangs on the wall from chains. It has a thin mattress covered in plastic.

"No. We are not nuke guys. The photos are in homage to what went on above us."

I look up to the ceiling, trying to imagine what Land is talking about.

"The Nevada test site. This is where we tested our nukes."

"Ahh," I say. "We're not at Area 51?"

Land doesn't answer me. He walks out the door. After a minute he returns holding a pile of clothes. He hands me several sets of old-fashioned gray baggy sweat suits, along with boxers, muscle T-shirts, and 1970s green-striped white sweat socks. The sweatshirts say ARMY in intimidating gold letters. "Area 51 covers a small part of the test site in the interior," he says. "We are just on the border, in Area 22." Land leaves the room again.

That's right. The president has confused me. I remember now that Slater had said I was going to Area 22.

Land returns with a prepackaged ham sandwich and a Coke. He sets them on a gray metal nightstand in the corner.

"Was this bunker built as a survival test for when the army exploded those bombs?"

Land looks out the door. He looks back at me. "Yes."

"But the bunker is under a public area."

Land moves long strands of hair out of his eyes and guides them back behind his head and shoulder. "Not always. When Emergence took over, they wanted to keep us secret from all the other government agencies, so they made the land above us public to better hide us. Well, at least our section—I think."

"So Emergence has to do with nuclear survival?"

"Something like that." Land looks out the door. He looks back at me. "You don't really know, do you?"

"What don't I know?"

He steps out the door. "Kitchen's at the far end. Need anything else, help yourself. My butler duties are over." He is gone.

I change and put my PPK on the nightstand next to the sandwich. I don't feel like eating. I fall into the bed. I'm exhausted, but the crazy events of the day race through my mind, and I have trouble falling asleep. To clear my thoughts, I think of all the ground above me. At first it's oppressive and claustrophobic, but I get used to the idea, and I begin to feel safe inside the earth's thick womb. I relax and wonder if Karen and Scotty are sleeping. Scotty is for sure. I imagine him, peaceful and innocent, breathing softly. Karen is probably awake, stewing. Hopefully I can gather enough information for a solid report and get back home in a day or two to patch things up.

What did Land mean by "our" section? That implies there are other Emergence areas, but he wasn't too sure about it. He seemed surprised I didn't know everything about Emergence. Maybe I'll be able to find out more if I act like I do.

There is a distant hum from the air vent. It is mesmerizing. I try to keep thinking about the secrets of Emergence, but in the pitch-black room I can't fend off my weariness. I drift off to sleep.

10

Even if we do damage some of the honest employees,
I must take the only method I know of whereby I think
we can secure a housecleaning.
—SENATOR JOSEPH MCCARTHY

WHEN I WAKE UP, the holster I had left next to me on the dented metal nightstand is empty. I put on a pair of sixty-year-old black high-top Converse All Stars that are a size too big. With my sweat suit on, I look like I belong in this 1950s bomb shelter. I march down to the common room and then into the kitchen. I can't find anyone.

I return to my room and sit at the edge of the bed with the door open. I hear footsteps. I lean out the doorway. X-ray has come out of his room. He walks away from me down the hall with calculated steps.

"Hey," I call.

He continues walking.

I follow him. "My gun. Someone took my gun."

He looks at me with annoyance. "No need for guns here."

That may be, but the fact that someone took it is

disconcerting. "You could have asked for it. Did someone have to sneak into my room and steal it?"

X-ray walks into the kitchen. Fluorescent lights illuminate the stainless steel cabinets and countertops. An old-fashioned coffee percolator hisses. X-ray draws himself a cup of coffee and doesn't offer me one. "Easier that way."

"Easier for you."

He takes a sip of his coffee. "You may be the liaison, but you're a stranger and you're untrustworthy. You'll leave that way, too. Do your job, fill out your reports, and be on your way." He sets the coffee on the counter and looks at his blurry reflection in the stainless steel. His eyes go cold. "You'll get your gun back on the way up. Just behave yourself."

X-ray leaves. I make myself a cup of coffee, uneasy after his comments.

I walk down to the lounge. Juice is on the couch, shuffling a metal Slinky back and forth. Flipper, Beach, and Clutch sit behind the old typewriters whacking away at the keys. They are still all dressed the same: clean, shaved, fastidiously neat. One of them groans when he sees me.

I sit down on a couch and take a sip of my coffee.

"Can I email someone?"

X-ray walks into the room. "No email," he says.

"Can I use the Internet?"

"No Internet."

"No Internet? Aren't you an intel center?"

X-ray hems and haws. "Not that kind of intel."

"So, you have no Internet, no TV, only a direct-line phone?"

Silence.

The one thousand feet of earth above me seems oppressive again. "No communication with the outside world?"

"None," Juice says. He looks disgusted.

"Shut up, Juice."

They're hiding something. I try to keep the conversation going. "You guys are doing some serious typing."

Silence.

I take another sip of coffee and then set it on a side table.

Land walks past the common room reading a book. After a minute he walks back the other way. He walks from one end of the complex to the other, back and forth, like a frustrated polar bear at the zoo.

I stand up and join Land in his walking. "Good book?"

He flips over the cover to show me. "*Fahrenheit 451.*"

"Hot," I say.

Land flips back open the book. "Third time reading it."

"Not much to do down here, huh?"

Land shrugs and returns to reading.

"Why all that typing?"

"Brochures," he says without looking up.

"Brochures about what?"

"Ask them." Land continues his walk.

I return to the lounge and stand behind the men typing. They are typing letters. I lean over Clutch. The return address label begins with BIG MAC.

"Big Mac," I say.

Clutch wheels around. "Hey. This is confidential."

"Relax," Flipper says. "The president and Slater sent him. He knows what's up."

I scoot closer to Flipper and Beach. They seem more agreeable. "You guys getting the good word out?"

"Absolutely." Flipper puts a new piece of paper into his typewriter. He twists the cylinder around to line it up. "We maintain correspondence with the membership. And with potential new recruits, of course."

"Of course," I say. "That's good work, but is that all that Emergence does?"

Silence. They continue what they are doing, ignoring my question.

"Oh, come on. You guys must do something."

Juice is fidgeting on the couch. He looks like he wants to talk. I look at him directly. "This is all you do?"

Clutch stands up and steps in front of Juice. "Keeping Big Mac members up to date with our policies and objectives is cohesive and good for the party."

"That's good," I say. "But do you have to be underground to do that?"

Silence.

I look to the gray steel vault at the end of the room. "What's up with that vault?"

Silence.

"Is it a secret stash of government gold?" I give a friendly laugh to show that I'm kidding.

Juice has fat circular lips that moisten when he talks. "Something like that."

Flipper walks over to the intimidating door. He reaches down and pushes a button on the wire. The Christmas lights blink in a new pulsing pattern. Flipper spreads his arms out in a grand presentation. "The Tunnel of Love."

The door is both scary and funny looking. I smile to hide my uneasiness. "Where does the Tunnel of Love go?"

Juice fidgets some more. He looks like he's been sitting in school an hour too long. I think he will talk. I think he wants to tell me something. "All those Christmas lights. Must be something special?" I say.

"Super special," Juice says.

"Stop it, Juicy," X-ray says. He stands at the room's edge. They all look toward him like he's the boss.

I ignore X-ray and try to keep the chatter going with the other guys. "That's a hell of a vault door. Don't they trust you guys?"

"Trying to keep us back," Juice says. Spittle has formed on his lips.

"I said stop it, Juice," X-ray says.

Juice stands up and is animated. "The door is to keep us

from . . . from fornicating." Spittle flies from his lips in all directions. "They've got our women in there."

X-ray steps forward and faces him. "Shut the hell up, Juice."

"Well, I can't stand it anymore," Juice shouts, spraying some more.

X-ray grabs Juice by the sleeve and pulls him out of the room. "Let's you and I have a little talk."

I wonder what Juice means about the vault. Is this some weird McCarthy science experiment? "What's this about fornicating?" I ask Flipper.

He replies in a low voice. "When our time here is over, we will enter the tunnel and meet our chosen women." He looks around, I assume checking for X-ray. "At the tunnel's end, there's a grand underground city just like our home in Utah, but with much, much more. That's what I believe."

"And when is your time here over?"

Beach stops typing. "Eight more days!" he says. "That's when we will have our Utopia Day." Beach's face lights up at the thought of it. "I don't think the city's underground. I think the tunnel emerges into a secret town above ground, one that's protected and secured on all sides by the government. We chosen ones and our descendants will live there for eternity."

Am I a fool for thinking this is all a hoax? Or do they all think that secretly, but smile and carry on so as not to ruin it for the others?

Flipper looks at me. "You are a Big Mac member, right?"

I rub my chin. "Uh, no. Not officially. I work for the president, but no, I haven't joined the Big Mac Party."

Beach stands up. "Well, how about it, Liaison? Are you ready to commit to a new spiritual journey through the vision of Senator Joseph McCarthy that offers a clear path to salvation and heaven on earth?"

"McCarthy," the others say reverently.

"Whoa," I say. "I've not heard anything about Big Mac being some kind of . . . McCarthy salvation plan."

"It's the truth, though," Clutch says sternly. "The rest of the public will know soon enough."

"Know what?"

X-ray has returned. He stands next to Clutch. His eyes are mesmerizing as he looks intently at me. "That Senator Joseph McCarthy's righteous vision for America is a truth that all pure citizens in this country are destined for."

I stare back at X-ray. His attempt to influence me with a hypnotic gaze has no effect. What they are saying though is incredible, and they're totally serious. These guys worship McCarthy. They don't just follow his principles; they actually worship him like a god. I wonder how and when McCarthy's ideas turned into a religion for them. The president is fighting against something crazier than even he can imagine. If these guys are tied in with the Big Mac Party, President Wright is fighting fanatics. American fanatics.

I smile my broadest grin. "Amen, brother. Sign me up. I'll be a member of Big Mac."

X-ray nods at me. He seems satisfied.

Everyone laughs in relief. They all talk at once. They shake my hand, pat me on the back, and say things like, "Welcome. Happiness. Liberty."

I smile. "Thank you. Thank you."

Slowly they return to what they were doing. I see Land. He has been watching us. He catches me looking at him. He returns to his walk and his reading.

I walk out of the lounge and catch up to him, smiling eagerly. "I've joined Big Mac," I say.

He glances at me, but continues walking and reading.

A phone rings. It's the hotline. X-ray walks quickly out of the lounge and into the library.

"You're not a believer?" I say.

Land stops and looks up, considering. "I'm not sure. I'm not a disbeliever."

"Clutch! Noodles!" X-ray shouts from the library. "We have to prepare for a delivery."

"Government one?" I hear Noodles say.

X-ray walks into the hallway and then stops. He looks like he is about to say something but then looks at me as if he's forgotten I'm there. "Yes, a government one." X-ray walks closer to talk to me. "Our major food delivery is tonight, and we have to do some inventory accounting. Excuse us." He turns and walks down the hall and into his room. Clutch and Noodles follow.

Later, I help Flipper prepare lunch. It's easy enough: Lipton noodle soup in a big pot with white bread and butter. Most of the men take their lunch and return to the lounge or to their rooms. Flipper sits with me at a long table in the kitchen. He is good-natured, and out of all the men here, he's made me feel the most welcome.

"How long have you been here?" I ask.

"Almost five years," he says without a trace of insincerity.

I almost spit out my soup. "Five years! But you get to go home on the weekends, right?"

Flipper smiles at my amazement. "Nope. We've all been here the whole time."

"But, but—why?"

He stands up and clears our plates and bowls. "Don't worry about it, Liaison. In eight days we have our Utopia Day, and we all get to leave."

"You must miss your family."

For the first time Flipper's smile leaves him. "Yes," he says. "I miss them terribly." After a brief moment the smile returns to his face. "But I'll have a new family soon."

I grab a towel and help him dry dishes. "The Tunnel of Love?"

"Yes," he says. He stares off, smiling at the thought, and says nothing more.

The rest of the day is uneventful. I play Chinese checkers, read some old magazines, but otherwise discover nothing else new.

At ten o'clock X-ray walks up and down the hallway. "Lights out!"

I head to my room and lie down in my bed. I'm now a member of the Big Mac Party. These guys send out letters and brochures to other members typed on old typewriters. They are down here for five years, but why? It has to do with the vault—the Tunnel of Love—and the women. There must be women behind that vault door. If so, do they live in a shelter just like this? What do they do? It's all so strange.

I'm getting sleepy. I try to forget where I am and think of Karen and Scotty. I see their faces in my mind and their images bring warmth to my chest. I fall asleep missing them.

I'm asleep for what I think is an hour or so when a low rumbling sound awakens me. The elevator is moving. I keep my light off and open the door slightly.

Noodles, Clutch, and X-ray walk down the dimly lit hall. Noodles pushes a dolly with a coffin-size pinewood crate. They push the crate into the shower room and emerge ten minutes later. I jump back into bed.

"We'll start first thing in the morning," I hear X-ray whisper.

11

*And wait till you hear the bleeding hearts scream
and cry about our methods.*
—SENATOR JOSEPH McCARTHY

AT FOUR IN THE MORNING I gather my government-issued toiletry kit—complete with beeswax, stale Crest, and Brut aftershave—and, wrapped in a towel, nimbly walk down the hall so as not to wake my sleeping comrades.

I enter the shower room and turn on the lights, shocking my pupils. I inspect the green, metal-enclosed shower stalls and can find no evidence of the crate. On the back wall are two dark green maintenance doors that blend in with the multi-shaded green mosaic tile.

The first door opens to a dark room with low humming machinery and an orgy of plumbing guts and pipes. The second door has a sign that says "Maintenance." There's a latch secured with an old gym combination lock. I pull on the lock, but it doesn't budge. I look around. Etched into the outside of a stall behind me are the numbers 23–12–31. I try the lock, twisting the faded orange face twice around right to 23, left once to 12, and then back to 31. The lock opens.

I walk into the dark room. I rub my hands over the wall. I find a switch and flip it. A dim grayish light reveals a toolroom. There are metal cabinets and shelves filled with power tools, rusty cans, and boxes of who knows what. A Peg-Board on one wall has hammers, chisels, and other tools hanging from hooks. What really grabs my attention takes up most of the tiny room's interior. A man lies facing up on a worktable.

The man has red hair. He wears flip-flops, silky red gym shorts that extend past his knees, and a white long-sleeve hockey jersey trimmed in red with a large Canadian maple leaf on the front. An IV tube drips solution into his flabby arm. His large chest rhythmically rises and falls as he breathes. He is either sleeping or in a coma.

I hear a door shut. There are voices in the shower room.

"Who left the light on?"

I look for a place to hide. The crate stands in a corner. I move the lid aside and step in. I pull the lid closed, hold it in place, and peek between the latticed boards.

The door clicks. Three men in scrubs and surgical masks enter. They wear square beatnik sunglasses to further hide their identities.

The surgeons lock down the man's ankles, legs, wrists, and arms with red rubber clamps. They tighten burlap straps around his waist and chest. They secure a square metal box clamp around the man's head.

One of the surgeons removes the IV and injects something into the man's arm with a syringe. The man wakes up. He screams and struggles against his confinement. Mozart's soothing Symphony no. 21 fills the room. One of the surgeons leans in next to the man's ear. "Relax," he repeats until the man becomes silent and still.

"Welcome." I recognize X-ray's voice.

The man's voice trembles. "Where am I?"

"That is not important."

"You're not stealing my organs are you?"

"We do not steal. That would be dishonest."

The surgeon who gave the first shot lifts up another syringe. He injects it into the man's arm.

"Ow," the man says.

"You'll be feeling just dandy in a moment," the surgeon says. I recognize Noodles's voice.

The man struggles against his restraints. "I want a lawyer. I demand to speak to a lawyer."

X-ray puts his hand on the man's shoulder. "Relax. All we want is a little information."

"I'll tell you everything I know."

"Great," Noodles says. "That's super."

"And then I can go home, eh?"

"Of course." X-ray pauses. "But 'home' can be such a nebulous term."

The man's kneecaps flutter. "This must be a mistake. What information could you possibly want from me?"

"Noodles?" X-ray says.

Noodles positions himself at the end of the table, near the man's head. He leans over and looks into the man's eyes. His sunglasses fall slightly down his nose. Their inverted faces are ten inches apart.

"Name?"

"Walter Moreau."

"French-Canadian?"

"Oui, monsieur."

The surgeon who has been silent so far laughs. "That's a good one." I recognize Clutch's voice.

"You are funny, Mr. Moreau," X-ray says.

"Let's be friends. Call me Walter."

Noodles continues. "Where did you cross the border, Walter?"

"Border?"

"Come on, Walter. We're pals, right?" Noodles straightens up and shifts over to Walter's side. "Walter, you were picked up for illegally trespassing on American soil. I know it might have seemed fun, but crossing the border is very serious. There's no need for us to get cranky, so I'll ask you again. Where did you cross the border?"

Walter's voice shakes. "Detroit."

"Oh, gee, that's great, Walter. Now we're talking."

"In the trunk of my buddy's Camaro."

"Sounds like a grand ol' time."

"We were meeting friends at a bar to watch a hockey game."

"But why did you feel the need to hide in the trunk?"

"The last time I went to Detroit I got arrested for fighting with a Red Wings fan. Judge barred me from the US for a year."

X-ray cracks his knuckles. "Now that's a no-no. These Red Wings, these are Communist cells?"

"This is crazy," Walter says. "The Red Wings are a hockey team."

X-ray walks directly toward me. He reaches out like he is going to open the crate. I brace myself, but his hand goes to the crate's side. I hear plastic or tape being torn off the wood.

X-ray returns to his spot. He opens a small plastic bag and unfolds some sheets of pink paper. "Excuse me. I misspoke. Walter, we have information here that you admitted to the border patrol that you were going to see the 'Red's Wing' in Detroit. Now is or is not the Red's Wing a Communist organization?"

"It's a typo. It's a mistake," Walter cries.

"Highly unlikely," X-ray says. "We are talking about the United States Border Patrol here."

"We know you crossed the border illegally as part of the Canadian invasion, and that you planned to rendezvous with the Communists in Detroit," Noodles says and then smacks his fist into his palm. "We want to know what your next move against the United States was going to be. Tell us about the invasion. We want to know whom you report to. We want to know about the command structure—names, places, everything."

Panic creeps into Walter's voice. "I don't know, eh. We were hoping to hook up with some chicks. If not, and we weren't too drunk, we'd return to Windsor that night. Louis drove, Eddie rode shotgun, and Michael sat in back. As I said before, I was in the trunk. I guess you could say Louis was in charge."

As a tool of the president's farce, I feel bad and responsible for Walter. He can't possibly know a thing.

"Enough!" X-ray shouts. "This is hogwash. The Macwacky is not working. Sometimes that happens. We need more extreme measures."

"I'm telling the truth, eh." Walter begins to cry. "What are you going to do, waterboard me?"

The sunglasses-wearing surgeons giggle in a funny way, like they are junior high kids at a birthday party. Noodles reaches up and pulls a power drill off the Peg-Board. "Waterboard? We have more fun than that here, Walter." Noodles plugs in the drill's cord. He then opens a cupboard drawer and pulls out a thin, shiny, metal drill bit. He fastens it to the end of the drill and positions it next to Walter's temple.

"Please, no." Walter's arm muscles flex as he presses against the restraints. Sweat lines his flushed face.

X-ray talks in a singsong tone. "A little exploratory drilling, Walter. If the pain doesn't make you talk, removing a strategic portion of your brain will make you better friends with us, and you will be more likely to answer our questions."

Walter screams.

X-ray takes the drill from Noodles. He flips a switch, and the drill begins to spin, adding a whir to Walter's screaming and the Mozart.

I burst from the crate. "Stop it, you bastards!"

The surgeons rear back in shock.

Walter screams.

The surgeon who I think is Clutch charges me.

I slam the crate lid down onto Clutch's head. He falls to the ground, knocked out cold. I jump over him and the lid. My towel falls off. I run around the table screaming like a naked banshee with my shower sandals clicking and flapping.

X-ray grabs the spinning drill and points it at me.

I stop, lift Clutch off the ground, and put a headlock on him.

"Drop the drill!" I yell.

X-ray stares at me, still pointing the drill.

I tighten my grip. "I'm warning you. I'll kill him. I'm a special agent trained for mortal combat. I'll kill Clutch and then you. Now drop that drill."

A pain flames in my neck like bees are stinging it. All my nerves electrify. Two metal rods touch my skin underneath the right side of my jaw. I turn and see Noodles holding the thin, foot-long rods. A wire extends from each rod and connects to a suitcase-size battery cell. Every muscle in my body contorts and spasms. I let Clutch go and he falls to the ground.

My vision wobbles. Only three seconds have passed, but time feels suspended. I see X-ray push the spinning drill bit into Walter's temple. I can do nothing. I see Walter scream, but can't hear him. Blood and pieces of flesh spray from his head. The room is sideways. I collapse to the floor. The pain dissipates. The horror remains.

"He's dead," I hear Noodles say through a fog that swirls in my brain. "You killed him."

"We should have tried more Macwacky," X-ray says.

Everything goes blank.

* * *

I wake up to see Noodles and Clutch placing Walter into the

crate. He is dead. I am latched to the operating table like Walter was before me. I hear the spinning drill next to my ear.

"Don't," Noodles says. "He's the liaison to the president."

I close my eyes and stifle a scream.

"That doesn't really matter much anymore, does it?" X-ray says.

"And you're willing to make that decision?" Noodles says. Silence.

I hear them leave. I open my eyes. The lights go out. I hear the door shut.

I lie in dark terror. I saw a man killed. I can't get the picture of that drill penetrating Walter's head out of my mind. I think of Scotty and Karen, and what a fool I am.

The hours pass, until I can't tell how many have gone by anymore.

These guys are torturing people for the government. Noodles asked X-ray last night if the delivery they were expecting was from the government. Do they torture for other organizations, too? More time passes. I think on the torture. Why would they do it? Messed-up patriotic reasons, I suppose. I remember the president's email. *Emergence program is Big Mac's greatest asset, but also a huge potential liability.* Shit. They're going to kill me for sure. I know too much. They'll never let me out. The plane crash. Fixer said I was going to die in the plane crash. The president probably thinks I've already died. Would they have told Karen and Scotty? I hope not, yet. Oh, shit. Please, God, let me out of here.

I hear the door open. This is it. I'm going to die. I start to hum "Frère Jacques," a song I used to hum as a little boy. The tune is nostalgic to me, and comforting. I hum louder.

"Shh," a deep voice says.

The straps around my arms and legs are released, and then the ones around my body fall away. I sit up. It is still dark. The mysterious person helps me off the operating table.

"Stay as quiet as you can," he says. It is Land. He grabs my wrist and tries to lead me out of the room.

I stand my ground. "What are you doing with me?"

"I'm saving you. Let's go."

"Why would you save me?"

"No time for discussion," Land hisses. "Would you rather X-ray be the one saving you?"

He's right. I've no choice. At least Land seems to be different from the others. "Okay, sorry. I'll go."

I let Land lead me. We pass through the showers and into the hallway. I hear pots clanging in the kitchen. It must be lunchtime. The typewriters are silent. Several of the dorm room doors are shut, indicating that some of the men are eating in their room.

"Shh," Land says. "The lounge was empty when I left. We don't have much time."

We walk quietly down the hall. Land peers around the corner. We enter the empty lounge.

Land guides me to the Tunnel of Love. He puts his finger over his lips.

A crash sounds in the kitchen.

Land punches a code into the vault door.

I hear footsteps approaching in the hallway.

Land grabs the vault's wheel handle.

"What are you doing?" It's Flipper. He approaches us quickly. "How do you know the code?"

"X-ray keeps the code for the whites. I keep it for the Cherokee." Land turns the wheel. A clank sounds. "They were going to kill Liaison. It ain't right."

Land gives a pull and the vault door slowly swings open. Land and Flipper look at each other for a moment. Behind the door a light flickers on inside a small chamber. There is another security door.

Flipper nods. "I won't tell."

Land hands Flipper a piece of paper. "The code, if you need it." Land and Flipper hug.

Flipper shakes my hand. "Godspeed," he says.

Land and I step inside the chamber and close the vault door. The lights go out.

12

One thing about a pig, he thinks he's warm if his nose is warm.
—SENATOR JOSEPH McCARTHY

A BEAM OF LIGHT from Land's small but powerful flashlight illuminates the chamber. Land places his hand on a numeric touch pad. He types in the code. The interior tunnel door opens. We gingerly step through into a dimly lit concrete tunnel that stretches as far as we can see.

Land and I start to walk. Our footsteps echo down the tunnel. "Where are we going?"

Land picks up the pace. "I'm going to my destiny. You're just trying to escape."

"What is Emergence? Some sort of secret black ops torture center?"

"Not at first," Land says. "Our primary mission is supposed to be to repopulate the United States after a nuclear attack or other cataclysmic disaster."

"Juice said there are women." My breathing quickens. Despite being stuck underground, Land is in better shape than me.

"The tunnel is supposed to connect to a women's shelter," he says.

"So there are seven women, too?" I say.

"Yes," Land says. "The men and women living in the shelters are the chosen ones. Every five years, like the men, six white women and one Cherokee woman are chosen for Emergence service."

"Quite the melting pot," I say.

Land shrugs like he has nothing to do with it. "1950s," he says in explanation. "It would have been all whites, but the Cherokee Nation got wind of the repopulation program and threatened to raise hell if we weren't included." His lips tighten. "That's what we were told. But I'm not sure of anything anymore."

"So that's our plan? To go to the women?" I say.

"The women, the Utopia, I don't know, okay? I don't know."

"Sorry," I say. "I'm just trying to understand."

"Me too."

"Do the women torture prisoners?"

Land scrunches his face like this would be an impossibility. "They do make the Macwacky, but torture—nah, I doubt it."

Macwacky. That's what they injected into Walter.

Land stops and looks at me. "We never knew about the interrogations until we got here. I never tortured anyone. Only the hard-core guys felt it was their duty to implement the aggressive interrogation techniques. The rest of us were meant to believe it was God's will, and we didn't want to mess with our chances of reaching the Utopia Day, so we didn't interfere with what was going on."

"X-ray, Noodles, and Clutch?" I say.

"Yes. Those three are the interrogators. They believe they're doing their job. They feel it's a necessary evil to protect their dream."

"The Utopia dream?"

Land looks uncertain about continuing. He quietly says,

"Yes. The dream that we will be allowed to live forever in some sort of Utopia."

Live forever. Here it is again. "What is this crap about living forever through the government?"

Land shrugs and starts walking again.

"Flipper and Beach talked about their home in Utah," I say. "Did they grow up together?"

"Yes. All the white men come from the same town in Utah."

"Is that where the everlasting life stuff comes from?"

Land rubs his temples like he is unsure. "I suppose."

I don't ask him any more questions. He's nervous and seems a little irritated with my prying. I suppose it's because he's unsure of what he believes, or because he's nervous about how reality will align with his expectations about whatever he'll find in this tunnel. He must have been thinking about this walk for the last five years.

We walk in silence for what I figure is about two miles when we reach a steel door in a cement wall.

I try the door. It is unlocked and opens to nothing but blackness.

Land shines his flashlight and we enter a large room with sofas like the lounge from the men's residence. Two halls lead off from each side of the room.

We continue to explore. There are large dorm rooms, with personal baths and showers. Each has a queen-size bed. Land looks at it all as if he's in a daze. He runs his hand over the bed. He looks into each room like he might find someone. Is this the women's dorm, or something else?

We return to the main lounge. Land's light reflects off something shiny in the corner. There are four old 1950s RCA television screens bolted by steel arms to the wall. A large professional-looking television camera from the same era focuses on a standing microphone before an American flag backdrop. We walk over to investigate. Next to the flag is a photograph of

Senator Joseph McCarthy. Engraved plastic plaques give simple broadcasting instructions. Black binders sit on a desk with names like "Emergency Broadcast Frequencies," "Speeches to Calm a Radiated Population," and "Clues to Detecting Subliminal Communist Telecasts."

Land lights up a door that says "Power Generator and Storage Area."

"Should we fire the generator up?" I ask.

Land pushes open the door. A neon safety light goes on. There's a small generator. I hear Land gasp. His light shines past the generator into the dark. I struggle to see what he is looking at. I see the word "Fizzle" spray-painted in black over metal. Land moves his flashlight around the metal. It's an atomic bomb. BUSTER ALPHA is written in block letters on the side.

"The bomb that never went off," Land says. "They stored it here."

Underneath the Buster Alpha name, someone has written "Completely made in America."

Land walks quickly out of the room. I follow.

On the opposite side of the main room is another door. I open it. Another tunnel stretches into the distance.

"This must go to the women," Land says.

"Shall we go to the women's shelter?"

Land looks disappointed. "We will be locked out from this side, just like we are now from the men's shelter." He takes a deep breath and looks around the area again. "This is our Utopia."

"So after five years, you all are supposed to hook up here? In these queen-size beds?"

"If there's no nuclear disaster, then yes, after five years we get married."

"Married?"

"Yes, to the one who has been chosen for us, and then we

live together, supposedly forever, in Utopia." Land shines his light around frantically and shouts. "But where is everyone? Where is Utopia?"

I see something in Land's erratic light beams. "There, Land. At the top of the stairs."

Land shines the flashlight into the corner and reveals a metal stairway. The stairs extend to a hatch in the ceiling. A sign at the top of the stairs says: *"In case of nuclear attack, remain at least one year. If not, and if resident time completed, remain no longer than one week. Maintain unit according to regulations. Please exit as couples at intervals of at least six hours."*

"That's where they went," I say. "Everyone before you."

Land and I walk up the stairs to a square landing. Above us it looks like there is a trap door in the ceiling. He pulls on the trap door, it opens, and metal stairs unfold down to where we stand. At the top of the unfolded stairs is a locked metal hatch. Land climbs up and enters his code into a keypad. It works, and he pushes open the hatch. In the dark space above, a metal fire-escape-like stairway zigzags up into nothingness.

Land shines his flashlight up the stairs. "Shall we go?" he says.

"You sure you don't want to try the women's tunnel?"

Land starts climbing the stairs. "I've been underground for five years. I don't know where this goes, but I'd rather go up."

We climb up the stairs and breathe heavily in the humid, still air. We climb and climb. Sweat pours from my temples and drips down my front and back. We take a break and then climb again. Finally, we reach a platform at the top. Another short ladder leads up to a thick manhole cover with a combination lock pad.

Land punches in the code and pushes on the heavy cover. The lid swings open on thick hinges. Bright light streams down, blinding us.

Land climbs out and I follow. We are in an antiseptic-smelling brightly lit room that screams *government*. The front wall has a window that runs the width of the room, like a newborn nursery. Sitting ominously in the center of the room are two shop tables with clamps. They look exactly like the table in the men's shower maintenance room, the table I was strapped to not long ago.

"What is this?" I say.

Land puts his hands over his face, and then removes them slowly. "It's not Utopia," he whispers.

13

Have you ever tried to spit sawdust?
—SENATOR JOSEPH MCCARTHY

THE TILE AND WALLS AND FURNITURE look just like they did
in the shelters underground. I walk over to the long window.
A guard in a black commando uniform stands outside. He
holds an automatic rifle. He walks past the window and then
turns around. At first I feel like ducking, but he doesn't seem
to see me. I wave at him. Nothing. The window is made of
one-way glass.

The hallway the guard walks down is painted sleek black
and has a silver metallic logo that says AREA 22. The floor
outside is a glossy white marble. I see computerized signs and
futuristic electronic screens down the hall. Outside this room is
the modern world. Inside, it is still 1950, just like underground.
This room must be too secret to let any workmen inside to
upgrade it.

A desk on the inside wall has papers and office supplies set
out with military precision. A nameplate says "Major Thomas
Pilgrim, MD." There is a small sticker after his name in red,

white, and blue that says *BM*. I open the desk drawer to neatly stacked rows of pens and pencils. The bottom-right file drawer is filled with personnel data sheets and military medical conference pamphlets. The top-right drawer is locked. I give it a few hard but unsuccessful pulls.

These young men and women have been brainwashed with McCarthy religion, ordered to torture for the government, and now what? This whole thing is all fucked up. I stand up and angrily kick the locked drawer, and it slides open. There are neatly categorized sleeves of microfiche. I randomly pick one and hold it to the ceiling light.

"What's that?" Land asks.

"Microfiche."

"Little fish?"

"No, microfiche. Haven't you ever seen microfiche? It's film with little pictures in it."

"Little pictures of fish?"

"It's *fiche*! Not fish." I sigh and look around. A tall metal cabinet stands next to the desk. Inside are lab coats and medical books. The top shelf holds papers and an Eye Com EC 1000 portable microfiche reader.

"I think we should leave," Land says.

"In a minute," I say. I plug in the reader and choose a microfiche slide from a section of sleeves titled "Emergence Termination Procedures and Orders."

I turn the knobs and documents blur uncontrollably around the screen like a bad college research paper flashback. I finally control it and stop on the following letter:

December 14, 2008
Office of the Judge Advocate General

TOP SECRET ** Military Tribunal LH4087-AREA
22-Emergence ** TOP SECRET

In application of President Roosevelt's Proclamation 2561 "DENYING CERTAIN ENEMIES ACCESS TO THE COURTS OF THE UNITED STATES" a TOP SECRET Military Tribunal was convened with Chief Justice of the Supreme Court, the Honorable Timothy M. Lancaster, serving as Judge Advocate General.

This Military Tribunal, LH4087-AREA 22-Emergence, operating within its authority under The United States, understands that in order to constitute torture, an act must be a deliberate and calculated act of an extremely cruel and inhuman nature. Specifically, Emergence Residents have intended to inflict excruciating pain through systemic beating, application of electric currents to sensitive parts of the body, and tying up or hanging in positions that cause extreme pain. Emergence Residents have utilized interrogation techniques that have been applied with minimal physical contact, such as poking, slapping, or shoving the detainee or the administration or application, or threatened administration or application of mind-altering substances or other procedures calculated to disrupt profoundly the senses or the personality. The tribunal recognizes that not all Emergence Residents participated in said activities, and also that if an Emergence Resident were to harm an enemy combatant or unlawful belligerent during an interrogation in a manner that might arguably violate before said guidelines, he would be doing so in order to prevent further attacks on the United States and could justify his actions.

However, the tribunal has determined that if aforementioned approved techniques were to become public, the Emergence program and credibility of the United States could be impaired, and given that the Emergence Residents have been previously declared dead due to various illnesses or accidents and are no longer categorized as United States citizens, they enjoy no protection under U.S. or international law. Therefore, to maintain ultimate secrecy, the tribunal authorizes AREA 22 Emergence Commander Thomas Pilgrim, MD, to permanently dispose of the following Emergence Residents:

Michael C. Sheehan, Anthony M. Ford, Mark T. Anderson, Luke A. Friedman, Christopher J. McHutchins, John T. Lamb, Chaman Dawes, Katherine Davis, Jennifer Watkins, Melissa Johnson, Sandi Hartford, Patricia Cross, Linda Smith, Julie Wilson.

Timothy M. Lancaster

The Honorable Timothy M. Lancaster
Chief Justice
Supreme Court of the United States

What a bunch of sinister legal loophole mumbo jumbo.

Chief Justice Lancaster has thrown a sucker punch, and my patriotic American gut feels it full force. Why would the Supreme Court's chief justice order the Emergence residents' death? Is he being framed? Paid off? Is he tied in with the Big Mac Party? Is Lancaster the leader? Does he follow the McCarthy religion?

"Land," I say.

Land is leaning over one of the tables. His hands grip the straps, his muscles are undulating, his face red with rage. A tear flows down his cheek.

"They kill the chosen ones," I say.

Land nods his head. He stands up straight and picks up the laminated sheet he has been looking at from the table. He walks over and hands it to me. "Our departure date," he says.

EMERGENCE RESIDENCE DISPOSAL PROCEDURE—May 2, 2013.

1. Greet residents at hatch with "Welcome to Utopia."
2. Administer disposal shot before they crawl out of hatch. Explain shot is required immunization to new viruses they have not yet been exposed to.
3. Assist sedated residents to table, unconsciousness will occur within thirty seconds. After unconsciousness

strap residents in for examination. Permanent unconsciousness will occur within two minutes.

4. Assist Dr. Pilgrim with required examination.

5. Utilize mobile cart to dispose of deceased residents'
bodies in crematory furnace.

I look to a stainless steel half door that is built into the wall
adjacent to me. It's a door to the crematory furnace.

Land walks across the room to the tall green file cabinets
that fill the side wall. He runs his fingers over the faded yellow
tags on the front of each drawer. He walks back and forth reading the names. He slowly opens one drawer as if he is afraid
of what is inside, reaches in, pulls out a copper urn, and backs
away in horror. "Mother of God."

Land frantically pulls another drawer open, and another,
and another, holding up urns each time. "These urns contain
the ashes from the chosen ones before us." He desperately reads
the names and looks into the file drawers. "It's everyone." Land
stands defeated. His head and arms hang in hopelessness.

"I'm sorry," I say.

Land stands still, too crushed to move.

"Land," I say. "You were right. We should go."

Nothing. Land continues to stand immobile.

"Land."

The outside door opens. I stand up and run to Land. I shake
him. "Land!"

A heavyset white woman in a business suit jiggles through
the door like a polyester-covered Jell-O mold. We freeze.

"How'd you get here?" she asks, her face panicked. She
lumbers as fast as she can over to a desk, lifts a phone, and
presses some numbers. A warning siren fills the complex.

Land bolts out of his sorrow-induced coma. He runs to the
filing cabinet and grabs an urn from the drawer he left open.

"Stay where you are," the woman commands.

A person in SWAT-like gear storms into the room.

Land runs toward the open manhole.

I grab the microfiche.

Land disappears into the tunnel stairwell.

"Stop!" the woman yells.

I run toward the opening.

A line of commandos files in and join the first.

I'm halfway down the hole. A shot rings out.

I close the lid and turn the crank to lock it. "Go!"

Land's flashlight spins below me as we rapidly descend. Down and around we go. Our feet clang against the metal steps until we reach the rendezvous room. We climb down the metal ladder. Land shuts and locks the hatch behind us. We run down the stairs into the common room. We are both breathing heavily.

I bend over and put my hands on my knees to rest. "This is one fucked-up program."

"And I thought it was so noble," Land says. "I was a chosen one. I was responsible for carrying on the Cherokee people."

I hear a distant sound from above, like raindrops hitting a tin roof. "They're coming. Should we hide?"

Land shakes his head. "They'll find us. We have to try to escape."

"The women's side," I say.

"No." Land heads for the door to the men's tunnel. "Stick with what we know."

"The vault door will be locked," I say.

Land makes a dismissive grunt, like he can't be bothered with such details now. He opens the door and starts running. I run next to him. We start off fast, but then slow to a jogging pace.

We run for fifteen minutes. My legs burn. There's a pain in my side from lack of oxygen. I hear shouts behind us. The tunnel door—I can see it, three football fields away.

The lights go out and there is nothing but black. We are trapped. Barking dogs echo behind us. I hear shouts and running footsteps.

The barking is louder and close. Land turns on his flashlight. Two German shepherds bound toward us.

"This is it," Land says.

I jump in front of Land. I slap my hands together and point my middle finger and PRAD at the dogs. Nothing happens. I slap my hands together again, harder this time. Nothing.

This ring is a joke. I angrily slap my hand as hard as I can against the cold cement wall. My middle finger tingles and then vibrates. A wail pulses down its length through my fingertip. The dogs are ten feet away and ready to pounce. I point my finger and the PRAD screams. The dogs silently yelp and squeal and then turn and run. The piercing sound beam screeches after them. The sound behind me, though, is manageable. "Run!" I shout.

I run toward the door, pointing my sound-debilitating finger behind me.

We reach the door and stop. "Now what?" I say. "They'll be back."

A click sounds, and then a clunk. The door opens. Flipper's head sticks through. That's right. Land gave him the code.

"I heard a crazy noise," Flipper says. "Is everything all right?"

Land and I barrel around Flipper. We pull him back through the doors. Land closes and locks the first door.

"What happened?" Flipper asks.

Land looks at my hand. "You have a magic ring."

"PRAD." I smile. "*P* for Puny. *R* for Range—"

"What the hell is going on?" X-ray stands in the lounge's entrance with his hands on his hips. He looks at the open vault. "Land, where have you been? Who gave you permission to enter the tunnel? What are you doing with this traitor—"

Land hands me the urn. He pushes the vault door shut and locks it. He walks toward X-ray calmly. "We had a problem, X-ray." Land is within three feet of him. "And to fix it—"

He lunges, but X-ray dives and rolls. X-ray jumps up and points my PPK at Land. Land puts his hands in the air and slowly backs up toward me. X-ray points the gun at me. "What are you holding?"

Land takes the urn from me and holds it like a football.

"Give that to me," X-ray says.

Land spreads his feet apart. "You'll have to shoot me."

X-ray contemplates. "Keep it. But don't think I won't shoot." X-ray motions with the gun. "You two. To the showers."

Land walks ahead and I follow. X-ray knows we were missing in the tunnel and that Land must have used his code, but I hope he doesn't figure out that Flipper was the one who let us back in. We enter the showers and then the maintenance room. Walter and his crate are gone.

"Are you going to drill us?" Land asks.

"I'm calling the hotline," X-ray says. "And we'll see what they say. Perhaps we will be drilling." He closes the door, leaving Land and me alone. I hear the combination lock click.

"We don't have long," I say. I notice a stainless steel half door on the bottom of the wall where Walter's crate used to be. "Another crematory furnace?"

Land nods. "Yes."

"What are we going to do?"

We are both silent. Land takes slow, deep breaths. I look around the room. The torture table sits eerily empty, waiting for its next victim. The tools on the walls and shelves look horrifying, now that I know their true purpose. The quiet is calming, and strangely, locked in this small torture chamber, it feels safe. I notice a large brown padded envelope on a low shelf next to my knees. EAGLE is written on the top of it.

The combination lock rattles and clicks. Land and I both

brace, ready for a fight. The door opens slightly. Flipper sticks his head in. "I've only got a second," he says.

Neither Land nor I say a word; we nod our heads and plead with our eyes for Flipper to hurry.

"I used your code to open up the emergency procedures file cabinet in the library. I found old blueprints. There's an emergency escape hatch."

"Where?" Land and I both say.

"Behind you, in the incinerator. It's an old escape shaft that they converted to a chimney when they put in the furnace."

Land sets the urn down, whips open the crematory door, and dives in. He's gone for ten seconds and then his head pops out. He's covered in soot. "It's open. There are metal stepping rungs, even."

"Good luck," Flipper says.

"They're going to kill you, all of you," Land says. "I saw it with my own eyes. They plan to kill you on Utopia Day."

Flipper smiles and shakes his head. He can't even fathom it. "You better go." He turns and leaves the room.

Land enters the furnace, holding his urn.

I vaguely remember Eagle being important. I grab the envelope, shove it inside my pants, and follow Land into the furnace.

The furnace is pitch black, and I make my way by feel. In the back of the furnace is an open flue. I squeeze through it and reach my hand up. I grab on to a metal rung that sticks out from the earth. I can hear Land breathing above me. I start to climb. It smells smoky. The rungs are slippery with ash, human ash, Walter's ash. I try not to think about it. Climb. I have to climb faster.

I'm having the greatest workout day of my life, and my muscles are crying in pain. Up and up I climb. Land is holding on to the urn, but still he's climbing faster than me. I'm not too far behind, though, and I keep a steady pace.

There's a metallic scraping sound above me. I hope Land

has reached the top. I feel cool air. I look up and see stars. I reach the top and pull myself out.

We stand on a pebbly roof. Night has fallen and it is dark. The back side of the neon Big Top Lounge sign shines before us. Land stares up at the sky. He opens his arms and spins slowly around, mesmerized by the world. He breathes in deep and looks at the moon, reveling in the reflected sunlight. Then he notices the sign.

"What is this?" Land says.

"Come on," I say. I'm in the lead now. I go to the roof's back edge, put my feet down, hang down by my arms, and fall on top of a garbage bin.

Land leans over and drops the urn into my hands. He then imitates my jump and joins me on the ground. I lead him around to the front of the Big Top. I stop before the main door. Our clothes, hands, and faces—everything is covered in soot. I open the door and quickly enter.

Land and I stand inside the Big Top Lounge against the back wall, in the dark, next to Cannonball's bar. An erotic show pulses onstage.

Land looks on in shock. "This was Grandma Ruth's Pancake Emporium when I went down."

"Times change," I say.

"To think this was going on above me the whole time."

Cannonball walks through the kitchen doors and stands behind the bar. Thank God he is here. Only one old man sits at the bar. All the other patrons sit and stare at the show. I notice big Joemore sitting in the front row. It seems like forever since I've been here.

Land and I walk up to the bar and sit down, a couple of dark shadows.

"Cannonball," I say.

"Whoa," the man sitting at the bar says. His eyes open

wide at us. He downs his drink and shakes his head. "Another, please," he says with slurred speech.

Cannonball looks at us with amazement. "Liaison dude. What the fuck?"

"This is Land," I say. "We escaped."

"Land the resident from down below? Holy shit. What happened?"

"I saw them torture and kill a man," I say. "And now they want to kill us."

"Who killed who what when?"

"A Canadian named Walter they sent down in a crate a few days ago."

Cannonball looks shocked. "They put people in those crates?"

"Don't play dumb," Land says.

"I—I didn't know. Maybe in my darkest nightmares I considered it."

"Walter was an innocent man," I say.

We pause in a moment of silence. Walter was chewed up and swallowed by an old McCarthy dog. I feel for Walter. I fear for the rest of us.

"The Emergence residents kill them?" Cannonball asks.

Land nods. "Yes, three of us anyway. They incinerate them, just like the Emergence program does to the chosen ones when they're done with us."

"We can stop it." I tap my high-tops where I've hidden the microfiche. "I've got proof."

"We better go," Land says. "They've probably figured out we're gone by now."

Cannonball frowns and nods his head confidently. "I'll take care of it." He motions us toward the door. "Wait out back."

"Why should we trust you?" Land says.

Cannonball's jowls shake. "You got anyone else trying to

help you? I'm going to try and save your lives, and risk mine too."

I start to leave. "Let's go, Land. Like before, we've got no other choice."

Land follows me. We walk around to the back side of the Big Top and stand hidden by the garbage bin. We rub the soot off our faces. We are still dirty, but not as crazy looking.

I hear footsteps. I look around the corner and see Cannonball running. His wide legs move with surprising speed, his tuxedo shoes clip-clop against the pavement. He races around the corner and stops. "Area 22 just called over. I'm supposed to look for you. They're heading here now."

A car starts up in the parking lot and races toward us, skidding to a stop.

"Move it," Cannonball yells. He runs to the car, opens the passenger-side door, and motions at us. "Get in."

Land and I pile into the backseat of a 1975 Cadillac Eldorado. Cannonball sits in the front. The car moves onto the highway.

Cannonball introduces us to the burly, bearded driver. "Everyone, this is Joemore."

It's Ninjenna's boyfriend. He seems even larger than the time I saw him onstage with the dancing girls. And today Joemore is not so animated.

Cannonball brings out his phone. "Any cell phones?"

Land and I say no.

Cannonball pries off the back cover of his BlackBerry and removes the battery. "Joemore?"

Joemore reluctantly hands over his phone.

Cannonball removes the battery. "We're going off the grid."

Joemore pulls onto the road and picks up speed. We've gone about three miles when I hear sirens. Flashing lights appear ahead of us. Joemore pulls the car to the side of the road. He turns around and looks at Land. "You didn't say nothing 'bout helping out Indians."

"Didn't think it mattered, Joemore," Cannonball says.

Joemore grunts. "It might."

Sirens wail as a line of government police cars, black SUVs, and a military Humvee race toward us, lighting up the sky with red, white, and blue.

"I'm out of here," Land says. He reaches up front and opens the passenger-side door.

14

I don't crawl. I learned to fight in an alley.

—SENATOR JOSEPH McCARTHY

"STAY INSIDE, LAND!" Cannonball screams. He reaches out and pulls the car door shut.

The government search team roars by with sirens blaring.

"Drive, Joemore," Cannonball yells.

Joemore casually pulls the Eldorado onto the open road.

"I thought you and I was friends, Joemore? What's this racist bullshit?" Cannonball says.

"Not racist," Joemore grumbles.

"Worse than racist," Land says. "Probably doesn't consider us human."

Joemore growls. "Indians stole my money."

Cannonball motions with his hand to the backseat. "Land stole your money?"

"Casino stole my money."

Cannonball's voice pitches higher. "A casino stole your money? And you're taking it out on Land, who, I can tell you, has been laying his life on the line for the United States?"

"Indian casino. Indian casino swindled me." Joemore says this as if it settles the matter.

Land laughs. "Being swindled don't feel so good, does it? Serves you right."

Joemore slams on the brakes and the car screeches to a halt. "Out!"

"Stay where you are," Cannonball says.

"Out!"

"If you kick him out," Cannonball says, "we will no longer be friends. And I remind you that this black-ass friend knows many of your darkest secrets and has until this moment kept them to himself, particularly from a certain ninja person you consider a girlfriend." Cannonball rocks his head side to side as if to say, *bring it on.*

Joemore groans, a deep guttural sound. The Eldorado begins to move.

Cannonball slowly smiles. "I knew you'd be practical."

"A practical racist," Land says. "I feel better already."

The Eldorado floats over the road effortlessly, gliding over bumps like they are cushions of air. I lean my head back against the soft leather seat. It is cool and comfortable, and I try to relax.

"Where should we go?" Cannonball asks. "Any ideas?"

"How are we supposed to know?" Land says. "I thought you were saving us."

"I'm not sure where I am now," I say.

"We're on the outskirts of the Nevada test site, fifty miles north of Las Vegas," Cannonball says.

"Vegas would be a good place to hide," I say.

Cannonball nods. "Anybody else got ideas?"

The car is silent.

"Vegas it is."

I look at the oversize packet that I have been clutching like a pillow. I run my fingers over the word EAGLE. I wonder what it means. I close my eyes and concentrate. The email President Wright showed me was from Eagle.

"How'd you get that?" Land asks.

"I swiped it off the shelf right before we climbed out the escape vent. Do you know what it is?"

"That's the Eagle envelope. It's filled with cash, pills, and drug vials."

"Cash? What kind of pills and drugs?"

"Variations of Macwacky," Land says.

"Never heard of Macwacky," Joemore says. "Sounds demented."

"You said the women make the Macwacky?" I ask.

"Ninjenna delivers those packets from the alien tourist shop," Joemore says.

"That's the women's side," Cannonball says.

Wind is whistling through an unsealed window. A stream of air flows through the slight fissure and pleasantly cools one side of my face.

Land's eyes are plastered to the window. Even in the dark he is trying to see as much of the world as he can. He talks slowly. "X-ray gives the Macwacky to the prisoners. It induces mental impairment, talkativeness, dizziness, and hallucinations. He then sends the packet with some of the Macwacky and cash back to the surface."

"Where I then get it," Cannonball says, turning around to face the backseat. He reaches for the packet. I hand it to him. "Vance Slater. Eagle is Chief of Staff Vance Slater."

Slater, always Slater. And to think the public views him as President Wright's lackey. "You sure?" I say.

"Oh yeah. Sometimes he picks up the envelope in person. Mostly, though, I send it to his attention in the classified mail. I had no idea what was in it."

"What would Vance Slater do with Macwacky?" I ask, thinking out loud.

Joemore is suddenly enthusiastic. "To totally flip someone out. Impair their cognitive abilities. Even mind-control them." He says this like it's the coolest thing and laughs.

Cannonball and I look at each other in mutual surprise. A look of understanding passes between us.

"Why would you say that?" I ask.

"'Cause that's what I would do." Joemore laughs. "You know, like, if I was totally evil."

Holy shit. It makes complete sense. The president is spaced out on Macwacky. Slater is in even more control than I thought. I hear cardboard ripping as Cannonball tears into the Eagle envelope. "Oh, wow."

Joemore looks. "Oh, yeah." He reaches toward the packet and Cannonball slaps his hand away.

Cannonball holds up a stack of hundred-dollar bills. "Cash. Lots of cash." He digs further into the packet. "Thirty-eight stacks."

Joemore whistles. "Three hundred and eighty thousand smackaroos."

With that kind of cash I could pay off the mortgage and rehab the kitchen. Karen, Scotty, and I could take a kick-ass vacation. Yeah, that's the first thing I'd do: take a month off and tour the country. The Grand Canyon, Yellowstone, the Redwood Forest, all the sights I've always wanted to see.

The car is silent. Everyone else must be thinking about the money as well.

"Where does the cash come from?" I ask Land.

Joemore laughs. "He probably runs casino games down there."

Land's hands curl into fists. I hear his knuckles crack. "Your bigotry will lead to a painful afterlife," he says.

"What the fuck?" Joemore says. "You got problems, Indian man."

Land looks out the window. "Respect and common decency. Got to defend common decency."

"Like each other or not, we have to help each other," I say.

"I'm sorry," Land says. "But if we were alone, Big Man, things would be different."

Joemore slaps his hand on the steering wheel. "You're right there."

The sooner these two are separated the better. "I'm still curious about the cash," I say.

"The crates," Land says. "The cash is in the crates when they arrive."

"Is it payment for the interrogation?"

Land nods. "Torture cash."

I reach my hands up front. "Can I see it again?"

Cannonball hands the packet back to me. "I saw an email implying that Emergence funded the Big Mac Party," I say. "That's how Big Mac makes money. Emergence must be a torture center for hire." I slap the back of the front seat. "The email was to Tim from Eagle. Tim must be Chief Justice Timothy Lancaster."

Cannonball whistles. "That's heavy."

Land takes the packet from me and inspects it. He runs his hands through the money.

"The question is," I say, "who is paying for the torture?"

"Lots of people want information," Joemore says. "Governments, corporations, the mob, jealous lovers—could be anyone."

"Some of the crates contained foreign military personnel and spies," Land says. "The types you would expect the CIA to want intelligence from. But others contained people from all walks of life."

"Like dope dealers and pimps?" Joemore says.

"Everything," Land says. "From hairdressers to city mayors."

"Big Mac doesn't discriminate," I say. "As long as it applies to torture, that is."

"As long as someone is paying," Land says. He opens his

window and the noisy air shocks me. He thrusts his hand out into the sky. I'm confused. He's waving something into the air. I see bills flying. Land is tossing the money out the window.

"Hey!" Joemore shouts.

The car comes to a stop.

Land and Joemore climb out of the car. Joemore tries to grab the package, but Land turns and runs down the empty road, throwing money into the moonlit air. He has ripped off the paper wrappings, and in the strong breeze the individual bills float away over the desert.

Joemore chases him. "Are you crazy?"

Land spins and screams as he throws the last of the money. "It's evil. All evil." He collapses to his knees, and buries his face in his hands.

The moon shines on white rocks from a dry creek bed that curves toward black, lifeless mountains beyond. A few bills are scattered about, but most have been whisked away by the strong breeze and float away into the night. Joemore runs after them, lumbering on his tiptoes, trying to catch them, like he's chasing bubbles. "Ahhh!" He trips and falls into a barrier of shrubs. He cries forth a profusion of profanity into the desert and laboriously removes himself from the prickly plants. Joemore walks back, defeated. "Stupid," he says.

"Doesn't concern you, Joemore," Cannonball says. "You'll get your pay either way."

"Hmph."

"Let's go." I turn and walk toward the car. The others silently follow.

We continue our drive in silence. I think about Emergence being a torture center that funds the Big Mac Party. There's no telling what an organization founded on such evil is likely to do. Hopefully, with my evidence and the president's help, the Big Mac Party will fail before it really gets going. I think about Scotty's school discouraging un-American lunches and foreign words. I think about corporations during McCarthy's time requiring employees to say loyalty oaths to the United States, corporations like General Electric, and the *New York Times*. The people of the United States can't fall for the same McCarthy tactics again. Can they? I continue to stew until the smooth ride of the Eldorado lulls me to sleep.

* * *

I awake to the dazzling galactic lights of the Las Vegas Strip. Vegas—Dan Tanna country. It's changed a bit. Land looks on in awe, his years of sensory deprivation obliterated by the spectacle.

Joemore pulls into the parking lot behind the Bellagio and parks amidst hundreds of cars. We sit quiet in the dark, the parking lot a peaceful reprieve. I roll down the window and take a deep breath of the cool desert air. It smells of New York strip and lusty hopes. I look at the stars and feel lonely and homesick. I could take off, but without any money or resources, I wouldn't have a chance. I realize, though, that I'm not ready to go home. I want to complete my mission. The torture must be stopped. The killing must be stopped. The Big Mac Party must be stopped.

"I want to call home," I say.

"No way," Cannonball says.

"I'll sneak into the casino, find a phone, and sneak out. No big deal."

"It is a big deal." Cannonball raises his voice. "Need I remind you? This is serious shit."

"No shit this is serious shit. You don't have to remind me."

Cannonball softens his tone. "It's just too risky."

I pull out and wave my Tri-Delta card. "I've got a direct number to the president. That's a call we can risk making."

Cannonball stares at me blankly.

"We can end this thing right now. I'll call President Wright and tell him what we know."

"And that will solve everything?"

I can see that Cannonball has some doubts about the president, too. "I don't know. Maybe he can send a helicopter or two to save us, and then he'll call in the cavalry to squash Emergence and the Big Mac Party."

Cannonball stares at me and then looks at the car ceiling, considering.

"We have to try. One phone call could end this mess."

"Okay." Cannonball opens the door and gets out of the car. "Stay put." He walks toward the casino and goes inside.

After a half hour, Cannonball is back. He throws me a small prepaid cell phone.

"Thanks."

Cannonball gives me sunglasses and a baseball cap that says BELLAGIO in glittering letters. He hands Land a cowboy hat and then gives each of us a shopping bag.

"Put the hats on, keep your faces down, and go into the hotel's pool and spa locker rooms to shower and change." Cannonball then gives us each a plastic magnetic card. "I bought you each a pass to the spa."

"What about me?" Joemore says.

"Throw away the phone when you're done with it." Cannonball peels off five hundred-dollar bills from a wad of cash. "In case of an emergency. Now get going and hurry back."

"Thanks."

"Thank the Big Top Lounge." He laughs. "I sort of borrowed our traveling funds from the safe."

I nod to Land. "Keep it away from him."

Cannonball laughs. "No kidding." He smiles, touches his earring, snaps his fingers, and points. "Good luck."

Land and I walk through the shopping mall until we reach the Bellagio's lobby. We are a grubby mess, still covered in grime, but with fancy hats and sunglasses we could possibly pass as just two more crazy Vegas characters. We find our way to the spa and use our key cards to enter a magnificent locker room. Land looks around at all the marble, glass, and gold-plated fixtures with amazement.

At this late hour the locker room is empty. I take a shower. The hot water rainfall from the oversize showerhead is luxurious. The dirt and ash falls away from my skin, and I begin to look like a normal person again. I step out of the shower, towel off, and feel invigorated.

I open my bag and look at the clothes Cannonball has purchased for me. I put on an extra tight pair of Gucci jeans, a white V-neck hooded linen shirt with gray embroidered cosmic circles for added flair, and a pair of rattlesnake skin cowboy boots. I put my Tri-Delta card and microfiche into my front pocket.

Land stands in cowboy boots and wears blue jeans, a flannel shirt, and the same cowboy hat.

I nod to him. "Pardner."

"We better go."

We walk back into the hotel.

"I'm going to make a phone call," I say.

Land nods. "See you soon." He walks off.

I walk through the hotel lobby with the hundreds rolled into my hand. There are people everywhere. I hear the casino and walk toward it. I'm drawn by the bells and whistles and look at all the blinking lights and crowds of people. One quick walk through the casino won't hurt.

I walk in. Bam! I'm there: *Casino Royale*. I walk with style past the pulsating tables, looking left and right as people look at me knowingly. Bond, James Bond. That's right.

I see an empty hallway leading to an exit. I walk into the hallway, pull out my Tri-Delta card, and call the president's number on the prepaid cell.

"Control," an official-sounding voice says.

"This is the EPLO. Connect me to the president immediately."

"One moment."

Good: my request didn't seem to faze the clerk, nor did he react as if I'm a wanted man.

President Wright comes on the line. "This better be good."

I hear Lionel Richie crooning in the background. "Mr. President. This is Special Agent Chris—"

"I know. They told me, Thompson. Have you found out anything?"

"Yes, sir. Shocking stuff, sir."

The president speaks distractedly. "Easy, Sylvia, please— just a moment, baby. What's this, Thompson?"

I wonder if the president is under the influence of Macwacky. "Torture, sir, and murder," I vehemently say. "Unspeakable things all ordered by Chief Justice Lancaster."

"Cheesehead Lancaster? Sylvia, please. Aroocha! You got proof, Thompson?"

"Yes, sir. Signed documents."

"I want to see them. Quit talking and fax them over."

How much control over the president does the Macwacky give Slater? Will the president be lucid enough to know what to do with the evidence? "Can't, sir. No fax machine."

"Email 'em then. PDF or Yahoo those suckers."

"Sorry, sir—they're on microfiche."

"Microfiche? Oh, Sylvia baby. Microfiche? Who do you think you are, Thompson—Sherlock Holmes? Oh, Jesus, Sylvia."

"Should I FedEx them?"

"No! Hell, no. Not you, Sylvia. I'm going to Phoenix tomorrow night. Meet me there."

Giving the evidence to the president in person makes more sense. Hopefully Slater won't be around, and I'll be better able to judge the president's mindset. "Yes, sir. How should I find you?"

"Criminy, Thompson! You're a secret agent. How much hand-holding do you need?"

"Um."

"Be in the Biltmore lobby at midnight. I'll send someone for you. And bring Wizkid with you. This damn fake invasion thing is backfiring on me, and Wizkid won't return my calls. I need his help."

"Okay, sir. How do I find Wizkid?"

"Oh, Sylvia. You're killing me, Thompson. Just find Wizkid. It shouldn't be too hard. Barracuda!" The phone goes dead.

A couple walks by and glances at me strangely. I want to call home. Maybe it's too big of a risk. I look around. No one else seems to be paying any attention to me. I want Karen and Scotty to know I'm okay. I want to patch things up with Karen. I haven't been gone too long. I'll make a quick call and then ditch the phone.

Karen answers. "Hello?"

"Hi, honey."

"Where are you?"

She seems excited, but I can't tell whether it's from happiness or anger. "I'm good," I say, pretending I misheard her. "Where's Scotty?"

"Where do you think? In bed—it's four in the morning. And I hope you didn't wake him up. He and Archie are going to play ball at eight."

"Archie?"

"Archie stopped by last night looking for his blue blazer."

I suddenly distrust my lecherous friend. "And he never left?"

The excitement in Karen's voice leaves. She's definitely just mad. "That's not funny," she whispers. "Yes, he left."

"Just joking."

"Archie and Scotty hit it off when he came over. Archie promised to come back and play basketball with him this morning."

"I bet." I take off my hat and slap it against my leg. Archie is making the moves on my family.

"Archie's worried about you, Chris. We all are. For all we knew you were gone for good. Calling from a whorehouse, and then nothing."

"A dance club," I say. "And I'm undercover. I told you it would be difficult to call."

"And where are you now?"

"I can't say."

We are silent.

A roar goes up from a distant craps table.

"What's that noise? What are all those bells and beeps? Are you in a casino?"

"Karen, listen. The casino has nothing to do with what is happening."

"Come home now, Chris. Stay away from these temptations. Stop gambling. Do you hear me?"

About a hundred feet away I see two gorilla-size men with suits, sunglasses, and earpieces walking purposefully in my direction. They don't look friendly.

"I'm not gambling. Listen, honey. I have to go."

"A strip club, and now a casino, and who knows what in between. I can't believe you've gone on some wild bender."

The two men weave their way between the crowded tables. It's possible a security camera has recognized me, or maybe they're just walking toward me because I look like I'm loitering. Either way, I don't want their attention. "I can explain, honey, but I have to go."

"I can't take it anymore!"

I hang up and drop the phone.

I walk quickly back into the casino, away from the approaching men. They're two tables away now. I turn to run and bump into a waitress. Her drinks fly and she falls into a blackjack table. Casino chips scatter to the ground. People dive for the chips from all directions, surrounding and blocking the two muscle goons. I turn and run.

I run in and out of rows of slot machines until I find an

exit. I'm at the front of the casino. The James Bond theme song runs through my mind. I spin around and stop myself; this is no movie. I run down the crowded sidewalk and around to the back parking lot. I find the Eldorado and jump into the back-seat next to Land.

"Go, go, go!" I say, and we're gone.

* * *

Joemore drives out to the Strip and carefully through Las Vegas. No one seems to be following us.

"Phoenix," I say. "President's orders." I tell them about the conversation with the president.

"ASU is right there in Tempe," Cannonball says. "And Wizkid is at ASU. It shouldn't be too hard to find him."

"The president and the Wizkid," I say. "Sounds like an after-school special."

We drive south on Highway 93. After two hours, we stop at a truck stop metropolis at the Interstate 40 intersection. We fuel up and pull behind a grimy store and restaurant called Oasis.

Joemore relaxes behind the wheel. The rest of us get out and stand next to the car, stretching our legs. The early morning sun is rising. The air is dry and cool. The sky is nothing but blue. Land looks toward the east. A distant roar sounds continuously from the vehicles on the interstate.

A screaming yellow Yamaha Supersport YZF-R1 motorcycle races into the truck stop. The rider, looking like a horse jockey, banks the motorcycle steeply around the final curve and pulls it up into a wheelie. It speeds toward us.

Joemore hurriedly unbuckles his seat belt.

The motorcycle returns to two wheels.

Joemore opens his door.

The motorcycle skids into a sliding stop.

Joemore steps out of the Eldorado and begins to run.

The rider drops the motorcycle, jumps at Joemore, and lands on his back. Joemore's face turns red as the motorcycle rider squeezes his neck in a double-armed choke hold. Joemore's eyes look to the sky. He crumbles to the blacktop, passed out cold.

The motorcycle rider removes her helmet and shakes down her hair.

"Hey there, Ninjenna," Cannonball says.

"What are you doing here, Butterball?" Ninjenna looks at the rest of us. I hadn't seen her face before. She is pretty. She runs her fingers through her dirty-blonde hair. A cute smile breaks through the intensity on her thin face. She nods to me. "Fixer's friend."

"Hi, Ninjenna."

"Seen Fixer lately?" she asks.

"Uh."

"What's going on here?"

"You tell us," Cannonball says.

Ninjenna takes off her gloves and throws them at Joemore's face. "This lug went outside his perimeter without permission."

"Perimeter?"

She flips her hair with the back of her hand. "If he wants a girlfriend as fine as me, he's got to play by the rules."

"How'd you find him?" I ask.

Joemore rolls over and groans.

"GPS locating device on his car," Ninjenna says.

Cannonball's eyes widen. He looks at me. I look at him. We understand the danger. We have to move, and not in the Eldorado.

Joemore struggles to his knees. He shakes his head.

"Next time it'll be worse," Ninjenna says. She walks toward the Oasis. "I need a break."

Cannonball paces beside the car. "Holy shit. A GPS locating device."

"Doesn't seem like she knows anything about our escape," I say.

Joemore sits up. He slaps his face and shakes his head. "I doubt she knows anything. She's been out of town." Cannonball sticks out his hand and helps Joemore up. Joemore rubs his neck and starts walking toward the Oasis. "I'll go talk to her."

Cannonball, Land, and I search the car for a tracking device but can't find anything. After a while, Joemore and Ninjenna walk out of the restaurant holding hands. We stop searching and stand together looking guilty. Ninjenna walks to the Eldorado, bends down by a tire, and reaches her fingers inside the hubcap. She removes a small black rectangular device about the size of a flash drive. She tosses it into a garbage can by the gas pumps.

"Joemore told me about what you all have been saying about Emergence."

"It's all true," I say.

She shuffles her feet. She believes it, I'm sure, but she doesn't like it. "So Fixer is really dead?"

I nod solemnly. "Fixer is really dead. The other Emergence men and women will be dead on May second if we don't do something."

"Seven days, counting today," Cannonball says.

"I'm leaving," Land says with fortitude. He looks to Cannonball and me. "I'm not going to Phoenix."

A moment passes.

Cannonball rubs his chin. "I think it's best if we stick together."

Land looks to the sun. "It's been five years. I'm going home."

A desert-warmed wind blows down on us from the cloudless sky. The dry air smells pure.

Cannonball touches his earring. "First place they'll look for you will be the reservation."

"If I make the reservation, they'll never find me," Land says.

"We stick together," Cannonball says. "We each have talents that can help solve this mess."

"No," Land says. "I have to be with my people. I have to connect with who I was before; to what is real." Land clutches the urn. "The Cherokee people need to know the truth."

Cannonball looks to the ground and shuffles his feet. "The president ordered Chris to Phoenix. Considering what we've all found out, I think it's our duty to follow that command."

Land takes a step toward Cannonball. "My loyalty is to the Cherokee people, first and foremost. I must deliver them the urn. He was one of us. He was Cherokee."

Land and Cannonball stare each other down.

"Let him go," I say.

Cannonball's head angrily jerks toward me.

"The government or somebody is going to look for us," I say. "It might be better to split up. If one of us is caught, the others will still know the truth."

Cannonball purses his lips and considers.

"I say again," Land says, "no one will find me on the reservation."

"Where's the reservation?" Joemore asks.

Land points. "Tahlequah, Oklahoma. Straight east on Interstate Forty."

Joemore walks over to Land. "You're okay. Sorry about the Indian thing."

Land shrugs.

"Take the bike," Joemore says.

"What?"

"The bike. Take the motorcycle to the reservation. Get you there quick."

"But the motorcycle is your girlfriend's."

Joemore spits on the ground. "I paid for the thing." He

flicks his hand at the motorcycle like he's pushing it away. "Take it. It will make me feel good."

Ninjenna straightens the motorcycle up and jumps on it. "Nobody rides my bike."

Joemore looks at Ninjenna like she's a spoiled child. "Fine," he says. "I'll give Land a ride then."

"To the reservation?" Land says.

"I can escort you guys," Ninjenna says. "You might need protection."

"That is kind." Land nods. He seems pleased. "What about Cannonball and Liaison?"

"We can find a ride," I say.

The anger has left Cannonball's face. "It makes sense," he says. "Splitting up is a good idea."

"It is settled then." Land shakes my hand. He nods to Cannonball and then walks toward the Eldorado.

Joemore walks behind him. He raises his hand in the air. "Later."

Ninjenna kick-starts the motorcycle. Land sits in the front seat of the Eldorado, the urn in his lap. He nods to us with solemn determination.

"Good luck!" I say.

Joemore starts the Eldorado.

Ninjenna revs the motorcycle and then pulls away. The Eldorado follows. Ninjenna speeds down the road, leading Land and Joemore into the barren desert toward the Cherokee reservation.

Cannonball and I walk between rows of semitrucks.

"Now what do we do?" I ask.

"Check that out."

Next to the last truck is a motor coach that says "Sun Devil Tours, Tempe, Arizona."

15

You're not fooling anyone at all.
—SENATOR JOSEPH McCARTHY

CANNONBALL AND I WALK over to stand by the Sun Devil Tours bus. College-age-looking kids walk out of the Oasis and meander lethargically toward us. They pay us no notice and climb onto the bus.

A wheat stalk of a driver stands next to the bus. Cannonball talks to him and finds out the bus is headed to ASU. He bribes the driver with a couple of hundreds, and we climb aboard. College men and women are scattered about, their backpacks littering the empty seats around them. In the middle of the bus, Cannonball and I take the only two vacant seats that are together. The students ignore us. They lean against the window or their backpacks and sleep.

The bus rumbles on, quiet but for the engine and the wheels running over the pavement. It has been two hours. A girl in blue jeans and a conservative pink polo shirt walks down the aisle handing out leaflets. "Tri-Delta, Alpha Tau Omega Spring Shooting Star Dance. Forty dollars a couple, twenty-five single.

Proceeds to benefit the Greater Phoenix Big Brothers Big Sisters program."

She stops near us. "Gentlemen?"

"We're not students," Cannonball says.

"Really? I would have never guessed."

"And dancing is not our thing," I say.

Cannonball elbows me. "Speak for yourself."

The girl has long brown hair and a pure face. She hands us flyers. Her eyes sparkle with energy when she talks. "We take donations whether you're a student or not." She is at once beautiful and cute. A nostalgic pain grips me as I long for my college days.

"And whether we dance or not?" I say.

She laughs.

I nudge Cannonball in the ribs. "We could make a donation."

"Oh, sure." He reaches into his pocket for some money. He hands her a fifty-dollar bill.

"Thanks. Very thoughtful of you," she says.

"Hope the dance is a success," I say.

"Me too. You guys live in Phoenix?"

"No, we're doing some recruiting at ASU," Cannonball says.

"Our rental car broke down," I say.

"Recruiting for whom?"

Cannonball sits up straighter. He is still in his bartender's tuxedo, sans bow tie. "Homeland Security."

"Are you looking for agents?" she asks.

"Not this trip," Cannonball says. "We're interviewing for more technical positions. Programmers and such."

Her eyes open wide, and she does a little hop. "I'm a computer science major."

"When do you graduate?" Cannonball asks.

"Next month."

"Anything lined up yet?"

"Couple things in the works, but nothing definite."

Cannonball hands her a card. "If you're interested, we'd be happy to look at your resume."

"Thanks. I'll send it to you." She turns and walks to her seat in the back of the bus.

"Do you really work for Homeland?" I ask.

Cannonball shrugs. "According to my card. What's your gig?"

"Tri-Delts."

"What?"

"Nothing." I pause and then say, "Customs Service."

Cannonball slaps his leg and laughs. "Now that's a bad cover. Sorry. Those guys are morons, huh?"

"Yeah."

"You're smooth at this," Cannonball says. "Not everyone is so calm under pressure."

"You think?" I sit up straighter. Maybe I am secret agent material. "Bond," I say softly to myself. "James Bond."

"What was that?"

"Thanks," I say responding to his earlier comment. "And you're obviously a pro."

Cannonball drops his head and suppresses a laugh. "Bond," he whispers. He giggles but then recovers and becomes serious. He reaches out his hand. "Real name's Derek Allen."

I shake his hand. "Chris Thompson."

"Don't think nicknames matter much anymore."

"No, we've done more than violate the nickname policy."

Derek laughs. "That's the truth."

"And the truth has been alarming to say the least."

Derek shakes his head. "The truth sucks. President Wright was right."

"Right about what?"

"That there was something sinister about Slater and Big Mac."

"Exactly how do you know the president?"

Derek chuckles. "The president and I go way back." He gives me a don't-doubt-me-it's-all-true look. "After I was done with the Marines—" I must look surprised. "Iraq. Two tours," he says.

"Wow. Thanks for, you know, your service," I say.

Derek nods. He seems appreciative. "When I got out, I landed a job at the Round Robin Bar at the Willard Hotel in DC. You know it?"

"Yeah, a real power joint," I say.

"President Wright—then Congressman Wright—was a regular there. We got to know each other pretty well over more than a few late-night drinks."

"So you guys have been friends ever since?"

Derek lowers his voice to a whisper. "Not officially friends, no. Eight years ago, the congressman recommended me to Slater. He liked my military background and helped me get a job with Homeland, and Slater must've liked me enough to get me the job with Emergence. I didn't think Congressman Wright knew exactly where I ended up. I had to go undercover and halt communications with everyone I used to know."

"That must suck."

Derek laughs. "Naw, not really." He looks around. "But then one time a couple years ago I'm at this show in Vegas."

"The Flamingo?"

"Yeah! I'm sitting in my seat and I get a tap on the shoulder. This hostess invites me into the VIP room, and there's the president with a couple of gals. Somehow he's found out that Slater assigned me to Emergence. We get to talking about Big Mac and the president's worries. The president is kind of hip that he's found someone he knows on the inside, but really I don't know shit. Still, we secretly meet each year to go over old times and such, and I try to give him whatever I know about Emergence."

"And you guys came up with that roast beef code."

"Yes! An emergency trust code."

"But Slater knows you know the president."

"I'm sure Slater's forgotten who introduced me to him. Even if he hasn't, I'm a peon anyway." He leans closer. "Did you know that when Slater was in law school he spent his summers as an aide to Timothy Lancaster?"

"Wow. It's still hard for me to believe that the chief justice is a part of Big Mac and the torture."

"Crazy, huh." Derek slaps his hands together. "Do you know what Lancaster's first job out of law school was?"

"That must have been a long time ago. Lancaster is ancient."

"In 1950 he worked for McCarthy."

"Oh, wow." I flutter my hands in the air and mimic the president. "McCarthyism. It keeps popping up everywhere."

"I wish it were funny."

We are silent.

"I can play the trivia game, too," I say. "I did a paper on McCarthy in school. You know he had thirty thousand books removed from libraries? Some of them they even burned."

"Dude didn't like books."

"That's true. He didn't like to read books, either. Except for one."

Derek bites his fingernail. "Don't tell me—*The Communist Manifesto* by Karl Marx?" He laughs.

"No. *Mein Kampf*, by Adolf Hitler."

Derek's jaw drops. "That dude didn't like books either."

"And guess what class McCarthy's worst grade in college was?"

"I don't know. Constitutional law?"

I laugh. "Close, but no. Legal ethics."

The dance-flyer girl comes back. It's about time this secret agent business had an upside. She is holding Derek's business card. "I just realized I forgot to introduce myself, Mr. Allen." She clutches her hands and talks nervously. "I thought, you know. You'd be more likely to read my email and resume if you knew my name."

Derek reaches his hand over. "Of course. I'm Derek Allen." She shakes his hand. "Nice to meet you."

"And . . . you are?"

She touches her forehead. "Oh, sorry. I'm Rachel Larson."

"Nice to meet you, Rachel. This is Chris Thompson."

I shake Rachel's hand. I feel guilty that we're leading her on about a job, but we need to have a cover.

"And you work for Homeland too?"

Cannonball smiles. "He's a Tri-Delt."

"A Tri-Delt?"

I'm embarrassed and feel guilty that a part of me wants to impress this girl. I wave my hand dismissively. "Small security division within the Customs Service."

She beams. "I'm a Tri-Delt too! The sorority kind, though."

We laugh.

Rachel takes a seat across the aisle from me. "You guys must be busy. With the national emergency and all."

"The what?"

"Don't you know? The president has declared a national emergency."

"I just didn't know that was public yet," I say.

"Oh." Rachel hands me her iPhone. "*Stealth Invasion—Illegal Aliens Storming the Border*," the headline reads.

"Is the Big Mac Party serious about this manifesto? It's a bunch of crap," she says.

The Internet article portrays the stealth invasion as I already understand it. It then says something about a Big Mac manifesto and lists some presidential executive orders, but I don't have a chance to read them. Maybe these executive orders are what the president meant when he said the invasion had backfired on him.

"Do you have a business card?" she asks me.

"My division isn't hiring."

Cannonball looks at me quizzically. "You don't have a business card?"

What is he doing? "Um, yeah. Sure, I have a business card." I pull out my Tri-Delta ID from the front pocket of my Gucci jeans. I hold it up for Rachel, careful only to reveal the front.

"Special Agent Tri-Delta Security. That's hilarious," she says. "But I'm sure it must be very serious."

Derek glances at the card. I put it quickly away. "Sorry, I only have one on me. And I need to keep it."

"So what are you doing if you're not interviewing?"

"Chris is here to see a particular individual," Derek says.

"A guy," I say. "Some computer science student they call Wizkid."

"Wizkid? Does he have a real name?"

Derek and I look at each other.

"Oh, I get it. Secret business, right?"

Derek and I don't say anything.

"Okay, then. Talk to you later." Rachel returns to her seat, I think feeling good about the conversation and her chances of getting a job interview.

"Don't you feel bad about bullshitting her?" I ask.

"I'll see to it she gets an interview."

"And a job?"

Derek starts laughing. "Big Top Lounge is always hiring."

"That's horrible." I try to shake the image of Rachel dancing at the Big Top Lounge out of my mind.

Derek laughs harder, shaking his seat as he does so. He raises his hands, circles them in the air, and gyrates his hips in a seat dance. "I crack myself up."

"Put it on your resume."

"Just might, Chris Thompson. I just might."

"You in a relationship?"

He sobers up at my question. "Yeah, I live with a lady in LA."

"LA?"

"Yeah. I commute. I'm month on, month off."

"She knows you work at the Big Top?"

"Hell no. She'd whoop my ass."

I laugh.

"Way to ruin my mood."

"I'm sorry. I just feel bad about that Rachel girl."

"Don't worry. I'll get her a real interview. The rest is up to her." He pauses. "And sorry about putting you on the spot. Just having fun—and testing you a bit, too."

I like Derek. We have a good rapport and seem to be on the same page about things. "Thanks," I say.

16

DEREK AND I ARE OFF THE BUS and walking around the Arizona State University campus.

"Should we just start asking people if they know a Wizkid?"

"There's gotta be a better way," Derek says.

"Mister Allen!"

We turn. Rachel is walking toward us with another girl. "This is Jenny," she says.

Jenny gives a short wave. She looks vaguely familiar.

Cannonball looks like he recognizes her, too. He is overly polite. "Hello, Jenny. Pleased to meet you."

"Jenny knows your Wizkid." Rachel gives us a proud smile.

Jenny rolls her eyes. "Randall Linquist. The geeks he hangs with call him the Wizkid."

"So you know how we can contact him?" Derek asks.

"I can give you his number." Jenny jumps behind Derek. She holds on to his shoulders and hides her head behind his back. "There's Randall now!"

"Why are you hiding?" Derek asks.

"We went on one date last year," Jenny whispers. "He's sort of been in love with me ever since." She looks around Derek and barely points with her finger. "There—he lives in Hassa dorm."

We look across the street to a brown brick seven-story dorm. People are walking in and out of the busy lobby.

Coming through the parking lot on a beat-up ten-speed bike is a tall skinny white student wearing blue jeans, a black T-shirt, and a ratty backpack. He lifts a leg over his bike frame and coasts, standing off to the side on one pedal.

"He's strange. Always on the move."

Wizkid slams into a bike rack with a jangled clank. His curly black mop of hair grooves with the motion.

"We better go," Derek says.

Rachel and Jenny start to walk away. "Okay, then. Come to the party if you guys are around," Rachel says.

"Sure," I say, knowing full well I wouldn't be going to a college party.

"Thanks," Derek says.

Derek and I head across the street toward the dorm. "I think Jenny is the president's daughter," he says.

I remember now: The president said his daughter was friends with Wizkid. I can't remember the last time I saw an image of her in the media, but she has definitely matured some since then. I look back toward Jenny and Rachel walking away. Just as I suspected; two Secret Service men tail Jenny from two hundred yards behind. I hope these guys are just her regular protection and don't recognize Derek and me.

Wizkid kicks his bike and runs across the parking lot toward the dorm.

Derek charges ahead of me to meet him. "Excuse me. Hey, buddy. Excuse me."

Wizkid has no choice but to stop when Derek blocks his way. He nervously looks at Derek and then at me. Wizkid's pasty white skin looks unhealthy, like he has spent too much time in front of a computer. His rail-thin body shakes when he talks. This is the genius who has created the fake invasions.

"Wha, wha, what do you want?"

"Relax," Derek says. "The commander in chief sent us."

"Are you Ba, Ba, Bowling Ball?"

"Close enough. Cannonball."

"That's right, Cannonball." Wizkid points at him. "Roast beef?"

"With red peppers."

"Okay." Wizkid starts shaking some more. "This manifesto of executive orders is bullshit."

"What orders?"

"Like you don't know. The Big Mac manifesto! The executive orders! President Wright double-crossed me. I suppose he sent you two because I haven't returned his calls."

A young couple stops to listen when they hear Wizkid mention President Wright.

"Is there somewhere more private we can talk?" I say.

"Who, who are you?"

I stick out my hand. "Chris Thompson."

Wizkid stares at me, fidgeting.

"Look," I say. "We're not sure what this Big Mac manifesto is that you're talking about, but President Wright wanted me to find you. He said the invasion had backfired on him."

He stares at us and jitters some more. "I'll give you ten minutes." He opens the front door with his ID card.

We follow Wizkid and take the elevator to the sixth floor. He rushes us into his room and closes the door. Dust particles float in the bright afternoon sunrays that stream through the drapeless windows. A musty odor arises from a pile of clothes on an unmade bed. Computer books and hacker magazines litter the warm room.

Wizkid's body seems to rebel against standing still. He fidgets. His left wrist twitches intermittently with a blink from his right eye. "I didn't sign up for this. My computer program was to be a joke. President Wright said he needed an outsider to test the system."

"I think the president intended more than a joke," I say.

Wizkid throws his twig-like arms into the air. "You think? The country thinks there's a full-scale double invasion going on."

I shrug my shoulders. "You did too good a job."

He shakes with angry contorted convulsions. "I, I, don't you pin this on me. I'm not evil. I don't want to be the Joseph Goebbels of the United States."

Derek laughs. "I think you're misrepresenting your relationship with the president. He's a decent man."

Wizkid scurries over to his desk and rifles through the mess around his computer. He holds up a piece of paper. "Says you, Volleyball. Look at this." He hands Derek the shaking paper.

Derek and I read an online printout from the *New York Times*. My insides begin to quiver like Wizkid as I read:

Big Mac Manifesto

In response to the mass illegal immigration threat from Mexico and Canada, President Wright has declared a national emergency and has instructed the Big Mac Party to coordinate the appropriate government agencies and implement the following executive orders. These executive orders are authorized by a reinstatement and amendment of previous executive orders and are enacted by the current emergency.

All citizens must register with the Postmas-
ter-General and carry a Big Mac-approved national
ID card at all times. Reinstatement of Executive
Order 11002—President John F. Kennedy.

Men ages 18 to 25 living in border states will be
drafted into large-scale work brigades to monitor, build, and fortify barriers along the borders
of Mexico and Canada. Reinstatement of Executive
Order 11000—President John F. Kennedy.

Illegal aliens shall report to specified deten-
tion centers. The FBI and all federal, state, and
local law enforcement shall enforce compliance
with this directive. Enforcement of Rex 84 Alpha
Ex plan—Colonel Oliver North.

Any citizen of natural lineage to current enemy
nations who lives within fifty miles of said enemies' borders should report to specified deten-
tion centers. Reinstatement of Executive Order
9066—President Franklin D. Roosevelt.

The president requests Congress to reactivate the
House of Representatives' Committee on Un-American
Activities. Executive Order 21068—President Oscar
I. Wright.

The government of the United States shall pre-
serve and enhance the role of American English
as the official language of the United States
of America. It shall be unlawful in the United
States to communicate, perform, or provide services or materials in any language other than
American English. Executive Order 21069—President
Oscar I. Wright.

All government employees, federal, state, and
local, are required to join or pledge allegiance
to the Big Mac Party and the American principles
it stands for. Executive Order 21070—President
Oscar I. Wright.

My spine tingles the same as when I read Chief Justice Lancaster's military tribunal judgment. Executive orders are essentially laws that do not require congressional approval. The Big Mac Party has used President Wright to put their spin on some old executive orders, as well as to reinstate and add a couple new ones of their own. Congress and the Supreme Court can nullify these actions, but that takes time and organization. If Slater has key members of Congress under his belt along with the Supreme Court, there could be no stopping Big Mac from issuing any order they want, which is exactly what they are doing.

Wizkid unwittingly helped create this mess. President Wright obviously wants his skills to help undo it. I need to calm him down and convince him to follow Derek and me to the president. "I admit these orders may be a little disconcerting," I say. "But I don't—"

Wizkid's hair rocks with agitation, energizing the dust particles around his head. "Disconcerting! Protests are breaking out everywhere. There's a mob by the library that will string me up if they find out my program caused this."

Derek looks troubled.

"This is not the president's work," I say.

"You're delusional," Wizkid says. "These are executive orders. Nobody but the president can enact them."

He is right, of course, but I hope he can understand that the president is only a pawn. "You can't just blame the president. There are people in the government who wield enormous power. Bad people. I know that now. The people we are fighting against. We've good reason to believe Vance Slater is influencing President Wright with a mind-control drug called Macwacky. We also have evidence that Slater and Chief Justice Lancaster run the Emergence program as a torture center for hire. They use the revenue to fund the Big Mac Party."

"Slater's a bad dude," Derek says. He stands straight, seeming to regain confidence that we can convince Wizkid to join us.

I touch Derek's shoulder. "The mock invasion fell right into Slater's hands. Whether the invasion was real or not, the national emergency has given him a chance to unleash this Big Mac crap."

"You mean like taking dictatorial control?" Wizkid says.

"Yes, like taking dictatorial control," I say. "That's why we can't give up. President Wright said the invasion had backfired on him. He undoubtedly wants you to help him end it. We have to help the president. We have to fight Big Mac."

Wizkid collapses onto the bed, disappearing under the mound of dirty clothes. He moans. "I'm ruined."

"Come, now," I say.

Dirty socks and underwear, coupled with an errant pair of jeans, fly through the air like smelly ghosts toward Derek and me. I was immune to my dorm room mess back in the day, but I now understand why Karen was disgusted with it. A smelly shirt hits me in the face. "Get the hell out."

"We have to stick together. Come with us and meet with President Wright."

The clothes continue to fly. "Six years of college for what? To become the most sinister man in the country?"

I swat flying clothes to the floor, now ankle deep. "The president plans on meeting us at the Biltmore tonight. He is sure to do the right thing." I hope this is the case. The president sent me on this mission for a reason. He knows he is a pawn, and I think he feels guilty about it—or at least he wants to be free from Slater's control. I now have the information that could put Slater away. Surely the president will be able to see the value of my microfiche evidence.

"This is a joke. You two are the best the president can come up with? Macwacky? Seriously? I think you're fakes."

Derek looks offended. "Macwacky is for real. We're for real."

I bring out my Tri-Delt card. "I have a contact number. We can call President Wright if you want proof."

I flip the card over, and we inspect the toll-free number below the Indiana University sorority house.

"The card may look silly, but this number is a direct line."

Wizkid jumps off the bed. He smiles mockingly. "Call it, then." He reaches for his cell phone and hands it to me. "Let's get your president buddy on the line right now and let him explain this whole mess."

I can't think of a reason not to. "All right." I dial the number.

Wizkid grabs the phone and looks doubtful. "I want to hear this." He puts the phone on speaker and sets it on the desk.

We listen to the other end ring. This time a computerized female voice answers the phone with consumer friendliness. "Thank you for contacting the United States Customs Service information line."

Wizkid laughs. "Just as I thought. We've all been duped."

Derek looks confused. "Who gave you this card again?"

"Shh."

The woman continues, "For new importation rules with Canada, say or press the number seven."

"This is stupid," Wizkid says.

"For Tri-Delta security authorization, say or press the number eight."

"Eight!" I smile triumphantly at Derek and Wizkid.

The line rings and then beeps. The woman's voice speaks again. "Please say your name."

"Chris Thompson," I say slowly.

More intelligent computer beeps sound. "Name and voice recognition verified. Please hold."

I point at Wizkid. "Ha!"

The phone rings and a nasal human voice comes on. "Please hold." We wait as ABBA music plays.

The music stops. "Thompson?"

"Mr. President?"

"No. Vance Slater."

"I prefer to speak to the president."

"You can talk to me first, Thompson. You do remember agreeing on that procedure before you left?"

"Vaguely."

"Very good. I'm glad you called in. We're going to send a car for you, and then we can have a nice debriefing session." Slater speaks in such a sweet voice it's maddening.

"No," I say. "I'm not going anywhere near you."

"You don't know who you're dealing with," Slater says, all sweetness gone.

"But I do," I say.

"You're in Tempe, Arizona, I see," Slater says calmly. "Who else is with you? Cornball? That Indian? That stupid Wizkid?"

"Where's the president?" I ask, but Wizkid grabs the phone and hangs up.

"This was a bad idea," he says. "They'll be able to find us now."

"You should have believed me," I say.

"Let's move," Derek says.

"I believe you," Wizkid says. He opens the door and leans out. "Hey, Surf. You going to class?"

"Uh, yeah."

Wizkid throws his cell phone down the hall. "Take this with you."

"Uh?"

"Just do it."

Wizkid shuts the door. "Now you two get the hell out of here. I'm disappearing."

"You can't run away from this problem. It'll come out you were behind this. Help us stop Slater now, or you may go down in history as the evil architect behind Big Mac." Wizkid looks up at me as I say this, and I can tell by the look in his eye that I've touched a nerve. "The president needs your help."

He stays stubborn. "Six years," he shouts. "What a loser I

am. I go on one date, and it just happens to be with the president's daughter. Wuh, wuh, one date, and suddenly the Secret Service comes down on me and the president wants to meet me and talk about patriotism, his daughter, and computers. I should have never told him about my fa, fa, fake invasion idea. But he was all keyed up on how he could create a harmless national emergency."

"So he could send someone like me to Emergence," I say proudly.

"Suh, suh, six years! I've never been invited to a party. Suh, suh, six years of geekdom, and I end up ruined with you guys."

"The country needs you," Derek says. "Help us deliver this evidence to the president, and you can help him end the invasion."

"I don't care. I'm vanishing and starting over. No more computers. I'm studying art, or something where I'll meet more girls."

"Say," I say. "What if we could help you meet some girls?"

"You guys?" He laughs. "I'd be better off calling the Geek Squad."

"I think you have," Derek says. "And look where that's gotten you."

Wizkid kicks some of the clothes from the floor up to his bed. "What's it to you, blubber ball?"

"Relax, guys," I say. "Wizkid, how would you like to go to a party being thrown by the Delta Delta Delta sorority?"

He looks up, but his expression is blank. "Big deal," he says.

"What if I told you there was a strong likelihood Jenny was going to be there?"

"We just saw Jenny," Derek said. "She was with the girl organizing the party. I think Jenny is going to go."

"Just stick with us for a while," I say. "It might be interesting."

Wizkid looks at his feet and then at me. He seems intrigued. "You're not shitting about this party?"

I pull out the leaflet Rachel had given me on the bus and hand it to Wizkid. I try to appear as sincere as possible. "Everything we've said so far has been true, hasn't it? And as long as we're at the Biltmore by midnight, we can go to this party."

Wizkid inspects the leaflet. "Alpha? Tuh, tuh . . . ATOs? I, I thought it was a sorority party."

"It's both. The Tri-Delts and Alpha Taus are throwing the party together at the Alpha Tau Omega house."

"Th, the, those frat guys are tough competition. They'll be all over Jenny."

"So you're just going to give up? Do you want to go see Jenny or not?"

"I got game," Derek says. "I could make a hell of a wing-man."

"Re, really? What will we say?"

"You can't plan it, man," Derek says. "You got to feel out the situation at the time. Follow my lead, and work your way into it."

Wizkid is considering.

"And you're sure Jenny will be there?"

"Pretty sure," I say.

"It's worth a shot," Derek says. "Party environment might be easier to talk to her."

"Like melting butter on hot toast," I say.

They both look at me blankly.

"What?"

"Let's move," Derek says, shooting Wizkid a get-a-load-of-this-guy look.

"Okay," Wizkid says, grinning back at him.

Wizkid grabs some stuff, and before he can change his

mind, we shuffle him out into the hall and into the elevator. We reach the ground, the doors open, and we exit the building as a team.

17

You can run away if you like.
—SENATOR JOSEPH McCARTHY

WE EXIT THE ELEVATOR into the quiet dorm lobby. Wizkid is calling for a taxi from the common phone in the information window.

"We really are going to go to that party?" Derek asks.

I look over to Wizkid to make sure he can't hear me. "Obviously I'd rather not, but we need him to stick with us. So maybe. We need to get him on a computer to see if he can stop this fake invasion and end the national emergency."

Wizkid hangs up the phone. We all walk outside and wait, looking up and down the street. I monitor the people walking by, watching for anyone suspicious, but they are all unconcerned students.

The cab pulls up and we climb in.

"Where to?" the cabbie asks.

Slater is going to be looking for us. We need our own transportation and a safe place to stay. "You know a good used-car lot?" I ask.

The air is on high, blowing a cool, cigarette-scented breeze around the cab. The cabbie turns around and looks at me. "What you looking for?"

"Something cheap. An old-time car lot, not a dealership."

The cabbie has one hand lazily on the wheel. He gestures at us with the other hand as he pulls out of the dorm's driveway. "Uno's got good deals. Have you there in fifteen minutes."

He drives us into east Mesa. The sun beats down on the hot wide boulevard. Palm trees line the sidewalks, making me feel like I'm on vacation. We drive by Manny's Brake Shop, Desert Custom Landscaping, and El Churro's Adobe Grill. A billboard that shows smiling Latina girls advertises Rosa's Salon. We pass a McDonald's, a Taco Bell, and a Bank of America.

The cab stops at Uno's Excelente Automobile Deals. Wizkid and I stand and look around, but Derek is immediately drawn to a pacific blue 1982 Dodge B150 conversion van. It has a Grand Canyon mural on one side and a howling wolf with a bright moon and stars on the other. Bond wouldn't dare—an Aston Martin DB5 it is not. A banner diagonally crosses the window: "Sale $1,199."

A Hispanic man with skinny legs and small overhanging belly walks out of a white hut-like office. He wears cowboy boots and hat. "Hey there, fellas. You like that one?" He walks closer. "I'm Uno." He opens his arms up wide to display his car lot. "And have I got some deals for you."

"How much for this van here?" Derek asks.

Uno points to the window. "It says eleven ninety-nine."

"I think you can do better than that," Derek says.

"For three men who arrive in a taxi, twelve hundred is a very good price. It's on sale."

"We'll take it," Derek says.

"Up in smoke," I say.

Derek brings out his cash. A white Cadillac Escalade pulls into the lot.

"Shit." Uno turns and calls out to his office-hut. "Get back to work, Manuel."

The Escalade's door opens. A skinny balding white man with a bulbous nose and oval sunglasses steps out. He has a Big Mac button on his pinstriped charcoal suit. "Good afternoon, Ohno."

Uno smiles politely. "I'm kind of in the middle of a deal here, Mr. Hochner."

Hochner holds up his hands. "Only a second—don't want to hamper your business. I just want to make sure you're making headway on the new chamber of commerce guidelines." Hochner pulls some typewritten papers from a folder. He looks at the papers and then around at the lot, and then scratches his head.

"It's only been a day since the order, Mr. Hochner," Uno says. "We're doing the best we can."

Hochner's eyes blink and he shuffles the papers. He looks around beyond the car lot and waves one arm. "Yes, well. I've got a lot of work to do to get this neighborhood Americanized and up to Big Mac standards."

Uno nods to his worker, Manuel, who is painting the wallboard on the back of the lot. "He's changing 'Excelente' to 'Excellent,'" Uno says. "Very English."

"That's good," Hochner says. He rubs his chin. "What about the Uno part?"

"We're changing it to Uncle Sam. We're now going to be Uncle Sam's Excellent Automobile Deals."

"That's perfect," Hochner says. "Very American. People will think you were born and raised here."

"I was born and raised here," Uno says. "I'm third-generation American."

Hochner opens his car door and climbs in. "That's swell, Ohno. I hope the rest of the neighborhood can hurry up and start fittin' in like you." The Escalade drives off.

Big Mac is using McCarthyism tactics to turn us all into white-bread Americans. They want to cook the great American melting pot until it boils into English chicken soup.

Uno shakes his head at Hochner's departing car, but then remembers us and smiles. "Let's go inside and take care of the paperwork."

"Paperwork? We don't care about any paperwork," Derek says.

"I do," Uno says. "All sales and vehicles are regulated by the state. And as you can see, Big Mac is coming down on me."

Big Mac in the White House. Big Mac in the Supreme Court. Big Mac in Scotty's school. Now Big Mac's fingers are swirling in local businesses—or the ones owned by minorities, anyway.

"What if we don't want to buy the van?" I say.

Uno looks disgusted. "Then don't buy it."

"No, I mean, what if we just want to borrow it with no paperwork?"

Uno looks at each one of us as if for clues. "Oh, I see." He rubs his chin. "Two thousand dollars."

"Two thousand dollars?" Derek says.

"Two thousand Uncle Sam American dollars. Plates are registered to me, and I have a feeling you're up to no good."

We all look at one another.

"Two thousand cash to borrow it with no paperwork. Return it or not, but in one week I report it stolen," Uno says.

Derek brings out his cash again. "Deal."

Inside the van, small track-lighting bulbs line the perimeter of the cabin ceiling, dimly illuminating the deep maroon wall-to-wall shag carpeting and the uncomfortable-looking built-in sponge bed with its red cigarette-burn-stained cover.

"Shotgun," Wizkid says as he climbs into the passenger seat.

"I'll drive," I say. I sit in a sheepskin-covered bucket seat on the driver's side. Derek sits behind Wizkid, across from a dilapidated faux-wood cabinet and sink.

I start the van up with a pop and a roar.

Uno stands outside his door. "Might need muffler work."

I point to the dash. "And some gas."

Uno shrugs. "Sometimes the battery runs low. You can always push it and pop it into gear to start it."

"Nice," Derek says.

Uno smiles as we drive off his lot. "Good luck."

"Where to now?" Derek says.

Wizkid shakes in his seat. "What about the party? I thought we were going to party with the Tri-Delts. What about that?"

"Sure, sure," I say. "We'll go to the party. But let's first figure out how we're going to sneak into the Biltmore and meet the president without Slater or any of his goons seeing us."

"I don't want to talk about the president and Slater. I want to talk about Jenny and the party. More to the point, I want to talk about why you think it's okay for us to show up at this party driving this molester van. Even for me this is a major step backward."

"Come on, Wizkid. This is a love machine," I say. I punch him jokingly in the shoulder. "You got to feel the vibe."

He glares at me, and I turn back to the road. It's full of people. I slam on the brakes, bringing the van to a halt twenty feet short of a stoplight on the edge of campus.

"Whoa, what's this?" asks Derek.

Hundreds of protesters overflow the cross street in front of us. They march slowly by, holding placards of peace signs, American flags, and President Wright and Senator McCarthy in Hitler mustaches. They burn signs that say "Big Mac Manifestos" and chant: "Wright is wrong! Wright is wrong!"

A line of policemen escorts the parade, keeping their distance.

A small group of white men in dark suits stand on the side of the street. They smile broadly and hold red, white, and blue Big Mac signs.

The protesters point at the Big Mac supporters and keep chanting, "Wright is wrong!"

The Big Mac people just smile and wave, like they are the happiest citizens alive. One of the men brings out a camera with a superscopic telephoto lens. He takes pictures of the protesters, and then slowly spins, taking photographs of the surroundings and the onlookers.

"We better split." I back up, pull a reverse three-point turn, and drive the opposite way.

"Can we talk about the Tri-Delts now?"

"I'm still worried about that meeting with the president," I say. "What if Big Mac captures us beforehand? Wizkid, I think you should work on ending the fake invasion now, just in case of any problems."

"He would need a computer," Derek says. "The university must have a computer lab he can use."

"I, I, I'd have to use my ID, Cannon Head."

"And if he does, Big Mac would find us in minutes," I say.

"What about the library? If they have a microfiche reader, I could print out my evidence, so we've got a backup."

"Too many cops around now, and the library wants IDs too," Wizkid says.

"You must have a friend with a computer," Derek says.

"No way." Wizkid pulls on his hair. "I'm not getting anyone else involved. Are we going to go to this party or not?"

I snap my fingers. Maybe going to the party is not such a bad idea. "I bet we could use a computer at the Alpha Tau house during the party."

Three presidential helicopters fly in formation overhead.

I point. "The president is in town."

"Like I was saying earlier," Derek says. "No planning necessary. Sometimes it all comes together."

"Okay," Wizkid says. "Let's drive to that party then."

I hadn't been to a college party in . . . well, since college.

After Karen was rejected by the Tri-Delts, we stayed away from the Greek scene. I wonder what Karen will think of me going to a party filled with young sorority girls—and Tri-Delt girls at that. She'll give me the guilt trip for sure, or worse. I think of Archie and worry. That hustler is obviously putting the moves on Karen. And she's certainly not giving me any assurance that his play is failing.

"Hey, Derek. You miss your lady?"

"Yeah. It hurts, you know?"

"Me too. And my kid."

"That's tough."

We ride in silence for a couple miles. I can't stop thinking about Archie and Karen. "Hey, Derek."

"What?"

"You ever worry your lady is foolin' around?"

"All the time. You?"

"Didn't used to, but she's really pissed about me leaving for this special mission crap. She doesn't believe it."

"It's hard to believe."

"And there's this single guy at the office who's been hanging around being all friendly and supportive-like."

"Oh, that is not good. You really are hurting, my man."

Wizkid groans. "Boo hoo. You saps are driving me crazy. I can't take it. I need to do something. I need a computer." Wizkid shakes uncontrollably. "I, I, I've never gone this long without a computer. You got a Game Boy? A programmable calculator? A digital watch? Anything? I can't stand it."

"Chill out," I say. "We're there."

"Party time," Derek says.

18

Oh, this helps me hold my liquor better.
—SENATOR JOSEPH MCCARTHY

DEREK PARKS A PLEDGE SPRINT AWAY from the Alpha Tau house.
The sun has just set, and the sky is a cool blue. The dry air still
smells of hot cement. We walk down a row of fraternity houses
until we reach Alpha Tau Omega, a three-story white-pillared
mansion. Long cement steps lead us to the front porch, where
two fraternity brothers with battleship arms block our way.
More collegiate-looking folks pass by unmolested.

I produce our ticket vouchers and offer to pay for Wizkid.

One of the frat guys scowls at me. "Where'd you get this?"

"We bought it, straight up."

"Yeah, but you wanted to donate, right? I mean, parents'
day is in the fall."

Derek steps in front of me. "Listen, you AT ogre. We bought
tickets to the dance, and we've been invited to the dance by
some honest Tri-Delt sisters. Now we are gonna dance." Derek's left foot points left, and his right points right. He poses his
arms like an Egyptian, and his body shakes like a worm. He

sticks his lip out and stares at the fraternity brothers as if to say, *take that.*

Wizkid shakes like a scared freshman on rush day. "Luh, luh, let's go."

One of the brothers steps forward and faces Derek. "Look, Snoop Dogg. I don't care how many tickets you bought. Alpha Tau is known for *sick* parties, and I'm not going to be the person to—"

"Mr. Allen!" Rachel and three friends come up the stairs. "Did you get my resume? Hi, Mr. Thompson."

"Hi, Rachel."

Derek smiles at Rachel. "Hey. Good to see you." He turns to Alpha Tau man. "Like I was saying, we were invited."

Alpha Tau man steps back. "Rachel?"

"Hi, Tom." Rachel smiles. "It's cool. They're with me."

Alpha Tau Tom looks to the sky and sighs. "Fine." He waves us in.

We walk through a grand foyer into a room decorated appropriately for the world's future players. A majestic chandelier overlooks a Queen Anne table. Fine antique furniture befitting an English lord's manor is placed throughout the room.

Wizkid looks around in awe. "We're at ASU? College students live here?"

"They do," I say. "And I'm sure they have a computer around here somewhere we can use."

We are directed down a hallway filled with portraits of Alpha Tau Omega power alums and out onto a cement back patio. A hunter green tent covers the back lawn. A dreadlocked four-man band plays reggae music in the far corner.

"I'm sorry," Derek says to Rachel. "I haven't had a chance to review your resume."

"Oh, that's okay."

Rachel's three friends stand their distance and eye us strangely through thick mascara.

"Don't worry. I'll get to it," Derek says. "Where'd you like to live when you graduate?"

"I've always wanted to go to LA."

A tuxedo-wearing redheaded pimple-faced pledge waiter offers us blue plastic pint cups filled with mango-colored liquid. "Special ATO island punch," he says.

Rachel, Derek, Wizkid, and I each take a glass.

"Anyway," Derek says. "We appreciate your help. I'll pass your resume along and set you up an interview with our LA office."

Rachel's face beams like she has won the lottery. Her smile transfixes me. "Oh, wow! Thank you so much."

"Let's dance," one of Rachel's friends says. The girl swings her arms and hips, sashaying out to the dance floor with the other two. Rachel stays with us. She's wearing a short skirt and a camisole. I find it hard to avert my eyes.

Derek takes a sip of punch. "Whoa. The island punch has some island rum."

Rachel puts her index finger across her lips. "Shh. Not officially."

Wizkid's glass shakes as he hurriedly drinks. He looks all around the party, searching for Jenny without success. A waiter comes by, and he grabs another drink.

"Do they not officially have any beer either?" I ask.

"Unofficially," Rachel says. "There are some hidden kegs in the basement."

I laugh. "Some things never change."

A worried look passes over Rachel's face. She raises her hands to her mouth. "Oh, you guys aren't here to bust us, are you?"

Derek and I laugh.

Wizkid grabs a third glass and drinks. Neither the plastic cup nor Wizkid's body shake anymore.

"We've bigger problems than college drinking parties," Derek says.

"Maybe not." I nod to Wizkid. "Hey, slow down there, buddy."

"Oh, you mean the invasion. And the Big Mac manifesto." Rachel looks at us uncertainly. "What's up with that?"

"We've got nothing to do with it," Derek says.

"Except that we're hoping to stop it," I say.

"Stop it? The invasion? The manifesto? What do you mean?"

Somehow Wizkid finds his way out to the dance floor. He dances in the middle of Rachel's friends.

"There are some bad people in the government behind the Big Mac manifesto," I say. Rachel waves to someone who is talking to Tom the bouncer. Tom stares at us with malice.

"I don't think he likes us," Derek says.

Rachel flicks her hand like she's shooing a fly. "Psh. Tom? Don't worry about him. He's a spoiled brat, but harmless. Now, about this invasion. I know Mexico and Canada say it's ridiculous, but if millions of illegal aliens are preparing to cross the borders, then maybe the executive orders in the Big Mac manifesto aren't such a bad idea."

I see Wizkid over Rachel's shoulder. His body moves in the strangest dance I've ever seen. He jiggles and jerks, and once in a while he bursts as if from an electrical shock, shaking violently with minute vibrations. His arms and legs splay in all directions, and his hair bounces like a gospel choir as his body cascades into the air.

"Personally," I say, "I think the orders in the Big Mac manifesto violate the Constitution. Executive orders were never intended to give the president ultimate power. Big Mac is feeding on people's fear of immigration, just as McCarthy did with Communism."

Rachel doesn't look convinced. "An invasion is scary. We're not too far from Mexico. I'm not afraid to admit that I'm scared."

Flustered, I laugh. "But that's just it. This whole invasion thing that Big Mac is using to frighten us is not real. It's completely made up."

Rachel laughs. "What kind of fool could make up something like that?"

Wizkid continues his spasmodic dancing spectacle, and I worry that his chances of attracting Jenny, or any young lady, will be ruined beyond repair. But curiously enough, the girls seem to like him. I stare at him. We all do. The whole party does. People laugh and scream, and urge him on. Wizkid is a hit.

I turn to Rachel. "Yes, it sounds foolish. But believe me, the invasion is a scam so that Big Mac can have an excuse to implement the manifesto."

"Why would they do that?"

Because everyone always wants control, I think. From the dress code enforcers at work to the neighbor lady who doesn't like my Home Depot plastic shed, everyone has an opinion on how everyone else should act. "Besides rounding up illegal aliens they don't like, and hassling anyone else they deem un-American, I think they want complete control."

"I don't know." Rachel looks at us with suspicion. "Why would you tell me this?"

"I'll tell anyone who wants to listen at this point. People need to know the truth."

"The only way you're going to believe us is for us to show you," Derek says. "Is there a way to get on the Internet here?"

"Yeah," I say. "If Wizkid can get to a computer, he can lay it out for you."

Rachel points toward the house. "There are computers in the library we can use."

We start walking toward the dance floor to reel in Wizkid.

"You'll see," I say.

I put a hand on Wizkid's shoulder and stop the electrified human dance machine. The crowd groans. Some even boo me. "You're a big hit," I say.

He does a sideways glide. "Can't touch this."

"Yeah, yeah. Hey, Rachel says there's a computer we can use."

"Now? I need a real computer, not some handheld thing."

"Yeah, now. They got real computers here. Work your magic and come back."

Wizkid is dejected. He's having his big moment and doesn't want to leave the dance floor. "Easy as that," he says sarcastically. "My program isn't that simple."

"Well, at least check it out."

"Don't take the Wizard," one of Rachel's friends says.

"We need someone to dance with," another says.

"He'll be right back."

"You dance with us," the third one says. She grabs my wrist and pulls me into the center of their triangle.

I haven't danced since my wedding, and I don't want to dance now. "Um."

"Good luck," Derek says. "The Wizard and I will take care of it." Before I can protest, Derek walks off with Wizkid and Rachel toward the house.

The girls start to dance around me as the steel drums reverberate Caribbean music. "Dance," they say.

I hold my hands in front of me, swing my arms slightly, and step from side to side in my white man's shuffle-no-matter-what-music-is-playing dance. Occasionally I snap my fingers.

One of the girls laughs and holds up her phone at me.

"Is my dancing so bad you need to take a picture?"

"No—video."

A waiter walks by and hands us some punch. We dance with the plastic cups in our hands. We dance for several songs.

I'm not sure how much time has passed. I look over my shoulder to the house, watching for the others returning from the computer room. Big Tom is staring back at me, a smug grin across his face.

"Attention! Attention!" a megaphone-enhanced voice roars. "Stay where you are!"

What did I do wrong?
—SENATOR JOSEPH MCCARTHY

THE MUSIC STOPS. The dancing stops. I look around bewildered, like everyone else.

Six skinny peach-fuzz-faced campus policemen walk in a line under the tent. They separate and stand at attention, remaining equidistant around the perimeter of the dance floor.

The crowd separates to allow a three-hundred-plus-pound doughnut in a campus police uniform to jelly-roll through. The ruddy-faced young cop walks over to me, looking at me through round frameless spectacles that seem to grow out of his chubby cheeks. His nametag says "Hubert Salsbury."

Pig squeals and calls of "Hueeeeey!" come from the crowd.

Hubert spins around looking for guilty faces. He speaks in a whine, as if he's inhaled helium. "Don't piss me off. Benefit or not, I'll stop this party now. I'll write you all up." He looks around again. The crowd goes silent.

"Now." He turns toward me. "What do we have here?"

"Can I help you, officer?"

Hubert takes the glass from me. He sniffs it and takes a drink. "Mmm, ATO island punch—loaded with rum."

I do not respond.

"Could I see your United States ID, sir?"

I freeze, but he doesn't press the issue. Instead he downs the rest of my punch in one swig, and turns to the crowd. "Who has a Big-Mac-approved national ID?" About a dozen patriotic do-gooders raise their hands. "Two weeks! Effective by executive decree, all citizens are required to have a Big-Mac-approved ID within two weeks."

"Bullshit!" A skinny boy with dark curly hair stands defiantly at the tent's edge.

"Arrest that man," Hubert cries.

Two campus cops descend on the boy and roughly cuff him. "I didn't do anything!" the boy yells. "What's the charge?"

"You're an agitator!" Hubert bellows to all who can hear. "That protest this afternoon was against the law. I have been empowered by the Big Mac Party to arrest all campus agitators."

A gasp goes through the crowd. I know it's terrible, but I'm relieved—he doesn't seem to be specifically interested in me. I look back toward the house, trying to decide whether I can make it safely there to join Wizkid and Derek.

Hubert spins around. "That's why I'm here. I want to know who was at that protest. Names. I want names. Who will tell me?"

Hubert struts around looking at all the faces. Everyone remains silent. "All right. I'll do it my way." He points at a girl. "Arrest her." He points at someone else. "And her." He points again. "Arrest him."

A cop walks toward each of the kids. They are about to put handcuffs on them.

"He was there!" I look up. Tom is pointing at me from the back of the crowd.

Hubert spins and points to me. "Him?"

"Yes. I saw him in the protest driving a van," Tom says.

Hubert leans back, puts his hands on his hips, and speaks in a sinister voice. "Very good. Very, very good. See, that wasn't so hard." He nods to his policemen. "You can release the others."

The faces of the kids Hubert singled out relax. A cop uncuffs the small curly-haired boy. The boy still looks defiant.

Hubert faces me. "Can I see whatever ID you have, please?"

"I, I don't have one."

Hubert turns to one of Rachel's friends. He grabs her plastic cup and takes a drink. "Mmm, s'more island punch." He turns to me again. "I am placing you under arrest."

Hubert's childlike cops close in on me. "What did I do?" I ask. "What are you arresting me for?"

Hubert squeaks, "No ID. Serving alcohol to underage sorority sisters and fraternity brothers. Consuming alcohol on campus. And taking part in an illegal demonstration. You are an agitator!"

The campus cops grab me and push me along. As the crowd realizes that Hubert only wants to arrest me, and that once he's done this the party can continue on, they turn against me.

I have to meet President Wright. I have to give him the microfiche. I have to tell him the truth. "This is bogus!" I shout.

Rachel, Wizkid, and Derek appear on the back porch just as the campus cops shove me in the back. Infuriated, I slap my hands together above my head to activate the PRAD. *Goldfinger!* The theme song plays in my head. "Enough of this!" I thrust my middle PRAD finger in fuck-you fashion at Hubert, his goons, and the crowd.

Nothing happens.

Everyone laughs.

I slap my hands again and point my middle finger. The crowd jeers and flips me the bird back. In a rage, I repeatedly clap and point my middle finger.

The people in the crowd clap their hands twice, flip me off, and shout "Fuck you!" They keep doing it, perfectly synchronized, like the cheering section in a college basketball game.

I try to break free, but the boy cops stop me.

"Bust him!" the crowd cries.

"This will never hold," I say. "You can't arrest me for going to a protest! You never even read me my rights."

Hubert shouts into the air, "To those of you thinking about protesting the Big Mac manifesto, all marching permits and any group gatherings"—Hubert points to me—"along with Miranda rights have been suspended."

I struggle uselessly as the mini-cops push me along.

"Let him go!" Rachel flies from the crowd and wraps her arms around my neck. "I believe you. They showed me. I know the truth." She tries to pull me in the opposite direction. "I don't think you guys have a chance, but I believe in your cause."

"Cuff him," Hubert shouts.

I try to get the PRAD working again, but it's no use. The police boys pull Rachel off of me and grab my arms. In a final struggle, she gets close to me and kisses my cheek. "Good luck."

Hubert makes a path and leads his boys and me out. There's no sign of Derek or Wizkid. The steel drums start playing again. The gleeful crowd claps and cheers, and the party resumes. Alpha Tau Tom winks at me in a final insult as I pass.

I'm put into the back of a hard-to-take-seriously campus police car. Hubert sits in the passenger seat, and a minion drives. Hubert drinks from a new plastic cup full of island punch. "Shouldn't have been so disrespectful," he says.

"I didn't break any laws."

"We'll see about that."

The damn PRAD had failed me. I guess Q hadn't manufactured it. Bond always has a bunch of gadgets. I have nothing but this dorky ring. Maybe it's only supposed to work once, but I don't recall President Wright saying anything like that. I have to get out of this somehow. I try to make up with Hubert. "Whatever I did, I'm sorry. It wasn't intentional I assure you."

Hubert and his minions laugh. "Going to a protest is 'bout as intentional as intentional can be."

"Listen," I say. "I'm sorry. Do you have to arrest me? I have a meeting with the president."

Hubert frowns at me. "President Milford? Of the university? He's not likely to be pleased at an old pervert crashing a sorority party. A lot of Daddy's-little-girls you were dancing with there. Daddies who wouldn't want the likes of you lurking around their princesses."

"And like they'd like the likes of you lurking around their princesses?"

"Ha, ha," Hubert belly laughs. "That—my good prisoner—is like, another matter."

We pull into a parking lot with a building that says "Campus Safety."

"I'm not talking about the university's president," I tell him. "I'm talking about *the* president, President Wright."

Hubert laughs.

"I've got to meet with President Wright. This Big Mac manifesto is horrible. He needs me to help end those executive orders."

Hubert and his minions laugh. "You are one loony-bird agitator."

"I am not loony! I need to talk to the president."

"The president issued those executive orders. Don't matter what you think."

"I've got information that will change the president's mind. His advisers are evil men."

"Yeah, yeah. Like we haven't heard that one before. Listen guy, I'm a real American and I follow the president through thick and thin. If he wants to draft a few video game punks to build walls and take other measures to keep the Mexicans out, then I'm all for it. So even if I could, I'm certainly not bringing some loony protester anywhere near the president."

"I'm a real American, too. And I happen to know the president. I need to talk to him."

"Ha, ha. I know the president, too. Ha, ha. Don't worry; you'll get your one phone call. You can call the president then. Ha, ha."

We exit the car, and they walk me into a building and down a hallway with posters of campus events and safety slogans. The place smells like paper and fresh cologne. They escort me into a large cement-walled room with a Mayberry-like cell cage in the corner. Computer-topped desks filled with stacks of paper sit, empty of people. Hubert opens the cage, unlocks my handcuffs, and shoves me inside. A lonely cot sits against the back wall. Hubert closes the iron door and punches a code into a keypad to lock me in.

"Bathroom break every four hours. Let me know and I'll escort you. If, that is, you've been quiet—otherwise, you suffer."

I sit down on the cot.

"I'll watch him, fellas," Hubert says. "Get back to the streets. And someone bring me some more island punch. Tell those ATO boys I'll head over to the party when I'm off at midnight."

The minions leave, and Hubert sits down at a desk and looks at a computer screen. He chuckles to himself. "Have to get word to President Wright. That's a good one."

"When are you letting me go? What's my bail?"

"Quiet over there," Hubert squeals. "Sheriff will book you and take you over to county court in the morning. You'll find out then. Say, you want that phone call?"

"No." I don't know what I want or who to call. I could try my hotline number again, but Slater is undoubtedly still having it monitored. I try to gather my thoughts. I'm in jail with no resources, and I can only hope the judge lets me go in the morning. Though I'm not sure that's likely, since I've been accused of attending a protest, evidently a serious crime now. And if Slater catches wind that I've been caught, I might be done for good.

Rachel was right. We don't stand a chance. I'm an amateur relying on James Bond movies for inspiration and tactics. I feel like giving up. If the judge lets me out tomorrow, I'm taking off back to Karen and Scotty. I'll FedEx the microfiche to CNN and let them figure it out. Hopefully, Wizkid was able to end the invasion. Maybe he and Derek will be able to meet the president. I lie down on the cot, stare at the ceiling, and doze off.

Clang! Clang! Clang! "Hey, Thompson." Hubert rattles his nightstick between the bars.

I jump with a start.

"Your wife's on the phone."

20

The President. He is their captive. The President is
not master in his own house.
—SENATOR JOSEPH McCARTHY

"YOU CALLED MY WIFE?"

"She called me."

"My wife called you?"

Hubert looks irritated. "Are you married to Karen Thompson from Wolf Trap, Virginia?"

"Uh, yeah."

Hubert hands me a cordless phone through the jail bars.

"Hello?"

I can hear crying.

"Hello?"

"Chris?"

"Karen?"

"Are you really in jail?"

This place doesn't look like a jail, and I hate to admit that I'm in one, but I still can't lie to Karen. "Well, technically. But it's more of a campus holding pen."

There is silence.

"Hello, Karen, are you there?"

Karen speaks softly. "This is the last straw, Chris."

Last straw? Last straw for what? "Come on, Karen. I told you I'm working. This arrest is all a big misunderstanding."

"It's not that, it's the strip clubs, the casinos, the drinking, and the carousing. Officer Salsbury explained the charges to me. They don't sound good."

Hubert smiles a Texas-size grin at me from his desk and nods his head slowly up and down.

I laugh. "Officer Salsbury. That's a good one." I smile at Hubert maliciously. "Officer Salsbury doesn't know what he's talking about. Officer Salsbury is an oversize juvenile delinquent that someone is letting play cop."

"He sounds very pleasant," Karen says. "In fact, he seems mature and quite articulate to me."

I give up, I sigh. "Can you help me get out of here?"

Karen talks distractedly in a singsong voice. "My days of helping are over, I'm afraid."

"What the hell is that supposed to mean?"

"I saw the evidence, Chris."

"What evidence? There's no evidence. It's a bunch of trumped-up charges if anything."

"I don't care what you've been arrested for. That's icing on the cake for me. I'm talking about your little dance party and girlfriend."

"Girlfriend?"

"Don't play dumb. I saw the video."

"Video?"

"Yes, video! Scotty constantly searches for you on the Internet. He found your dance party and arrest on YouTube."

Oh, shit. "I, I—"

"You looked crazed—fighting police officers! And all those obscene gestures."

"I was trying to activate the PRAD." I say this like it should explain everything.

"And I saw that girl hanging on you and kissing you. I'm not a fool."

"That was only Rachel, she's just a—"

"Is she the Tri-Delt?"

"Um, she is a Tri-Delt. But—"

"I knew it. How could I be so stupid to trust you?"

"Honey, I can explain. The president gave me a secret ring. I was trying to use the ring's secret power to escape these campus cops this Alpha Tau frat guy Tom sent after me. You see, it's all perfectly logical if you'll take the time to hear me out."

"I've heard enough. Scotty and I are moving in with my mother. We'll be gone if you ever come home."

"Are you serious?"

"I rented a truck. Archie is going to drive it and help us move out."

Moving out? Archie? My head spins. "Archie? I told you to stay away from him."

"Archie's a good man, Chris. He's just a doll. He took Mother to tea the other day at the Park Hyatt. She adores him."

"Archie? Your mother?" Has the world gone crazy?

"He doesn't live too far from Mother's house, you know."

"Listen, Karen. Archie is a nice enough guy to yuck it up with around the office and such, but he's no one to get involved with. Seriously, he has loose morals. I don't trust him."

Karen laughs. "Oh, I don't think so, Chris. Archie is nothing like you."

"You're still a married woman, I remind you."

"A humiliated one," she yells. "YouTube proves it to the world."

Hubert walks toward the cage. "Time is up."

"Karen, I have to go. Can you call me a lawyer at least? I need help."

"You're on your own, Chris." She hangs up.

Hubert reaches in and grabs the phone. He smiles. "Tough night."

"Leave me alone."

I feel horrible. I wonder if other secret agents are able to hold a family together. I think of Bond. I guess not.

Hubert walks back to his desk. "YouTube video is not too bad. Only caught a glimpse of me, though. If I'd known, I would've been more aggressive. I could have clubbed you on the head. Now that would've been something."

I sit down on the cot. "I want my phone call."

Hubert leans back in his chair and puts his feet on the desk. "You just had it."

"She called me."

"Doesn't matter."

I jump up and grab the jail bars. "You're a fat-ass buffoon."

"No piss breaks for you."

"I don't care! I'll piss all over the place." I'm infuriated. "It's still the truth. You're the pervert. You're the fat awkward slob at the party who stands around and ogles the girls who will have nothing to do with him, and never will."

Hubert puts his feet on the ground and stands up. He grabs his nightstick and walks toward me, slapping the stick in the palm of his hand. "You've really done it now."

But then the door to the room bursts open. Two plastic-faced men in suits and sunglasses walk in with President Wright.

Hubert's mouth falls open. He drops his nightstick to the ground, straightens up, and salutes.

More plastic-faced men enter. They take up positions along the walls and look like they have always been there.

I beam. "Mr. President." Yes. Victory. I'm about to be avenged. I'll tell him the truth, give him the microfiche, and I'll be on my way home. *Die Another Day!*

"There you are, Special Agent Thompson," President Wright says.

I'm elated. Hubert continues to stand at attention, saluting. I walk back and forth in my cage and point at him. "Who's laughing now? You're going down, Hubert. Hueeey. Hueeey."

Hubert's face turns red, and a bead of sweat rolls down his cheek.

"At ease, officer," the president says.

Hubert ends his salute, but still stands at attention.

The president turns to me. "Thompson, that YouTube video was an embarrassment."

"I was trying to activate the PRAD." I point to Hubert. "He arrested me for no reason. I tried to explain to him that—"

The president waves his hand in front of me dismissively. "I'm not talking about that. I'm talking about the footage before your arrest. I'm talking about your dancing."

"My dancing?"

"Worst dancing I've ever seen."

"Sir, I need to talk to you."

"You ever see James Bond dance, Thompson?"

"Tango to the death in *Never Say Never Again*," I say.

President Wright scrunches his face and shakes his head as if to nullify what I've just said. "Special agents don't dance," he says emphatically.

"Sorry, sir. Now about Emergence."

"Was a disgrace to the profession. Special agents remain cool and on the outskirts. Dancing is not for them. Special agents leave the dancing to the pros—like me."

I try to catch the president's eye, but he has a faraway look. "The Emergence program, Mr. President. It has gone awry in a horrible way."

"Hit it, Sparky," the president says.

A plastic-faced man steps forward and holds up a hand-size speaker device. Michael Jackson's "Billie Jean" pulses from it.

The president raises one knee to his chest and points his opposite arm to the side. He slides to the right and repeats the move with his opposite leg and arm. The plastic-faced men all do the same in perfect rhythm with the music and the president. President Wright spins around and points at Hubert. "Come on, fat boy."

Hubert looks shocked and confused. He hesitates and then lifts his knee high in the air and joins the dance.

"That's it," the president says.

I have to admit that Hubert can dance pretty well. He slides and moves with the president, perfectly synchronized with the dancing plastic-faced men. A big smile breaks out on his face.

President Wright croons with Michael Jackson. "Ooh hoo."

They shake their legs and bodies, and the song ends. The president reaches his hand in the air to high-five Hubert. "My boy."

Hubert reaches up and slaps the president's hand.

President Wright claps his hands and points at me. "That's how you dance, Thompson."

"Mr. President, please. I respectfully request a word."

The president walks briskly over and stands next to me. The iron bars separate us. "What's up?"

"Emergence, sir." I speak with passion; I don't care if Hubert can hear me or not. In just minutes I'll be out of here. "Emergence is an underground torture center utilized by Vance Slater and the Big Mac Party. Remember that email? Slater is Eagle. Emergence farms out their illegal and torturous interrogations for profit. That's how Big Mac makes money. These are evil men. They're trying to take over the United States. We can expose Slater and his cronies, and then you can end these crazy executive orders." I feel the heat in my face.

The president grimaces. "Torture, you say?"

"Torture and death. The prisoners never get out alive. I saw an innocent Canadian tortured and killed with my own eyes."

"Canadian, huh?"

"Does it matter?" Something's wrong with his eyes. I begin to speak faster. "Mr. President, get this; the chief justice of the Supreme Court, Justice Lancaster, orders the torture and deaths. In your email, Tim is Chief Justice Timothy Lancaster. Can you believe it?"

President Wright scratches his head. "Justice Lancaster?"

"Yes, Cheesehead Lancaster. Remember? I told you on the phone." I dig out the microfiche from my pocket. "I've got the proof right here. You have to stop it."

The president takes the microfiche and holds it up for inspection. "I can't see anything."

"It's there, trust me. We need to find a microfiche reader is all."

The president sticks his face between the bars. He whispers to me. "It's all so confusing."

I take a deep breath. "Mr. President, I think Vance Slater is secretly giving you Macwacky."

The president shakes his head. "No secret no more. Macwacky. I love my Macwacky."

"You have to try to regain control," I plead.

"Take more now. Macky macky fun fun."

"Slater is mind-controlling you! Don't you see? You sent me to Emergence because you didn't trust him. Snap out of it! We have to stop Big Mac."

The president looks at me long and hard, and I see, or hope I see, a glimmer of recognition. "Patrick Sheehan."

"Patrick Sheehan?"

The president's eyes begin to glaze over again. "Star, Utah."

"Okay, okay. Patrick Sheehan, Star, Utah. What about them? What does that mean?"

I lose him. A tear comes out of his eye and turns into a stream. The president sobs. He grabs the bars and shakes them. "It's all coming apart. It's breaking up. It's breaking up."

"Get a grip. It will be okay."

"You have to help me, Thompson." He shakes the bars and moves two feet over and shakes them again. "Help me. Get me out of here. Thompson, get me out of here." He crumples to the floor whimpering, the microfiche still in his hand.

"The microfiche, sir. Put the microfiche in your pocket."

He rolls over and moans.

Vance Slater marches into the room. Two United States Marshals and a medical team enter with him. The white-coats rush to the president. They ease him to a sitting position.

Vance Slater walks to President Wright, bends over, and snatches the microfiche from his hand. He smiles at me.

"Bastard," I say.

The medical team lifts the president to a standing position and, escorted by the plastic-faced men, walks him out of the room.

Slater turns the upside-down American flag that adorns the lapel of his charcoal-colored suit back to its full glory. He wipes his brow and brings the bulk of his personality down on Hubert. "I'll be taking this prisoner off your hands, son."

Hubert, to his credit, realizes an opportunity at hand. "I'm sorry, sir, but I cannot release the prisoner until I receive orders from the judge to do so in the morning."

Slater glares at Hubert and seems to see him for the first time. "This is a national emergency matter, officer—" Like a bold bulldog, Slater thrusts his face toward Hubert's chest and reads his nametag. "Officer Salsbury, we are counting on local law enforcement to do their duty during this crisis."

"Yes, sir. But according to my criminal justice class that I just received an A in, if my department made the arrest, then this prisoner is my responsibility until a judge orders otherwise."

Slater turns to the marshals. "Leave us." The marshals nod and then exit the room.

Slater takes a step closer to Hubert. Their chests are less

than an inch apart. Slater stands taller, but Hubert is wider. "Do you not know how important this is?" Slater says. "Did you not just see the president of the United States in this room only moments ago?"

"I did." Hubert smiles a slight grin. "I saw President Wright quite clearly. I even danced with President Wright. He's a *very* good dancer." Hubert curves his lips and widens his mouth into an intimidating smile.

Slater takes a step back. "Interesting." He places his hand on Hubert's shoulder. "You're a promising young officer, Salsbury."

"Yes, sir."

"Perhaps you could play a greater role in this emergency?"

"Yes, sir. I would like that, sir."

"Root out some campus agitators and that sort of thing."

Hubert sways his head. "That's small time, sir—already do that."

"Border patrol more your style?"

Hubert grins.

Slater's eyes widen. "Be in charge of a work brigade division, chase down some Mexicans? How them beans sizzle?"

"Yes, sir."

"Probably make five times as much as now. Get yourself a fancy armored SUV with tinted windows loaded for bear."

"Oh, sir. Yes, sir!"

Slater puts his finger on Hubert's chest. "You saw nothing here."

"No, sir."

"The president was never here."

"What president?"

"Excellent." Slater pats Hubert's cheek, sending a rapid-moving flesh ripple to his eye and ear. "I'll be back in an hour with your new assignment. Need to make arrangements for transport. I'll take my prisoner then."

"Yes, sir."

"Marshals will be outside. You have some time alone to clean up here. I want no evidence. The president was never here. There was never a prisoner here tonight."

"Yes, sir."

Slater walks by me. "Need to eliminate those YouTube videos," he says to himself.

"What are you going to do with me?" I ask.

"You. You were supposed to be part of the president's little liaison ploy to find out what was going on at Emergence."

"Dastardly deeds of the worst kind."

Slater sniffs. "So you say."

"I do say, and others do too. You can't get away with this, Slater."

"Well, we have you." Slater laughs. "And by others, if you mean your fat meatball friend and the geek, they shouldn't be too hard to track down."

There's nothing I can do. I'm done for. We're done for. The country is done for. I'm demoralized. Karen is leaving me. Big Mac is going to take over. "I have rights," I say feebly. "I want a lawyer. I demand to speak to a lawyer."

"You're a dead man," Slater says. "And dead men have no rights."

"I'm alive as alive can be, you'll find out."

"I think not," he says smugly. "You died last week in that terrible plane crash with Fixer. I have the death certificate to prove it."

My hands are jittery. My voice quavers. "What are you going to do with me?"

"Send you back to complete your mission. Back to where you're supposed to be. Back to Emergence." He laughs. "You can find out what's going on there."

"You bastard. I already know what's going on there."

Slater walks toward the door. "Not everything. X-ray has

a few more things he'd like to show you." He laughs again. "Good-bye, Thompson." He points at Hubert. "You're with us one hundred percent now. Capiche?"

"Capiche," Hubert says.

"I apologize for using an Italian word," Slater adds as he closes the door behind him.

"You have to help me," I say to Hubert once Slater's gone. "This guy Slater—he's drugging the president. He's subverting the Constitution. You saw what was going on."

"I saw nothing," says Hubert. "I heard that I'd be making a lot of money and tooling around in a badass SUV." He starts shredding papers that I assume have to do with me. "I've got work to do, so shut the hell up."

I sit down on the cot and wonder what to do. I'm never going to see Karen and Scotty again. They'll never know what happened to me. I lie back, rest my head on the pillow, and stare at the ceiling. Hubert continues to shred papers. I still have the PRAD; maybe I can lure Hubert into the cell and disable him with it. He wanted to beat me up before the president walked in; maybe I can antagonize him again.

An air vent in the ceiling, two desks behind Hubert's, glistens with a large drop of water. The drop grows larger and then falls through the air, landing on a stack of papers on top of a desk. Another drop forms and falls. And then another.

"Hey, Hubert."

"Shut up."

"Your ceiling is leaking."

Hubert looks around and notices the water. The drops are increasing in frequency. He walks over and clears the papers off the assaulted desk, climbs on top, and reaches up to investigate the vent. Water drips on his forehead. He touches the vent. It comes loose, falls on his head, and bounces to the floor.

Rubbing his skull, Hubert looks up into the airshaft. There

is a puff and a hiss. A dart flies out of the opening and lodges in Hubert's neck. His mouth opens and he gasps. He crawls off the desk, pulls the dart out of his neck, bends over, and collapses to the floor.

21

I'm back in shape.
— SENATOR JOSEPH MCCARTHY

A MOP OF HAIR FALLS out of the air vent. I see the upside-down
smile of Wizkid. A small light is strapped to his forehead. He
puts his index finger over his lips. He dangles his arms out of
the opening. A small computer tablet rests in one palm. He
presses his index finger to the screen and a click sounds in the
jail door.

I jump up, push on the bars, and open the door. I walk
into freedom and toward the air vent. In order to turn around
Wizkid hangs face down as far as his arms will let him, flips his
legs out like an acrobat, and then pulls himself headfirst back
into the air vent.

I stand on the desk, reach up, and pull myself into the vent.
The cool metal closes in around me. It smells of dust. Wizkid
begins to crawl. His feet push the computer tablet toward me
as he moves forward.

"Leave it," he whispers.

We crawl to a bend and turn left. I try to be quiet, but the
thin metal reverberates with every movement. Wizkid is more

nimble. After thirty feet we reach a main vertical airshaft. A rope ladder hangs down from it. Wizkid pushes the headlamp to me. I point the light on him and watch him climb until he disappears. I strap the light to my head and follow.

When I reach the top, Wizkid and Derek grab my arms and pull me through an opening they have cut into the air vent.

"Careful, the sheet metal is sharp," Derek says.

We stand on the roof looking at one another next to a heating/air conditioning unit the air vent feeds into.

"Nice work," I say.

Derek points to ropes, lights, knives, tranquilizer-dart kit, and other equipment. "We went shopping."

Wizkid excitedly shakes my hand. "Thank you, dude. That was awesome."

I feel such relief. "I should be thanking you," I say. "That was a great rescue."

"No, the party I mean. Jenny showed up after you were arrested. We danced. She really digs me now."

"That's great," I say. "But did you end the invasion?"

Wizkid looks at me like I'm the rudest person in the world. "I'm telling a story about Jenny." His face lights up again. He can barely contain his joy. "She likes me! She asked me out. We're going to a vampire movie on Thursday."

"But Wizkid. We have—"

"And I have you to thank."

The smile on the kid's face is heartrending. I hate to ruin his mood. "Sorry, Wizkid, but I don't think that date is going to happen."

"Oh, I think it is," he says.

I look at both of them. "Guys, listen. President Wright, and then Vance Slater, came to see me."

"You saw the president?" Derek asks. "Are we cool?"

"No. Slater has upped the president's Macwacky dosage. He's in total control. And he took the microfiche."

"So, President Wright is in on all this?" Wizkid asks.

"Not *in*," I say. "The president is half out of his mind on Macwacky. He doesn't know what he's doing, and I don't think he gives a rat's ass anymore."

"Me either," Wizkid says and spins. "Oh, Jenny. Jenny, Jenny, Jenny."

"Slater was going to send me back to Emergence," I say. "Said he was going to round you two up as well."

Wizkid looks at the moon and sings, *"Jenny, won't you be mine?"*

I give up on Wizkid and look to Derek. "He said I was a dead man already. They're going to waste us and nobody will know."

"Jenny, won't you be my lady?"

"Why are we standing around talking like fools?" Derek says. "We gotta move."

Derek and Wizkid wear maintenance uniforms; black pants, thick gray polyester button-down shirts, and black vinyl belts. They have red oval nametags sewn above their shirt pockets. Derek's says "Sol." Wizkid's says "Bob."

"Nice," I say.

Derek reaches into a large duffel bag. "We have to do this quick. Marshals have been walking the streets." He tosses me a uniform.

My nametag says "Larry."

He hands Wizkid a baseball cap. "Put it on. Keep that distracting chia-head under control."

Dark mountains are outlined in the distance. The campus spreads out before us. The roof of an identical concrete university building is only five feet away.

I peek over the edge and can find no one watching. "At the count of three. One—two—three."

We run and jump. Sol, Larry, and Bob, the flying maintenance men.

We land safely and make our way down the roof stairwell.

On the ground level, I open the emergency exit door and an alarm sounds. We hurriedly walk several blocks to the center of campus.

Derek takes a seat on a bench. "This is the spot."

Wizkid and I sit next to him. Occasional groups of late-night partygoers walk by.

"We look a little strange here," I say.

Wizkid fidgets. "I'm used to it."

I feel like bailing. "My wife's moving out. I need to go home."

Derek punches me in the shoulder. "You can't give up now."

I punch him back. "Did you not hear me? I'm risking my marriage on this death quest. I'm risking Karen and Scotty's lives, too! Slater was going to kill me. What if he uses them to get to me?"

"Life is risk," he says, gently.

I stand up, perturbed. "What do you know about it, Derek?"

Derek shoots me an angry glance, but he quickly returns to normal. "You just got out of jail," he says. "Relax. Think about it in the car." He points. "Here we go."

A beige Toyota Camry, a car designed to look like every other car in the world, pulls up to the curb.

We pile into the backseat. Rachel is driving; one of her friends sits in the passenger seat. It's Jenny. She gives us all a big toothy smile.

"Jenny!"

"What's up, Wizard?"

"Doing the maintenance thing."

"You're cute."

"You're cute."

"I said it first."

"What's the plan?" I ask.

"The party van broke down, and the ladies here graciously offered to help us," Derek says.

"Very nice of you," I say. "Don't you have a Secret Service tail, Jenny?"

"I sent those chastity guards to Cancún on my credit card. You can't have any fun with them around." Jenny shrugs. "Daddy ditches them all the time."

"We've been circling for an hour," Rachel says. She wears jeans and a white T-shirt. I find it hard not to look at her as she concentrates on driving.

Jenny looks at Wizkid. "Was it a difficult mission?"

Wizkid nods. "And dangerous."

Jenny clasps her fists to her chest. "This is *soo* exciting."

Too exciting. "Let's get out of here," I say.

"What do you think we're doing?" Derek says.

"Where are we going?" I ask.

Derek throws up his hands in frustration. "I don't know! We're just going, okay?"

"We need a plan."

"I know, I know. Let's make a plan."

There is silence.

I slap my knee. "Wizkid."

Jenny twirls her hair with her finger. "The Wizard!"

"Wizkid, did you end the invasion?"

Wizkid sighs. "Don't you think, Larry? Do you think we would risk busting you out of the slammer if this whole mess was coming to an end on its own?"

"Yeah, Larry." Jenny chomps on her gum. "Don't ya think the Wizard woulda thoughta that?"

"My name is Chris." I slap my thigh. "You had time to dance all night and didn't stop the invasion?"

Jenny gives me a mean look. It's irritating.

"You were supposed to end the stealth invasion and stop the illegal crossings in the government mainframes. The border patrol and their computers would have picked up on it right away. Word would have spread, and the hysteria and the impetus for the Big Mac manifesto would have ended." I spread my hands apart. "That was the whole reason for going to the party."

"The government blocked my hacking after ten minutes," Wizkid says quietly.

"We have a big problem if you can't get on the Internet."

"I can get on the Internet. It's the border patrol mainframes I'm talking about. They've figured out my tricks. I can't get in anymore to stop the invasion."

"They've got smart dudes working for them, too," Derek says.

"Not as smart as the Wizard, though," Jenny says.

"Think you can crack the border patrol's block?" I ask.

"I don't know. Maybe. Might take a few days, or weeks. Who knows?"

Silence.

I think about President Wright and his craziness at the jail. James Bond and M have an elegant back-and-forth rapport. I try to imagine President Wright talking to Bond; it staggers the imagination.

"The president was trying to tell me something," I recall. "In a lucid moment, he said 'Patrick Sheehan' and 'Star, Utah.'"

"A lot of help that is," Jenny says.

Jenny is getting on my nerves. But then again, if we get rid of her, Wizkid is sure to go as well.

"No, let's consider this," I say. "In the shelter, a couple of the men were reminiscing about their home in Utah. In fact I remember now that Land mentioned all the white Emergence residents came from the same town in Utah. Maybe Star, Utah, is that place. I'm thinking we should go there."

"And do what? Slater took your evidence," Wizkid says.

"We can tell them what we know."

"They'll think we're crazy," Derek says.

"They must have contact with the government somehow. Maybe this Patrick Sheehan is there. Maybe he can help us."

"I don't know," Derek says. "Sounds like a long shot."

"We have no other shots. If we can convince the town of all the bad shit going down, at least we can gain some allies—allies that could have valuable information about Emergence."

Silence.

"Let me see a map," I say.

"We don't have a map," Rachel says.

"GPS?"

"Derek disabled my car's GPS," Rachel says. "I think it's broken for good."

"Relax," Derek says. "It's an easy fix."

"And he made us leave our phones," Jenny says.

"We need a map," I say.

"Gas station should be coming up," Rachel says.

At a BP gas station, Jenny and Wizkid walk holding hands into the mini-mart to buy a map. I pray no one recognizes her. Derek follows. "I'll get some munchies," he says.

I step outside to stretch my legs and lean against the car. I wonder if Star, Utah, is real, or if it's some mystical place that exists only in President Wright's mind. Suddenly Rachel is in front of me. Her hands are holding mine. "I totally believe in what you're doing," she says. Her green eyes look into mine. She moves her face close. Her beauty is unnerving. She presses her body against mine and kisses me long on the lips. She's a Bond girl! *Honey Rider, Vesper Lynd, Pussy Galore, Plenty O'Toole, Mary Goodnight, Holly Goodhead, Strawberry Fields*, I can't take it! I kiss Rachel back. Or maybe I don't. I can't tell. Our lips linger, in any case.

I look up. Derek is standing outside the mini-mart staring at us, his arms piled high with bags of chips and cookies.

What am I doing? Embarrassed, I open the back door and guiltily climb into my seat. Jenny and Wizkid run out chasing each other and sit in the back with me. Derek sits in the passenger seat, Rachel drives, and we are off.

Jenny opens a Rand McNally United States Road Atlas. "It has all fifty states and parts of Mexico and Canada."

"Our mortal enemies," Wizkid says.

I reach my hand toward Jenny. "Let me see."

I look at the index and find the coordinates for Star, Utah. It's real. It's located in the Wasatch National Forest in an out-of-the-way mountain valley by Dead Horse Peak. "Star, Utah, is about twelve hours away."

"Okay," Derek says. "I guess it's worth a try. Let's go see what we can find out."

"That's too far for the girls. They shouldn't be involved," I say.

And I shouldn't be involved with Rachel. And Karen shouldn't be involved with Archie.

Derek nods to Jenny. She is snuggling up to Wizkid. "I don't think she cares."

"I'm in," Rachel says. "We can drive you there."

What am I going to do about Rachel? What would Bond do? That's a stupid question. Maybe I don't want to be all Bond.

Rachel drives. There are two hours of silence. Derek and Wizkid fall asleep. Jenny leans forward over the front seat and she and Rachel quietly talk to each other.

"It's in my backpack," I hear Rachel say.

Jenny reaches into Rachel's backpack and pulls out an iPad. "I need to check Facebook."

"Are you going to friend Wizkid?" Rachel asks.

Jenny giggles. "First thing."

Derek jerks awake. "Whoa, what are you doing? Where'd that iPad come from?"

Jenny's face glows from the light of the iPad's screen. "You said no cell phones. You didn't say anything about iPads."

"It was implied. What are you doing?"

"Checking Facebook."

"Shut it off," Derek says immediately.

Wizkid wakes up. "What's going on?"

Derek points at Jenny. "She has an iPad with cellular data. And iPads have a built-in GPS. The government will be able to track it."

McCarthy would have had a field day with modern electronic equipment.

"It's Rachel's," Jenny says.

"We have to get rid of it," Derek says.

"No way. I'm not giving up my iPad," Rachel says. "My whole life is in there."

"They won't be tracking Rachel," Wizkid says.

"They will if the president's daughter signs into Facebook from her iPad," I say.

Rachel starts to slow the car. "I'm not ditching my iPad. You guys can get out and find your own ride if you don't like it."

"Okay, okay," Derek says. "We'll take the risk. But you can't log in to Facebook or anything else."

"Better yet, turn it off and save the batteries," I say. "We may need it for an emergency or something."

Jenny groans. "God, you guys are boring." But she turns the iPad off.

Derek, Rachel, and I take turns driving throughout the night. In the wee hours I catch Jenny playing a game on the iPad. "Turn that off," I hiss.

Jenny plays the game for another minute and then turns it off. "What a pain in the ass," she says.

In the early morning, about fifty miles away from Star, we pull into a rest stop. Tall green mountains surround a grassy area and a restroom facility. A fast-moving river gurgles pleasantly at the bottom of an embankment. I sit on a picnic table with Wizkid.

"Think I could use the iPad to contact my wife and kid?" I ask. "I'm dying to see that they're okay."

Wizkid ponders, and then looks to the sky as he gets an idea. "I can reroute a Skype call through a dummy server in Florida. If the government is watching your family, they won't have a clue it's you."

"But what if they're tracking this iPad?" I say.

Wizkid shrugs. "Then our escape is blown already." He gets up and walks toward Jenny and Rachel and returns with the iPad. He types on it. The screen goes blank, and lines of code scroll over it. He types some more and brings up the Skype app. "What's your wife's email?"

To be safer, I give Wizkid an email account we set up for Scotty. Wizkid types, and then stares at the screen. "Your son's on the computer. He replied."

"That's my boy."

Wizkid hands me the iPad. I hold it steady in front of me. I see a blue screen with my mug in a small square section. It is 6:00 a.m., 9:00 a.m. on the East Coast. The blue screen dissolves, and Scotty's face appears.

Wizkid gets up. "I'll give you some privacy."

My heart warms to see Scotty. "Hey, buddy."

Scotty's face breaks into a huge smile, full of adult and baby teeth juggled together. "Hey, Dad!" He covers his mouth and looks around. "Sorry—can I say that?"

"Say whatever you want, buddy. We're secure. How have you been?"

"Good. We live at Grandma's house now."

"I heard. That's great that you and Mom can be with Grandma while I'm gone."

"When are you coming back?"

"Soon, buddy, soon."

"Did you get arrested?"

"Temporarily, sport. It was all part of the mission."

"That's what I thought."

Jenny walks by and looks over my shoulder. "Is that your boy? He's so cute."

"Chip off the old block," I say.

Jenny motions Rachel over. "Come here and look at Larry's cute kid."

Rachel walks over and leans on my other shoulder. "He's beautiful—those eyes. I wish I had those lashes." She waves to the iPad. "Hi, sweetie."

Scotty beams a huge smile. "Hi."

"This is Rachel and Jenny, Scott. They've been a big help on my mission."

Karen's face suddenly appears sideways on the screen. "You're the one."

Jenny jumps back. "Ah. I'm out of here."

Karen sits down in front of the computer. "Go to the other room, Scotty."

"Bye, Dad."

"Bye, Scotty."

Karen adjusts her pink bathrobe. Her hair sticks out in a frayed knotted mess. She wears black rectangular reading glasses. Two white splotches of pimple cream are on her left cheek. A Breathe Right strip clenches her nose. "You're the sorority girl in the video. You're the one who was kissing my husband."

"I, I—" Rachel doesn't know what to say.

"This is Rachel," I say.

"You little homewrecker. Are you sleeping with my husband?"

Rachel looks guilty. "No," she says meekly.

Karen's eyes widen and it looks like she's daring Rachel to confess.

Rachel recovers and goes on the offensive. "Sleeping with your husband? Gross! He's old. He's like forty."

Karen stammers. "He's thirty-eight. You're not sleeping with him?"

Rachel raises her voice. "No. He's nice and all, but besides being old, he's kind of pudgy."

"Pudgy!" Karen cries. "Old! You dumb Tri-Delt. You don't even know what a good man is."

"Dumb Tri-Delt?" Rachel puts her hands on her hips. "Who are you to be calling me a dumb Tri-Delt? You has-been. Probably never was. Ended up with Mr. Geeky-and-Nice."

"Ladies, please."

"No offense," Rachel says to me.

Karen points at the screen. "Chris, you just go ahead and sleep with that bimbo."

"What?"

"You heard me. Give her everything you've got." Karen's head tilts side to side. "She can't handle my man."

Rachel flips her hand at the screen. "You're crazy. Good-bye." She walks away.

"Karen, what are you saying? Relax. Get ahold of yourself."

Karen takes off her glasses and puts her face in her hands. She starts to cry. "I don't know. I can't take it anymore. I miss you."

Maybe she's not fooling around with Archie. I think about my kiss with Rachel and my attraction to her. I feel horrible. I'm glad, though, that Karen admits to missing me. "I miss you, too, honey. It's unbearable."

"I know, I know. I'm sorry. I thought you were fooling around."

Finally we are talking on the same wavelength. "Honey, this mission has exposed me to some seedier elements, I admit. But I'm still the same man you married."

She puts her glasses back on and sniffles. "I wish you were here."

"I wish I was there, too. Everything has gone haywire. You see the Big Mac manifesto?"

"It's unbelievable," Karen says. "And they want me to take a loyalty oath at work."

"But you work at a dentist's office," I say.

Karen shakes her head. "That's not the worst. The House Un-American Activities Committee has subpoenaed me. It has something to do with you and apple pies."

The apple pies. I knew they'd come back to haunt me. "I'm sorry. They're using you to make things difficult for me. Don't worry, though. I'm going to stop them."

"How? By yourself?"

I try to sound confident. "I've got a couple of friends. We're sort of wanted by the government, now. We could use some help."

Karen puts her hands to her face. "Oh geez, Chris. What are you going to do? Should Scotty and I just get in the car and drive west?"

"That's a good idea," I say. "Forget about the subpoena. Don't tell anyone. You might not be safe there anymore any-way."

"Oh, no."

Scotty's voice calls from the next room. "Uncle Archie is here."

"Archie? Has he nowhere else to go?"

Karen whispers. "Not really. But where are you?"

"Star, Utah."

"Okay, got it. Hold on—Archie wants to talk."

Archie's face replaces Karen's. It grows large and tilts. His mustache fills up my screen as he investigates the computer.

"Back up, dude."

"Can you see me?"

"Sit down, Archie."

His face comes into focus.

"I see you."

A cheerful goofy grin spreads across his face. "What's

up, hound dog? Having a good run from what I've seen, Mr. Player."

"Why aren't you at work?"

"Vacay, my friend, vacay. Two weeks off for the Arch."

"Vacation? And you're spending it at my house?"

Archie looks around. "This is your mother-in-law's house."

"Oh, right. I forgot." I slap my forehead. "My wife moved out of my house. What the hell do you think you're doing?"

"Nothing, hound dog, but I'm happy as a clam. I—"

"I can see that. Ruining my marriage must be a big party for you."

Archie's thick eyebrows form into a V of shock and consternation. His bottom lip moves up and down like a guppy's. "Wh, wh, what are you talking about?"

"I'm talking about you worming your way into my life. I'm talking about you moving my family out of my house. I'm talking about you making a play for my wife."

He points his finger at the screen. "I've done nothing but support your family in their time of need. Karen's a little upset, to say the least. I've been trying to reel her back in for you, if anything. And it's not that easy talking you up and thinking of excuses with all these stunts you've been pulling."

I find it hard to believe. "Are you serious?"

"Straight up, brother."

It's too suspicious. "Why are you being so helpful?"

"We're friends, right?"

I pause. I guess when you get down to it, Archie's the closest thing I have to a friend. "Okay, sure."

"And friends help each other out. You'd do the same for me."

I pause and consider. I'm not sure I would. I decide to be conciliatory though. "Okay, I'm sorry. Thanks for your help."

Archie's eyes widen. "I've met someone."

"Like a girl?"

"Like a woman. That's what I've been meaning to tell you."

"That's great, Arch. Can I talk to Karen?"

"I think I'm in love."

"Is she from work?"

"No—"

The screen goes blank. I move my finger over it but it's dead. The iPad has shut down from lack of power.

"Hey!" I shout to Rachel and Jenny. "The iPad is out of power. All the game playing you were sneaking last night drained the battery."

The rest area has no facilities, only a few picnic tables on a grassy area overlooking a mountain stream. I walk over to the car and hand the iPad to Jenny, who is sitting on the hood holding hands with Wizkid. Rachel stands leaning against the Camry door.

"This is serious stuff we're dealing with here," I say. "When I asked you not to drain the battery, I meant it."

Jenny looks at me venomously.

"From now on, listen to what I say. And try to be team players."

"Up yours, Grandpa," Jenny says. "You're not my boss."

"Yeah, take it easy on her," Rachel says. "We're doing you a favor."

"Like I'm supposed to save Rachel's iPad battery"—Jenny jumps off the hood—"so that you can use her iPad to chitchat with your bitchy wife."

"Hey, now. I'll have none of that."

"Your wife is a rag," Rachel says.

"A total bitch," Jenny says.

"Stop talking about my wife. She's a very refined woman."

"Fooled me," Rachel says.

"Yeah, is she undercover too?" Jenny says.

Rachel laughs. "Must have taken hours to look that bad."

I'm furious. "Listen, you little sorority airheads. You little I'm-too-good-for-anyone, I'm-so-pretty, I'm-going-to-fake-doing-good-deeds-so-I-can-pretend-to-have-some-integrityto-impress-my-fake-all-we-care-about-is-looks-friends. Let me tell you something about real life—"

Rachel gets in the car. "Come on, Jenny."

Jenny opens the front passenger-side door. "Wizard."

"Hey," I say.

The car starts. Wizard runs around to the other side.

"What are you doing? You have to stay with us, Wizkid."

He climbs into the backseat behind his new girlfriend. "Yeah, right."

The doors shut, and the car begins to move. I run behind. "Wait. I'm sorry. You're right, you're right. My wife's a bitch."

Two duffel bags fly out of the back windows. The Camry pulls onto the road and turns 180 degrees to face the direction we came from.

Derek and I are stranded.

22

I think you might be an expert on that—what a pixie is?
—SENATOR JOSEPH MCCARTHY

DEREK TRUDGES UP the grassy embankment. He has been walking down by the river. "Where is everybody?"

"They left."

Derek can't believe it. "They left?"

"I got too bossy with them—pissed them off."

"Are they coming back?"

"I don't think so."

"Damn, Thompson. What are we going to do now?"

I sit down at a splintering picnic table. "I'm sorry."

"Wizkid, too? You pissed him off?"

"I don't know. Didn't matter. You saw how he's leashed up."

Derek sits down across from me. "Damn, Thompson."

"I know, I know." We're stuck and are going to have to hitchhike to Star. And who in their right mind would pick up two grown men?

We sit and think. The sun warms the morning chill. A breeze picks up and rustles the aspen leaves in a pleasing mountain rhythm.

"Nice here," I say.

Derek breathes deeply through his nose. "I love the smell of pine."

"We should get out of these maintenance clothes," I say.

"Little suspicious."

"Yeah."

Derek reaches down for a duffel bag. "Khakis and polos. I know my pants fit, but I had to guess again for you. Thirty-six by thirty-two?"

"That'll work. A little baggy, but better than those Guccis."

"I've got razors, soap, and deodorant. There's a tranquil spot a ways down the river. You want to go for a swim and clean up?"

"Probably a good idea."

We grab the bags and walk along the riverbank until we find the place Derek has in mind. The river widens here into a large oval pond. The riverbanks are shady, but the sun shines in the middle, revealing translucent dark blue water. Derek strips down, takes two steps into the water, and dives. He emerges and slaps his face with both hands. "Whooh." He looks to me. "Come on."

I strip out of my maintenance uniform and dive in. The water tingles like tiny sharp icicles as it engulfs me. I break through the surface and shake my head. "Oh, oh, oh."

Derek laughs and swims.

I dive again and swim for as long as I can hold my breath.

Derek treads water and looks into the crisp azure sky. "Refreshing."

"Painfully refreshing."

We swim in silence, each in our own thoughts, enjoying the beauty of the clear water, green forest, and surrounding mountains.

After a few minutes Derek breaks the silence. "You still worried about your wife?"

"She's staying with her mom," I say.

"She still mad?"

"At first, but I think we cleared some things up."

"That's cool."

"Yeah, hopefully we're back on track. But I'm still worried about Archie."

Derek shakes his head and sighs in sympathy. "And your boy? How's he doing?"

"He's good—never doubted me for a second."

"That's got to feel good."

It does feel good. I dive under the water and glide in its smooth timelessness. Scotty's not always going to be so enamored with me, and I dread the day when I will no longer seem cool to him.

I come up for air. "You'd make a good father, Derek."

"I don't think I have the patience."

I think about how Derek calmly dealt with Joemore and the Alpha Tau bouncers, and how he good-naturedly lets the Cannonball jokes roll over him. "Trust me. You've got plenty of patience."

I look up the mountainside to a hawk circling above. A distant roar from rapids downstream adds to the peaceful sleepiness of the place. "Kind of a sanctuary here," I say.

Derek looks around. "Beautiful, simply beautiful."

"Nice to get away from it all, even if it's just for a moment. Out here in nature—no rules, no government, no pressure. It's freedom. We can do whatever we want."

Derek jerks his neck toward me. "Are you hitting on me?"

I laugh and slap my hand into the water. "No, good God, no."

He laughs. "Now I'm offended."

"Don't even start."

After our swim we clean up and dress. The pants fit, and we actually look respectable; like businessmen at a conference resort. We walk along the river and back up the slope to the picnic area.

"I suppose you want a plan?" Derek says.

"Yes, exactly. We need a plan."

We sit down at our picnic table.

"Fifty miles away." Derek points with his thumb. "We can start walking and try to bum a ride."

"Why are we doing this? Why don't we hide out and then escape to Canada, lie low and let someone else deal with this?"

"Like who?"

"I don't know. Why is Emergence our problem? This is dangerous stuff we're messing with."

Derek grimaces. "Like I don't know it."

"All right then. Why don't we let it all blow over? We're a democracy, right? The people have the power. They can kick Big Mac out if they don't like it."

"Did you read those executive orders in the Big Mac manifesto?" Derek clenches his fists. "Do you think Big Mac will have fair elections? And what about the boys? The boys at Emergence have . . ." Derek looks up and counts softly to himself. "Counting today, six days to live. Are we just going to let them die? The Emergence program is over sixty years old now. Who knows how long the torture has been going on? Oh, sure, let it blow over. Maybe in another sixty years some schmucks with bigger balls and more pride than we have will take care of it."

"And less brains," I say.

"Less brains? Oh, I get it. Look, if you want to turn in your boxers for panties I won't hold it against you."

I laugh. "Don't let Ninjenna hear you say that." Derek is right, of course. We have to do what we can to save the Emergence residents. As long as Slater and Big Mac are around, I'm in trouble.

Derek lets an ant crawl from the picnic table up his finger. "Next week is their Utopia Day. The new chosen ones enter the shelter and the current chosen ones go into the tunnel and meet their stupid utopia."

"And their death." We have to fight Big Mac. I hold up my hand. "You made your point. I'm in—just discouraged."

Derek sets the ant into the grass. He looks past me. A blue

Honda minivan pulls into the rest stop carrying a young white couple and two kids.

"This is our chance," Derek says.

The minivan pulls into a parking space.

Derek stands up and walks toward the Honda. When he is about twenty feet away, the minivan backs up and leaves the rest area.

Derek walks back scratching his head. "I don't think they've ever seen a black person. They looked at me like I was Bigfoot."

"You could be right. Not many African-Americans around here."

"That's bullshit."

I open my palm to him. "But what were you doing? What kind of tactic was that? You walk straight at them, a stranger in a rest stop? Doesn't matter who you are—it would have scared the hell out of me, too."

Another car pulls into the rest area. An older man drives a tan Ford Taurus wagon.

"You're up," Derek says. "Let's see those Customs Service tactics."

The man steps out of the car and walks toward the river. He glances at us, unconcerned, and takes in the view.

"Well?" Derek says.

"Patience."

The man wears navy dress pants and a white short-sleeve button-down shirt. He runs his hand through the short-cropped gray hair above his ear. He sits down at a picnic table, facing outward, and looks up, contemplating the mountainside.

I stand and walk at a nonthreatening angle to the riverbank. I look out meditatively for several minutes.

The man stays put. He looks like a military man, like he can handle any trouble sent his way.

I walk along the bank until I'm within thirty feet of him. Again, I take in the view for several minutes.

The man stands up.

I look to him naturally after noticing his movement. "Mighty fine day the Lord has given us."

He nods. "Indeed."

"Know of a town around here called Star?"

"Reckon I do."

I nod to where Derek is sitting. "We've business there."

"Not likely."

"I mean, we hope to do business there."

"That's not likely either."

"Not much of a happening place, then?"

"Not so friendly a place." He cocks his head and raises an eyebrow. "To outsiders, at least."

"I see."

"I don't think you do. I suggest you go to Taylorville. Plenty of business there."

"You must live in Star."

"I do. And I suggest you take my advice."

I take a chance. "We're with the government. A secret division within the government. And we're familiar with the reality of Star."

I half expect him to run, but instead he stays and rubs his chin. "Used to work for the government myself. Secret division, as you say." He looks around to his car and the empty parking spaces. "Say, how you boys end up here?"

"The execution of our plan hit a snafu, and now we're stuck."

The man chuckles. "That's working for the government all right. Brings back some memories."

I stick out my hand. "I'm Chris Thompson."

He shakes my hand. "Samuel."

"Derek!" I wave for him to come over.

Derek jogs and then slows to a walk when he nears us.

"This is my partner, Derek."

They shake hands.

"So," Samuel says. "Why you government fellas come to Star? We rarely get personal visits.

"We have information that'd best be told in person," I say.

Samuel looks back and forth at us. "Like what?"

I pause, wondering how much to tell him.

"Best we go to town first," Derek says. "Speak to the leadership all at once."

Samuel raises an eyebrow, but does not say anything.

"Would you mind giving us a lift?" I ask.

Samuel shuffles his feet. "Town's very protective, as you may know. Not like us to bring in strangers on a whim, no matter how good their story sounds."

We stare at each other. It's not an angry stare or a friendly one; both of us are just trying to figure out the situation.

"Our story might be of interest to some boys' parents," Derek says.

Samuel perks up at this. "What do you mean, boys?"

"Special boys," I say. "Young men who have gone to work for the government. You know anyone like that?"

Samuel scratches his face and looks me in the eye. "My son works for the government. His name is Daniel. You ever hear of him?"

"Doesn't ring a bell," I say. "What's his last name?"

Samuel's eyes squint. He looks me up and down, assessing me. "He's the only Daniel. If you're with the program you've been hinting you're with, then you'd know him."

"People's names change," I say. "You have a photograph of Daniel?"

Samuel sighs. He seems unsure but then nods his head and reaches in his back pocket for his wallet. "Haven't seen him in nearly five years." He flips open the worn brown leather wallet to a picture of a handsome young man.

His haircut is different, but I immediately recognize the person in the photograph. "Flipper!"

Samuel steps back. "Only a few people know his code name. You know my son?"

"I saw him a few days ago."

And just like that, Samuel's cool demeanor breaks. "You saw him! You saw Daniel?" He puts his shaking hand on my shoulder. "How is he?"

I think of Flipper telling Land and I about the escape shaft in the incinerator, saving our lives. "He's good, really good. He's a very nice kid."

"Yes, yes. That's my Daniel. And the other boys? Have you seen the other boys?"

Bingo. It appears that the white men at least are indeed all from Star. "I've seen them. Everyone is well."

Immediately, Samuel walks toward his Taurus. "Come with me. I'll give you a ride, straight away."

We ride in the Taurus on a two-lane road, heading deeper into the mountains. We are silent, but the change that comes over Samuel is obvious. He taps on the steering wheel and sways his head to a silent song known only to him. He smiles on and off.

Samuel pulls off on a gravel road that has two NO TRESPASSING signs posted on each side.

"Is this the entrance to your house?" Derek asks.

"Road to town. One way in, one way out."

The road curves down the mountainside and eventually becomes paved.

"So, Star is completely hidden?" Derek asks.

"Not so much hidden. Just private. I told you we keep to ourselves."

Samuel turns in to a driveway and stops. "See that river down below? Cross that bridge, and that's the town."

I see a church steeple and buildings along a main street that runs up perpendicular from the river. Roads, lined with houses, splinter off from the main street. A canopy of pines, elm, and aspen protect the hamlet-like town.

"I'd like to invite you to my home first. Would that be agreeable?"

"Sure," I say.

"Give me a chance to talk to some folks and arrange things."

"We're in your hands."

"Plus, I'd like you to meet my wife. I want her to hear your news and have a chance to ask you questions. After word gets out, you're going to be very popular around here."

I think about meeting X-ray's family and wonder whether being popular is a good thing.

The driveway opens through the trees to a small white Dutch-lap-sided cottage with red shutters. A small grassy front yard area is neatly trimmed.

Samuel parks the car and we get out. The view behind the house is tremendous. Bright sunlight streams into the valley below. A sharp diagonal shadow from the mountainside cuts across the river. A white pebble walkway leads to the front door. Wild mountain bluebells grow on the outskirts of the lawn. An old tire hangs by a rope from the limb of an elm tree. Samuel sees that I notice it. "Daniel is our only child. Even if he has children, we can never expect to see them."

I do not respond, as I do not know what to say.

Samuel opens his front door. "Barbara?"

"Sam, is that you? Is everything all right?"

"Yes, it's me, Mother. Can you come here? Are you dressed?"

"I should think so!" A woman with short gray hair, octagonal wire-rimmed glasses, and a floral-print dress rounds the corner from the hallway into the entrance. She holds a dust rag in her hand. "It's nearly noon."

She stops when she sees us. "Oh."

"We have guests."

She looks at us suspiciously. "I see."

"Derek and Chris, this is my wife, Barbara."

I nod. "Hello."

"Pleased to meet you, ma'am," Derek says.

She pauses for a moment to look us over. "Come in and have a seat, then." She guides us toward a solid-green fabric couch. Derek and I sit down together. A coffee table rests in front of us.

"Would you gentlemen like something to drink?"

"No thanks," we both say.

Samuel sits down in one of the two matching green recliners across from us. Knitted checkered blankets are draped over the seatbacks. Samuel rocks in his chair, his arms lazily flung over the armrests. "Please, sit down, Mother."

Barbara sits down on the edge of her chair. She clasps her hands in front of her.

A 1950s RCA TV with a rabbit-ear antenna sits on a walnut stained cabinet at the far end of the room. A sixteen-by-twenty-inch frame containing a picture of Flipper sits on top.

"These boys work for the government," Samuel says. "We got to talking, and I showed them a picture of Daniel." He flips open his wallet and shows me again. "And Chris here says . . ." Samuel puts his hand toward me.

"I say, 'That's Flipper.'"

Barbara's eyes widen. She puts her hands to her face. "You know my son?"

Samuel beams as he watches his wife's reaction. "He does," Samuel says. "Tell her more. Tell her what you told me."

"I saw him a few days ago. He's doing well. I spent two days with him."

"In the shelter?"

"Yes."

"And you saw the other boys?"

"Yes, the six from Star and the Native American."

Barbara sidesteps the coffee table, reaches out, and places her hands on my cheeks. She kisses my forehead. "Bless you." She pauses and looks at Derek. "And you. You know my son, too?"

"Know of him, but we've never met. I work the entrance above the shelter."

Barbara scoots over to Derek. She places her hands on his cheeks and kisses his forehead. "Bless you, too." She sits back down on her chair, takes off her glasses, and begins to cry. "I can't believe it. I'm so happy, and yet it hurts. I miss him so much."

Samuel stands up and places his hand on her back. "It's good news, Mother. Our Daniel is well."

"Yes, yes." She rubs her eyes and puts her glasses back on. "Let's have lunch."

We go into a small kitchen and sit in spindle chairs around an oval pine table. A rectangular picture window reveals a spectacular view of the valley.

Barbara makes us ham sandwiches and serves potato salad from a faded blue Tupperware container. The cabinets, appliances, and cookbooks are all circa 1950. We drink whole milk. Derek and I finish our sandwiches, and Barbara makes us more without asking. For dessert she cuts us pieces of chocolate cake from a tray on the counter.

When we are finished, Barbara asks me questions about her Daniel. Samuel remains silent, listening, seeming sure that his wife's questions will be thorough.

I tell them everything I can remember about Flipper. How he spends his time. What he eats. How he looks. What he reads. When he sleeps. No incident or detail is too minor for their interest. They revel in everything I say and seem so happy I can't bring myself to tell them the truth right now. The truth that Daniel is supposed to die in six days.

Another picture of Flipper hangs on the wall in the kitchen.

Next to it is a photograph of a girl about Flipper's age. She has long brown hair and a friendly smile.

"Is that Flipper's—I mean Daniel's high school sweetheart?"

"Oh, no. That's Cheryl, his fiancée."

"Is she in the women's shelter?" Derek asks.

"Yes, they meet next week on Utopia Day. We are so excited for them. She is perfect for him."

"Have you met her?" I ask.

"No, but we talk with her family. They are good people from Idaho. We speak every week. Only thing keeps us going sometimes," Barbara says.

"Idaho?" I say.

"Yes, that's where the chosen women come from." Barbara looks at me strangely. She looks at Samuel, who is squinting at me like he did at the rest stop.

I wonder how Samuel would react if I told him the truth. Would he believe me? Would he turn us in to the authorities? We need Samuel and Barbara's trust. "Of course," I say. "But I only work with the men."

Samuel stands up and looks at the pictures. "The thought of Daniel and Cheryl meeting and loving each other for eternity fills us with hope and indescribable joy."

I look at Derek. He purses his lips and looks away. Should we tell them? Or is it better to let them live on, naively happy for as long as they can? It feels right to sit here with Flipper's parents, to comfort them, but we can't sit here all day. Flipper and the rest are in danger, and so are we. We have to do something. We have to move.

"You boys have blessed us," Barbara says. "To know that Daniel is doing well on the path toward his salvation is of great comfort."

"Do you know a Patrick Sheehan?" I ask

Samuel is squinting at me again. "Why do you ask about Patrick?"

Derek and I look at each other. So there is a Patrick Shee-han here. "I'd just like to talk with him," I say.

"I'm sure Preacher will also want to speak with you fellas," Barbara says.

Derek looks at me, concerned. He's had it with the McCarthy religious stuff, too. We need to speak to someone official, someone who knows what really is going on. "Or the mayor," Derek says. "Could we speak to the mayor?"

"Certainly," Barbara says. "Preacher is the mayor."

"I'll take you to town," Samuel says. "Might be busy. This week we are having the Emergence Festival for the new boys going into service on Utopia Day."

Barbara looks out the window into the sky. "There's an Emergence service today to pray for the current boys' everlasting Utopia." She returns her attention to the kitchen and starts wiping a countertop.

"The service is at church this afternoon," Samuel says. "We can give you boys a ride. You can see Preacher then."

"I'm calling Elizabeth," Barbara says.

"We don't want too many people to know about us," I say.

"Just Elizabeth," Barbara says. "She'd just kill me if she found out I didn't ring her right away."

I look at Derek. I nod to Barbara. "Okay, just Elizabeth." I hate to call attention to ourselves, but what else can I do? We don't want to appear as if we're hiding from anyone.

Barbara picks up an old rotary phone hanging on the kitchen wall. She goes through the long process of dialing. "Hello, Elizabeth? You'd better sit down."

She tells our story to Elizabeth and points to another picture on the wall. I look. The six boys from Star currently at Emergence stand in a line, their arms around one another in brotherly affection. They are full of youthful hope and energy, and they don't look like they could harm anyone. Even X-ray looks innocent. What a sad fate awaits these boys.

Barbara points at one of the boys. "Did you see him?"

"Yes, I saw all of them."

She holds her hand over the mouthpiece. "What was his code name?"

"Juice."

She brings the phone back to her mouth. "He says Peter's code name is Juice."

A scream echoes from the phone. Barbara holds it away from her. "Oh my goodness!" comes out of the speaker.

"But don't tell anyone else, Elizabeth. They want to talk to Preacher first." Barbara hangs up the phone.

After the phone call we talk some more. Barbara's desire for information is endless. I tell her the same stories over, and she relishes in them again.

We hear a car door shut and the doorbell ring.

"It's Jeanie and Art," Samuel says from the front room.

Barbara points to X-ray in the picture. "Lester's parents."

"Two more cars are pulling up," Samuel says. "Elizabeth wasn't exactly quiet."

"Word travels fast around here," Barbara says.

The phone rings. Barbara answers. "I can't talk right now."

Samuel speaks with X-ray's parents through the screen door. Their voices grow loud. "Is it the redemption day? Are they the messengers?"

"I don't know." Samuel forces the door closed and locks it.

The phone rings again.

More cars arrive. Aunts, uncles, siblings, parents, cousins, old sweethearts and friends—Barbara announces them all as they pull in along the side of the drive.

Samuel paces in the living room, looking out the window at the cars and people. "We need to get you boys to Preacher. He can handle this."

23

We are dealing with a far more sinister type of activity.
—SENATOR JOSEPH McCARTHY

PEOPLE APPEAR IN THE BACK WINDOW, looking in and trying to see us, their heads barely above the bottom sill because of the drop in elevation.

"I better give 'em a ride to Preacher before our friends tear down the house," Samuel says.

"Hurry," Barbara says.

"You fellas ready?"

"Yes, sir," I say.

"Thank you for lunch," Derek says to Barbara.

"Yes, thank you. Very kind of you," I say.

"My pleasure. And thank you for everything," Barbara says. She gives Derek and I each a kiss on the cheek.

Samuel opens the front door. The crowd outside cheers.

"Let's go." Samuel leads the way through the crowd. "Back up! Out of the way!"

People enclose us. They touch us on the shoulder and shout names. "Do you know—?" They wave pictures of young men in the air. Some are old black-and-white photographs with guys in suits, square-rimmed black glasses, and flattops. Others are bright colored prints with high school boys in wild shirts with long hair.

We make it to the Taurus. Derek and I sit in the backseat. Samuel slowly pulls through the crowd. "Get out of the way!" he shouts through a slightly open window.

People run to their cars and form a line behind us. We pull onto the road and descend toward town. Lights flash on and off, and horns blare behind us. People wave their arms out their windows like an ecstatic parade of fans following a team bus home from a high school state championship.

We descend the mountain and cross the bridge. We drive down Main Street. The buildings are small, neat, and discreet, with names like "Hardware," "Drugstore," and "Grocery." There are no restaurants or specialty stores.

"Pretty basic," Derek says.

"Don't want to encourage the tourists."

"But no restaurants?" I ask.

"Good cooks can make money on the side out of their homes." Samuel waves his hand. "Plenty of tasty spots around."

I notice pictures of young men throughout town. They are in store windows and front doors. American flags fly from every lamppost and surround Big Mac signs. Poster boards are painted with slogans: "*Better Dead Than Red*," "*Live Free or Die*," and "*Go Home, Commie!*"

Cars are in front of us now, and we inch along. The cars behind us continue to create a cacophony of jubilation. People on the sidewalks wave and walk with us. At the third stoplight, more than halfway through town, we stop. A white wood clapboard church is one block down on the right. It has a black roof and a simple steeple at the front. People are crowded all around the entrance.

"Maybe this is not such a good idea," Samuel says. He turns the car left.

"Where are you taking us?" Derek says.

Samuel ignores him. He picks up speed and takes a quick right and pulls in front of a limestone building. Etched into the stone above the door are the words STAR POLICE.

Samuel gets out of the car. "Come on."

Derek and I get out of the car and look at the police station. We look at each other. Should we run? A crowd is heading toward us down the street.

Samuel is at the entrance to the station. "Let's go."

It's the crowd or Samuel. We follow him into the police station. He shuts and locks the door behind us.

Three desks sit on black-and-white-checkered tile. The desks are covered in paper. The walls are littered with community service announcements and safety recommendations. A hallway leads to a small jail cell.

A tall skinny officer in cowboy hat and boots stands up from behind a desk and walks toward us. "Quite a ruckus you've caused, Samuel."

"You know what it's about?" Samuel asks.

"Word's all over town—ninety percent fiction by now, I suppose. They're talking like this is it, the redemption day. The day when all past chosen ones will return to show us the way to our salvation."

Samuel points at us. "These two have information for Preacher."

"I don't know what you boys are selling, but I ain't buying it. People around here believe some crazy things."

"That so?" I look at a nightstick hanging on the wall behind the policeman's desk. "P. Sheehan" it says in white letters on the base. This must be the Patrick Sheehan President Wright mentioned. Has Samuel brought us to the police or to talk with Patrick Sheehan? Maybe both.

"These boys asked for you, too," Samuel says.

Patrick's head jerks backward a little. His eyes open wide in surprise.

"I don't want to hear your mantra," he says quickly. "My brother was selected to work with you fellas in the shelter ten years ago. I was all jacked-up proud at first, but as the years gone by I began to wonder, you know?"

I remember the military tribunal document from the microfiche that authorized the chosen ones' deaths. One of the men listed was Michael Sheehan.

"Any others like you?" Derek asks.

Patrick turns and glares at us. A trace of fear flickers in his eye. "Is that what this is, an inquisition against nonbelievers?"

"Absolutely not," I say. "We're here to tell the truth."

"Let's hear it then. I want the truth."

I glance at Derek and then ask, "Are you Patrick Sheehan?"

"That's what my nametag says. That's your truth?"

"Your brother was Michael Sheehan?"

Patrick turns to face me. "What do you mean was?" he asks slowly.

"I'm sorry, Patrick. I've seen evidence that your brother was killed five years ago by the government."

Samuel gasps.

A look of pain envelops Patrick's face, but he remains hard and stoic. "I ought to put a bullet in your motherfuckin' government heads right now."

"We've got nothing to do with it," I say. "We're trying to stop it from happening again. It's all a big evil government conspiracy."

Patrick's face softens a little. "I've always feared so. Poor Michael."

"The president sent us to find you," Derek says.

"President Wright?"

Derek opens his eyes wide. "Roast beef sandwich?"

Patrick looks at him quizzically. "With red peppers?"

Derek slaps his hands together. "I knew it. You're one of us."

"One of who?"

"One of the good guys," Derek says.

"A trusted special agent," I say. "That the president is relying on to stop this mess."

"What about all the other chosen ones?" Patrick asks.

"Same fate as your brother, I'm afraid," I say. "The president sent me to the shelter as an EPLO, a liaison. I discovered that some of the chosen boys torture prisoners to raise money for the Big Mac Party. The chosen ones are killed at the end of their service to hide the evidence."

"Do you have proof?" Samuel asks quietly.

"I had it, but Vance Slater took it." I look at Patrick and Samuel pleadingly. "I'm telling the truth. I'm just an ordinary guy that really has no stake in the matter, other than that I'm a concerned citizen."

Derek slaps me on the back. "A real American."

I nod to Derek. "Thanks, man."

Patrick clenches his jaw.

Samuel is pacing, clutching his hands. I don't think he knows what to believe.

"Why does everyone believe they live forever?" I ask.

Patrick's face turns red. "Because you government scumbags keep hinting that. And the checks keep coming."

"What checks?" Derek asks.

Patrick looks toward the window and then back at us. "All the chosen ones' paychecks keep coming to their loved ones."

"Which implies they're still alive," I say.

"Yes," Patrick says. "Odds are that some should have died by now, but the checks keep coming, indexed for inflation, and sometimes even with bonuses."

"What's your role in this?" I say. "How'd you know President Wright's password?"

Patrick turns and opens a drawer in his desk. "I wrote the president a letter about a year ago. It was a million-in-one shot, but I had to complain to someone."

"Complain about what?" Derek asks.

"My brother," he says coldly.

"Oh, yes, sorry."

"I wanted to know what happened to my brother. I told him I had doubts about the whole Emergence program."

"Blasphemy," I say.

Patrick pulls out a letter from the drawer. "'Bout six months ago I get this letter from the White House."

"Pony Express," Derek says.

"It was a handwritten note signed by the president."

"Impressive," I say.

Patrick flips his hand into the air, shaking the envelope. "I thought it was a big joke. The letter says that he understands my frustration, and that he has questions about Emergence as well. President Wright signed his name and then wrote, 'p.s., you can trust roast beef with red peppers.'"

"Mm, mm," Derek says. "In a panini is the best."

"Until today I thought some White House staff member was having a joke at my expense."

"The letter is legit, all right," I say. "President Wright even remembers your name. He told me to find you."

"Wow. Wonder why."

"I guess he figured you were a friend," I say.

There are scratches and tapping on the door and windows from outside. People's faces peer through the glass.

A pounding reverberates through the door. "It's Preacher. Let me in!"

We all look at one another.

"What do we do?" I say.

"You guys came here. What'd you have in mind?" Patrick says.

Derek goes to the window and looks at the growing crowd. "Not this. It feels like a lynching."

"Best go with Preacher. You don't have much choice," Samuel says.

There is more pounding on the door. "I said let me in!"

"Do you think he will believe us?" I say.

Samuel shrugs. "I don't know if I believe you."

Patrick walks to the door. "Judgment time." He opens it and Preacher pushes his way in. Patrick slams and locks the door.

Preacher is a tall husky man in a white robe. A stars-and-stripes hood is draped around his shoulders. He has brown hair streaked with gray and parted in the middle, long enough to cover his ears and three quarters of the back of his neck. Preacher smiles a chemically enhanced set of pearly white teeth at us through a closely trimmed mustache and beard. "Gentleman, you have brought us good news?"

"For some," I say. "Perhaps we should speak in private."

"All should be shared," he says. "Don't worry—we are good at keeping secrets."

Derek whispers to me. "I hope so."

"Is it the redemption day?" Preacher asks.

"I don't think so," I say.

"We bring the truth," Derek says.

"A step, no doubt, to our redemption day?"

"I'm not so sure about that," I say.

"You are merely messengers then?"

"You could say that," Derek says.

"All these people," I say. "I don't think what we have to say is—"

Preacher holds up a hand. "I've heard what you've said already. It is good. Do not worry if the rest is not as exciting. I have, shall we say—a certain flair. I'm sure we can make it interesting."

Preacher opens the door. "Come, messengers. Come to our Emergence celebration!" The crowd cheers.

"I still think a private meeting would be better," I say.

"Nonsense. It is not our way." He holds his hands to the

crowd. "And the messengers will come and impart the good news unto all the faithful."

"Amen!" the crowd cries.

Preacher walks us outside. The people separate for him, and we follow him through the crowd. We walk two blocks, leading the people to the church. At the church, cement steps reach up from the sidewalk to sinless-looking oaken doors. Beyond the oak doors, a simple Protestant-style church welcomes us. Tall thin Gothic windows filled with stained glass line the sides. Rather than old biblical images, the windows portray American patriotic themes: air force jets in formation, baseball players, farmers, and construction workers. American flags are in each of them. Sunlight illuminates the stained glass and brightens the left side of the church.

Backbreaking dark wood pews are filled with chatting people. The low murmur quiets as they spot us. All heads turn in silent expectation.

Preacher turns around and looks up. A balcony filled with people overlooks us. He spreads his arms in the air and nods to the organist, who sits at her post in the balcony. She bows her head to the altar and moves her arms and hands. Glorious music reverberates throughout the church.

Two altar boys walk down the aisle, part, and light candles on both sides of the chancel. Another altar boy holds a gold metallic cross in front of us. Next to him an altar boy holds an American flag. On a nod from Preacher, they begin walking down the aisle.

"Follow me," Preacher says.

The music changes. The crowd stands. Preacher walks down the aisle. Derek and I follow. Everyone sings, "*Onward Christian soldiers, marching as to war.*"

Behind the altar a red, white, and blue cross painted with stars and stripes floats in midair, suspended by thin cables. On the wall behind the altar and cross hangs a gold-encrusted frame decorated with an eagle. The frame contains a reverent black-and-white photograph of Senator Joseph McCarthy. He has slicked-down thinning black hair and thick, brooding eyebrows. His razor-thin lips smirk as he looks down on the congregation with accusing benevolence.

We walk up three steps to the right of the altar. Preacher ushers us to a small pew. On the opposite side, a blue-robed choir sits in stadium-seating pews. In the front row on both left and right pews sit six young men dressed in white button-down shirts and black dress pants. A proud parent sits on each side of them. These must be the new Emergence recruits.

Preacher steps into the pulpit. He smiles and holds his hands up to the congregation like he's about to give a benediction. The music and singing stop. "Friends, it's so nice to see all of you again on this day of Emergence celebration. A day in which we shall celebrate the calling of our new chosen ones."

The congregation applauds. The chosen ones look around and wave.

Preacher grabs the pulpit and leans forward. "Friends, in 1950, as you know, our town was chosen for its purity, chosen for its values, chosen for its undying love of America, chosen for its hatred of Communism, Fascism, or any godless evil movement that would undermine our American way of life. Yes, friends, our patron saint, Senator Joseph McCarthy, chose us."

The congregation, the chosen ones and parents, the choir, the organist, the altar boys, ushers, and Preacher, all raise their right fists in the air and shout, "McCarthy!"

Derek and I flinch from the power of their exultation.

"Our town was chosen for a program. God helped our fore-fathers found America, and if the evilness in the world causes the human race to destroy itself, then through God, *we* will rebuild that world with the vision of Saint McCarthy."

"McCarthy!" they shout.

"And to this program we have sent our finest boys; young

men in the prime of life, young men who represented pure American values. We send these chosen ones to this noble program. And through this program, with the help of science, God, and America, the chosen ones have achieved their salvation. Through the signs shown to us and through the revelations of our divine oracles, we believe—our chosen ones have attained everlasting life! Such are the fruits and abundance from the program started by Saint McCarthy."

"McCarthy!"

Preacher raises his fist into the air. "The checks keep coming!"

"The checks keep coming!" the congregation shouts.

"This program. This program we know as Emergence." Preacher bows his head. The choir jumps up, points at the photograph of McCarthy, and sings in a crescendo, *"Emergence, Emergence, Emergence!"*

Preacher puts his palms out to the congregation and motions for them to stand. He points with them at McCarthy. Everyone sings, *"Emergence, Emergence, Emergence!"*

Preacher motions for all to sit down. A buzz rings throughout the congregation.

"Brothers and sisters. This week we celebrate the coming Utopia Day. The day the chosen ones in the shelter will reach their Utopia, the day the new chosen ones will begin their sacred journey, the day fifty-six years ago our patron saint, Joseph McCarthy, passed unto his own Utopia."

"McCarthy!"

"We also believe the chosen ones will return one redemption day. The day we will be rewarded for our faith and sacrifice. On that day we will join the chosen ones and their families in eternal life. And though today might not be the redemption day, it is a special day! Today messengers have been sent to us, messengers with good news, messengers who will confirm that our chosen ones are doing well, messengers who will strengthen

our faith and renew our spirit in the principles of Saint McCarthy—"

"McCarthy!"

"—and the fruits of the Emergence program and the Big
Mac Party."

He motions for everyone to rise with the choir. They sing
again, "*Emergence, Emergence, Emergence!*"

Preacher points to me. "To share the good news, I present
to you—a messenger."

Derek whispers to me: "Good luck."

I stand and walk toward the pulpit. Wild applause erupts.

Preacher puts his hands in the air and lowers them slowly
to quiet the congregation.

I step into the pulpit, put my hands on the smooth dove-white
painted wood sides, and lean forward. A lake of parishioners
looks up to me with hopeful minnow faces and salvation-ready
souls. This is my chance. I must convince them of the truth.
To legitimize myself, I will appeal to their patriotism and tell
them of my role in service of President Wright. I will speak of
my time in the shelter and reveal the horrible atrocities. I hope
that I can shock them out of their religious stupor enough that
they will want to help us save their boys and bring down the
Big Mac Party. If this town turns against Slater's organization,
we may have a chance.

I tap the PRAD nervously on the pulpit rail. I clear my
throat. "Ladies and gentlemen, citizens of Star. I am an EPLO—
an emergency preparedness liaison officer."

They all nod their heads knowingly, which surprises me.

"Last week I was sent by the president of the United States
to act as a liaison to the Emergence program."

"*Emergence, Emergence, Emergence!*"

I inhale, and Preacher jumps up and interrupts me before
I can talk. "Brothers and sisters! Let us recite together chapter
three, verse twenty-one, from the Big Mac Book of Creation."

He lifts his arms into the air, and the people respond in unison. "And in times of a national emergency a liaison shall be sent forth by the president unto the shelter."

"Amen! Brothers and sisters." Preacher motions for me to continue.

I want to avoid another Emergence song outburst, so I say. "This same program we are referring to, this program started by McCarthy—"

Fists shoot up into the air, including Derek's. "McCarthy!"

I take a sharp stare at Derek. He shrugs and smiles.

"Yes, yes, McCarthy," I say.

"McCarthy!"

"Jesus," I say in frustration. Then I begin again. "Citizens of Star."

They look up to me with rapt attention.

"Recently I spent two days in the shelter you refer to in that program you are so intimately involved with."

A few zealous smiles disappear from the most joyous of the lot when I avoid saying "Emergence."

"I stayed in the shelter with the six chosen boys from your town."

The smiles return.

"And with the chosen one from the Cherokee reservation."

I pause.

"I am happy to report that the chosen ones in the shelter are alive and well."

The congregation explodes with applause. They smile and nod to one another.

I hold up my hands. "Yes, yes. They are well." I pause. "As you know, the initial aim of the Emergence program was to—"

"*Emergence, Emergence, Emergence!*"

I clench my fists. "—was to ensure the population continuity and goals of America."

Many look to the picture of McCarthy when I say this.

Now to shock them. "But citizens of Star. I must tell you that something has gone horribly wrong." I point to Derek. "My friend and I are witnesses. Witnesses to evidence that proves—" I look to Samuel and Barbara. They stand in the back vestibule among others and stare blankly at me. "—to evidence that proves, unfortunately, that the chosen ones are killed by the government when their service in the shelter is complete."

The congregation falls deathly silent.

I point at them. "Your sons have been deceived into committing crimes for the United States government—crimes of torture and murder."

A fat balding man stands up. "Liar!"

I ignore him and raise my voice. "I speak the truth. Your sons have fallen victim to the same crimes. Your current chosen boys will die on the Utopia Day."

Another man stands up to speak. "This is no messenger!"

I shout him down. "Torture and murder!"

An old lady stands up in the second row. She raises her fist. "McCarthy!" she croaks.

"McCarthy!" they cry.

I feel the heat rise in my face. I see all their eyes at once. I see Fixer's bloody face, Walter screaming on the torture table, Scotty's Big Mac sticker, President Wright's foggy eyes, Slater's mocking leer. The stained glass windows swirl. My face sweats and temples pulse. I throw my arms at them.

"Damn McCarthy!" I shout.

"McCarthy!" they cry.

"The Big Mac manifesto abuses executive powers." I raise my fist. "We're heading for Stalinistic Communism!"

"Blasphemer!" the old lady shouts, pointing at me.

Samuel hustles down the side aisle. "I believe him."

"Blasphemer!" someone else shouts.

"My boy is a chosen one," Samuel shouts. "I want to save my boy! We need to save our boys!"

"Hear, hear," shouts someone from the crowd. A few other people take up the chant.

"Blasphemer! Blasphemer!" shout the rest.

"Save your boys!" I shout.

"Blasphemer! Blasphemer!"

The church erupts in shouts and cries and insults. The cries of "Blasphemer" outnumber my small flock of converts by a huge margin.

They push and shove each other. Samuel quickly becomes swallowed up in the crowd.

Preacher, the opportunist, joins the winning side. "Faith in the Emergence!"

"*Emergence, Emergence, Emergence!*" his believers sing.

Preacher points at me. "Silence the blasphemer."

"Silence! Silence!"

"Faith in the Emergence."

The faithful exit their pews. They walk toward me and point at me as they sing. "*Emergence, Emergence, Emergence!*"

"Silence the blasphemer!"

The congregation sings the Emergence chant continuously as they edge toward the altar area.

I feel a tug on my shirt and turn around. The choir has me surrounded. I see Derek running for an exit door in the back corner behind his pew. He stops and looks at me and claps his hands and flips me off. He does it again and looks at me, exasperated.

I push three eighty-year-old choir members aside, lower my shoulder, and run like a fullback through soft housewife flesh. I break free and dart toward the exit. But I stop midway, turn, clap my hands, and point my middle finger at the encroaching crowd. Alleluia. The PRAD shrieks like a hound out of hell.

Take that, Q. God bless America. The parishioners cover their ears, turn, and fight for the back door, or fall to a fetal position.

"Beelzebub!" someone yells.

Derek and I exit out the side door and clamber down cement stairs to a perfectly manicured lawn.

Patrick comes out the front of the church. "This way."

24

*It is dangerous for a national candidate to say things
that people might remember.*
—SENATOR JOSEPH MCCARTHY

PATRICK STANDS NEXT TO HIS SQUAD CAR motioning frantically
at us to come his way.

Derek and I sprint toward the car. Patrick gets inside and
starts the engine. He turns on the lights and blares the siren,
which stuns the few parishioners who have exited the church.

Derek and I dive into the backseat, and Patrick speeds away.

"Nice speech," Derek says.

"A lot of help you were."

"I'm the only black man within a hundred miles. They were
mad at me just for sitting there."

"You could have done something."

"Man, you did enough," Derek says.

"Didn't exactly convince them," Patrick says.

"A few of them," I say.

Derek touches his earring, snaps his fingers, and points. "I
found the exit."

"And you were leaving without me, I noticed."

"I figured you could handle those powder puffs on your own."

We drive over the bridge and leave town. Patrick turns off the lights and siren. "Probably be fired for this."

"You're doing the right thing," I say.

"I've thought about what you said in there. It hurts, but it makes sense."

"It makes no sense," Derek says.

"Does it ever?" I say.

"What you guys say is believable," Patrick says. "More believable than this everlasting McCarthy crap."

We failed to convince the town, except for Samuel and a few others. We're back to square one, and Slater's bound to hear about our public performance and come after us. "We need a plan," I say.

"Slater will be on our tail soon," Derek says. "We need a place to hide."

We are on the highway now, following the river, curving through the mountains. Patrick drives, silent, listening to Derek and I talk.

"Land said no one would find him on the reservation. Maybe we should go there and regroup," I say.

"Ninjenna and Joemore might still be there."

"Then we'd have a team. Together we could devise a plan to save the Emergence residents."

Derek laughs sarcastically. "That's being a little optimistic. We're kind of a ragtag bunch."

"Come on, Derek. We're pros. Look at all we've done the last few days. Masterful escapes with intelligent strategy and pinpoint execution! We're basically super spies at this point, just as good as Bond. We'll figure out something. We have to try, at least."

Derek doesn't look impressed with my assessment. "Too

bad Wizkid ditched us." He looks out the window at the passing scenery. "Okay. Going to the Cherokee reservation in Oklahoma is not a bad idea."

"I can't take you that far," Patrick says. "But I can drop
you at the bus station in Salt Lake City."

"We certainly appreciate it," I say.

Derek touches my arm. "We're low on funds."

Patrick reaches into his pocket and tosses his wallet to us.
"'Bout six hundred in there. Take it."

"Really? You sure?"

"If I can help avenge my brother, then that's nothing."

"Thanks. You're helping to save the current boys, too."

"I wish I could do more."

So do I. We need more help. We need someone on the outside. "The press needs to get wind of this."

"My lady is friends with an investigative reporter in LA,"
Derek says. "Naomi Woods. She's always tracking down stupid
stuff."

"Okay, good. We'll try to contact her as soon as we can."

After a two-hour drive, Patrick pulls to a curb in downtown Salt Lake City.

Karen and Scotty won't find me now if they make it to Star.
I lean my head into the front seat. "My wife and kid might be
showing up in Star. Could you help them out? They might be
in danger too."

Patrick nods. "Be glad to. I keep a pretty good eye on the
entrance road. I'll try and spot them before Preacher or anyone
else does."

"And Wizkid, too," Derek says. Derek goes into a long
explanation about who Wizkid is and what he looks like. "If
he happens to show up, tell him we've gone to the reservation."

"Sure thing," Patrick says. "Now hurry up—the search for
you is undoubtedly on by now."

I shake Patrick's hand and exit the car.

"Good luck," I say.

"Don't worry. I'll find your family a safe place to stay. Star is a good place to hide." Patrick laughs. "That is, if you haven't made a spectacle of yourselves like you two."

"That's awfully nice of you. Thanks for everything." I shut the door and Patrick drives off.

Derek and I walk toward the station. We enter a 1930s WPA Art Deco train station that also serves as a Greyhound bus depot. An opaque glass ceiling dimly covers the station with natural light. The sleepy room is empty but for a few people who sit or pass through silently. I sit in a pew-like bench while Derek goes to the ticket counter.

Two men in SWAT gear walk with a police dog through the atrium lobby. Occasionally they stop and talk to people. I feel uneasy. The SWAT guys approach a man reading a newspaper. The man tries to get up, but they grab him and handcuff him. The man is shouting. "I didn't do anything! Somebody help! Please help!" The SWAT men lead him off down a hallway.

"Damn!" Derek's voice echoes throughout the cavernous station. He walks over and sits down next to me, disgusted.

"Problem?"

The two SWAT men are back, walking around the station.

"You need a Big Mac ID to buy a bus ticket," Derek says.

I nod toward the SWAT guys. "That's not our only problem."

Derek sees them coming and sits up straight. They stop in front of us. "Gentlemen," one of them cavalierly says.

"Hello, officers."

They carry Heckler & Koch MP5 submachine guns and wear black baseball caps that say BORDER PATROL in gold stitching.

"Can I see your IDs, gentlemen?"

"The thing is, officer," Derek says, "is that we were robbed on the way here and have no IDs."

"Come with us."

"We're not doing anything wrong, officers," I say. "Surely it's not a crime to be without an ID?"

"Actually, it is. But you're coming with us either way."

We follow them down a hallway off the main atrium and into a small fluorescent-lit office. Another SWAT man sits behind a desk. Standing to the side is the man I saw taken away in the atrium. He is wearing an orange jumpsuit.

The SWAT man behind the desk shouts through a door into a back room. "We got two more, Hazel."

The SWAT men who brought us in stand guard at the door. The man behind the desk sifts through some paper forms. "Gentlemen, by the authority vested in me through the Emergency Powers Act and Executive Order 11000, I hereby draft you into Border Patrol Service Work Brigade BP0137CAN."

"We've been drafted for not having IDs?" I say.

"Bullshit," the lone man in the jumpsuit says.

The man behind the desk scowls at us. "I don't care about IDs. I have a quota to make."

Derek nods to the man in the jumpsuit. "That's right. Bullshit."

"Don't worry, gentlemen. We'll provide clothing, and room and board. Hazel! I got one medium-pudgy and a medium-fatso."

"Hey," Derek says.

The man nervously taps his fingers against the desk. "Relax, gentlemen. Your three-month tour will be up before you know it, and you'll lose the weight while you're at it. Border patrol builds character."

"We're nowhere near the border," I say.

A short elderly lady emerges from the back room holding two orange jumpsuits.

"Hand over your personal belongings and jewelry," SWAT man says. "Strip down to your Skivvies and put these on."

The old woman drops the jumpsuits and leaves the room.

I stand up. "This is outrageous." They don't know they're dealing with a superspy with secret weapons. I clap my hands and flip them off.

Nothing.

I try to clap again, but feel a sharp pain in the side of my head. Everything goes black.

25

I AWAKE SITTING in a bus seat. The bus is moving, and it is
dark but for a few dim lights. Derek sits next to me, wearing
an orange jumpsuit like mine. The bus is filled with identically
dressed degenerate-looking souls.

I run my hands over the baggy jumpsuit. "How'd I get in
these?"

"You were a bit groggy, but they managed," Derek says.

I look out the window but can't see anything in the dark.
"Where are we going?"

"Been on the road two hours now. On our way to the
Canadian border."

"Shit, shit, shit."

"They didn't ask who we were. They just wanted bodies. At
least we have a cover, now."

"What difference does it make? They've got us. We're in
prison, from what I can see."

Derek laughs. "We're hiding right under their noses."

I shake my head. It hurts. I suppose Derek is right, but I don't want to give him the satisfaction. "The glass is always half full with you."

"Full is always better."

I hold my hands up and spread my fingers. "My PRAD. Damn it. They took my PRAD."

"That thing got you in as much trouble as it helped."

"Are you serious? The power in that ring saved us. What will we do now?"

"You'll think of something, Frodo."

Derek is getting on my nerves. "Why the hell are we going to Canada?" I ask him.

"Just to the border. We're going to build a wall, they say."

I rub the knot that has formed on the side of my head.

"Big guy whacked you pretty good."

"We gotta figure a way out of here."

The bus drives north all night through Idaho and into Montana. In the morning we stop at Sunburst, Montana, about eight miles from the Canadian border.

The border patrol has overtaken the town. Thousands and thousands of orange-jumpsuit-wearing men are being bussed in and out or are milling around the compound under the watchful eye of machine-gun-toting SWAT men. We drive through a gate and a double-razor-wire fence. Construction crews work on new barracks. They have erected row upon row of white painted army-style structures that go on for as far as I can see.

Derek and I exit the bus and stand in line for a bowl of greasy potato soup. We wait in another line for a duffel bag full of supplies and a bed assignment.

We walk on new sidewalks through manicured grass-seeded dirt and past several buildings before we find our barracks. Inside, we walk between never-ending rows of bunk beds and angry men. It smells of fresh paint and stinks of bad body odor.

We stop at our bunk. Derek throws his duffel bag on top. "I call top bunk."

"I'm top bunk."

"What are you talking about? I just called top bunk."

"Look at the number," I say. "I've been assigned the top bunk."

"What difference does it make?"

"It makes a big difference. You can't go breaking the rules in a place like this."

Derek starts climbing; his large body makes the ladder look childlike. "Watch me."

I grab his collar and halt his ascent.

"Hey." He looks at me with his eyebrows furled. "Just what do you think you're doing?"

His smugness is irritating. "I never get top bunk. My whole life, I'm always stuck on the bottom bunk."

"Get over it." He tries to swat my arm away, but I resist.

I have more leverage on the ground and I lean back and pull him off the ladder. He stumbles, and then we face each other. "I've finally been assigned the top bunk, and I'm going to take it," I say.

A crowd of orange-suited men accumulates around us.

Derek pushes me in the chest. "Take it then, try it."

"Take it," someone shouts.

I stomp my foot. "I order you to let me have the top bunk."

The crowd around us laughs.

Derek laughs, too. He puts his finger into my chest. "You can't order me, Customs Service. I'm Homeland Security. I give the orders."

I stomp my foot again. "I'm in charge. I'm under direct orders from the president. The commander in chief. I'm in charge."

"You fags are nuts," someone shouts.

I grab the front of Derek's jumpsuit. "Give me the top bunk."

He grabs me by the front of my jumpsuit. "Never."

We spin around and around, shoving and wrestling while the men laugh and egg us on. I trip and Derek throws me down on the bottom bunk. He dives on top of me and puts me in a headlock. "Who gets the top bunk?"

I feel like I'm suffocating and struggle to say, "I get the top bunk."

From out of nowhere, three SWAT dudes attack and separate us. We stand up guiltily. One of them waves a scanner over the bar code on each of our uniforms. He looks into his handheld computer. "Just off the boat, I see." He brings out a thin wire rope from a leg pocket and runs it through Derek's belt loops. He runs the other end through my loops and locks the ends together so that Derek and I are connected, with only a foot of space between us. "You two need to learn to get along."

The men whistle and jeer.

"Beat it," the SWAT man shouts at them. He types into his computer. "Twenty-four-hour work punishment for you two. Catch the six p.m. bus." He scans our bar codes again to confirm our obligation. "My advice would be to rest up until then."

"How?" Derek asks. "We're connected."

"Who gets the top bunk?" I ask.

"No one gets the top bunk," the man says. "Figure it out. You two are Siamese twins from now on."

The SWAT men turn and march away.

Derek and I sit on the bottom bed in silence.

"Do you feel the anger in this place?" I finally say.

"I can feel my own anger."

"These men are angry."

"So are we."

"We need to ignite that anger."

"We did. And look where that got us."

"No. Not our anger. Don't you understand? We should

create a disturbance, ignite an uprising. That's our ticket out of this place."

Derek sighs. "None of your ideas ever seem to work."

"You got an idea?"

He sighs again. "I'll think about it."

We rest as best we can, lying side by side on the bottom bunk. At six o'clock we board a gray school bus with the same men we rode with from Salt Lake City. The bus drives us to the deserted border town of Sweet Grass and to one of the most incredible sights I have ever seen. We get off the bus and stand stupefied. Most of the town has been razed to accommodate the border wall. Calling it a mere wall is a failure of description. The wall is a black monolithic fifty-story Teflon-looking skyscraper that stretches as far as the eye can see in both directions. American flags that look like they have been made from seamstresses on steroids fly from the top. Crisscrossing green laser beams shoot diagonally upward, forming a checkerboard-patterned neon wall into space. It is awesomely fearsome and smells like bad future.

"You'd have to be Superman to get over that wall," I say.

"Or Super-Can." Derek laughs. "Get it, Super-Can? As in Canadian."

"Shut up over there," a guard shouts. He points to us. "Yo, newbies—this way."

Derek and I shuffle over to him. Derek is still chuckling to himself.

"Newbies get a tour of the top," the guard says. "Enjoy it—you'll be underground the rest of your stay."

"Underground?" Derek says.

"Have to stop those tunnel-digging Canucks," I say.

"Silence." The guard looks to Derek and me and smiles when he notices we are chained together. "Already been in trouble, huh?" He points at his eyes and then at us. "I'm watching you two."

The guard walks us inside the monolith and we ride in a stainless steel elevator to the top. We exit into a cold whipping wind. Country-size American flags flap together, crackling like a Boy Scout bonfire. We walk along a five-foot-wide cement path. Robotic lenses scan the Canadian landscape to the north. Human spotters are stationed every five hundred yards with powerful binoculars. They watch over the beautiful panoramic evening scene on both sides of the wall.

The guard leans with his back against the edge, facing us. "This twenty-mile-long prototype wall was completed last year. Thanks to Big Mac's quick response to the current national emergency, funds and cheap labor have been appropriated to extend the wall, which is now known as the Forever United against Canada—or FUC—Wall, from coast to coast. The FUC Wall will prevent Canadians from infiltrating our borders and polluting our American way of life."

"Thank God," I say.

The guard glares over at us.

Derek stands up straight. "Thank God for America," he says. "And the FUC Wall."

The guard thinks for a moment, but fails to grasp the sarcasm. "Yes," the guard says. "Thank God for America and the FUC Wall."

Loudspeakers blare around us. "Canadian in water vessel spotted." A short whooping alarm sounds.

Derek and I go to the edge and stand next to the guard. We look out a half mile to a round lake. A lone Canadian fisherman is rowing in a small boat. The robotic-sounding loudspeakers call out the fisherman's actions.

"Alert yellow. Threat to crossing, medium."

The fisherman casts out a line.

"Projectile launched. Threat of contact, low."

The fisherman reels in the line and starts rowing again.

"Vessel approaching, destination indeterminate. Threat to crossing, medium."

The whooping alarm sounds. "Enemy combatants spotted."

"I have to report to my station." The guard runs toward a spotter.

Someone points. "Out there." Two hunters in bright orange vests walk down a gravel road. They have rifles slung over their shoulders.

The speakers sound. "Weapons in possession—possible WMDs."

"Super-Can!" Derek says.

The alarm sounds again.

"Alert red. Threat, high. Clear the deck. Clear the deck."

Another guard appears from the elevator. "Let's go, newbies. Move, move, move!"

We hustle into the elevator.

The guard nods and smiles. "Always exciting up here. Don't be alarmed—we'll handle it."

The elevator doors close, and we descend to the ground. We walk out of the monolith.

"We're safe," I say.

"For now," Derek says. "No telling what those maple-heads have in mind."

I laugh. "They'll be shooting hockey pucks at us next."

We board the bus and drive a mile along the wall. They drop us off at a mine shaft entrance. Tired, soiled workers come out of a metal cage elevator. New men replace them and descend into the mine.

We are given miner caps and lights. They scan our bar codes as we enter. When a guard scans ours, he says, "Twenty-four hours. See you tomorrow."

We descend with a group to a dimly lit earth-smelling tunnel that is braced with a hodgepodge of boards and cement.

"This way, newbies." We follow a tough miner boss who holds a quarter-inch wire. "This is a sensor cable. We're running these from the wall deep into the ground. They will immediately detect any excavating activity by the Canadians."

"How far down does it go?" Derek asks.

"Classified—but far enough, I assure you."

We reach an area with drilling machines spread five yards apart. Pipe protrudes from the ceiling into the machines and then into the ground below. The boss puts plugs in his ears, and we do the same. He holds on to the two handles of a drilling machine and turns it on. It roars and vibrates, and the pipe slowly spins.

"Take a post, men. Press the button and apply downward pressure. Not too difficult."

The men separate and claim machines.

Derek and I have no choice but to stand together next to one machine.

The boss barks at us. "What are you two lovebirds doing?" He walks over to inspect. "Christ. Stupid guards always slowing down production with their games." He grabs an ax from the wall, places our connecting wire against a wood post, and chops the wire in half. "Now get to work."

I scurry down the line and find my own machine. I press the red button and grab hold. The sounds and vibrations are earth shattering, and I worry the tunnel might collapse.

We work on in the dust and oil. It smells of sweat, dirt, and cold rocks. The machine shakes every bone in my body. A rock splinter hits me in the face, stinging my cheek. I taste blood on my lips. My jaw vibrates, and it feels like a hammer is pounding against my temples.

After two shaking rock-splintering hours, the burly boss returns. He flips a switch, and the machines all stop at once. "Break time—fifteen minutes."

I stumble down the tunnel and collapse next to Derek. Someone passes out water, and I gulp greedily. "Twenty-four hours of this might kill us," I say.

"That may be the point," Derek says.

We return to work. Blisters form on my hands and then

break, leaving my palms raw and in pain. My arms no longer feel like my own; they are painful cords barely guiding a mad jackhammer. I somehow survive for another two hours. We again have fifteen minutes to rest. Derek has a faraway look in his eye. Perhaps he is thinking back to Iraq and his days as a Marine. He looks like a warrior, and it gives me strength.

Derek and I repeat the hellish routine for three eight-hour shifts. I am dizzy, delirious, claustrophobic, and somewhat psychotic. I am in hell.

The torture ends, and we somehow make it back to the barracks. We feast on potato soup, bread, and cheese until I feel ill. We shower and are given a second set of jumpsuits. Exhausted, and forgetting we are no longer attached, we crash together in the bottom bunk.

"I don't think we can get out of here," Derek says. "Let's serve our three months and go from there. Slater might have forgotten about us by then."

"Not likely."

"If we're caught trying to escape, they may keep us here forever."

Derek can't give up. I won't stand a chance on my own. "What about the boys in the shelter? Their time is up. You want their deaths on your hands?"

Derek pauses and considers. "You know, it's not like they're innocent college kids. They've been torturing and murdering people for years."

"Not all of them. And it wasn't like it was their idea. They were under orders."

"And that makes it right?"

I think of Flipper and his parents, the chocolate cake Barbara served us. "I don't know. That's not for me to decide. All I know is that those boys are going to die, and that Big Mac is taking over. We should do what we can."

Derek groans.

"Come on, Derek." I punch him in the arm. "Where's that optimistic spirit? We're the good guys. We can do it."

Silence.

"I know," Derek says. "I'm just tired is all."

"Me too. We should go to sleep."

"So get out of my bed. Get up there on top."

"Really?"

"Really. Man, I couldn't climb up there if I wanted."

I know what he means. I can barely make it up the ladder myself. I plop into the bed and sleep like the overworked prisoner I am, dead to the world, without thoughts or dreams.

* * *

We sleep late and make our way to the cafeteria building in the compound's center. It's a monstrous room where men with trays form a long line as they wait for powdered eggs and hash browns. They sit, crowded, at lined-up rows of white plastic-laminated picnic tables. Our shift starts at 6:00 p.m.

"I think starting an uprising is our best option," I say.

"We better think this through," Derek cautions.

"I've thought it through. And we're more likely to get away if there's a mass escape."

Derek takes a sip of orange juice from concentrate. "I'm just saying that we'd better plan this out to the last detail."

"You can't plan riots." I raise my arms up in the air. "They just erupt. They're spontaneous." I jump up on the table and look out over six hundred eating workers.

Derek puts his hand over his face.

"Oppressed workers!" I shout. "We have been drafted against our will. We are Americans. We have rights. We have freedom. Let's exert our rights against this oppression!"

An old hippie-looking dude with hair down to his waist and a beard to match stands up and shouts. "Right on!"

"Yes!" I shout and point at the hippie. "There is a freedom fighter! Who else is with us?"

The men in the cafeteria look sullenly into their food.

Two guards at each end of the room remain stoic, staring straight ahead.

"Come on, people. Enough is enough. Let's fight Big Mac together."

Someone clears his throat behind me. I turn around and look at three guards. They motion for me to step down and I do.

"I, I, I just got off a twenty-four-hour shift. I, I, I'm a little out of sorts."

"Open up," one says. He opens his mouth wide to demonstrate.

I open my mouth, and they shove a small round beanbag inside. It's attached to a leather strap, which they wrap around my head and fasten with a small lock.

The guard smacks the side of my head. "That should keep you quiet for a while."

The guards leave, and I sit down next to Derek.

He bursts out laughing.

I open my eyes wide and make a growling sound.

Derek pounds the table and laughs some more. "You sure have a way with words."

"Grr," I say.

"You really ignited their anger."

"Grr."

He hits the table again and laughs. "Jesus over there was with you, but that's about it."

"Grr."

"Spontaneous uprising—nice plan."

Your turn next time, I think. "Grr, grr."

"Okay," Derek says, somehow reading my thoughts. "Time for plan C."

* * *

I spend a silent, drooling, miserable day listening to Derek.

At six o'clock we board the bus for the mine. Derek and I are at the stop early. I've been exhausted all day, but now that we are about to execute our plan, the adrenaline kicks in and I'm hyper-alert. We board the school bus first and walk to the rear. A lone guard sits in the last seat. Derek and I sit in the seat before him.

When we reach the mine, I walk off the bus last. As I descend I turn and try to talk to the guard walking behind me. "Grr, grr."

I step off the bus and continue my gibberish as the guard exits.

"Move along, I don't have time for this," he says.

"Gurble, gurble, grr." I try to talk with my hands and pantomime nonsense. I speak louder. "Rahh, grr."

The guard is agitated. He points his finger at me. "Look, buddy, I have no idea—"

Derek crashes the guard into the side of the bus. He kicks out his legs and punches him hard in the stomach. The guard crumples to the ground. In a split second, Derek takes the MP5 submachine gun out of the guard's hands and pulls the Smith & Wesson semiautomatic pistol from his holster. He hands me the pistol, and we both jump back on the bus.

Derek sits behind the bus driver and points the MP5 at his head.

I stand on the steps and point the pistol out the door. I reach back, pull the handle and close the folding doors.

"Drive," Derek says.

The bus pulls out of the mine, and the workers cheer. The guard jumps to his feet and chases after us. He stops and speaks into the radio strapped to his chest.

The driver is an old frail white man with wispy gray hair. His hands shake on the wheel.

"What's your name?" Derek asks.

"Calvin, or just Cal."

"Friends call you Cal?"

"Yes, sir."

"Then we'll call you Cal. We mean you no harm, Cal. Just keep driving south."

"Yes, sir."

"You have anything sharp?"

Cal reaches into a side bag and pulls out a pocketknife.

I cover Cal with my pistol while Derek works on the leather straps around my neck. The knife breaks through, and I spit out the beanbag.

"Whew. Man, oh man. What a relief. Yeah."

"Welcome back."

"Boy, did that suck."

Derek smiles. "It wasn't so bad."

"For you."

"Kind of nice, actually."

"Sorry to ruin your day. So where does your plan C go from here?"

Derek sits square behind Cal.

I sit in the seat across from him.

Derek pats Cal on the shoulder. "Cal here is going to drive us all the way to Washington, DC, where we can raise awareness as to the slave-labor conditions we faced here in the mines at the FUC Wall."

I smirk. "Easy as that."

"Easy as that." Derek puts his head low, leans over to me, and whispers. "We'll pull the old slip along the line somewhere. If we can somehow trick or convince Cal to keep driving the bus toward DC, then we can catch another ride to the Cherokee reservation."

I frown, about to ask him how we could possibly ever convince Cal to keep going if we're not on the bus, but just then the bus radio comes to life. "Operator Olsen, come in," says the voice on the radio.

"Is that you?" Derek asks.

"Yes, that's me. Calvin Olsen."

"Go ahead and answer," Derek says. "And speed this thing up."

Cal increases the speed of the bus to seventy miles per hour. He reaches for the radio microphone. "This is Olsen."

"What's going on there, Olsen?"

Cal looks quickly back at Derek. Derek nods for him to talk.

"I think I've been taken hostage."

Silence.

"You think?" the speaker says.

Cal looks around. When he realizes we aren't going to say anything he talks. "I know. I mean, I have. I have been taken hostage."

Silence.

"How many are there?"

Derek taps Cal's shoulder. "Don't tell him."

"What do they want?"

"Tell them to stay away," I say. "No vehicles, no road-blocks, nothing."

Calvin relays the message, and we drive unencumbered for several miles before the radio voice returns.

"You there, Calvin?"

Cal picks up the mic. "Still here. Everything is good."

I notice a helicopter high in the sky. It comes closer and follows us from a short distance. "Helicopter is following us."

"Tell them to move that chopper away from us," Derek says.

"Move the chopper away," Cal says.

"How old are you, Calvin?" the speaker asks.

The chopper moves closer to us.

Derek and I look at each other. He shrugs.

"I'm seventy," Cal says.

"The terrorists who have taken you are bad people, Calvin. Who knows what they may try to do? Innocent Americans may be in danger."

"Tell them to move the chopper," I say.

"Move the chopper," Cal says.

"You've lived a good life, Calvin. Are you prepared to make the ultimate sacrifice for your country?" the radio voice asks.

"I'm a retired math teacher. I drive a bus part time. I don't know what you're talking about."

"One strike, Calvin. The chopper can obliterate the bus with one strike, and the threat to the United States will be neutralized. Are you prepared to make the sacrifice, Calvin?"

"They're nuts, Cal," I say. "Tell them you want to live."

Cal presses the microphone button and in a soft raspy voice says, "I want to live."

"You want to live?"

"Yes."

"Damn it, Calvin." The speaker pauses. "Are you saying you want to live?"

"Yes."

Silence.

"Calvin?" the speaker says.

"Yes, Calvin here."

"Okay," the speaker says. "For the last time, I want to confirm that you want to live."

"I want to live."

The radio voice is silent. The chopper flies higher into the air before veering off and vanishing.

Derek slaps Cal on the back. "Good job, man."

Cal wipes his brow. "I don't know what's happening to this country."

"Us either," I say. "And we aim to do something about it."

We drive on in silence for a peaceful while until the radio voice speaks again.

"Come in, Calvin."

"Calvin here."

"Calvin, the life expectancy of the American male is seventy-eight years," says the radio voice. "For you, that's eight more years. Eight years of fourteen-hundred-a-month Social Security payments, plus two thousand a month from the teacher's retirement fund, plus eight hundred a month from your part-time bus job. Stay with me now, Calvin. When you die in eight years, your wife will only get a portion of your Social Security, which will be nine hundred and fifty dollars a month until she dies, which is expected to be in another fifteen years at her then age of eighty-two. Are you following this, Calvin?"

Cal looks irritated. "What's your point?"

"The point is that the present value of all these payments, discounted at a fair risk-free United States Treasury geeeearunteed interest rate of three percent, is forty thousand eight hundred and twenty-three dollars. Calvin, in the case of your unexpected death in valiant service to your country, we have been authorized to offer you triple value for your expected payments, or a one-time lump-sum payment of one hundred twenty-two thousand four hundred and sixty-nine dollars. That's a lot of money, Calvin. Imagine what your wife could do with that. Imagine how happy she would be. And all because of your careful planning."

Cal grabs the microphone. "I told you, I want to live."

"Calvin, Homeland Security, the IRS, the FBI, the CIA, the United States Armed Forces, the United States Border Patrol, the United States Park Rangers, the Montana Teachers' Retirement System, the United States Treasury, and the Social Security Administration all deem this more than fair compensation and have signed off on your early demise under valiant service to your country."

"I want to live, you asshole!"

"Sorry, Calvin, but unless that bus stops and the terrorists surrender in the next two minutes, the aforementioned plan will be activated, and you will expire under operation School Bus Stop—Torch and Burn—No Terrorist Left Behind."

Three Apache helicopters appear on the horizon in front of us.

"Nuts," I say.

"I think they're serious," Cal says.

Derek puts his MP5 down. "What kind of country wastes hostages?"

"And so quickly," I say.

Derek punches the back of his seat. "I mean, taking hostages is an internationally accepted tactic to begin negotiations."

I put down my gun. "Stop the bus, Cal."

"Morons," Derek says.

The bus comes to a stop.

"Tell them we're surrendering," I say.

"They surrender," Cal shouts into the mic. "We surrender. Don't shoot."

The speaker crackles. "Leave the bus. Arms in the air."

The Apaches turn and leave. Black Suburbans, Humvees, and Crown Victorias appear and surround us.

I lead the way out, my arms in the air.

"Nice to meet you, Cal," Derek says. "Sorry about the inconvenience."

Cal nods. "It was eye opening. Thanks for sparing me."

"Enjoy your eight years," I say.

Guards surround and cuff us. A chain runs down from our handcuffs and connects to a chain between our legs that attaches to cuffs around our ankles. They push us into the backseat of a Crown Victoria. Two guards sit up front, and we drive off, escorted by Humvees fore and aft.

"What were you two thinking?" a guard asks.

I can't tell him what we were thinking. We were thinking that we were invincible super-spies. Despite astronomical odds against us, we believed that as freedom fighters and overall good guys, we would be destined to prevail. We're idiots. The fight leaves me, and I can feel my body again. My arms and legs are in pain. My hands are still raw from the jackhammer. Derek and I remain silent, looking at the floor. I close my eyes and would like to sleep, but I am too tired and in too much pain.

"No one tries to escape," the guard says. "You do your three months and you're done. It's not that hard. Now you're screwed."

"What's going to happen?" I ask.

"Up to the commandant. Ain't going to be good—he's a hard-ass."

We drive back to Sunburst, through the gate, and down the main road past the rows and rows of barracks. The barracks come to an end, and the road curves into a grassy area filled with trees landscaped to perfection. A stately red-brick manor house sits upon a hill. We drive up the circular drive and come to a stop.

The car doors open and Derek and I are pulled out and surrounded by guards. They walk us into the house, and we shuffle to keep up, but it's difficult because my legs are so tired. We walk past a waiting area through French doors into an expansive office. A testosterone-inspired mahogany desk sits before us. Behind the desk, floor-to-ceiling mullioned beveled windows reveal a garden and pond.

An icicle of a woman sits behind a petite desk in the corner. She speaks as if we are intruding. "Have a seat. The commandant will be here momentarily."

Derek and I sit before the muscle desk. A guard sits on each side of us, and the others stand along the wall. We sit so for forty-five minutes. Even the usually disciplined guards impatiently shift.

A side door opens. A guard appears in it. "All rise for the commandant."

Everyone stands, and the guards enter, followed by the commandant and another guard.

The commandant looks like a fat Nazi SS trooper. He is dressed in all black with knee-high riding boots. He has a short horsewhipper in his hand. A captain's cap with an eagle medallion tilts slightly on top of his head. Dark aviator sunglasses cover his eyes.

He lumbers his large frame over and stands behind the desk.

Derek and I look to the floor.

The commandant leans over the desk and places both his hands in the center.

Derek and I look up.

A huge grin breaks across the commandant's face. He reaches for his sunglasses and dramatically pulls them off.

I look into the chubby face of former ASU campus cop, Officer Hubert Salsbury.

26

Traitors are not gentlemen, my friend.
—SENATOR JOSEPH McCARTHY

HUBERT SLAPS THE DESK and laughs. "Well, well, well. What have we here? This is a very interesting development."

I don't care anymore. "How's it going, Hueeey?" I say with a sneer.

The rest of the room looks at me wide-eyed.

Hubert reaches across the desk and smacks me across the face with his whip.

"Ow!"

"A little respect for the commandant, now, Special Agent Thompson. Oh, ho, ho!"

Hubert has reopened a mining wound. I feel blood dripping down the side of my cheek. "What lunatic made you commandant?"

"I think you know the answer to that." Hubert points his whip at my face. "And if it weren't for your embarrassing escape, I'd be down near Mexico rounding up real border-jumping criminals. Instead I was sent up here to Paul Bunyan land to scare away lumberjacks."

"Seems like you're doing pretty well," I say.

Hubert slaps his whip into his hand. "Not too shabby, I admit. But now with you two little nuggets, I'll be golden." He looks at Derek. "You must be Cannonball."

Derek looks at Hubert evenly, without a trace of emotion. "I can explode at any time," he says.

"Ho, ho. A comedian."

"How can you be so underhanded?" I ask. "Didn't they teach you any morality in those criminal justice classes at ASU?"

"Plenty. But the morality of the world is that the strong persevere. Survival of the fittest—that's the moral to life, regardless of the means."

I notice a small cross hanging from a thin silver necklace around Hubert's neck. I look at the necklace intently and nod at the cross. "'Turn the other cheek' mean anything to you?"

Hubert smacks his whip against the desk. "Get 'em out of here!"

The guards grab our arms.

"What are you going to do with us?" I ask.

Hubert laughs a quiet, evil chuckle. "Right now you guys are Big Mac's number one target. I'm going to make a few calls and parlay my little find into something really grand—maybe a DC post."

"Maybe you could be a Cub Scout master," I say.

Hubert flings his hands into the air. "Get 'em out of here. Put 'em in the hole."

The guards look confused. One of them finally says, "Um, we don't have a hole, Commandant."

"Dig one then, idiots."

The guards grab our arms and lead us to the door.

Hubert calls to us as we exit. "Didn't appreciate that

tranquilizer dart—made me look like a fool. I'll get my revenge, mind you. Think about that while you're in the hole, suckers."

The guards drive us to the barracks closest to the manor house. It serves as a guard command center.

They sit us down at a table in a break room.

"Heck with Baby Huey," one says. "I'm not digging any hole."

"Who does that peach-fuzzed balloon-head think he is?" another says. "Only been here two days and he treats us like crap."

"Careful. They say he has connections—all the way to the White House."

We sit in the break room for an hour, and the guards are nice enough to feed us. They bring in two cots. "There you go. Welcome to the hole."

We sleep that night on the cots as the guards take turns watching us. In the morning we eat breakfast with the guards like family. I wonder what Hubert has in store for us. Soon we will be in Slater's control, and that will be it. A guard's cell phone rings. "Yes, sir. We'll be ready." He hangs up. "Solves the hole problem. We're moving these prisoners in twenty minutes."

"Where to?"

"Don't know, but we're supposed to prepare for at least a three-day trip."

True to plan, in twenty minutes we are ushered outside. A three-vehicle caravan pulls up, a Suburban sandwiched between two Humvees. The black Suburban has dark tinted windows. "Commandant" is printed in white lettering on the side.

Hubert steps out of the passenger side of the Suburban. "I got my badass SUV, as promised."

"If the Tri-Delts could see you now," I say.

Hubert points at me. "That's right, that's right."

I sit behind Hubert. Derek sits behind me in the third seat. A guard drives, and a guard each sit next to Derek and me.

"Settle in for a long drive, boys," Hubert says.

"Where are we going?" I ask.

"All the way to Nevada. Area 22. You boys are going to be the special guests at a big meeting—hee, hee."

"I'm honored." When I was stuck in the jail cell at ASU, Slater said he would send me back to Emergence. Looks like he is keeping his word. I try to think of a plan. Hubert is the key. We have to figure out how to trick him again. "I look forward to speaking at this meeting about the conditions at your FUC Wall. Did they invite you to the meeting, Commandant?"

"Oh, yes. I am invited. I'm a very big wig, now, you see. Hee, hee. And I don't think Mr. Slater plans on letting you two do any talking."

"Wow, Mr. Slater!" Derek says. "That's one big wig."

"Yes, indeed," Hubert says with pride. "And not only Mr. Slater, but someone else very powerful wants my sage advice." He rubs his hands together. "I'm not supposed to say anything, but the top, top dog will be at the meeting as well."

Why would Slater bring President Wright to Emergence? The answer hits me before I finish the question. It's obvious. Tomorrow is May 2, the Utopia Day, the chosen ones' day to enter the Tunnel of Love and meet their death. Slater is bringing the president, Derek, and me to Emergence to kill us, too. No. Slater has control of the president; killing him will only cause problems. Unless the vice president is a Big Mac insider? No, that doesn't make sense—if that were true, Slater would have had the president killed a long time ago. Perhaps the simple answer is that Slater needs to keep an eye on the president wherever he goes now.

Hubert rubs his legs. "I swell up if I sit for long periods." He takes his shoes and socks off. "My feet sweat too." A miserable moldy stench fills the Suburban. Hubert leans back and places his feet on the dashboard. "First class."

We drive this way for hours, into the late afternoon.

Hubert's cell phone rings. "Yes, sir—got it." He holds the phone to his ear and turns around to look at us. His face goes pale. "Um, yes, sir. No problem, sir. You can count on me." He hangs up and whispers something to the driver.

In fifteen minutes, we turn from our southerly direction onto a road heading west. We enter a town called Atomic City. Out-of-business stores line the dust-covered streets. A lone bar with Atomic City souvenirs in the window has a single neon sign that says it is open. The caravan comes to a halt. Everyone exits the vehicles, including us.

Hubert has a conference with two guards and then returns to the Suburban. This time, he sits on the driver's side.

The guards open the back door of the Suburban and fold down the seats. They produce two straitjackets and wrap them tightly around Derek and me.

"What the hell, Hubert?" I yell.

He smiles out the open driver's-side window. "Going for a little drive. Revenge time."

Perspiration forms above my upper lip. We're not going to make it to the Emergence meeting. They're going to dump us somewhere. I struggle against the claustrophobically tight straitjacket.

They wrap duct tape around our legs from our ankles to our knees. We are immobilized. Two guards pick me up and put me in the back of the Suburban like I'm in a body bag. Three men lift Derek and do the same. We lie on our backs with our heads to the rear of the vehicle. As a final insult, they duct-tape our mouths shut and close the door.

The Suburban moves. Hubert laughs and squeaks. "Only you and me now, boys."

We drive for ten minutes.

"Shifting to four-wheel drive. Off-road time, boys."

The Suburban shakes and bounces, jarring Derek and me uncomfortably around.

"Whoo hoo."

The Suburban dips and it feels like we are racing down a hill. We flatten out and the ride is smoother. We come to a stop and the engine turns off.

The rear door opens and Hubert's face grins down at us. He reaches in and rips the tape off our faces.

"Ow."

"Jesus."

"That's right. I want to hear your pain."

Hubert grabs me by the shoulders and pulls me out. I land on the ground with a dead thud. Derek comes out the same way and lands partially on top of me. Hubert goes back in the Suburban and starts the engine. The Suburban slowly rolls away from us.

Derek and I squirm around until we are lying next to each other on our stomachs. He has dirty sand all over his face. I can taste the same on mine.

"Is he leaving us here?" Derek asks.

The Suburban stops and Hubert gets out holding a rifle.

"No. He's going to kill us," I say.

"How can you sound so resigned about it?" Derek asks.

I don't know. The fight has gone out of me. I feel nothing. I lift my head. We are on a sandy bank in the bend of a fast-flowing river. The sun is about to set, and the few kite-like clouds on the horizon are pink.

"I'm sorry," I say. "Sorry for everything."

Hubert approaches us. "Too bad, boys, but our plans have changed. Evidently they don't want you at the meeting in Nevada after all. I'm supposed to put you out of your misery."

Hubert pisses me off. I feel again. "You'll pay for this, you big fat bastard."

Hubert laughs. "Au contraire, mon frère. I will be hand-somely rewarded for this."

"Go to hell," Derek says.

"Now, now, take it like men." Hubert puts his hands together. "Say your prayers—you have sixty seconds."

I think of Karen and Scotty and my dead parents and grandparents. I think of Karen and Scotty. I curse myself for agreeing to this mission. I think of Karen and Scotty. I forgive everyone I've ever hated and pray to God for forgiveness. I think of Karen and Scotty.

"Bye-bye, boys."

I shut my eyes, and my ears scream as the gun goes off. I open my eyes and look to Derek. His lips are quivering uncontrollably. Tears stream down his cheeks. He is sobbing.

"Ha, ha. Sorry, boys, just testing the gun. Get ready for the real shebang."

I look up and see a small speck on the horizon in the orange setting sun. The speck grows larger as it approaches us. It's a Black Hawk helicopter.

"They're coming for you, Hubert," I say.

Hubert looks up and around. "What's that?"

"Don't you see that chopper?"

He puts his hand to his forehead like a visor. "What of it?"

"You really think they're going to let you live, too?"

"Yeah," Derek says. "After you waste us they're going to waste you. You know too much about us."

Hubert looks shaken. "They wouldn't."

"Don't you watch any spy movies?" I say.

He squeaks softly. "We had a deal."

I laugh. "Too good a deal for you. Let me guess—they agreed to all your outrageous demands."

"Damn," Hubert says.

"Untie us," I say. "Our only chance is to fight them together."

A laser-guided Boeing SLAM-ER missile shoots from the Black Hawk and heads straight for us.

Hubert runs and dives into the sand.

The missile whines and plows into the Suburban with a terrific explosion. The heat and fumes make me nauseous.

The Black Hawk circles around and hovers. Slowly it begins to descend. It lands fifty yards away from us.

Hubert stands up and runs.

"Hey!" I shout. "Untie us. Don't leave us."

Hubert dives into the river like a walrus and swims frantically away. He goes underwater and reappears in the center. I watch as his head bobs. The current carries him swiftly downstream. He rounds the bend and disappears.

The Black Hawk's engine turns off, and its rotors slow to a stop. A figure emerges, and spiderlike blue-jeaned legs run toward us in the sand. A black mess of hair bounces to the runner's gait and flies back in the breeze.

"Wizkid," I shout.

Derek is too excited to speak coherently. "Hey, hey, hey, what, what?"

Wizkid reaches us, panting heavily. "Sol? Larry? What's up with the new digs?" He begins unfastening Derek's straitjacket.

"What about me?" I ask. "Why is he first?"

"He didn't insult my girlfriend."

Derek's arms are free. He goes to work on the tape around his legs.

Wizkid unfastens my straitjacket and then helps me with my legs.

Derek and I jump to our feet.

After being so close to death, I'm elated to be alive. Endorphins pulse through my brain. I hug Wizkid. "Thank you."

Derek is ecstatic as well. He jabbers on incomprehensibly and laughs and laughs.

We raise our fists into the air, shout, and hug.

Derek gives me a shove and laughs. "You pissed your pants." He points at my wet crotch. "You big wuss. You were so scared you pissed yourself."

"Me?" I point at him. "You blubber baby crying sack of shit—look before you speak."

Derek looks down at himself and discovers that he too has pissed his pants.

"What smells?" Wizkid says.

Derek looks over his left shoulder and then his right. He looks thoughtfully toward the sky. "Um, I may have shit my pants too."

Wizkid and I start laughing.

Derek laughs too. "I guess I was pretty scared."

"Scared as I've ever been," I say.

Derek punches me in the shoulder. "I thought you were a dead man."

I punch him back. "I thought *we* were dead men."

"We *were* dead men." Derek puts both his hands in the air. "Give it up."

I put my hands up and clasp his.

"We went to the brink and back," Derek says.

"We faced death together," I say.

"You all need to end this lovefest," a deep voice says.

Samuel, our gray-haired escort into Star, Utah, stands before us. "We should skedaddle out of here," he says.

"How'd you get here?" I ask.

Wizkid points to the Black Hawk. "Who do you think flew that beast?"

"Let's go," Samuel says.

We walk toward the chopper.

"How'd you get a Black Hawk?" Derek asks.

"We sort of requisitioned one," Wizkid says.

"How the hell do you requisition a Black Hawk?" Derek says. "Doesn't seem possible."

"In the dark of the night, anything is possible," Samuel says.

"Ye, ye, yeah," Wizkid says. "This Black Hawk no longer officially exists."

"You erased its records?" I ask.

Wizkid smiles proudly. "Yep."

"So you can get back into the government mainframes?"

"Didn't you listen to what he just said?" Derek says.

"I know, I know. I just wanted to confirm it."

The wind blows Wizkid's hair in front of his face, but he doesn't seem to mind. "Um, the army's mainframe, anyway. Border patrol is still giving me problems. The invasion continues."

I look at Derek. "You see?"

We reach the Black Hawk. The green flying monster looks awesomely tough.

"Samuel," I say. "You actually know how to fly one of these?"

"Of course. I told you I worked for the government. Who do you think taught your friend Fixer how to fly? I'm the best pilot in the world."

"I guess you did," I say.

We climb into the helicopter. Samuel sits in the captain's seat.

"Take copilot, Chris," Wizkid says.

I'm not fighting anymore about bunk beds or seats. "No. That's all right. You can sit there."

"No way." Wizkid straps himself in a side harness. He closes his eyes. "Can't stand this thing. I can't look."

They have brought apples and water. Derek and I drink and eat.

"Why did you blow up the Suburban?" I ask. "We could have been inside."

Samuel shakes his head like it was nothing. "Naw, I had it figured out." He fires up the Black Hawk.

"Still, a bit excessive."

"Naw." He clenches his fist and pounds it in the air. "Hit 'em hard with a bang. Shock and awe! Remember? Never fails."

The Black Hawk lifts off the ground.

"You the man," Derek shouts.

Samuel points straight out the front window. "Back in the game." A change has overcome him. He has transformed from an easygoing retiree back into whatever secret force the government had trained him to be.

The Black Hawk tilts and races forward.

Wizkid's eyes are closed, and his white knuckles clench his harness.

"How the hell did you find us?" I ask.

Samuel points his thumb to the back. "Patrick found your friend there coming into Star. Evidently his girl dumped him, and he was trying to find you guys. Patrick brought him over to stay with Barbara and me."

"Sorry about Jenny," I shout toward Wizkid.

Wizkid continues to grimace. "Just tell me when this ride is over," he says.

Samuel shouts over the Black Hawk rotor's *whup whup*. "I let him use my computer. We were able to contact a couple old friends of mine in the government. Figured out something was going to go down in Atomic City. Indications hinted that you two were involved and in trouble, so we took a chance."

"Did you really need a Black Hawk?"

"It worked, didn't it?"

"Yeah, but . . ."

"But you can never be overprepared. Besides, I've got other plans."

"I'm guessing that you believe our story, and you aim to save your son."

Samuel shakes his fist. "Damn right. Tomorrow's Utopia Day, a day that used to inspire great hope and pride for me and all the citizens of Star. Now I look on it with dread. I have to save Daniel. We have to save all the boys—and the women too. We have to do everything we can."

The cockpit computer displays and electronic dials come to

life as the sun goes down. It all seems so confusing, but Samuel pilots the Black Hawk with an easy confidence. He's a man on a mission, a warrior in combat mode.

"We also heard there's some big meeting with Slater, and possibly the president," Derek says.

"I don't give a flying saucer what nincompoop is there," Samuel says. "I plan on going in hell's bells, whooping ass on whoever's responsible, and saving my boy."

The plan sounds reckless to me. It's the plan of an over-zealous old fighter with no qualms about sacrificing himself. We have until tomorrow; perhaps we can refine the mission somewhat.

"Where are we going?" I ask.

"We've got friends who live on an isolated ranch in Idaho. It has an airstrip. We'll be able to refuel and spend the night. You two look like you could use the rest—and you're going to need it."

We fly over rolling, unpopulated land, chasing the fallen sun.

"Oh, I forgot," Samuel says. "Your family showed up."

The blood rushes to my head. "They did?"

"Patrick reeled them in as well. They're safe at my place."

I ask Samuel questions about Karen and Scotty.

He holds up his hand. "Whoa, now. You have to ask the kid. It all went down when I was obtaining the chopper. I never actually saw your family."

I turn to ask Wizkid, but he still looks petrified and unable to communicate.

Samuel points into the distance. "There she is. Coordinates are right on."

I look out the window but have trouble seeing in the twilight. Samuel lowers the Black Hawk and a ranch comes into clearer view. He swoops in low over buildings and a thin black-top runway. We turn and hover. A spotlight near the end of the runway flashes twice.

"We're good," Samuel says.

He slowly moves the Black Hawk in and sets us down on the grass between the runway and a small hangar.

When the engine shuts off, Wizkid tumbles out and kisses the ground.

A man about Samuel's age approaches. A cowboy hat enhances his height, and a cattle-fed belly sags over an oval chrome belt buckle that holds up his blue jeans.

"Stay here." Samuel walks over to the man. They shake hands and pat each other on the shoulder. They talk for a few moments and then walk over to us.

Samuel holds up a hand. "No introductions. Our host has generously offered use of his hangar tonight. There's a small room we can sleep in that has a shower." He looks at Derek. "There's a water hose behind the hangar—might be better for you in your current predicament."

Derek nods and, embarrassed, looks to the ground.

The rancher takes a moment to eye each of us. He doesn't seem impressed and looks rather uncertain. "Samuel says y'all are Big Mac believers, and I appreciate that, but I'm sure ya understand. We don't mix much with strangers."

Wizkid, Derek, and I don't say a word. We stand and listen, and try to appear respectful.

"I have a couple of rules." The rancher removes his hat and uses it as a pointer as he gestures around the property. "Rule number one. Under no circumstances are you to leave the hangar area. The grounds and ranch house are strictly off limits." He points his hat at each one of us. "And under no circumstances are you to have any interaction with my wife or daughters." I hear Wizkid gulp. "In the unlikely event that you encounter my wife or daughters, you shall look to the ground and remain silent." The rancher puts his hat back on. "Are we good?"

Wizkid, Derek, and I nod.

Our host nods back. "I'll bring some clothes for you two." He turns around and walks off.

We walk into the hangar. Bright lights illuminate a smooth, clean concrete floor. An American flag hangs high from the ceiling's peak. Posters of airplanes line the light-yellow aluminum walls. A polished single-engine Cessna shines at one end. The rest of the hangar is empty, but there is easily room for two more small planes.

The rancher brings out blankets and pillows. He gives Derek and me oversize boxers, T-shirts, and blue jean overalls. "Keep 'em."

Derek grabs his new clothes and walks out to use the hose.

The rancher shows us into a multipurpose room. There is a small kitchenette with a coffeemaker. Underneath a high rectangular window a circular card table sits close to a wall. Worn chairs and a sofa sit before a wall-mounted flat-screen TV. The whole room is covered in a thin beige carpet. "Make yourself at home." The rancher nods and leaves.

I take a seat in a chair. Samuel sits on the couch. Wizkid fiddles with the coffee machine.

"About tomorrow?" I say to Samuel. "Let's talk about the details."

Samuel looks toward me like a father would to a defiant son. "I thought I made it pretty clear."

"Yes, I know you did. But I'm just wondering exactly how we are going to fly a Black Hawk helicopter into a secure zone, capture the bad guys, and save the chosen ones below ground."

"Exactly like that. Exactly like I said. With guns a-blazing and God at our backs."

"But." I pause. "We have to obtain evidence. Otherwise we're the criminals."

Samuel is losing his patience. "So obtain the evidence." He tilts his head and raises his eyebrows. "You know where it is, right?"

"Well, I, er, I know what the room looks like, but—"

"Son, these Big Mac fellas don't understand diplomacy. It's going to be war—blood, chaos, and crap! Full-press destruction. You can't sweat the details."

"I can," I say.

"We know we're in the right, right?"

"Yeah."

"So the forces of good are on our side." Samuel puts his hand on my shoulder. "Don't worry—you'll know what to do when the time comes."

I'm not so sure. I absentmindedly try to spin the missing PRAD on my finger and squeeze my knuckle.

Samuel goes to fuel up the Black Hawk and check on her systems.

Derek walks into the room looking like a sloppy farmer. Wizkid and I laugh.

"Overalls are a little big," he says.

I walk over to a bookshelf that is next to the circular table. It's filled with old paperbacks and framed photographs. I look at a small photo of the rancher and his family. He stands on their front porch next to his wife and three beautiful girls.

Derek looks over my shoulder. "No wonder the house is off limits."

"We're nothing to worry about."

"Don't forget, Wizkid is a player."

I laugh. "That's right. I forgot."

I point to the photograph. "The oldest girl looks familiar."

"I think she was at the sorority party," Derek says.

"No, no. Her hair is longer, and she is younger here, but that's Flipper's fiancée. Remember the photo from Samuel's house? This rancher's daughter is a chosen woman in the women's shelter."

Samuel comes back. "Chopper's ready to go. Lights out."

Derek, Wizkid, and I claim areas on the thinly carpeted floor and prepare to sleep.

I close my eyes. Derek is snoring already. I whisper to Wizkid. "Wizkid—you saw my family?"

"Yeah, your kid is smart. He could be a fine hacker someday. I'd be happy to show him the ropes."

"Thanks, but no. Mrs. Hamilton is teaching him just fine." I pause a moment. "How is Karen?"

"Worried—really worried."

"I figured."

Wizkid sits up. "Sorry to pry, but what's the deal with that dork she's hanging out with?"

"Dork?"

"Guy with a bushy mustache. Always seems to be lurking around, always has something to say."

I can't believe that buffoon came with them. "Archie."

"That's it—Archie. He drove your wife and kid in his RV."

"RV? Archie has an RV?"

"Old Winnebago—four-wheel drive."

I thought things between Karen and me had been straightened out. I felt good after our last conversation. Am I being fooled? Stomach acid burns in my chest. "Where were they sleeping?"

"In the RV."

"The three of them? Where exactly in the RV were they sleeping?"

"I'm sorry, man. I don't know."

I sleep fitfully, worrying about Karen and that stooge Archie, supposedly my friend.

* * *

"Turn on the TV!"

It's morning. The rancher marches into the room. He retrieves a remote control from a small cabinet underneath the flat screen. He points the remote and the TV comes to life.

Vance Slater stands large before the camera. He wears an

impressive-looking black suit with a red tie. His hair is impeccably groomed. Behind Vance stands Chief Justice Timothy Lancaster. He wears his robe and leans on a cane.

"Citizens of America," Slater says. "Due to security reasons, I am speaking to you from an undisclosed safe location. Joining me is Chief Justice Timothy Lancaster. Also joining me via video from the White House is Senate Majority Leader Lance Pearlman and Speaker of the House Joiner Dixon. From the Pentagon we have Joint Chiefs of Staff chairman General George McGuffin with the other members from the Joint Chiefs of Staff." The TV is split in two as the men Slater introduced are shown from the Pentagon and White House. They nod and say a chorus of hellos. The screen returns to Slater. "I wish to announce that President Oscar I. Wright has officially resigned as president of the United States of America due to mental health reasons. The president has been having episodes that detrimentally affect his duties, episodes that we are no longer able to control."

The president runs into the camera's view. He runs around Slater and Lancaster laughing like a wild hyena. Two men in white suits chase him. The president dives into a sofa and does donkey kicks high into the air. The men in white suits try to subdue him, but the president runs up a stairwell and then back down again, laughing all the while.

Wait a minute. I recognize that room. It's the rendezvous room underground at Emergence, where the tunnels meet and the chosen men and women are supposed to hook up. Slater must be using the broadcast station.

The president is caught and led away. The room's attention is brought back to Slater. "Due to our war with Canada and Mexico, the president's resignation has forced the Big Mac Party to declare martial law. Additionally, because of incendiary un-American influences from Canada and Mexico within Congress, Chief Justice Lancaster has declared the current Congress of the United States unconstitutional. Vice President Carlson and other recently sworn Big Mac loyalists have elected me, Vance Douglas Slater, as Chancellor of the States for all America." Slater pauses. "Gentlemen, do you agree?"

The screen reverts back to the men in Washington, DC. They all say, "I do."

"Thank you," Slater says. "I will now take the oath of office."

Slater steps in front of the American flag and the photograph of Senator Joseph McCarthy that I remember as part of the shelter's broadcast station. Chief Justice Lancaster places a Bible in front of Slater. Slater puts his left hand on the Bible and raises his right. Lancaster starts reciting an oath of office, which Slater greedily smiles and repeats.

I look around the room in shock.

The rancher wipes a tear from his eye. "It's a great day. A true America has risen again. Excuse me—I must enjoy this joyous moment with my family." The rancher leaves the room.

Slater finishes the oath and the camera switches to the DC men clapping. Slater addresses the camera again. "Thank you, America. We will be great again. I would now like Joint Chiefs of Staff chairman General George McGuffin to say a word."

General McGuffin stands tough in full regalia. His wide, erect frame takes up the whole TV screen. "America would like to inform the world that this afternoon, we will conduct an underground nuclear test. This test is necessary because of our current war and because of our need for precise tactical nuclear weapons to control and secure our land borders to the north and south." The general steps back, and the TV screen switches to a CNN newsroom.

A banner across the top of the screen reads *WANTED FOR TREASON*. Underneath the banner, photographs flash of Derek, Wizkid, and me.

Samuel turns off the TV.

I stand up and pace. "They're at Emergence, underground, in the rendezvous shelter. I'm sure of it."

Samuel stands up with me. "What's that malarkey about detonating a bomb?"

"Buster Able!"

"Buster what?"

"Buster Able. It's an old nuclear bomb stored in the rendezvous shelter. They're not testing anything. Emergence has served its purpose to Big Mac. They're going to blow up Emergence, kill all the chosen ones, and destroy all the evidence at once."

Derek slaps his hands together. "We better move."

"Now," Samuel says.

A high-pitched scream comes from the direction of the house.

I look around. "Where's Wizkid?"

27

This is the era of the Armageddon—that final all-out battle between light and darkness foretold in the Bible.
— SENATOR JOSEPH McCARTHY

"GET IN THE CHOPPER," Samuel says.

We run to the Black Hawk and pile in. Samuel brings her to life. He pulls back on the stick and lifts her ten feet off the ground. We circle around the hangar toward the house.

A woman stands on the front porch with a baseball bat in her hand.

Wizkid is running away from the house in a zigzag pattern. The rancher stands aiming his rifle at him.

Samuel swoops the Black Hawk down, and the rancher dives to the ground. We pass over him and spin around before Wizkid.

The rancher stands up and aims at us.

Samuel presses a button and the two 30mm autocannon machine guns tilt and rotate.

The rancher, recognizing our superior firepower, lowers his gun. He shakes his fist and stares at Samuel. "Communist!"

Samuel drops the chopper to the ground. We motion wildly for Wizkid to jump aboard. He looks uncertain at first, but then runs and climbs in. He crawls to his side spot, fastens his harness, and closes his eyes.

"What did you do?" Derek asks.

The Black Hawk lurches into the air.

Wizkid screams.

I put my hand on his shoulder. "Relax, man."

He breathes deeply. "I thought I was a goner."

"What did you do?" Derek asks again.

"I went for a walk and ended up by the farmhouse."

"We were told to stay away," Derek says. He puts his hands against his cheeks and opens his eyes wide. "That was the only rule we had to follow. You could've been killed."

Wizkid puts his head down and pulls on his hair. "I know, but I saw this suh-suh-smoking hot girl walk across the front porch into the house."

Derek looks at him scornfully. "And you couldn't resist?"

"I don't know. I think her mom saw me looking through a window."

Derek shapes his hands against his eyes like binoculars. "You were peeping them?"

"I, I, I was going to go to the front door and introduce myself." Wizkid looks up and around at us. He shrugs. "But I thought I'd see what I was dealing with first."

"Yeah," I say. "'Cause that's how you meet girls, Derek, you peep at them first."

Derek laughs. "Kids nowadays."

Wizkid shuts his eyes and clams up.

I climb up into the copilot's seat next to Samuel. "How long will it take to reach Emergence?"

"About four hours."

"Do we have enough fuel?"

"We should." Samuel points his thumb out the window. "This baby has an extra three-hundred-and-fifty-gallon tank."

The Black Hawk flies low to the ground, swerving in and out of canyons and valleys. The snow-tipped Rocky Mountains glare with reflected sunlight. Fresh morning-blue sky covers them. A river meanders through the green beneath us, flush with mountain spring water.

"Why so low?" I ask.

"Nate is bound to report us. I'm trying to avoid radar."

"Nate's the rancher?"

Samuel nods. "We were friends because of our kids, but he's just too deep into the faith to see any other possibilities."

We race along, a rogue bird over America, hoping to save the chosen ones' lives. And our own, too—if we cannot bring down Big Mac, Chancellor Vance Slater will never stop until we're dead.

* * *

It's been three hours. A red light blinks on the console. Samuel puts his flight helmet on and adjusts the microphone.

I put my helmet on as well.

An official-sounding voice is calling us. "Renegade Black Hawk come in. Slammer, Slammer, are you there? Renegade Black Hawk come in. Slammer, Slammer, are you there?"

I point at Samuel. "Are you Slammer?"

He grins. "Slammin' Sammy, back in the day."

"Don't answer."

He frowns at me. "I'm not a fool. They can jabber all they want."

We continue on in silence while the radio voice calls for Slammer.

Samuel turns and talks to us. "Twenty minutes away. Ready yourselves." He points at Derek. "Firearms are in the back."

Derek comes up with two Mini-Beryl 96 close assault rifles. They are coal black and compact with pistol and front grip. A curved magazine hangs down in the middle. It looks like a pimped-out AK-47. "You ever fire one of these?" he asks me.

"No."

Derek places the Mini-Beryl in my hands. "Nothing to it," he says.

My senses are alert. My eye twitches, and I concentrate on steadying my hands as I hold the gun.

"Relax." Derek grabs my wrist and moves my hand. "Hold the front grip for stability. Safety off, butt in the shoulder, aim, and go for it. Can you handle it?"

For the first time I recognize the futility of our mission. I'm an amateur holding a professional killing tool, and I'll be going up against people who know how to use weapons like these. We are going to die. I take a deep breath. *Bond, James Bond.* I smile at Derek. "Sure, I got it."

"I need more," Samuel says.

"More what?" Derek asks.

"Guns, man! We're going to war. Bring me more guns."

Derek returns to the back for knives, grenades, handguns, and another Mini-Beryl rifle. "That enough firepower for you, General?"

"Enough to get us started." Samuel sets the assault rifles next to one another and pockets the other weapons in his flight suit. "What about the kid?"

Derek looks at Wizkid. He sits frozen with his eyes shut. "A gun is probably not the best thing for him."

"Probably not," I say.

"Probably not," Samuel agrees.

Three F-18 fighters buzz over us with a roar. They shoot up into the sky and bank away in formation.

"Here we go," Samuel shouts.

"Slammer, come in," the radio continues.

"Bam, bam, Slammer here." He adjusts his headset microphone. "They've found us. Silence doesn't matter anymore."

"What's the situation, Slammer? Are you a renegade? What are your intentions?"

"Negative renegade. We have a hostage situation here. I've been taken hostage and forced to fly this helicopter by two escaped border patrol conscripts." Samuel looks at us and smiles.

"They don't play the hostage game," Derek says.

I point to the sky. "Apaches above." I count two Apache helicopters matching our movements.

"No sense in hugging the dirt anymore," Samuel says. He lifts the chopper into the air between the Apaches. He salutes them. "Howdy, friends."

The radio voice comes back on. "Are the hostage-takers middle-aged men—one white, pudgy with black hair? The other African-American, fat, and bald?"

Samuel looks at us and laughs. "That's them. Couple of softies."

"One moment," the radio voice says.

Samuel banks the chopper hard to the left. Our consorts are slow to react. "Almost there," he says.

"Slammer, how old are you now?" the radio asks.

"What?"

"Repeat, Slammer how old are you?"

I take my helmet off and throw it in the back. "We're done talking," I yell. I motion for Samuel to take off his helmet. He does.

Two miles away, helicopters and fighter jets circle and criss-cross the sky like a swarm of hornets. We are two thousand feet in the air. Samuel slows our speed to sixty-five knots. Below the circling planes and helicopters stands a thin two-story black rectangular building. Humvees and limousines are parked around the building. I feel the roar of the chopper in my bones, but the noise seems quiet as I concentrate.

"Area 22," Samuel says.

Derek shouts. "There! There!" He points out the side of the chopper.

We are one thousand feet away. Helicopters and airplanes converge on us to protect the building. Samuel banks the Black Hawk sharply and veers away.

I see what Derek is pointing at. A line of moving vehicles stretches down the two-lane highway for as far as I can see. There are cars, motorcycles, jeeps, minivans, station wagons, and campers of every description. There are thousands of them, and they are heading for the black building. Is it a protest? Has the public figured out the secrets of Emergence, too? Or is it some crazy desert festival searching for extraterrestrial life?

"What in tarnation?" Samuel says. He lowers the chopper, circles around, and comes in line with the front of the caravan.

A familiar yellow Yamaha Supersport YZF-R1 motorcycle leads the way. We are close enough to see the helmetless rider's face. He hugs the bike low, and his long black hair flies back in the wind. It's Land! Warrior paint covers his cheeks, and a rifle is slung over his back. Behind Land is the Cadillac Eldorado. Joemore is driving; his sleeveless, meaty arm hangs out the open window. A slim figure all in black sits next to Joemore. I can't see her face, but it must be Ninjenna.

It looks like the whole Cherokee Nation is following Land and the Eldorado. Land tilts his head and looks at our chopper with menace.

I wave to him through the glass frantically.

Land looks at me closer and sits up in surprise. He recognizes me.

I point ahead of us and pound my fist into my hand. I repeat this motion.

Land smiles, lifts a hand off the motorcycle and salutes us.

Joemore raises his fist in the air toward us as well.

"Whoo!" I yell. "It's Land." We have a chance now. I'm fired up. This is fun. Eat your heart out, 007.

Samuel lifts the Black Hawk higher into the air over Land's army. Two television-news helicopters fly beside us. I look down and spot TV news vans in the caravan as well.

"The press is here," I say. "I guess a full-on Native American uprising is still news."

"Slater's misguided army will be reluctant to shoot at us now," Samuel says.

When we come closer to the building Samuel slows the Black Hawk and hovers. The circling airplanes occasionally roar by us. Other Black Hawk helicopters hover over the building, facing us.

Land moves the motorcycle aside and falls in behind Joemore. The first vehicles trailing Joemore and Land are Chevy duallys that have Cherokee men crowded into their pickup beds. The men crouch low, their rifles pointing out.

The Eldorado smashes through a lowered gate and a closed fence. Land and the other vehicles pour in. The guards, recognizing that they are overwhelmed, do not resist. The caravan encircles the building. Their swarming numbers rapidly increase until the whole area is filled with Cherokee warriors.

The Cherokee army posts flags. They beat drums. Men stand on top of their vehicles whooping and hollering, raising their weapons into the air.

The Eldorado circles around and leaves the fenced area. It heads east; a group of twenty vehicles follow.

Derek points. "They're going to the Big Top Lounge," he says. "See it out in the distance?"

Samuel turns the Black Hawk around and speeds away. He climbs to a higher altitude and does a sweeping bank turn until we face the building again.

Two Apaches are on our tail. Fighters swoop over us. The Black Hawks over the building reposition themselves to thwart us.

"You boys ready?" Samuel asks.

"Ready for what?" Derek asks.

Samuel waves his hand around in the air, exactly as Fixer had done when we took off in the DC-10. "Ready to get this party started."

Derek sticks his head between Samuel and me. "The

Cherokee Nation seems to have it under control. Can't we just watch?"

"Baw!" Samuel says. "They need a spark. We came this far—let's have some fun."

"Rock 'n' roll," I say, caught up in the moment. We're going in; no anxious second-guessing. The air is sweltering and feels electric. Sweat stings my eyes and I wipe my brow with my forearm. Adrenaline rushes through my body and I love it. This is the excitement I craved and dreamed of. A few days ago, I would have been scared to the bone and cowering next to Wizkid. Now I relish the anticipation, and the action about to happen. *Quantum of Solace!*

"Strap yourselves in, boys," says Samuel. "Here we go."

The Black Hawk dives and accelerates. The engine whines and I'm pushed into my seat. Samuel banks it hard left and then right in a diving S curve.

Wizkid emits a high-pitched scream.

Something explodes outside the Black Hawk. We lurch and turn on our side. My head compresses into my chest. My mouth is dry and the air smells toxic. Samuel was wrong about their reluctance to fire on us.

Wizkid continues to scream.

"First blood!" Samuel shouts. "Shots fired. Let the record show we were fired on first—taking retaliatory measures."

The Black Hawk levels off.

Samuel shouts at me. "Man the cannons!"

I look around. "What?"

"Grab that stick. Press the orange button."

Another explosion goes off near us.

I grab the stick and look at him. "Now?"

"Wait! When I say."

The Black Hawk banks, swerves, dives, and rises, and might even roll. I can't tell in the confusion.

Wizkid continues to scream. His eyes are closed, and he clutches the side of his head.

"Fire now!"

I press the orange button and hold it.

Samuel presses some buttons, and rockets shoot forth from both sides of the Black Hawk.

I feel the vibrations and can hear the throaty *rut-tut-tut* of the mounted cannons.

We break through black smoke in front of us, and I see four helicopters that had been blocking our way explode.

Samuel dives us through the airborne debris. A fighter jet heads for us. There's a clear path to the Emergence building.

An explosion goes off in the rear of the Black Hawk. Warning bells and whooping noise fill the cockpit. Smoke fills the cabin. The Black Hawk starts to spin.

Wizkid, Derek, and I scream.

"Hold on, boys!" Samuel yells.

The Black Hawk straightens out, but we wobble and dive as we sweep over the Cherokee Nation and toward the building. We're going down. This is it. Cherokee warriors stand on vehicles and cheer us with their weapons in the air. I raise my fist to salute them. I feel the glory. "Yeah!"

Samuel somehow positions us over Emergence headquarters. The engine dies. The Black Hawk tilts sideways, and falls.

28

*But the record, my good friends, is that the damage has been done
by cleverly calculated subversion at home, and not from abroad.*
—SENATOR JOSEPH McCARTHY

WE CRASH THROUGH THE ROOF of the building. Dust and debris
fill the air. I cough and unbuckle. I look around. Everyone looks
a little dazed, but okay. "Go, go, go!" I yell.

Derek drops out of the chopper into the room below.

Wizkid continues to scream. He holds on to his harness
with his eyes closed.

I climb out my door and stand on the green metallic side
of the Black Hawk and look out over the roof. The Cherokee
Nation is attacking the building in force. I hear their shouts
and cries.

Samuel climbs over to Wizkid. He slaps him in the face
and unbuckles him. Wizkid opens his eyes, but appears shell-
shocked.

I drop into the room below and help Samuel lower Wizkid.
We walk him to a corner and let him sit down. He curls up into
the fetal position and closes his eyes.

"Let's go," Samuel yells.

I motion toward Wizkid. "We can't just leave him."

Samuel looks disgusted. "Are you going to haul his ass around? This is war."

I guess Samuel is right. Wizkid is probably safer here anyway. I pat Wizkid on the shoulder. "You're okay. Stay here. We'll be back."

Samuel, Derek, and I march into the hallway with our assault rifles.

Alarms sound and the sprinkler system sprays water into the empty hallway.

"Downstairs," I shout.

We run for the stairs and scramble down to the ground floor.

Outside I see guards walking from the building with their arms up, surrendering.

We run down the hall, and I bump into Land coming through the main entrance.

"Land!"

"Liaison, Cannonball." Land gives us each a manly hug. "My friends."

"Wonderful timing," I say.

"We saw you arrested on YouTube and figured you were a goner. Decided to take matters into our own hands."

I look around. "You have a lot of friends."

Land nods. "Those ashes I took—" His eyes narrow. "They were definitely from one of our chosen ones. We identified some dental filling pieces." Land opens his arms and turns around. "That riled everyone up."

"Boy, did it ever," I say.

"Called the press to witness this, too," Land says.

"Quit the chitchatting," Samuel says. "You two can have a tea party later. We've got to save the chosen ones."

"This way," I say. I run toward a room with a long window in the wall.

"Good memory," Land says.

We reach the window but can't see in because it is opaque from this side. Land tries the door, but it is locked. There are noises and a commotion inside the room. Someone is shouting commands.

"Get back," Samuel says.

Land holds his rifle in front of him. "I'll take out the window to distract them."

"I'll go in low." Samuel points to Derek. "Follow high."

Derek puts his hand on my shoulder. "Stay back, Chris. Let the professionals handle this."

"What? The hell with that. I'm going in with you." I'm disappointed. Hadn't I proven myself? I don't think Bond could have done any better until this point. I clutch my shaking gun and am about to argue, but Land cries out and runs. He points his rifle and shoots at the window, shattering it, and whoops and hollers as he passes.

Four armed guards stand in a line facing the door. I see the head of Chief Justice Timothy Lancaster disappear into the hatch that leads to the tunnel. Vance Slater stands next to the hatch, waiting to step in. The guards open fire on us.

Land fires back from the far end of the window.

Samuel kicks open the door and falls to the ground shooting.

Derek leans around the doorway and fires his Mini-Beryl.

The sound of gunfire deafens me.

Derek's body flies backward and lands on the floor against the far wall of the hallway.

The gunfire stops.

I can hear cries and moans from the next room. I run to Derek. He holds his upper arm. Blood spreads across his T-shirt. First Fixer and then Walter. Am I bad luck? Derek can't die. Not now. Not after we've made it this far.

Samuel runs into the room. He disarms the guards. Two are

dead. One lies on his side, a bloody mess, gasping for breath. The fourth has escaped into the tunnel.

The pursuers from our escape last week have cut off the hatch's lock handles. Land opens the lid and enters the hole. Samuel follows him.

I rip Derek's T-shirt open from his neck. Skin, muscle, and blood mushroom out of his upper arm. I take my T-shirt off and wrap it around his arm as tight as I can and hold on.

Derek pushes me in the chest with his good arm. "Go. I'll be all right."

Cherokee men flood into the hallway with hunting weapons; .22s, .30-.30 rifles, and double-barreled shotguns. One kneels down next to us. "I'm a paramedic," he says. He immediately takes hold of the shirt wrapped around Derek's arm and begins tying a skillful knot.

"Go," Derek says.

I stand up. "You sure?"

"This is nothing." Derek reaches his right hand up. "Give 'em hell."

I hold his hand. "Okay, see you soon."

I run into the room and turn to yell at the Cherokee men. "This way!" I crawl through the hatch and down the ladder to the metal stairs. The open hatch dimly lights my way as I run down. Land's and Samuel's flashlights move far below me.

Gunfire rings from the bottom and echoes throughout the stairwell. I increase my speed and descend recklessly into the dark. I wonder what tricks Slater has underground. There might be escape tunnels or secret weapons. This could be our only chance.

The men behind me catch up, and we descend the stairs as a snakelike mob clanking our way down until the next hatch. I open the lid and peer in. Someone has turned on the generator, because the lights are on. Samuel stands next to the door that leads to the men's tunnel. Land is guarding a pale, droopy-faced man. The man is Chief Justice Timothy Lancaster. His normally neat, side-parted hair is a scraggly mess.

The door to the women's tunnel flies open. A dark-skinned Cherokee woman stands with six white women. The white women are wearing floral-patterned knee-length dresses. They stare at the scene before them.

A woman with straight long hair says, "A supreme leader!" She runs toward Land and screams. "Stay away from Leader Lancaster." The other women run behind her.

Land doesn't know what to do. He holds the gun like a hockey stick and braces himself. The lead woman jumps on Land's torso and tears at his face with her fingers.

I recognize the woman. It's Flipper's fiancée.

I climb down through the hatch and rapidly descend the stairs. The men pour through behind me.

Land is spinning around with Cheryl. The other women are pulling on his arms, trying to bring him down.

"Cheryl!" I shout.

Cheryl looks up, surprised, and relaxes for a second. It's all the time Land needs; he pushes her off him.

The Cherokee men overwhelm the other women. Two or three hold on to each one.

"What's happening?" the Cherokee woman asks Land.

"Sky?" Land's features relax. His eyes look tenderly upon Sky. "I'm Land. Our people have come to save us."

Sky looks around. "But why?"

"I will explain later. Please just trust me, and your people."

The residency area continues to fill up with Land's men.

"Hey, Sky!" A Cherokee man coming down the stairs waves at her. "Remember me?"

"I remember." Sky smiles. "You were a foot shorter though, Jim."

The white women stop struggling, but they still look confused and suspicious.

Land nods to Samuel. "Slater went that way, down the men's tunnel."

I motion to some of the men. "Help Samuel cover the door." I nod to Lancaster. "Some men take him upstairs and guard him." Four men grab Lancaster and escort him back up through the hatch.

I say to Land, "Let's put the women in the back room."

"With the bomb?"

"Guns are more dangerous than that Buster Able right now."

"Eat shit." A heavy woman with short bobbed hair and a tough-set jaw stares at me. "You can shoot us now, because we ain't moving."

I ignore the woman and open the door to the back room. There sits Buster Able in all its faded glory. Chains are now wrapped around it. A man is strapped spread-eagled against Buster Able's wide belly. "'Bout time, Thompson," a raspy voice says.

"Mr. President!" I run to him and try to loosen his constraints, but they are too tight, and the padlock securing them is thick.

The women file in, subdued by the sight of President Wright tied up.

"Forget about the chains. This thing is going to go off. Get everyone out of here!" The president speaks coherently and with authority. He nods behind him.

Around the room are some metal file cabinets and a desk that were not here before. It takes a second for me to realize it, but the desk is the same one that contained all the microfiche. They have moved all the evidence down here.

"Fuck," Land says. Against one wall are urns, stacked two deep from the floor to the ceiling. "The chosen ones," Land explains to the women. "This is the Utopia. Death is the Utopia."

Behind the bomb, a laptop is set up. Wires protrude from it and enter into a small open hatch inside the bomb. I look into the hatch and see a small silver box with blinking blue and red lights.

"Don't touch a thing, Thompson," the president shouts.

I back away. A countdown timer fills the computer screen. The timer just dipped below nineteen minutes.

"Are you okay, sir?"

"Just dandy. Never felt better. Slater took away my Macwacky today so that I could be fully frightened by the big kaboom. He's got issues, that one."

An explosion sounds.

The president screams like a high-pitched little girl.

The door from the men's side blows open. Samuel flies backward to the ground. Smoke fills the hallway and oozes into the room.

A gun appears out of the smoke and fires indiscriminately. It's my PPK. X-ray races into the room, firing wildly. His blond, pomaded hair is stuck on end like a punk's, giving him a fierce look, but his blue eyes are wide like a frightened boy's.

Without thought, I aim my Mini-Beryl 96 assault rifle, pull the trigger, and put a string of bullets in X-ray's head.

Ten more guns fire after mine and riddle his body with more bullets. X-ray collapses to the floor.

I drop the rifle. What have I done? I kneel to the ground, my head spinning with adrenaline. My hands shake uncontrollably. I think of X-ray's smiling face from the chosen boys' group photo in Samuel and Barbara's house. He looked happy to be going to Emergence, like any American kid about to go to college. X-ray had no idea what awaited him. Was it his fault he had gotten twisted up in Slater's plan and had to torture people? My stomach turns, and I think I might vomit. Damn James Bond.

Samuel picks himself up off the ground and steps over to me. He grabs me by the shoulders and lifts me to my feet.

"I'm done," I say. "Bond is gone."

Samuel picks the gun up and places it in my hands. He slaps me in the face. "Toughen up. We're at war."

Land puts his hand on my back. "Let's go. I'm with you."

I stand up. Land's courage strengthens me. "Okay." ·

Samuel raises his assault rifle in the air. "After me, everybody. Ready? Move!"

He charges through the door. Land and I follow close behind.

Samuel pulls up and stops. Three feet away, through the smoke and dust, stands his son. Flipper has a pistol in his hand. Vance Slater stands behind him. Juice, Noodles, Beach, and Clutch stand behind Slater with makeshift weapons: a fire extinguisher, a butcher's knife, a vacuum cleaner pole, and a golf putter.

Samuel lowers his gun.

"Shoot him," Slater says to Flipper.

Flipper lowers his pistol.

Slater's face is red with fury. "Shoot him!" he screams. Spit flies from his lips.

Samuel smiles, and a tear forms in his eye. Slater grabs Flipper's arm and tries to wrestle the pistol from his hand.

Anger arises within me; anger at Slater for bringing me into this mess, anger at him for leading such a twisted program, anger at him for hijacking the presidency, anger at him for killing innocent people, and anger that because of him, I have killed someone.

I lunge forward and punch Slater with all my justified might. My fist lands on the side of his face, and I feel his jawbone crack. A tooth flies out of his mouth and he collapses, limp, to the floor.

Shouts come from the tunnel. The group from Land's army that broke off to the Big Top Lounge has made its way through the men's shelter and is now arriving. Joemore and Ninjenna are leading them. They come to a halt, surrounding the chosen boys.

"I surrender," Flipper says.

The rest of the chosen boys put their hodgepodge of weapons down. The guard does the same.

Samuel approaches Daniel and they embrace. "You're not surrendering, boys," Samuel says. "You're being rescued."

"Good to see you, Dad."

Samuel and Daniel, arm in arm, talk excitedly with each other.

Land's men tie Slater's hands and feet, string him up to a long pipe, and carry him like a shot deer.

"Hey, Liaison," Juice says.

I wave.

"What happened to X-ray?"

I pause and look at them without emotion. "Shot dead," I say.

"Get out of here!" the president is screaming from the back room. "An atomic bomb is going to blow us all to bits."

"The president's right," I say. "Everybody up top and get away from here."

"Is that really the president?" Joemore says.

People hurriedly climb the stairs. The men let the women go first.

"Yes, really the president," I say. "And there's a two-kiloton atomic bomb about to go off, unless we can find somebody to deprogram it."

Ninjenna whistles. "Who knows computers? Who knows how to defuse a nuke?"

"Where's that Wizjumper?" Samuel says.

"No time," I say. "He's up top and we only have—"

"Fifteen minutes!" the president says.

"Make way!" Ninjenna darts between the men up the stairs. She leaps up, bypassing the fold-out stairs, grabs on to the hatch, and flips herself through. She's gone.

"Bring the camera in here," the president says.

A modern camera is now set up on a tripod at the broadcast station. I lift it up and try to bring it into the bomb room, but the video cables are too short, and I have to stop before the door.

"Broadcast!" the president shouts.

Joemore goes to the broadcast station. He reads the simple big-block-lettered instructions that are on the placards. Joemore flips two switches, and a red ON AIR sign lights up.

Only Slater, Joemore, Sky, Samuel, and Land remain.

I turn the camera on President Wright. "You guys get out of here."

"I'm seeing this through," Land says. He runs into the room and starts working on the president's chains.

Joemore shrugs and then runs to help Land.

"I stay with Land," Sky says. "We live or die together."

Slater lies on the ground, his legs and hands still tied to the pole. His eyes are now alert. Samuel grabs him by the neck. "How do you turn the bomb off?"

"I don't know, traitor," Slater hisses as blood oozes out his mouth. "I will die a martyr. This place will be gone, and Big Mac will continue on. General McGuffin will take over as chancellor." Samuel kicks Slater in the stomach.

"Go," I say to Samuel. "You just saved your son. Don't make his life miserable by dying unnecessarily."

Samuel nods. He kicks Slater again and then runs up the stairs.

Joemore and Land aren't having any luck prying the chains loose. "Five minutes," Joemore says.

I focus the camera on the president.

The president yells so that the camera can hear him. His voice echoes like that of a god. "People of the United States. I am President Wright, the commander in chief. Although I find myself chained to an atomic bomb, I am fully coherent and am of sound mind. Vance Slater has been drugging me for the past several months. The Big Mac Party has illegally taken over the government. I am broadcasting from a shelter in Area 22 at the Nevada test site. I order all military personnel not to follow any orders from anyone they have seen in the broadcast this morning, or anyone affiliated with the Big Mac Party. I order the FBI to arrest those individuals. I order the FBI to Area 22. I also ask the governor of Nevada to order members of the Nevada National Guard and the Nevada State Police to Area 22 as soon as possible after safety allows. This bomb I am on will detonate—"

The camera tumbles to the ground. The lens shatters, and knobs fly off.

Slater laughs. He has spun around. The video cables attached to the camera are wrapped tightly around his legs.

Joemore marches into the room. He grabs Slater's head and slams it into the ground. Slater is knocked out cold again.

I run to the computer. "Three minutes! We should yank out the wires."

"No, Thompson. That will detonate the bomb for sure."

A throaty screeching sound comes from the hatch. It sounds like a leaf blower and it's getting louder. I hear screaming as well. The blower sound and screaming intensify. The screaming sounds like Wizkid. The leaf blower now sounds like a motorcycle. Ninjenna is racing down the stairs on her motorcycle with Wizkid. Maybe we do have a chance.

They sound close. Land runs up the stairs. Skinny legs plop down the hatch. Land grabs Wizkid and, holding him over his shoulder, runs down the stairs and into the bomb room.

Wizkid still looks like he's in shock, but after seeing the bomb and computer he instantly grasps the situation. The sight of a computer seems to give him strength. He shakes out of his stupor.

"Sixty seconds!" I say.

Wizkid flops to his knees and his fingers fly over the computer keys.

Joemore spits. Ninjenna walks in. She holds Joemore's arm. Sky hugs Land.

"Motherfuckers," the president says.

Time ticks by and slows down. This is it. I try to think of the James Bond comparisons, and I know there are some—they should be easy, but nothing comes to mind. Scotty, Karen, I love you.

Wizkid's hands fly up. His eyes and face scream panic. "I can't do anything." He holds five fingers in the air and counts. "Five, four, three, two, one."

Land rips the wires from Buster Able's guts.

"Zero!"

A hiss comes from the bomb, and then a click. And then— nothing.

* * *

We all stare at one another. Everyone looks scared to death, like we have been reduced to our elemental selves, like we are naked, ready to meet our maker.

Land leans over to the words painted on Buster Able, "Completely made in America," and kisses them.

"Derek!" I start to run. "I'll go get help."

"You want a ride?" Ninjenna calls.

I run up the stairs as fast as I can. I have to take a quick gasping break, and then another. I run and break for ten minutes and then pull myself through the top hatch.

I look around. The room is empty but for Derek sitting on the ground. He stands up gingerly and gives me a light hug. "You made it."

A blood-soaked bandage wraps his arm. He looks weak.

"What are you still doing here?"

He shrugs. He holds on to a cell phone. "All good?"

"All good," I say. "The bomb is a dud. Once a fizzle, always a fizzle."

Derek talks into the phone. "Naomi? Yeah, all clear—no bomb."

I hear helicopters landing outside. Land's men come back in and fill the room. Cameras and reporters are soon swarming everywhere.

I explain the situation to Land's men, and in a minute several are heading back down the chute with bolt cutters in hand.

After twenty minutes, Land's men emerge from the tunnel carrying the microfiche desk, file cabinets, and urns. They carefully stack the urns and then return to the tunnel for more.

The reporters attack the files. Derek nods to an African-American woman in front of a microfiche reader. She has short-cropped hair and large red glasses. "That's Naomi Woods, my reporter friend."

Naomi talks excitedly into a cell phone. "Lancaster and Slater authorized the deaths. Others are implicated here, too."

"Naomi," Derek says. She looks and he points at me. "This is Chris Thompson, the one I was telling you about."

Naomi grabs stacks of microfiche and puts them into her briefcase. Other reporters are anxiously doing the same. Some have portable scanners and are emailing documents to their newsrooms.

Naomi walks over to me. She sticks a recorder in my face. "Special Agent Thompson, we understand that you're the one who uncovered this conspiracy?"

Other reporters rush over and surround me. Microphones and cameras point in my face. I don't feel like talking. I just want to go home. "No comment," I say.

"Are you going to keep it all a secret, too?" Naomi asks.

I see Land climb through the hatch. He pulls Slater out of it. Joemore follows, and they hold Slater tight.

She's right. I've the chance to expose Slater and his Big Mac cronies and I should do it. I stand shirtless in blue jean overalls with an assault rifle in my hand. I face the press. "These facilities and underground bunkers are part of a secret program that started under Senator Joseph McCarthy in the 1950s."

The reporters scribble furiously or jostle with one another to keep their microphones close to me. Their bright lights are hot and blinding. A buzz goes through the crowd as I delve deeper into the story and they realize the implications of what I'm saying. I tell them the facts, but I can't stop talking. I'm filled with a passion I can't explain. "McCarthy hijacked the country by being a bully and ignoring the rules. We think that is all in the past, but the persecution has happened again. And it will be attempted in the future! Men like Slater, Lancaster, and McCarthy will keep popping up. We must remember that we are a democracy, and that the people have the power. Our officials need accountability. Our current checks and balances are not strong enough to stop a renegade."

I stop. I'm out of breath. I'm preaching. "You get the idea."

A reporter says, "So, you discovered all this because you were battling an invasion that didn't exist?"

"Yes," I say. "It was a formidable farce."

The reporter takes notes. "Formidable farce. That's good. I'm going to use that."

Wizkid and Ninjenna climb out of the hatch. They stand around the hole, reach down, and help pull up President Wright.

The reporters and cameras leave me and rush over to the president.

A reporter returns and hands me his cell phone. "It's for you."

I put the phone to my ear. "Hello?"

"Hey, hound dog."

"Archie. How the hell did you reach me here?"

"I called work, you see. Glenda knows someone at the State Department who has a cousin who works for the Associated Press. Anyhow, she calls someone at ABC in Las Vegas and—"

"I got it. Where are you?"

"Vegas, baby."

"Let me talk to Karen."

"We all just saw you on TV. Nice duds, by the way. Are you supposed to be a farmer or a male stripper?"

"Didn't you hear me?" I feel my face becoming warm. "I want to talk to Karen."

"She can't talk. She's getting ready."

The hairs on my neck bristle. I wonder what she is getting ready for. "Where are you at?" I ask.

"Yeow. We're at the Hitch 'Um Up Wedding Chapel."

Derek's knees buckle, and he faints next to me.

I lean over Derek and feel his pulse. Someone splashes water in his face. The paramedic is back. He holds something to Derek's nose. Derek shakes his head and comes to.

"Are you all right?" I ask.

"Couldn't be better," Archie says.

Derek smiles weakly. "I'll be fine."

Two medics bring in a stretcher and put Derek on it. I hold on to his hand and halfway listen to what Archie is saying.

"I got to go," Archie says. "It's my big day, you know."

"We did the right thing," Derek says.

I squeeze his hand. "We did."

What the hell is Archie talking about? Big day?

"We're getting married, dude," Archie says.

"Let's get together after all this is over," Derek says.

"That's a great idea," I say.

"Oh, dude. I'm glad you think so," Archie says. "That's a big relief."

Then it dawns on me. Married? It feels like Buster Able has detonated. Holy shit—Archie's going to marry Karen.

They start to carry Derek off. He winks at me as they do. "It's been fun."

"You're the best," I say.

"Thanks, man," Archie says.

"Not you, Judas. Now wait just a minute. I object to this wedding."

"But, but you just said it's a great idea—and it's a little late to object now. And besides, you're supposed to be dead."

"Dead? That's crazy," I say.

"Karen got an email yesterday confirming your death in a plane crash," Archie says matter-of-factly.

"I'm alive. I'm alive," I say. "And you can't get married. I object to this marriage."

"Sorry, man. Anything goes in Vegas. Doesn't matter who objects."

"Now you listen to me, Archie—"

"Gotta go." Archie hangs up.

"Hey, hey, hey!" I scream into the phone even though I know he is no longer there.

29

I DESPERATELY LOOK AROUND the room. "I gotta get to Vegas. My wife's getting married." No one seems concerned with my problem. "Hey, hey. My wife's getting married!" I'm beginning to hyperventilate. I crouch down and hold my knees. I might vomit. Finally, Land walks over to me. He puts his hand on my shoulder. "Easy, Liaison. What's wrong?"

"I have to go to Vegas." I gasp for breath. "Like now."

Samuel and Daniel come over. I look at them pleadingly. "I have to stop my wife from getting married. How can I get to the Hitch 'Um Up Wedding Chapel fast?"

Samuel raises an eyebrow. "I don't know what you're talking about, but my son is safe because of you. I will help you in any way I can."

Medical technicians file into the room. "Emergence residents, please gather over here," an elderly female nurse says.

Samuel and Daniel hug. "Go, son," Samuel says. "We'll catch up later. I'm going to help Chris."

Daniel walks back to his group. A line of FBI and Nevada state law enforcement personnel file in. A short stocky woman in SWAT gear that says FBI in bold white letters on the back holds up a badge. "FBI. This is an investigation site. We are locking this facility down. The perimeter is secure. No one is allowed to leave until after they have been interviewed."

The press groans.

"All Emergence security and personnel report to conference rooms B and C for interviews. Members of the press and Emergence bunker residents remain here. Members of the Cherokee Nation and all others, proceed to the front lawn."

"How long is this going to take?" someone asks.

The FBI woman looks at her handheld computer. "If everyone cooperates, we should have you out by morning. Settle in for a long night."

The press swears and complains.

"Night!" I say. "What am I going to do?"

Land's men do not seem concerned. Nor does Land. "Time is not important," Land says. "We've got a job to do, and we're not leaving until we get our chosen ones' remains, and we're satisfied things are under control."

"I gotta leave now," I say.

Samuel starts walking. "Come on. Let's check things out." Samuel, Land, and I walk to the main entrance of the building. A circular drive surrounds a set of flagpoles and runs up to the glass entranceway doors. A manicured lawn spreads out beyond. Federal personnel and vehicles encircle the premises in a tight perimeter.

There's no way out. I clench my fists. "Damn it."

"This is nothing," Samuel says.

I look at Samuel and wonder whether he has flown one too many missions. "How can you always be so confident?"

Samuel pokes my chest. "'Cause confident people get things done. Now go up to the second-floor room we crashed the copter into, climb onto the roof, and I'll meet you there."

Myriad problems come to mind. "How are you going—"

Samuel holds up his hand. "I may be retired, but I'm still the best." He pauses. "Trust me. These guys will be easy."

"But—"

"Do you want to stop that wedding or not?"

"I do," I say. "I can't survive without Karen."

Samuel pushes me away. "Two minutes—on the roof."

I walk down the hallway toward the stairs.

"Chris," Land calls.

I stop.

Land points. "I'm going back to the evidence room."

"Of course. I'm sorry." I walk toward Land and shake his hand. "Thanks for everything."

He pats me on the back. "Thank you."

I turn to walk away. "We should have a reunion sometime," I say.

Land smiles. One of the only times I have seen him do so.

I walk down the hall. Wizkid walks warily toward me. A Cherokee man holds his arm.

"Wizkid. You all right?"

He looks up at me. His eyes are tired and unfocused.

The man touches his arm. "A little too much excitement. He's suffering from a combat-stress reaction."

"No more helicopters or motorcycles," Wizkid says.

"We did well," I say. "You did well. It's all over now."

Wizkid nods slowly.

I reach out and grab his hands. "I have to go. They're going to take care of you. Rest up now." I let go of his hands. "We'll catch up later."

Wizkid looks up. A lazy smile appears on his face. "Later, dude."

I laugh. He'll be all right. I turn to run up the stairs, but a large hand grabs me by the shoulders. "Not going to say goodbye?" Joemore asks.

Ninjenna stands arm in arm with him.

"Good-bye," I say. "Thanks so much, you two."

Joemore grins. "Good-bye."

"We should all get together sometime," I say.

Ninjenna's hand flies out, and she grabs my nuts through my overalls. "You've got cojones, Chris Thompson. I'll work with you anytime."

"I was thinking more of a social situation," I say in a strained voice.

"So was I." Ninjenna lets go of my crotch and pats me on the arm. "See ya."

I run up the stairs and into the room. The front landing skids of the Black Hawk touch the floor. The rest of the helicopter angles up and out the ceiling and roof.

Feeling better, I approach the Black Hawk and climb inside. Two FBI agents are investigating the helicopter. One searches the cockpit, while the other kneels behind the copilot's seat. "What are you doing?" one says.

"I forgot something."

"You came in the Black Hawk?"

I start climbing back toward the tail.

"Hey, wait. What did you forget?"

I climb faster and pull myself out the back hatch. "I think it's on the roof."

The FBI agent closest to me starts climbing. "You're messing up an accident site. Get back down here."

I pull myself up onto the roof and walk away from the Black Hawk. I hear the *whup whup whup* of another helicopter.

The FBI agent's head appears through the break in the roof.

A white-and-red medevac helicopter rises over the side of the building and hovers toward me.

I run back to the FBI agent, lean down, and shove him in the shoulders to push him back into the Black Hawk. He falls, reaches back, and grabs my overall suspenders. I fall with him, but twist and throw a quick uppercut to his face. He releases his grip and falls into the Black Hawk. I push with my legs, do a little hop, and fall on the roof, inches from the opening.

The medevac helicopter hovers a foot from the roof. Samuel looks to me expectantly from the pilot's seat. I rise up and run toward the open side door. I jump up and in. The helicopter lifts toward the sky.

"I knew you wouldn't let me go it alone," a voice says. Derek lies on a stretcher on the port wall of the helicopter.

I spread my hands wide. "We're partners, right?"

Derek touches his earring and points at me. "You're the best." He laughs. "As good as Bond."

I know he's joking, but I feel like crying.

A harried-looking medic sits beside Derek. His hand steadies a pole holding an IV bag. The medic points at Samuel. "He, he hijacked us! He, he beat up our pilots."

Samuel banks the helicopter sharply and increases its speed. "Look out, Vegas, here we come."

"Ah!" the medic yells.

The IV is reviving Derek. "Go, Slammer, go," he says.

"Who are you guys?" the medic asks.

"Good question," I say. "But it's a long story."

*　*　*

Samuel expertly lands on Las Vegas Valley Hospital's rooftop helipad. I try to help the medic carry Derek.

Derek refuses our help and sits up. "I can walk." The medic holds on to his IV as Derek climbs out of the helicopter. Two hospital orderlies appear with a wheelchair. They insist that Derek sit down.

I shake his hand. "Good-bye again."

"Get out of here. Go save your marriage." Derek waves as they wheel him off. "Call me soon."

I yell at him. "We should have a reunion."

"Sure, sure."

I jump into the copter and Samuel lifts it into the air.

"Hitch 'Um Up?" Samuel asks.

"That's the place. You know where it is?"

"I asked on the radio. It's down the Strip, past the airport."

Within five minutes we are there. It has only been a half hour since we left Emergence. I hope I'm not too late.

Samuel lands in the near-empty parking lot of the Hitch 'Um Up Wedding Chapel. A faded green-striped Winnebago is parked in front of the entrance. The chapel is shaped and decorated to look like the top half of a covered wagon. Hitched to the wagon front are two giant oxen statues. One wears a tuxedo. The other wears a wedding dress. Their noses touch.

I lean forward in the cabin to say good-bye to Samuel, but he scowls at me. "Go. We said our good-byes. I'll return the chopper, and we should be good."

I jump off the helicopter. "Thanks." I turn to walk away. I stop. "Hey—"

Samuel points at me. "I know—we should have a reunion." He lifts the helicopter off the ground.

I wave. "Exactly."

I run into the chapel. There are wagon wheels, rustic trail benches for pews, and a cast-iron pot full of pork and beans along the side. A cowboy-dressed preacher stands up by the saddled-up-sawhorse altar. It's all so confusing.

And then I see him, and I focus. Standing beside the cowboy preacher, in an old-time faded-blue Western-tuxedo getup, is Archie. His eyes are lit up with excitement. A whale-size grin, which enlarges his puffy cheeks, is spread across his face. His thick cheesy mustache incenses me.

I start for him. I run down the aisle and hop onto the wooden benches. I run on top of the last few benches and launch into the air.

"Dad!"

"Chris!"

"Hound dog!"

I land on Archie, and we fall to the ground. I wrap my hands around his neck and choke him with all my might. Hands tug at my back. The cowboy preacher slaps me with his toy whip. I can hear Karen and Scotty pleading with me to stop. It's all to no avail. I'm out of my mind.

Archie knees me hard in the groin. The fight sails out of me. I release my grip, and Archie pushes me off. I lie on my back and look at the arched-beam supports of the chapel wagon.

Karen, Scotty, and Archie appear over me. Scotty smiles. Archie rubs his neck. Karen looks concerned.

"I object," I whisper.

"What are you saying?" Karen asks.

"I object to this wedding."

Karen touches the side of my face. "But, whatever for, honey?"

"Huh?"

Another face appears over me. It's my mother-in-law, June. Archie grabs her hand. "We're in love, hound dog." He leans in and gives June a kiss on the cheek. She is wearing a conservative champagne-colored dress. Her smooth olive skin blushes.

I sit up. "What? Mom? You and Archie?"

"I told you I found a real woman," Archie says. "June flew out this morning. We couldn't stand to be apart any longer."

"But my mother-in-law?" I shake my head. I stand up and straighten my suspenders. I'm still shirtless. I look to Karen. "And you approve?"

"Why not? Older men marry younger women all the time. What's wrong with an older woman marrying a younger man?"

"Nothing. And that's great . . . but, Karen, it's your mom. And Archie."

Archie slaps me on the back. "You're going to be my son-in-law. It'd mean a lot to me if you called me Dad, hound dog."

"Dad?"

"Yeah. And I'll call you Son. That's endearing, don't you think?"

I feel woozy.

The preacher cracks his whip. "Let's hitch 'um up."

I hug Scotty. "Good to see you, sport."

"Is the mission over, Dad?"

"It is, buddy, and the good guys won."

Scotty smiles. "I knew you'd do it."

I hug Karen and kiss her. I can tell she is happy to see me, but she's a little standoffish. I think she has to get used to me again.

"You've changed," she says.

"You think?"

"I saw your speech on TV."

"Too preachy?"

"No." She looks at me seriously. "I didn't know you had such conviction, Chris."

"I was pissed off."

"A lot of people are. And they feel the same way. You could run for office."

I laugh. "Yeah right. In my overalls?"

Karen looks me over. "Well, uh, yeah," she says. "Those do scare me a little."

I run my hand through my hair. "At certain times in the last few days, I've felt unstoppable."

Karen looks at the ground. "We're going to be way too dull for you now."

"No." I pause. I'm not sure how to say this, so I just blurt it out. "I want you to know, I shot and killed someone."

"Cool," Scotty says.

I pat his head. "No, son, it was not."

Karen looks shocked. Her expression changes to one of concern. She touches my arm. "Did they deserve it?"

"I don't know. He would have killed some innocent people. Only God knows what we deserve."

The cowboy preacher cracks his whip again. "Let's hitch 'um up."

"You can be my best man," Archie says. He excitedly positions me where I'm to stand. "And Scotty, you can give your grandmother away."

"Hitch 'um up." The cowboy preacher cracks his whip.

* * *

Scotty walks his grandmother down the aisle, and the ceremony begins. Karen cries, I remain dumbfounded, and Archie and June are married. It all goes off without a hitch, as they say.

The next wedding party begins to arrive. We take our celebration out to the parking lot.

I walk away with Karen to have a moment alone. She's as beautiful as ever. Her black hair falls down to her shoulders. She wears a strapless navy blue evening dress. I feel giddy to be with her again, but I have to come clean. "I have something else to tell you."

Her head snaps, and she looks at me with suspense. "It's that Tri-Delt," she says accusingly.

"Only a kiss," I say as innocently as I can. "She surprised me with a kiss."

"That's it?"

"That's it."

Karen looks relieved. She laughs. "Did you kiss her back?"

"No." I fidget. "But I didn't exactly pull away, either."

Karen raises an eyebrow. "Did you enjoy it?"

I close my eyes and try to think of a correct answer. I reply with the truth. "Maybe. Yes. I'm sorry."

Karen laughs at my discomfort. She raises her nose skyward. "Archie kissed me as well." She puts her arms around my neck. "It was only a kiss. And I *did not* kiss him back. And I did not enjoy it."

I laugh and we kiss. Archie interrupts us.

"Come look at the Winnebago. I want to check you out. She has a few quirks you may have to get used to."

"What do you mean 'check me out'? What are you talking about?"

Archie's big grin returns. "June and I are going to have a little honeymoon here in Vegas." He winks at me. "Thought you could drive the Winnebago with Karen and Scotty back home."

I look at the Winnebago and imagine all sorts of disasters.

Archie pats me on the back. "While June and I are getting down at the Hard Rock, you and the family can spend some quality time together out on the road. You know, away from it all."

I wince and try to push the thought of Archie and June 'getting down' at the Hard Rock out of my mind. It's difficult. But he has a point. Bond is done. It's time to be alone with my family.

I look to Karen and Scotty. "What do you all say? Shall we have an RV vacation?"

Scotty jumps with his arms in the air. "Yeah!"

Karen laughs. "Why the hell not?"

"Sounds like a plan," I say.

"Can you drop us off at the Hard Rock?" Archie asks.

"Sure enough," I say. "Everybody in the Winnebago. Let's get this party started."

30

I'm happy to have this circus over.
—SENATOR JOSEPH McCARTHY

THREE DAYS AGO we dropped off Archie and June at the Hard Rock and said our good-byes. I've finally begun to relax. I didn't see President Wright again, but he went on television, rescinded those crazy executive orders, and did his best to get the government back in order. He also publicly granted me "a month's leave, wherever the hell you are, Thompson." Karen, Scotty, and I plan to take that month and leisurely tour the country on our way home.

Through the Winnebago's sink window I see Karen and Scotty sitting by the fire. We have just finished eating roasted hot dogs, and I'm inside breaking Hershey bars for s'mores.

My cell phone rings. "Hello?"

"Hell of a show, Thompson, hell of a show."

I stand up straight. "It all started with you, Mr. President."

"I always had a bad feeling in my stomach about Slater," President Wright says. "This may be my proudest moment, though I'll probably be impeached or have to resign because of it. Having your right-hand man controlling such a sinister program certainly doesn't look good."

"Hopefully the truth will be believed," I say.

"You mean the truth that even though the country's philandering president was whacked out on hallucinogens, he still did the right thing in the end?" He sighs. "I think resigning may be my best bet."

"You might be happier."

"That's true, Thompson. I could spend some time with the family. Hell, maybe even have some more kids."

I laugh.

"I cancelled all those crazy executive orders."

"I saw."

"Good. Then you're taking your month's leave, I hope?"

"All of it," I say.

"Good, good. You know, before I resign, I think I'm going to sponsor some laws limiting the power of the presidency. That'll be a first, huh?"

"Very forefatherly," I say.

"Hopefully we can make it happen before they kick me out of here."

"Yes, sir. Good luck, sir, Mr. President."

"Thank you, Thompson. Stay in touch."

"Of course, sir."

"Things get hairy, I might need you to testify." Before I can say anything, he hangs up.

I step outside the Winnebago into the cool pine-scented air of Grand Teton National Park and join Scotty and Karen around the campfire. I carry graham crackers, marshmallows, and Hershey bars. "S'mores anyone?"

The sun is setting and the magnificent Grand Tetons cast a shadow over the beautiful deep blue Jackson Lake. Tomorrow we can go hiking or canoeing, or perhaps do nothing at all.

The sun disappears, and the stars shine down on our crackling fire.

"Is it fun being a secret agent, Dad?"

I put my arm around Karen. "*Intense* is a better word."

"I think it'd be fun," Scotty says. "Better than working in a boring office."

Karen kisses my cheek. "Working in an office can be exciting, Scott."

Scotty stands up, ducks, and covers. He aims a pretend pistol at the trees. "I want to be a secret agent. I want to be like Dad."

Karen and I laugh.

"Do you think you'll be a secret agent again someday, Dad?"

A shooting star arcs across the sky.

I laugh. "Son, sometimes you just don't know."

ACKNOWLEDGMENTS

FOREMOST, I would like to thank my wife Renée and our sons, Calvin, Cooper, and Colin for supporting me during the countless hours I spent on this novel.

And to my parents, John and Pat Lundy, for their help and support.

The book would not be possible without the wisdom of my mentors for this project, Mary Yukari Waters and Kira Obolensky, or the incredible insights of my editors, Jeanne Thornton and Aaron Hierholzer.

I would like to thank Spalding MFA professors, Robin Lippincott and Eleanor Morse. Their writing guidance has been invaluable.

And to all my other friends and cohorts at the Spalding MFA program—cheers!

The great fiction writer and MBA, Alan Larson, has encouraged and guided me from day one. Thank you Alan for your sound judgment, enthusiasm, and friendship.

The following people have in one way or other selflessly

given their time to help bring *Happy Utopia Day, Joe McCarthy* to fruition: Margaret Bailey, Jameson Cole, Annamaria Formichella-Elsden, Mardelle Fortier, Steve Jansen, Alicia Johnson, Nath Jones, Heidi Kuhn, Lawdon, Janet Lane, Teri Lavelle, Laura Haley-McNeil, Jennifer Prentice, Scott Prentice, Sheila Parr, and Anke Shulte.

To give an accurate sense of creeping McCarthyism in this book, I've relied on several outside sources. Chief among these are Robert Shogan's *No Sense of Decency: The Army-McCarthy Hearings: A Demagogue Falls and Television Takes Charge of American Politics* and Stanton M. Evans's *The Untold Story of Senator Joe McCarthy and His Fight Against America's Enemies*. Additionally, to provide realism to the government-authored memos found in chapters 3 and 13, I have utilized modified text from the following sources:

- The Department of Defense's *Manual for Civil Emergencies*, June 1994, chapter 6, "Emergency Preparedness Liaison Officer Program" (http://www.cdmha.org /toolkit/cdmha-rltk/PUBLICATIONS/dm3025chap6. pdf).

- *Military Tribunals: The Quirin Precedent*, March 26, 2002, a Congressional Research Service report by Louis Fisher, senior specialist in Separation of Powers, Government and Finance Division (http://www.au.af .mil/au/awc/awcgate/crs/rl31340.pdf).

- "Memorandum for William J. Haynes IT, General Counsel of the Department of Defense (Re: Military Interrogation of Alien Unlawful Combatants Held Outside the United States)," Office of the Deputy Assistant Attorney General, US Department of Justice, March 14, 2003 (http://www.fas.org/irp/agency/doj /olc-interrogation.pdf).

All quotes from Joseph McCarthy are, unfortunately, accurate.

ABOUT THE AUTHOR

J.T. LUNDY lives in Naperville, Illinois, where he writes novels and screenplays, and attempts to help his wife manage the chaos of raising three growing boys. He likes to read, write, travel, and eat good food. A graduate of Indiana University, he also holds an MFA from Spalding University and an MBA from the University of Chicago.